SHAKETOWN
The Madam's Daughter

**A Tale of San Francisco's
Victorian Underworld**

Joanne Orion Miller

Other books by Joanne Orion Miller

Little Black Book of Maui and Kauai (Peter Pauper Press)
Spotlight Delaware (Spotlight Series/Avalon)
Spotlight Maryland's Eastern Shore
  (Spotlight Series/Avalon)
Chesapeake Bay Handbook (Moon/Avalon)
Maryland-Delaware Handbook (Moon/Avalon)
Pennsylvania Handbook (Moon/Avalon)
Best Places Marin (Sasquatch Books)

Shaketown is a work of historical fiction. Apart from the well-known people, locales and events that figure in the narrative, all names, characters, places and incidents are products of the author's imagination or are used fictitiously. Any resemblance to current events or locales, or to living persons, is entirely coincidental.

A publication of
Quile Press, USA
www.Quilepress.info

ISBN: 978-0-9906391-0-7

*"To all us gals
what takes care of ourselves,
everywhere"*

—Miss Opal Boone

"Too proud to beg, too honest to steal,
I know what it is to be Shabby Genteel"
—"Shabby Genteel" Harry Clifton, comic song 1878

BOOK 1
The Making of a Madam
&
The Chinaman's Fate

Chapter ONE - August 1889

Michael's dour face appeared around the corner of the butler's pantry: "He'll take you along, sister." He didn't wait for a reply.

Cayley lifted a cut crystal bowl up into the cupboard and inhaled sharply. She was as jumpy as a small child about to be let out from school, knowing the schoolyard held bullies as well as freedom. A small thrill rippled through her; she pushed it back down. *It wouldn't do to think on why the Mister favors me,* she thought. It was more than an hour's walk home from her duties at the Rolifer's. And she hadn't saved enough to take the Hyde Street car down the hill. Mr. Rolifer had offered to take her along with him before; an unusual kindness to a day girl. It wouldn't do to refuse him, either. The first time she was invited to ride in his fancy carriage, she shook out her skirt in a merry mood, picked up her belongings, and smugly congratulated herself on her special treatment. But now she wasn't so sure of herself.

As she stepped out the service door, the chill she was already feeling doubled in the wet air, and she turned back to the pantry to borrow a shawl from Moira, the housekeeper. "It's cold as iron in January out there, with fog on the move," Cayley said shyly, eyes on the floor. Her roughened hands held tightly to the bundle of cast-offs Mrs. Rolifer had given her.

Moira made her lips thin and shook her head. "You know what the weather's like here in summer. Tell that husband of yours to buy you a decent coat. Here, you can use my old blanket, but I'll be needing it, so mind you, bring it back. Get going before 'his lordship' changes his mind."

Cayley went out the back and made her way through the narrow service alley to the portico in front of the house. Michael had brought up the Rolifer's fine black carriage, led by the dappled mare, Stilly. The carriage's brass fittings glowed bright from the lamps lit on either side. Rolifer himself emerged from the large oak front door, walking quickly while pulling on thin leather gloves; he adjusted the collar of his heavy wool coat around his thick neck. His sideburns extended all the way to his collar. He didn't look at Cayley as Michael helped him mount the carriage and handed him the reins. Rolifer stared with disgust at Michael's malformed hand, and the boy quickly jerked it down. He usually wore special gloves that his mother made to cover the stubby fingers grown together like hooves.

Embarrassed, Michael kept his eyes on the ground. "Are you along, girl?" he said gruffly. Pity stabbed at Cayley's heart, but she quickly turned her face away; she knew pity was almost as bad as the laughter of the other children when Michael was little. He helped her up beside Rolifer; she wrapped the blanket close about her shoulders as they lurched forward.

The fog was broken: thick and impenetrable in some parts, sheer as silk organza in others. Cayley liked how the streetlamps glowed in the dark night above her as the wheels of the carriage stuttered down the cobble street. *You can smell the sea,* she thought, and took a deep breath with her eyes closed.

"What's your name, girl," said Rolifer, without much interest. He focused on the horse's ears.

"It's Cayley, sir. As I told you before, sir."

He looked over at her, then swiveled his head forward and snorted. He pulled onto a level street and reined the horse to a stop. "Did you?" he asked.

"Yes, sir." Cayley kept her chin level and looked directly at Mr. Rolifer. Her armpits grew damp inside her tight sleeves.

"You'd think I'd remember, pretty little thing like you," he said. His teeth peeked out from under his thick upper lip in a fleeting smile. "Never mind," he said. He shook Stilly into action, and the horse pulled forward again. "You work in the kitchen."

"And house, yes sir. I'm a housemaid, not just the kitchen, sir."

"Mmm" he said, looking ahead. His right hand dropped to her thigh. Cayley jumped, though it was more a reaction than a surprise. He had done this before. The last time, it frightened her. If she said anything, she surely would lose her job—Henry would be hard on her for that. Rolifer kneaded her thigh like soft dough. "Pretty little thing," he said. She gulped for air, and tried to ignore the melting sensation between her legs, and the shame that flared from her heart to her throat.

As they reached the main part of town and pulled on to O'Farrell Street, gas lamps illuminated the windows in nearly every building. It was as if they had reached a fairy city; the homes and buildings were glowing inside and out, and the alleys made dark reference to the narrow spaces between. Rolifer awkwardly worked his hand up under Cayley's blanket and wrapped it around her forearm, his fingers playing on the underside of her breast. He never took his eyes off the horse, and neither did she. Finally, he withdrew his hand. Cayley continued to look straight ahead, and swallowed hard. As they reached the upper end of Market, other carriages began to appear from the side streets, announced by the soft thudding of horse hooves on packed earth. Rolifer pulled over and waited for Cayley to climb down. He set off without a word.

She stood in the middle of the muddy street, clutching her bundle of cast-offs with one hand. She felt soiled. Shaking off like a wet pup, she turned and began to walk up Market, all the while wondering how she had brought the Mister's attentions on herself and what she should do about it—or could do about it. In minutes, she reached the alley where she was fated to rescue a man in a plaid suit.

Chapter TWO

Cayley clutched the blanket around her shoulders as she backed away from the light of the street lamp. A man was making pitiful sounds and rolling on the ground twenty feet away in the unlit alley. She looked around—the crowd thinned to a few hunched figures in the fog at this end of Market Street. There were no coppers in sight. She took a few hesitant steps around the pool of light. The man on the ground was trying to sit. He appeared to have blood streaming down his face, black in the half-light. "You there, help me," he said.

She gingerly made her way over, hitching up her wide grey skirt above the puddles. Against the wall, barrels of rotting fish parts caused her to hold the corner of the blanket over her nose. She kept glancing about, watchful for the return of the hoodlums who beat the man to the ground as she was passing. It could be a trick, after all. Not that they would have anything to steal except the second-hand clothes Mrs. Rolifer had given her. But after the foolishness with her employer minutes ago, she knew very well that possessions weren't the only valuables a girl might lose. The man on the ground was well dressed—not a vagrant, as she feared. He wore an old-fashioned derby and a brown plaid suit: showy, but not worn. She took him under one arm and tried to lift him. He was likely twice her size; she staggered under his weight, banging his head against the wall. He groaned and cursed under his breath. Just then, a dark figure hesitated at the entrance to the alley, silhouetted by the light where she had stood a moment before. Cayley froze.

The stranger appeared to be alone. She called out, "Sir, please come help!" The person at the entrance didn't move. Her breath caught—what if these men planned to rob her or worse? "Please sir, there's someone hurt here," her voice wavered as she called out again. "Please, I can't do it alone." He came toward her, keeping his back to the brick wall, edging along and moving slowly. Out of the gloom she was surprised to see it was a

Chinaman, dressed in the uniform they all seemed to wear, a dark square jacket and pants, a round cap. Whites and Chinese seldom had dealings together. "Do you understand me?" she said.

"Yes," he said. "I speak English. What has happened to your friend?" His accent was musical and elegant, a little like that of Mr. Henley, who came from London to visit her employers. "Oh, I don't know him. I was passing by and saw some men beating him."

"If you're done chatting—," said the man on the ground.

The Chinaman took one arm and Cayley the other, bringing the man to his feet where he wobbled about. "Can you take me to my place?" he said. "It's right down the street." He looked from one to the other. "I'll pay you."

They each took a side and walked him awkwardly down Market a few blocks to a doorway hung with the painted sign of a Blue Rooster. When they got him in the door, the bartender rushed to take him from their arms. Overhead, gas chandeliers illuminated the room, though the air was hazy with smoke; their entrance barely made a ripple in the conversations and laughter. Cayley's hunger surged at the smell of roast meat and seafood stew, mixed strangely with sweat, over-heated woolens, and the acid reek of whiskey. She couldn't see the tables for the smoke and bodies in between.

"Boss! You awright?" said the barman. He had an enormous handlebar mustache that was so stiffly waxed it seemed to have a life of its own when he spoke.

"Jaysus, Riley, of course not. Thick-headed fool! Take me in back. Get Ellen." Riley shouldered the man's weight, edging Cayley out of the way.

"Well, sir, if you've no more need of me, I'll be getting on home," said Cayley to their retreating backs. She could imagine her Henry back at the flat, tapping out minutes with his heavy boot until supper was on the table.

"Wait, you hold up there, girlie," said the man. "Get rid of the Chinaman, though. They's bad for business."

"That's a fine way to treat someone who helped you," said Cayley, and immediately regretted her outburst. Henry often told her to hold her tongue.

The man with the bloodied face waved his fingers at the barman, who went and opened the till, took out a few bills, and held them up to the Chinaman's face. "Now get outta here," he growled. The Chinese man took the money, held his head up and looked carefully at each of their faces—especially Cayley's—as if memorizing them; he turned so quickly his queue flew out behind him. Then he was gone.

"Help me get him into the office," said Riley, and he and Cayley supported the man through a narrow doorway into a dim room. They sat him on a red velvet couch, the impressions of a hundred backs and bottoms worn into the pattern. The polish on the carved wood arms was rubbed thin. The man told Riley to go watch the till before the customers ran off with it. A roll-top desk stood in one corner, with messy piles of papers stacked all around it; a few were held down with empty glasses, others with a chunk of brick or some other odd piece of masonry. A flickering gas lamp illuminated the room, and wall sconces further served to light the darker corners. It had a dusty, male odor that made Cayley jumpy and alert.

"I'll be going too, I guess." Cayley stood near the door.

"Nay, stay and have a drink with me. I insist."

"Sir, I'm a married woman and all, I shouldn't even be here."

"Ellen!" he bellowed. A tall, pretty redheaded girl a few years older than Cayley came in from the other room. "See, there's another woman here—it ain't what you think." He turned toward the girl. "Get us a couple of whiskeys, Ellen. One for you, too. Say, this here little girl saved my life!"

"That so," said Ellen, with a wide-faced grin. "Did she fight off an invadin' horde, then, Mr. Max?" She went out for a moment and returned with three brim-full drinks in her hands. "Who roughed you up, anyway?"

Mr. Max shrugged. "Lots of people need money these days." He downed half his whiskey in one gulp. "How about you, girlie—" he turned toward Cayley. "You must be on your way home from work, one of them big houses on the hill I figure. Am I right?"

"You're a mind-reader sir, truly."

"No 'sir'—you can call me Mr. Max like they all do in here. And I can call you...?"

"Cayley—Mrs. Henry Wallace that is."

"Well, Mrs. Wallace. So, you work up the hill?"

"I do. I'm a house servant for Mr. Rolifer, the well-known lawyer, and his Missus." Cayley raised her chin as she said it.

Max chuckled as he looked into his glass. "Oh, yes, the well-known-lawyer-Mr.-Rolifer. He comes in every once in a while. Do you like your work, Mrs. Wallace?" he took a sip of his whiskey, eyeing Cayley steadily over the rim of the glass. Ellen returned with a bowl of hot water and a rag. She proceeded to dab the cut on his forehead; he winced and tried to wave her away.

"Worse than a bawling baby," she said. He winced again. "And twice as ugly."

"It's all right. I'm glad to have it." Cayley looked at the honey-toned liquid in her hand. "My husband, Mr. Wallace, he's a fireman, you know." She took a dainty sip of whiskey, and coughed twice as it ripped down her throat.

"A fireman! Now he has plenty of work in this town does he not?" He elevated his hand, indicating that Cayley should drink up. "That's my good whiskey, you know."

"Oh, that's very true, sir, very true. On both counts."

"Mr. Max, please. No need to 'sir' me."

"Sorry."

"Don't be—I don't get much respect around here, even though I'm the one rattling the till to feed this crew." He gave Ellen an exasperated look. "Rolifer, you say?"

Ellen continued to dab the blood from his face.

"Yes si—Mr. Max"

"He comes in, working the bar circuit with those other nobs. I'd like to see him in here more often. Here's an idea rolling around in my noggin—" He tapped the side of his head with two fingers, which caused him to grimace. "Another whiskey, Mrs. Wallace?"

Cayley felt warm for the first time in days. The tension in her shoulders seemed to drain out her tired feet; she found herself liking this plain-talking man and the gentle red-haired girl who looked at her so open and friendly. The cross around Ellen's neck glinted in the light. Cayley discovered her glass was nearly empty. "Don't mind if I do."

The bartender, Riley, brought the bottle in and topped off the glasses, then hurried out again, his mustache twitching as if trying to escape.

"I'm thinking that I should have the finest barmaids on the circuit. Now I've got my Ellen here, pretty as a copper penny and sharp as broken glass, that one! The men like her well enough."

Ellen sat on a corner of the desk and crossed her ankles so that a bit of her white leggings showed above her boots. "Well enough, indeed," she said, bringing the corners of her mouth and one eyebrow up.

"Can't go letting you get too swell-headed, dearie. Anyway, I get a good look at you in the light Mrs. Wallace, and I say, well, here's a blond one to be the other bookend! You and Ellen could jolly up the old boys, build us all a hell of a business, and make some money for your selves, too. What do you say?"

The muscles in Cayley's jaw worked a little; she was conscious of the heavy smoke filtering in from the main room. "Mr. Max, I'm a married woman. I'm no fancy woman—no insult to you, Miss Ellen—but I can't be taking on such disrespectable work. Mr. Wallace wouldn't have it, and who could blame him."

Ellen laughed, a sound like church bells pealing. "I'd have a lot more to confess to Father Mullin on Saturday if I did half what you think I do!" said Ellen. "No, darlin', I just serve drinks and let 'em look at me. If anyone gets too bold, I turn the serving over to Riley, and that's the end of it. I work for the money, which is good; especially the tips, the little extra bit of money they slip you if they like you—if you give them a little twinkle.

It's fun, with naught to thrill the good Father. Not that I ain't tempted now and again," she laughed and winked at Mr. Max.

"No fooling around, strictly on the up-and-up, my dear," he said to Cayley. "What do you make at the Palace of Rolifer?"

Cayley's face reddened and she suddenly found the sticky rim of her glass very interesting. "I don't think that's any business of yours, si…Mr. Max."

"That bad, eh?" He looked at Ellen. "We could use you right away. If you want to work here, just come in around 4 p.m., and you'll work until 11. And I'll pay you ten dollars a week plus whatever you can get on the side. Ellen will show you what to do. Think about it."

"And no more calling anybody 'sir'," said Ellen. "Not unless you want a bigger tip."

Cayley controlled her face. The money was nearly three times what she made now. Her head whirled with whiskey; she rapidly blinked back tears at the memory of little Daniel. *God keep his tiny soul. Henry and me could put aside some and try for another baby. And I could help my mother, too.* "Look here," said Cayley. "I appreciate the offer, and I'll put my head to it. The money's good all right—though twelve a week would be better." She hoped her face wouldn't burn an even brighter shade of fiery pink and give her away. She set down her glass and looked into Mr. Max's eyes, "But what I'd really appreciate is a few dollars out of the till like you give the Chinaman. A bird in the hand, and all that."

Max laughed and gestured to Ellen. "All right then, Mrs. Wallace. You can contemplate on this."

Cayley made her way unsteadily out of the Blue Rooster, clutching three coins, a gold and two silvers. A fortune! There was a lot of bread and pork in twelve dollars. But Henry would raise Cain himself if she even mentioned working at a place like the Blue Rooster, though there didn't seem to be anything going on that shouldn't. She walked determinedly down Sixth Street, placing one foot in front of the other, holding the blanket tight around her shoulders to shield her from the icy fog. Working for

the Rolifer's was a good job; she was lucky to have gotten a position at all thanks to her brother Michael being the stable boy.
She wasn't blessed with education or the proper manners to be a
shop girl. Ahead lay the flat she and Henry shared with another
family. The lamps that winked through the windows of the modest wooden houses seemed to shine like happy little stars.

Well, Cayley thought, *Henry wouldn't have to know, would
he? Oh Lord, no. What am I thinking? Sure the devil has me in
his grip thanks to Mr. Max's fine whiskey.*

Chapter THREE

Wo Sam kept his head down and walked quickly north from the Blue Rooster to the darker streets on the outskirts of Little China. He stepped inside a deserted doorway and crumpled the bills the barman had given him into a pouch he wore under his jacket. No sense tempting fate—and the white devils that roamed the streets looking for trouble. What in the world had made him stop to help those two in the alley? He thanked whatever gods watching over him that he didn't walk into a beating. *It was that woman,* he thought. *A woman calling out for me.*

He pushed aside his loneliness and made his way to Dupont *Gai,* then up a tiny side street to Sacramento *Gai.* The other men he saw were Chinese who moved purposefully through the narrow alleys or whites with their hats pulled low, there for the opium, gambling, or girls. There were no women on the streets—those few that lived here finished shopping hours ago, and the rest were in the cribs, waiting for customers. He entered an unmarked doorway, and walked slowly to his room in the *ui kun,* the boarding house provided by his employers, the Yeung Lo Company.

He shared the room with Wo Kim, a cousin also from Pearl River Village near the South China Sea. Once inside the doors—even inside the boundary of Chinatown—Sam relaxed a little. At this late hour, the smells of dried fish, ginger and incense, and the multi-toned, guttural pitches of Cantonese coming from dozens of closed and curtained doors reassured him. The room assigned to him was comfortable, in spite of the limited space for his books, ink and brushes. He was hardly in a position to complain: most of the rooms were shared by four or more men. His privilege stemmed from the fact he spoke and read excellent English. His father sacrificed to send him to the English school so Wo Sam could come to Gold Mountain as a scholar, teacher, and accountant to serve the governing board of the company. And he wouldn't be here forever, only a few years. His passage was nearly worked out, and soon he could afford to send even more money home to China.

Wo Kim sat cross-legged on a rush mat in the neat room, sharing tea with another of the residents, Ling Hai. The older man stroked his thin white beard; his scalp showed under the strands of hair, wound back into a snowy queue. Ling Hai had been with the Company for many years, starting out as a laborer and working his way up to the position of foreman. He took the boys under his wing when they arrived. The mats Sam and Kim used as mattresses were rolled up against the wall; the room was bare of furniture except for four dark seating cushions, an oil lamp, a small chest and low table. Both men greeted Wo Sam formally, then continued their conversation.

"I don't see how we can avoid it," said Kim. He cradled the dark pottery tea bowl in one pale, unblemished hand; two fingers of the other hand supported the bottom.

"The white devils..." agreed Ling Hai. "We can't rely on *lo fan* law to protect us. Wo Sam, what does a learned man think?"

"You're talking about the tongs again?" Sam sat to join them, arranging a small blue pillow on the floor.

"Yes," Kim said. "I know this is not your favorite topic."

"Before tonight, I might have continued to discourage you. But I don't know myself anymore."

"Cousin, has something happened? Are you all right?" Kim's smooth forehead wrinkled in concern.

"Only a minor thing—I helped a white man who had been beaten. No one is safe anywhere." Sam decided not to mention the humiliation of being thrown out of the bar like a common cur, though his jaw clenched at the thought.

"But it's better than it was a few years ago." Kim looked for confirmation at the older man as he poured tea for the others and then for himself. Ling Hai nodded.

"Yes, it was much worse before we came. It's still possible to make much money here, and the war at home—I worry about my father and sister all the time." Sam brought the steaming cup to his lips. "Ah, *Xi Hu Longjing*," he said. "Most refreshing." His memory darted back to the walled yard of his family compound, his sister Li's small plump hands open to capture the pink petals of the plum tree as they floated to earth around her. His mind recalled a line from a poem: *Flowers, after their nature, whirl away in the wind.*

"Better to worry about yourself these days, cousin," said Kim. "I'm thinking about joining Chee Kong. The leader is very powerful."

Ling Hai made a deep rumbling sound in his throat, "Lord Low Yet is very impressive. Soldiers, women—everyone in town knows him and the white guards don't even try to harass them."

"With respect, Ling Hai; Chee Kong is no longer the political organization it was in China. Now, they run opium, girls, gambling." Sam took a delicate sip of tea.

"They would welcome someone like you, who can read and write English as well as the white devils," said Kim.

"You didn't hear a word I said, little cousin!" said Sam, a half-smile on his lips.

Footsteps in the hallway signaled the return of another of the house residents. The men paused in their conversation until the house was silent once again.

Sam touched his lips with his free hand. "Tell me, both of you: do you feel you must join a tong to protect yourselves from other Chinese?"

Kim and his friend looked at each other and nodded. "It's not the way it used to be, before the Exclusion acts," said the older man, stroking the thin beard on his chin. "We could rely on the Six Companies then. They were respected. But they've lost face. No one will go to them with complaints. They're like a toothless old woman."

"It's impossible to go out safely among the whites, but it is possible to live safely here in Little China if we align with a benefactor," said Kim. "A small handful of rice is better than none, as long as we must stay here."

They could hear the footsteps of other men crossing in the hallway outside their door. The whale oil lamp in the room guttered and bounced their shadows against the walls.

"Even if the benefactor is little more than a criminal?" said Sam.

"I would make friends with a tiger if he would protect me from other tigers," his cousin retorted.

"What if he wants you to be a tiger, too?" said Sam. "And rip the flesh of others who are not in your clan?"

"Sam, it's not that bad. Don't you ever go to women? Take a pipe now and then to relieve the monotony? Play a little *fan-tan* to summon your luck? You know these are simple pleasures, only evil when they are misused. That's all it is."

Wo Sam's eyes dropped to the floor in front of his black canvas shoes. He could not admit to his younger cousin that the women in the brothels sickened him, painted like orchids in a hothouse, beckoning him with voices sweet and sticky as opium. There were no other women here, no one to arrange a marriage to—they all were owned, bought and sold like cattle. He shuddered slightly. Maybe there was something wrong with him. No, he did look, he did—he couldn't bring himself to touch. He wanted to take his money, go home to his village by the river, and have his father speak to the marriage broker about a proper wife for a scholar. And opium...what a waste of time! Precious time he would rather spend reading his favorite Tang poets or observing the fine brush strokes of masters. *Fan-tan*, though...luck wheeling in and out of the door. A great, golden wheel, so like life.

"That's all it is," agreed Sam. "If you say so."

"Ling Hai has already spoken to the Chee Kong for me," said Kim excitedly. "Perhaps they'll let you take the initiation if you agree to read English papers for them—they'll pay you well, I'm sure. You can make money from the company and the tong, both."

Sam balanced his teacup on the tips of the fingers of his left hand and twirled the pale porcelain cup with his right, turning a quarter turn with each movement. "If they pay me, we'll see," he said. "If it means I can leave this place sooner and begin my life away from these ignorant while devils, it might be worth it. But I will not take part in the tong's evil works, and neither should you."

Ling Hai smiled down into his cup, but kept close the knowledge of how sweetly seductive power might be to an ambitious young man.

Chapter FOUR

Cayley opened the door to a cold, dark flat, and relief flashed through her followed by an equally powerful surge of anger. *Henry's either out working or working at getting drunk,* she thought as she fumbled about for the lamp and matches. At least she would be able to get her sewing done without having to fend off his meanness or his liquored-up lovemaking, or worst of all, to endure his silence. Since the baby died, they had little to say to one another. She planned to take in her favorite of the lawn shirtwaists Mrs. Rolifer had given her, but discovered she was low on thread and needles both. She reluctantly gathered her own well-worn shawl about her and went around the block to her mother's row house on Howard, tucking one of the coins Mr. Max had given her in the little fabric pouch she wore inside her skirt.

Cayley entered the flat without knocking. Though it was late, Lizzie Pearson was still doing close work in the kitchen, using the light from the open stove and a lamp both to see her stitches in the darkened room.

"I figured you'd be up, still," said Cayley as she emerged from the darkened hall. "I wish you wouldn't sit so close to that fire, Ma. It's dangerous."

"Shhh," her mother cautioned, and nodded toward the corner, where Cayley's youngest brother and sister lay entwined in each other's arms on a makeshift bed on the floor. Cayley reached down and pulled the quilt up to their chins. The piecework quilt was so old the stuffing was grainy, and leaked out like dust from the seams when she moved it.

"I'm to be borrowing some thread from you," whispered Cayley. Mrs. Pearson looked up, and Cayley could see brown circles beneath her dull eyes. "Looks like you're working late a lot these days, Ma."

"Somebody has to keep these bellies full," said her mother. "I'm lucky to have extra mending when the factory closes." She kept her eyes on her work, pulling the needle through the fabric at a quick, steady pace.

"So, I thought Eddie and Mary and them was working."

"Was. They both got let off when the powers that be found they could hire the Chinee for almost nothing. Damned heathens! Forgive me, Lord, I know they have to eat too, but they make our lives miserable! Now I'm carrying the load. Maybe I can get Mary work down at the factory, with luck. But Eddie..... He's too old to run telegraph messages and not good for much else." She bit off the end of a thread and wiped her graying hair off her face. "Don't even ask me about your Da." She looked up quickly at Cayley. "Don't say a word."

"Bad luck," said the girl. She knew better than to ask if her father had shown his face in the house at all, much less brought home any money from his infrequent bouts of work. The question would bring on her mother's unhappy wailing over having married "a sodden mick fresh off the boat instead of a good local lad." He seemed to show up regular enough to bring another baby into the world, though. *It's our lot in life, ain't it,* she thought. The all-too-familiar smell of boiled cabbage soup that lingered in the kitchen soured her stomach—she could imagine her mother begging for the discarded leaves from the greengrocer.

"Well, at least you have Henry, and work in a good house, thanks to your brother," her mother said. "When them Rolifers took him in, it was a real blessing—a bed in the stable and steady job was more than I prayed for when our Michael was born. He always seemed to cotton to animals more than people anyway." She reached up and pulled Cayley down to kiss her forehead. Her face was damp against Cayley's cool skin. "You're the best of all my own." Her mother laid the handwork down on the table and rubbed her left hand with her right. "It's hard times, but we'll all be all right. The good Lord will see to that."

"Here, Ma." Cayley produced the gold coin from her coat pocket. "A present for you, for all your hard work."

22

Her mother looked down at the coin in Cayley's hand for a long time, as though she didn't recognize what it was. Then she looked up at the girl and squinted. "Where would you be getting a ten-dollar gold piece, daughter?"

Cayley smiled innocently. She made up her explanation on the way. "Mrs. Rolifer gave it to me, as she forgot to pay me last week, and she said I did such a fine job of setting up for her big party two days ago. And I also did mending for her. And I took over for Moira in the nursery for a few days when she was sick."

Her mother raised one eyebrow and looked down again at the gold piece, taking it carefully from Cayley's hand as though it was hot. She set it in her palm and rubbed the raised surface with her other thumb. She nodded, "Well, God be praised. This week we'll be seeing a pig up close for a change instead of just hearing the squeal." Her eyes watered. "Sitting too close to that stove, I am. What color thread is it you're needing, girl?"

***

When Cayley left her marriage bed before dawn the next morning, she wriggled out from under Henry's heavy arm, eliciting nothing more than a beer-tinged grunt. *I should tell him about the Blue Rooster*, she thought, but she knew he wouldn't be around for hours, seeing as how he came in after she was already abed. *Just as well—it might be naught more than a puff of smoke, and no sense causing trouble for nothing*. She took the lawn shirtwaist she had worked on with her to the Rolifer's, along with her best black skirt. Better shoes would have to come later, but the skirt would pretty well cover her feet. She folded the clothing and the blanket she borrowed from the housekeeper the night before into a burlap sack, and walked quickly to Market Street, then up the hill.

Cayley did her morning chores then rubbed all twenty settings of the table silver until the cloth was black. To distract herself from the mindless work, she let her eyes wander up to the shelves of the cupboard and chose a fancy porcelain soup tureen, covered in pink roses. She imagined Mrs. Rolifer giving it to her as a reward for a heroic deed—saving one of the children from drowning or some such disaster. The harsh voice of Moira, the housekeeper—admonishing one of the other servants—brought her back to her task and the unpleasant truth that she'd see such treasure only if it was broken in twenty pieces. Cayley scrubbed her hands free of the tarnish that clung to them until they were rough and red. "Moira, do you mind if I leave the crystal 'til tomorrow? I'm not feeling at all well, and a little extra sleep would do me."

"The Mister giving you a ride down the hill again?" asked Moira, a nasty smile rising out of her mouth. "Such a kindness to a day girl."

She don't miss much, thought Cayley. *She probably thinks I'm having a high old time cozying up to the Mister.*

Moira wiped her hands on a blue cloth hanging from her waistband. "I don't know whether to scold you or warn you, girl. You're barely 18 and too pretty for your own good. Be careful of yourself. I've surely noticed the Mister's eyes following you around the room when Mrs. Rolifer's own are glued to her embroidery."

"It's not like that, Moira." The thought of Rolifer's hand creeping up her leg as they silently rode along in the carriage filled her with an odd mix of shame and titillation. "No ride for me today, Ma'am. I'm on my own two feet. And the better for it." She left by the back door, picked up her skirts and skittered down the slick cobblestones toward Market in the long afternoon light, establishing an even pace. In 40 minutes, she reached the level streets of town. Even though the thickening fog pierced her thin shawl, Cayley stepped up onto the walkway from the street, and paused to look in the shop windows. The latest styles were displayed at the dressmakers, along with a bit of ribbon or gewgaw to buy for a few pennies to mend the skirt Mrs. Rolifer had given her. There was a frill that would pretty up her shirtwaist. The windows were dim, but the streets were beginning to come alive. Carriages, from simple carts to elaborate two-pony landaus passed each other; packed cars of the Market Street Cable Railway clanked past.

On the walkways, prosperous-looking men strolled, dressed in gleaming top hats and closely cut dark suits. Servants and shopgirls, eyes down, scurried homeward; street performers set up their shell games and card tables. She nodded to the man with his tinkling musical box, and hesitated a moment to watch a dancing dog in a clown outfit, then hurried past the fire-eaters and jugglers before they could pass the hat. Cayley's eyes plummeted to the ground in front of her when two fancy women passed; she turned after they were well by to stare at them. They always had the most beautiful dresses, shiny satin in blues and greens—and even red—with lace trims. No cloth she could buy would ever catch the light like that. Cayley crossed over Market, skipping to miss the streetcar that clanged angrily in the middle of the roadway.

A few of the saloons were already wide open, and men stood in front, smoking cigars and talking loudly. There were no women, of course. No respectable women, anyway. Cayley now knew what it was like in there: warm as the sun, the banquets loaded with food free for the price of a drink; brightly lit, shimmering mirrors and chandeliers made of the same crystal as the bowls and vases she polished at the Rolifer's. She drifted toward the Blue Rooster, and shyly passed through the crowd of suited men near the door.

"Say there, Missy," said one of the men, cigar clenched between his teeth, his thumbs in his waistcoat pockets.

Cayley covered her mouth with her hand and knocked at the door; she asked Riley for Mr. Max or Ellen. "We won't be opening for another hour," said Riley. "You're an eager one." He smiled, his luxurious upper lip quivering.

"I'm wanting to make sure there's a real job here," she said. "Before I quit my old one and I'm out in the street on empty promises."

Riley told her to sit and wait, and half an hour later, Ellen walked in, and shook out her shawl by the door. "Well, look what the cat dragged in," she said, a big grin on her face.

"I'm here to see if Mr. Max is serious about that job," said Cayley.

"Oh, he means it all right. Are you here to work tonight?"

"I guess," Cayley shrugged. "I don't know what I'm supposed to do, but I'll pick it up quick."

"Come here, then, and I'll learn you a few of the finer points," said Ellen, who moved behind the bar and began to explain the different liquors, how to measure a drink, how much you might get away with watering it, and so on. "You can always come and ask me or Riley if you're confounded," she said. "We also have to make sure the food gets out proper," and she took Cayley by the hand and led her to the kitchen, alive with clattering pots, pans, and Italian phrases shouted above the din. All the men were burley, dressed in undershirts. Steaming pots of bubbling food were spiced by the odor of perspiring bodies.

"Are they all Eye-talians?" Cayley asked Ellen.

"Max hired Chinee before the troubles started—now he's afraid they'll attract more trouble; you've already had a demonstration of that. Besides, the Itals—they cook almost as good as the Chinee—and they're just as loud." The women helped the cooks carry out the big platters and arrange them on the table. The kitchen boss spoke little English, but everyone seemed to know what needed to be done, and did it quickly.

"The laundryman at the Rolifer's is Chinese." Cayley set down a platter of cold oysters on the half shell, served on a bed of coarse salt. "I didn't have much to do with him, really. He worked in the basement."

"They're just people, I guess. But when Kearny started all that yellow peril folderol a few years ago, it gave the bad sort a target for their fun. Did you eat yet?" said Ellen.

Cayley shook her head. "I left the Rolifer's early, and I don't usually eat there anyway."

"Here, have a little now. Get a plate." She pointed toward the stack. "There won't be any time to eat later, and there won't be any left after the hogs are at the trough."

Cayley took a little terrapin soup in a shallow bowl, drank the thin soup without a spoon, and then loaded the bowl with slices of roast beef. She would have kept eating, but when Mr.

Max came in, she almost wiped her face on her sleeve in a hurry to get rid of the bowl. Cayley remembered she was wearing her best shirtwaist, and backed into the kitchen, where she hurriedly dabbed at her mouth with one of the kitchen rags. The kitchen man smiled without showing his teeth and winked at her—she scurried out.

"You look like a schoolmarm," said Mr. Max. "Our patrons will get a good laugh out of that!"

"Be easy on her," said Ellen. "It's her first night, and after you pay her the royal sum you've offered, she'll be able to dress like a queen. Won't you darlin'?"

Cayley smiled thinly at Mr. Max and nodded vigorously. "What's wrong with the way I look," Cayley whispered to Ellen. "This shirtwaist belonged to Mrs. Rolifer, herself. It's very fine lawn, very elegant, and I worked on it so it fits perfect."

Ellen took a towel from behind the bar and wiped down spills on the buffet counter. "I think that's what Max has a problem with. He likes his girls to be a little...you know...showier. But I think you're dressed beautiful and proper, and I might get myself one of those outfits, too."

"You're mighty sweet," said Cayley. "I'm lucky to be working with such a nice girl. Were you a housemaid before you came here, too?"

Ellen washed her hands in a bowl of water behind the bar. "No, I didn't even have skill for that, I'm afraid. I came to the back door looking for clean-up work in the kitchen, and the head cook brought me up to the front. I guess it was his idea that Max hire women to serve at the bar. I didn't care—I was just glad to find work, and I like it well enough. It's not like down in the Barbary where they expect you to do more than hand them a drink and a smile."

Riley opened the doors. The street outside was in twilight, with a faint golden glow coming from the gas lamps that were being lit in succession by the lamplighter. Riley greeted the man as he passed by the door. The fog hadn't moved in yet, but the damp in the air softened the smell of horse droppings on the street outside. Cayley wiped her damp hands on her skirt and stood close to Ellen. "My husband doesn't know I'm here," she whispered. "I left a note saying I had to serve at a party tonight at the Rolifer's."

"Hmmm," Ellen said, keeping her eyes on the door. "That might be a problem." She looked over at the tiny blond woman. "Not because anything might happen to you here, of course." Ellen smiled and touched the side of her upswept hair. "What sort of man is he, your husband?"

Two men in derbies came in the door and headed for the bar, eyeing the food on the table all the while. "Tell me later," said Ellen. "Watch what I do." She went up to the men, who had already ordered from Riley. He set down a couple of heavy-bottomed glasses and was pouring from behind the bar. "Gentlemen," said Ellen, "why don't you go over to the buffet and pick something out, and I'll bring your drinks. Sit down and make yourselves to home!" Cayley noted how the men looked at Ellen apprehensively, then more boldly, taking in the curves of her body with their eyes. They looked at each other and nodded, slid off their stools and headed for the buffet. As they turned their backs, Riley added a dab of water to each drink. Ellen grabbed a tray from behind the counter, picked up the glasses and followed them to a table where she chatted them up—"Do you live here in town?" she asked one, and patted the other on the shoulder: "You look like you're in the silver business, and doing mighty well, too," and so on.

Another group of three approached the bar, and Ellen nodded to Cayley, who swallowed nervously and approached the newcomers. "Gentlemen," she began, and the evening was swept into a blur of new faces, appreciative looks, and flirtation. A few of the men would treat her with a curious politeness; others would put an arm around her waist from which she would quickly twist away, laughing all the while. *It's just being a good hostess, like Mrs. Rolifer,* she thought. *As if I were in my own home, but with better food, drink, and company—much better company.* Once during the next few hours, Ellen stooped to whisper in her ear, "Remember, if anyone forgets he's a gentleman, tell Riley."

And they separated to continue their conversations and service of food and drink. Riley would ask Cayley how many rounds, and proceed to make the whiskey more watery with each round. Cayley now went to the door when newcomers came in to greet them, and caught Mr. Max's smile and finger-waved gesture of approval and encouragement. He came over to her.

"Well, you're a natural, Missy." The cut on his head was a grim reminder of the night before.

"It's hardly like work, except I'm on my feet," she grinned at him, and winked. "Though I guess I shouldn't tell you that, should I?" She turned to greet the men at the door.

"Am I paying you too much, ten dollars a week and all?" He said to her back.

She stopped and remained rooted to the floor, not turning around. "Thirteen and I'm worth twice that!" she said, surprised with her own boldness.

"Right," he said, "twelve," and coughed. "You have work to do."

Ellen cut her off before she reached the door. "That one's mine," she said, and nodded toward the fair-haired man who had just entered. His suit was the color of doves, and fit him like it grew out of his skin; unlike most of the men, he was completely clean-shaven—and handsome as a theater actor.

"Oh ho," said Cayley. "A special one, eh?"

"I think so. Say Bill!" Ellen smiled so wide she lit up the room as she swept toward him. He held out his arm and she flew under it as if sheltered from a storm.

Cayley turned back into the crowd, waved, laughed uproariously at jokes she had heard a hundred times, flattered, smiled, wheedled, and occasionally patted the cheek of a sodden drunk.

That night, other bar owners on the circuit wondered what happened to their regular influx of customers as a vortex developed around the Blue Rooster. At around 11 p.m., Cayley headed for the door, only to walk into the somewhat unsteady path of Mr. Rolifer and his cohorts. She took breath in, sharply, as he stared at her.

He squinted, opened his eyes, and squinted again. "My wife has a shirtwaist like that," he said. "But she doesn't fill it out quite as well."

"Gentlemen," Cayley said, and led them to the bar.

Chapter FIVE

A metal door with peeling yellow paint, indistinguishable from several others on Washington Street, served as the entrance to the Chee Kong meeting hall. Ling Hai pushed the door open and stepped inside, followed by his two friends.

"State your names," said the man seated next to the door.

"Wo Sam."

"Wo Kim."

"Ling Hai, a member of this organization."

The group of three men was waved ahead to the first archway, where a man armed with a long-barreled revolver swung his body in front of them. Arms crossed, he said, "What is your business here?"

Coached by Ling Hai, the three said in unison, "Overthrow the Manchu, restore the Ming." The man stepped aside, and the initiates and their escort moved to the next set of arches. The walls over the arch were painted bright red; golden dragons wound up pillars on either side of the opening. Intricate carved wood screens spanned the arch. A small door between the pillars swung open, and the men stepped through. Two guards stood at the opposite end of the room in front of another portal. Sam and his companions removed their blue cotton garments and unplait their queues. They donned gowns of five colors and capped their heads with red turbans symbolizing the Ming Dynasty. They progressed through the next door.

Sam leaned over to his cousin and whispered, "I don't see the wisdom of replacing one greedy Emperor with another," but he was glared into silence by the guards who stood outside a gauntlet in the next room. The guards crossed their swords at waist height to form a low alley, and, as Ling Hai stepped aside, the two young men dropped to their hands and knees and crawled under the swords. At the end of the gauntlet sat the *Ah Mah,* Mother—actually Low Yet, Lord of the secret society. He sat on an elaborately carved rosewood chair, his small plump hands on each arm. The oil on his short English haircut shone in

31

the dim light. Once through the alley of swords, Sam and Kim stood in front of the *Ah Mah*. A man at his side held out a scroll and read off 21 regulations and declarations of brotherhood and loyalty ("all members must share with each other in times of need," "all members must never reveal these secret vows"), which the cousins agreed to uphold. They then pricked their thumbs with a knife and squeezed a drop of blood into a glass of wine that contained the blood of other members. Both swore to keep the secrets of the tong to death. Kim wrinkled his nose, and sipped, as Sam had done.

A member of the tong indicated to Sam and Kim that they must crawl under the *Ah Mah's* elaborate carved chair, a symbolic act of rebirth as a new tong member. Wo Sam caught his collar on the underside of the chair and had to tug at his robes, sprawling flat on his face. He felt more foolish by the minute, and wouldn't have been surprised if everyone in the room burst out laughing at his pratfall. They remained stone-faced, which only added to his discomfort.

"Do you renounce all allegiance to Emperor, family and clan?" asked the *Ah Mah*. Sam looked at Kim. Both men nodded. The two were escorted to an altar to light incense and burn gilded paper, and to offer wine and tea to the spirits of the monks who died in the Manchu takeover centuries before. At least in this, Sam was comfortable.

When they were done, the entire membership entered the great hall, filled with dusty sunlight streaming through massive rafters. In unison, they chanted 36 oaths, most having to do with restoring the Ming Dynasty back to power. To affirm their loyalty, Sam and Kim purchased a symbolic gift for the tong: a gleaming black bantam, wings flapping, was carried into the hall. The cock's entry was brief; a knife was drawn across its throat on the stone altar.

After, tong members milled about welcoming the two newcomers. Kim flushed, a wide grin decorated his face as men came up and clapped him across the back. Sam merely nodded. The man who read the 21 regulations approached Sam and leaned slightly toward him while looking away. "*Ah Mah* wants you to attend him at his home tomorrow morning." He leaned back and gave Sam directions, to which Sam nodded dumbly.

As the two young men made their way back to the boarding house, Sam walked ahead, keeping a furious pace.

"Slow down, cousin. Enjoy the cool night," Kim admonished.

Sam stopped and whirled around. "What have you gotten me into?"

Kim looked surprised, and a little puzzled. "Are you worried about all the promises, cousin?" He brought his hand to his mouth, as if to hide a smile.

"We are honor-bound to these people now. Tomorrow, I must go to the *Ah Mah's* house! What will he ask of me?"

Kim shook his head. "It's only a game, Sam. Dress up and shout slogans like school. Think of all the new connections—new opportunities for work and friendship. You always take everything so seriously!"

"And you don't take it seriously enough. Schoolmates do not carry pistols. They don't run whorehouses!"

Kim sighed, exasperated. "You'll see, it's the right thing. You just have to calm down. It's an honor to go to the boss's house. Don't worry! Besides, I didn't get you into this—you wanted to make more money, remember?"

But Wo Sam had planted a strong seed of doubt in his own garden, and was not happy he had done so.

Early the next morning, he waited before the carved door on Dupont *Gai*. A small woman dressed in a plain gray jacket opened the door and inquired of his business in the common Cantonese dialect of Little China. He said he was summoned by the *Ah Mah,* and gave his name. She shut the door without a word; moments later, she let Sam in and told him to wait again while she departed.

She returned shortly and led him through a dark wood-paneled hallway, then turned left at a screen and stepped into an open courtyard. The courtyard was swept clean, empty except for barrel-sized stone urns in the corners and a large porcelain

33

fish bowl in front of the door of the room they now entered. Behind a carved rosewood desk, the *Ah Mah* sat, brush in hand, working on a text in characters. He nodded as Sam bowed. The woman disappeared back into the courtyard, and Sam remained standing.

The *Ah Mah* spoke in precise Cantonese syllables, as if addressing a large audience: "You speak and write English, is that correct?"

"Yes, Sir," said Sam, and bowed again.

"I need someone I can trust to read the documents I get from the English. I do much shipping business with them. You understand that I must have complete confidentiality?"

Wo Sam bowed again.

"Now that you are one of us, I also expect unquestioning loyalty. You can start today?"

"Sir, I have duties as scholar and accountant for the Yeung Lo Company."

"They brought you over?"

"Yes Sir."

"Then you will continue with them during the day, and come here in the evening."

Wo Sam bowed low, and the *Ah Mah* called for the woman to show him out.

***

"What happened?" said Kim, grabbing Wo Sam excitedly by both shoulders. "What did he want?"

"He wants me to go over his contracts with the white devils—that's all."

"Is his house worthy of the leader of the Chee Kong?"

"He is very wealthy. It may sound silly, but seeing his compound made me homesick. He had a courtyard, just like at home, but the rooms are furnished with rosewood and teak; silks cover the walls and furniture—much fancier than my father's house."

Later that night, after Wo Sam had eaten at a teahouse around the corner from the *ui kun*, he made his way back to the

34

Ah Mah's house. The same servant let him in again, and led him across the courtyard to another room. On the way, he heard the murmur of women's voices from behind one of the doors.

On the table were a number of sheets of paper with writing on them. Wo Sam hoped his English was up to the task, and wondered what would happen if it wasn't. The top paper consisted of a contract with the Chee Wo Suey Company—the tong's business name—and Edson Container, agreeing on the importation of a certain number of boxes of paste ink. *This is far too much money for even the finest ink*, thought Wo Sam. *This "paste ink" must be opium*. The prices and charges were outlined, and figures given in American dollars and *yuan*. Sam took an abacus from the table and worked with the figures—the numbers agreed.

By the tenth contract, his eyelids grew heavy and he longed to put his head on the table. *One more*. The numbers did not agree. *I must be tired*. He worked out the figures again. The numbers still did not agree. Chee Wo came up short on reimbursement for the paste ink it had brought for the Selmar Manufacturing Company in San Jose. Sam put the contract on top and made his way to the front door. The courtyard was silent.

Chapter SIX

In the morning before he went to his day work, Sam stopped by the *Ah Mah's* house and asked to see him. He was brought in and made to wait, afraid he would be late returning to the Yeung Lo Company. Finally, he entered the *Ah Mah's* receiving room, and told the story of the contract and error. The contract was brought to him, and he went over it again, showing the *Ah Mah* the differences in numbers. The *Ah Mah* seemed unimpressed, and dismissed the young man, telling him to return that night.

When he did, his chamber had a steaming pot of tea waiting; the woman servant checked in with him every hour to refill the pot or bring him rice to eat.

By the end of the week, Sam had found four discrepancies in agreements between the Chee Wo Suey Company and its American contractors which amounted to considerable sums of money. He personally brought each one to the attention of the *Ah Mah*, and on the following Monday, found an envelope with a twenty-dollar gold piece in it on his desk. The next day, the *Ah Mah* summoned him early in the morning.

"I want you to negotiate a contract for me," said the *Ah Mah*. "My man, Po Wen, speaks for me with Chinese, but you and he will go together to talk to the Americans. You will go tomorrow." The *Ah Mah* looked toward the doorway; "Po Wen? Come."

Wo Sam held his breath. He was to work at Yeung Lo the next day. What would he tell them?

Po Wen, dressed in deep blue satin, entered the room. He was close to Sam's father's age. He bowed deeply to the *Ah Mah* and nodded to Sam without meeting his eyes.

"This is the boy you will take with you tomorrow."

Po Wen bowed again. "Though you know best, my lord, it is unnecessary to trouble yourself by adding another person to the tasks you have set before me."

The *Ah Mah* said nothing. When Po Wen looked up, he quickly averted his eyes and bowed more deeply. "As you wish, my lord."

The *Ah Mah* waved them both away. In the courtyard, Po Wen looked beyond Sam's face and said, "Meet me tomorrow at noon on the corner of Spofford Alley and Washington *Gai*. You will not speak to the people we are meeting. I will do all the talking. You will listen. Do you understand?"

"Yes, sir."

***

The next day, Sam hurried out of the Yeung Lo building to the meeting place without saying anything to his coworkers. Po Wen saw him, and without formally recognizing him, began walking in the opposite direction; Sam hurried to keep up, but stayed several paces behind, as propriety dictated. They went into a storefront on a street just beyond the boundaries of Chinatown. Inside were three hair-faced white men dressed in tall hats and dark, close-fitting suits. One of the men—a short, sharp-faced fellow named Montrose—began to talk about "units," and "cost per unit." Po Wen looked serene, but his gaze traveled toward Wo Sam and back toward the men. Wo Sam bowed deeply to the older man, and asked if he might have the privilege of translating the white's poor English into decent Cantonese. It wasn't long before he was also translating Cantonese into English for Po Wen, when it became obvious that the older man's command of the language was tenuous. An exchange was agreed upon, and a price; Montrose wrote everything down in English and handed it to Po Wen, who waved it over to Sam. Sam read the document, and pointed out a correction. Montrose laughed uncomfortably, showing jagged, tobacco-stained teeth; he corrected the error. They parted ways, the Chinese leaving first.

Po Wen walked in front of Wo Sam, but the distance was much narrower. At one point, the older man stopped and Wo Sam walked up behind him but did not pass him. "Your parents taught you well," he said. "Where is your home?" Wo Sam named his village on the Pearl River. The older man nodded. "Where did you learn to speak English?"

"In Hong Kong, at the British school."

"Very useful."

"Yes, sir" said Wo Sam, "But I confess, at first I thought the Americans were asking to buy eunuchs."

The older man placed his hand on his chest and laughed. "Very similar," he said. "these 'units,'" as they call them, are women. Almost eunuchs. But much more valuable, at least here in Gold Mountain. I will speak to Lord Low Yet of this meeting. You will write up this contract in characters so I may present it?"

"Yes, sir."

Po Wen narrowed his eyes. "I think you will be very valuable, too."

Chapter SEVEN

California Cayley and Red Ellen of the Blue Rooster had become an attraction within a few weeks, and San Francisco's men-about-town came in to joke with them, beg a kiss, or win a bet on who would be the first to bed the flirtatious Miss Cayley. Ellen was already taken of course—she only had eyes for Bill Duarte, the gambler from Sacramento.

Cayley had never ridden so high. It was a celebration, a performance every night. And she made more money than she had ever seen. She went to the tailor on Market Street—where she could only afford ribbons and trim before—and ordered a silk evening dress she kept at the bar. Before she went home at night, she reluctantly peeled off the bright satin and changed back into her plain shirtwaist, coarse wool jacket and skirt.

Giddy with her newfound popularity, she quit Rolifer's at the end of her third week at the Blue Rooster. She told her mother, brother Michael, and husband that she was hired by guests of the Rolifer's to serve dinner at their home every night, sure the Rolifer's would say nothing to Michael—they properly kept the servants at arm's length on personal matters. Cayley turned over slightly more money to Henry than she did before. She felt enormous pride in handing her mother frequent gifts of coin along with sacks of groceries for the young ones; she saved whatever remained in a cigar box under her bed.

Since neither her husband nor her brother would ever drink alongside the merchants and other wealthy men who patronized the Blue Rooster, they'd never find out. And she really wasn't doing anything sinful, unless protecting those you loved from dark thoughts was a sin. Coloring up the truth gave her a strange devilish pleasure—the secret knowledge of something truly her own.

"I'm surprised that Mister Rolifer hasn't put a hand on you," said Ellen. "He's always eyeing you like a hungry bear when he's in here. Not that you would do anything, of course."

"He hasn't said naught to me beyond a compliment or two. And he's married, silly, like me."

"He 'recognize' you yet?" Ellen's voice dripped scorn.

Cayley tugged on the blonde curls over her ears. "I think he does, but he's never said. Probably too embarrassed to tell his cronies I quit being his servant to come work here. I guess he thought it was all right to be familiar with me when I worked for him, but I would likely speak up now."

"It's funny how they respect you more when they don't own you. Isn't Rolifer's wife one of them Decency League gals?"

"She is. Not a bad sort, though. Gave my brother work when no one else would have him."

Ellen leaned back against the bar and winked, "Is she as ugly as they say? That'll drive you to decency."

"She won't be posing for any fashion books, but she's good at running Rolifer's house for him," said Cayley. "At least she knew how to boss the servants. I was tired as a dog with ten pups when I was doing their housework and had to come home to my own, too!"

"You married for love, though, didn't you? That's what I want to do." Ellen turned to the bar and leaned on her elbows, cupping her chin in her hands. Riley suppressed a laugh, and she whipped a corner of a bar rag at his retreating behind.

"More or less. Less, if I tell the truth," said Cayley. "He asked me, and it was the thing to do—get married, have kids like my mother and every other woman in the parish. Get out of a crowded house, make a crowded house of my own. Henry had steady work. He was from the neighborhood, older than me, a big Irishman with a big laugh. He was sweet on me right away." Cayley touched her cheek with her fingers and was silent for a moment. Then she shrugged. "After the baby died, none of that seemed to matter. We don't have much to laugh about, like we used to. Oh, it's not his failing, not really. I suppose we're just getting on with it, like everyone else." Ellen put her hand on her friend's shoulder, and Cayley smiled up at her. "Maybe I was meant for a higher purpose."

"Like comforting poor, lonely Mr. Rolifer?"

"What a wicked one you are, Red Ellen!" Cayley turned to her, clasped her hand and together they went out to talk to the men at the tables.

At the end of the evening, Cayley changed into her plain clothes, draped her new wool coat over her shoulders, and walked ten blocks home on the dimly lit streets. With each step, she added up the money she made over the last few weeks, including what she was paid tonight. She was able to afford a hack! But how could she explain that to Henry?

She elbowed her way through the entry door, stepping into the odor of boiled potatoes and diapers, the homely scent of her neighbors, the McClatchys. Henry had taken to eating there nights, or at the bars he frequented with his fireman friends. They lived close to the firehouse, so he would come home for meals, even on duty days. Instead of being out or asleep, he stood in the doorway to their flat with his arms folded across his barrel chest, a scowl on his face. Cayley knew trouble when she saw it, and kept her head down as she tried to go around him. He had a yeasty smell that meant he'd downed enough beer to sweat it out—but he wasn't half-leaning over, so that was a good sign.

He stepped to the side to block her way. "I know your secret, girl."

She backed up and looked up at him. His once-handsome face was darkened by sun and drink. "And what secret's that, Henry?"

"Don't play the coy one with me. It's all over the firehouse, and I'm the fool. The last one to hear. My wife working as a bargirl, a common hoo-er."

Cayley felt her knees go watery. "Now just a minute, Henry. Let's talk this out. Who are you going to believe, those scatterbrains you work with, or me?"

"Why should I put my trust in whatever cock-and-bull story you're handing me? I looked in the door of that rich man's bar tonight and saw you flouncing around, all dressed up fancy. You can't tell me you haven't shamed me and my name." He stepped forward and grabbed her forearm so tightly the flesh bulged out the sides. Cayley winced but held her tears.

"Flouncing around, as you put it, is all I do. I serve drinks there, and I'm making good money, too—better than scrubbing an outhouse for rich brats."

He pulled her toward him so his face was above the top of her head. The dark stubble of his chin scraped against her bonnet. In a sinister whisper, he said, "If you're making such good money, and you've got nothing to be ashamed of, why didn't you tell me then?"

"I wanted to tell you. I considered it every day. Maybe I figured you'd not believe me—that you'd act like this. Henry, listen. First, let go, you're hurting me."

He jerked her forward, hesitated, then lightened his grip though he kept his hand on her arm. Mrs. McClatchy opened her door and stepped into the hall. "Everything all right here?" she asked.

"None of your business, Missus, get back inside!" snarled Henry.

"Well, you've no right to be making such a ruckus." Mrs. McClatchy stuck her nose up in the air, stepped back into her apartment and slammed her door shut.

"Let's go in and talk this through, Henry," said Cayley. "You're right, it's not the neighbor's business." They stepped inside the doorway. The room was cold, with a single lamp burning. It sat on the rickety table next to the rocking chair. An empty mug sat next to it. "Jaysus, it's cold in here," said Cayley.

"Don't try to wiggle out of this," said Henry. He shut the door behind them. "How could you, the mother of my son, my wife. A common hoo-er."

"It's whore, Henry, not hoo-er, as if it matters. Me and the other girl, Ellen, we just serve drinks, That's all. I swear! I helped the owner after he was robbed on the street, and he offered me a job. It's never been more than that."

"Do you expect me to believe that? Everybody knows what goes on in those bars."

"Well, everybody is wrong, Henry. The whorehouses are a few blocks over. They go there after they get liquored up at the bar. That shows what you and your friends know."

He drew up and slapped her across the face with the back of his hand. His arm led with so much power that she fell against the wall; the pins protruding from her hair scraped off bits of pale green wallpaper as they pressed painfully into her head. She lost her breath for a moment; then the tears started. She covered her face with both hands. "Jaysus, Henry. For the love of God!"

He stood, clenching and unclenching his fists. "How do you expect me to face people?" he asked. "How do you expect me to face our families and the boys?"

Cayley raised her face slowly from her hands. "Henry." She felt the flesh of her cheek starting to swell, making one side of her face seem twice the size of the other. "Is there anything wrong with wanting a little more than we've got? Is there anything wrong with wanting to live in a place of our own, that doesn't reek of rotten food?" Her voice began to rise. "Or of having enough money so that we don't have to scramble for a bit of coal for heat, and a God-damned warm coat?"

"I'm supposed to provide those things, and I do." He lowered his head as if expecting a blow himself. "I do the best I can."

Cayley dropped her hands to her sides, where they hung limply. "Ah Henry, I know you do. And you're not to blame for the state of things as it is. But look around you. Just look."

His face was set grim, and he looked steadily at her from beneath his lashes. Then he smirked and nodded. "You want another baby, don't you? Why didn't you just say so?"

Cayley sighed. She felt exhausted. "I'm not going to raise a child I can't afford to feed and keep warm. I'm going to keep working there," she said flatly. "We need the money."

"Like hell!" He moved toward her. She slid against the wall away from him.

"Why don't we talk about it tomorrow, in daylight?" she said. "We both need to cool off a little. I'll go talk to my mother. She'll straighten me out."

"That's a good idea. She'll talk sense to you, your mother."

Cayley packed a sack with clothing in it. She thought about reaching under the bed for the cigar box, but decided against it.

"I'll walk you," said Henry.

"No, it's not far."

His eyes narrowed.

"I'm going there, I really am," Cayley said. "Where else would I go?"

"I'll walk you," he said. He left her at her mother's door, two blocks away.

***

"Cayley, look at you!" Her mother tentatively touched Cayley's cheek, but the girl jerked away. "What is it this time?"

Cayley could hear her brothers and sisters in the back room—childlike snores mixed with the rustle of bodies three to a bed.

"I'm working at a bar on Market, Ma. It's a nice bar, I serve drinks there. I'm not doing anything wrong. I quit the Rolifer's."

Her mother sighed and shook her head from side to side. "The shame of it! And you've hidden this from Henry as well as me, I take it?"

They sat down at the battered wooden table, but were forced to whisper as Cayley's youngest brother and sister were again sleeping by the stove.

"He found out, though, and here's the proof." She pointed to her cheek. "Now how do you suppose he got word?" Cayley stared hard at her mother's worn face.

Her mother pressed her lips together, raised her right hand and looked first at the palm then at the back of it as if examining it for truth. "You know how those firemen talk amongst themselves." She stood up and put the kettle on over the banked coals in the stove. Hesitating, she turned around and sat down again at the table, placing both hands flat on the worn wood. "Maybe it was a word from your brother. Now I'm not saying it was! When Michael was here the other day, he said he saw you go in one of them fancy bars on Market." She quickly added, "None of us listened to him, though. Your brother can be in his own world."

"He seems to be in this world well enough. What would Michael be doing on Market Street at night, anyway?"

"Some errand for the Rolifer's I suppose." Cayley's mother raised one shoulder. "Why are you surprised by Henry? What decent man would allow his wife to work down there amongst that crowd?"

"What decent man beats his wife?"

"Cayley! He runs hot, does Henry. He's a good man, with a steady job. What can be going through your head? Being down there among them nobs has given you airs. Henry is right; you don't belong there. Go back to the Rolifer's and beg for your job, if, pray to God, they haven't already found someone else. Go home and beg your husband's forgiveness. He's the one who has to face everyone because of what you've done, after all." Cayley's mother stood up and began to pace the floor. "I'm ashamed of you, girl. I thought I raised you right." She continued to walk back and forth, her faded skirt twirled about her legs at every turn, her face a mask of worry. "Too good to be a servant now. Too good for the likes of us."

"You don't seem to mind the extra money I give you every week," said Cayley tightly.

Her mother stopped and turned toward the girl. She raised both hands to the level of her heart, and opened her mouth as if to speak. Then she shook her head and resumed her pacing. "I've no more words for this," she said. "You must to do right by your husband."

Cayley put her forearms on the table, and stared at the uneven grain of the wood. She had grown up eating at this table, crowded elbow-to-elbow with the other children. "I'm tired Ma. I'm tired of not having any say. I'm tired of nobody even listening when I got something to say. I'm not just a wife, or daughter, or a few extra coins in the church basket." Cayley opened her right hand, as if offering. "Times are changing, Ma. What about Miss Nellie Bly? People read what she has to say in the newspapers. She's not much older than me, and she don't come home to

45

a sharp slap or scrub plates for pennies. Is it asking so much to have a say?"

"You're living in a made-up world, daughter. That writer girl must come from money, or have some special pull to be working at that fancy job. She's schooled. It's not for the likes of us."

Cayley covered her face with her hands for a moment then looked up. "Let me sleep, all right, Ma? I can bed down with the kids here on the floor, and we'll talk again tomorrow." She stood up, pulled a bit of the quilt out from under her sister, and put her bag down as a pillow. By dawn, she was gone.

Chapter EIGHT

Fog was light in the lower mission, though Cayley noted heavy white clouds on the bay extending from the water onto the docks. She made her way to a boarding house just below the slot, but it was more than she could afford. They recommended a place on Clay Street, on the edge of the Chinatown—a run-down neighborhood, but a fairly safe place to stay. The boarding house called itself the Washoe Hotel, and though Cayley had to step around a few grizzled drunks, she could afford a room all her own—a luxury she had never dreamed of. It wasn't quiet; but no place she had ever lived was quiet. At least it didn't stink of boiled offal, and the man at the desk told her of a Chinese place nearby where she might get a meal of rice and meat for a nickel. Cayley walked to it, but had no idea what to order; she mimed a bowl, and the man brought her a steaming bowl of broth with meat and noodles in it. A strange breakfast, but it tasted wonderful and filled her. When she went back to her room, she was able to sleep for several hours before walking to the Blue Rooster.

"Did you fall down the stairs?" Ellen asked. "No, don't answer that. I'll bet I can guess. Mr. Wallace objected to your behavior, did he?"

"Does it look too bad?" Cayley was changing into her "work dress," and Ellen was helping her tighten her laces.

"We'll powder it up a bit. I'm surprised he let you come."

Cayley turned around, took a breath and closed her eyes. "He didn't. I ran away from home, though finding me is easy enough."

Ellen's mouth dropped open. "Cayley! Where are you staying, then?"

"At a boarding house on Clay. It's all right for now. In fact, and I'm a little surprised at this myself...it feels...good! I've never slept alone one night in my life. I have to get an advance from Mr. Max, as all my savings are home under the bed."

"My God, you've left your husband! I don't know whether to hip hooray or take you to the doctor to see if that wallop he gave you addled your brain." Ellen laced her fingers in front of her waist. "I'm worried about this."

"You and my mother both, I'm sure. I didn't think about it much—I only thought about getting away from his temper. I'm hoping he'll come around when he realizes I'm serious about working here."

"Well, let's just stay calm for the time being. I'd invite you to my place but for my aunt—she doesn't know what I do for a living, and it's easy enough not to tell her." Ellen stepped around behind Cayley and resumed pulling in her corset ties. "If she figured it out, she'd throw me in the street for sure."

"Oh, that's all right. I like where I am, for now. It's like I told my mother. I want to be like that Nellie Bly girl. She's as brave as can be, and bold too. Did you read that story she wrote about the insane asylum? If she can stay inside a madhouse for 10 days just to write about it, I can live on my own for a few days until Henry and them come around. I know they'll see what I'm doing makes sense."

***

Ellen and Cayley met before work and walked the shops. The newest sensation in the bookstores was the Oz book—it seemed that every shop in town had a tin man or cowardly lion in the display. Laphard's had an entire Emerald City in one window, made from cardboard and glitter. Cayley bought herself a copy and she and Ellen read it together at the bar before the door opened. "I don't care if it's a child's story," said Cayley. "I started working when I was old enough to stand up and never had the luxury of reading time; there was no money for books anyhow. I'll take my pleasure in it now. I'm going to make a little library in my room, and buy a new book every month."

Henry had been seen outside the door of the Blue Rooster a couple of times in the week since Cayley moved out, but he didn't enter, nor would he speak to her though she beckoned him in. He stood like an island, twisting his cap in his hands while the street whirled around him. She refused to go outside to talk to him. *If Henry would just screw up his courage and step inside, he could learn the world outside Irish town ain't all bad*, she thought.

On the third week, Cayley's brother Michael came to the bar and called her to the door. Hunched over, cap pulled low, Michael hid his malformed, gloved hands in his pockets; he appeared to be trying to make himself as small as possible. Jostled by passersby, he nearly toppled into the street as they stood outside on the narrow sidewalk. Michael brought a message from Cayley's husband: "Henry says you've shamed him beyond all measure; that you've become a fallen woman."

"Mother of God! That man's head is as solid as a brick!"

"If you won't come 'round to his will, sister, he intends to file for divorce, though he knows the Church won't recognize it."

Cayley's face collapsed like a crumpled balloon. "Oh Michael. How could he think so little of me?"

"He's set on his course." Michael kept his eyes on the sidewalk and jammed his hands more deeply into his pockets. "And he's right to do so. He might take you back. You can still save yourself by leaving this place."

"Save myself indeed. Well I'm set on my course too. And I suppose I have you to thank for all this…spying on me and tattling like a spiteful child."

"I was only doing right." He nodded firmly and clenched his jaw, avoiding her eyes. Behind him the lights in shop windows were being extinguished; down on Powell, shouts of doormen hailing hacks at the Baldwin Hotel rose above the street din.

"If either of you would listen to reason . . . Well, that's asking a lot, isn't it? I'm not leaving here. Come inside and see for yourself how innocent it is."

Michael looked up past Cayley into the brightly lit interior of the Blue Rooster. "I'll not set foot in such a place," he said.

She could see the longing pass over his face like a cloud blown by a soft wind.

He turned his gaze to the dusty toes of his boots. "They'd only laugh at me."

"Oh Michael, I'll take you into Mr. Max's office—you can watch from there and no one can see you."

He shook his head no without looking up.

Cayley rubbed her forehead. "Go home, Michael. Tell him if he won't take my word for it, there's naught I can do about it." She wished she could lie down in a field of poppies and just sleep, like Dorothy and her companions in Oz. But she also knew that if she wanted the sleep of dreams, there was plenty to go around a few blocks away in Chinatown—anyway, she preferred the laughter, gaiety, and high emotion of the Blue Rooster. "And this foolishness about a divorce...." she threw up her hands in exasperation. "That's plain crazy talk. Henry's as stubborn as a rusty bolt!"

"He'd say the same for you, sister."

Neither Michael nor Henry showed up at the Blue Rooster in the days that followed. When Cayley asked her mother of any news of them, she said, "Moving out was a grand insult to Henry. I haven't heard a peep from him, and Michael's not been home at all." Her mother set the cloth bag with bills and coins Cayley handed her on the table, then tucked wayward strands of hair into the white cotton cap on the back of her head. "A mother might be proud that her girl's doing well on her own. But why don't you come here to home instead of staying in that foreign place?"

"Ma, you know there's no room for me here. And Henry won't have me as I am. So I have to stay put for a while."

***

Cayley lay on the thin mattress in her room at the Washoe Hotel and listened to the night noises rumbling through the walls. She thought, *Am I a fool to throw away what little I have on a fancy job and a few dollars?* She missed the warmth of Henry in their little bed, and his sweetness when he was in a fine mood. *But I have to be steadfast. I'm seeing roses bloom on the cheeks of the young ones in my mother's house. It's worth the little discomfort I have to put up with to help my family. And the patrons treat me mighty well at the Blue Roo. We've had two good years together, Henry and me. They'll all come around, in time.* Cayley pressed her lips tightly together at the thought.

She began to arrive at work earlier and leave later than ever, turning the pages of her latest book—"Around the World in 80 Days"—while sipping a glass of Mr. Max's good whiskey.

One morning, after finishing her morning bowl of noodles at her breakfast spot, she went to the counter to pay and discovered she had left her change purse back in her room.

"I'll cover you, dearie. I'm plenty flush today."

Cayley turned to the tall smiling woman standing behind her. Though it wasn't unusual to see whites on the border of Chinatown, Cayley had noticed the woman and her friends once or twice before in the café, remarkable in the richness of their clothes and the light-hearted manner in which they conversed. They had nodded to her before, but not spoken. Cayley smiled back.

Chapter NINE

"Opal Boone, that's me." The voluptuous brunette touched the tip of her broad hat as a man might do. The deep-purple ostrich plumes that flared from the crown quivered.

"Oh, thank you Miss Boone. I'm so embarrassed. I live around the corner at the Washoe. I have the money, just not with me...."

"Call me Opal, dearie." She laughed out loud and gave Cayley's shoulder a playful tap. "No need to be so formal. I seen you around here a lot."

Cayley laughed, more out of embarrassment than anything else. "Well, thank you, Opal. If you want to wait here, I'll go home and get the money real quick, and come right back."

Opal turned to her two women friends who were seated nearby. "That's what they always say," she said in a loud stage whisper. The other women shook their heads and winked at each other. Cayley had no idea what to say in reply, so she stood there, smiling uncertainly.

"Oh, I'm just having fun with you, honey." Opal looked back at Cayley. "We were about to leave anyway, and we'll walk past your place on our way home. Safety in numbers!" she added, grinning.

As they stepped out the door, a Chinese man passed them on the way in. Cayley looked at him and hesitated, then turned her head away as he passed by her into the restaurant.

"What was that about?" said Opal. "Friend of yours?"

Cayley shrugged. "I thought I knew him, but I wasn't sure."

"He's a good-looking man. For a Chinese." Opal narrowed her eyes appraisingly. "On the other hand, it's a bad idea to cozy up to too many of the oriental persuasion these days."

On the street outside, Cayley felt like a sparrow among peacocks. It passed her mind that maybe these ladies might be the right kind of friends—they definitely looked prosperous and spoke well, like the ladies who visited the Rolifer's. Opal and her friends were dressed in fine warm wool jackets, skirts and shirtwaists, in the slim new style from Paris. The hand-worked passementerie on Opal's jacket would have cost Cayley a month's wages. "If you don't mind my asking," said Cayley, "I can't help but wonder why you eat at that place. You look like you're used to much better."

"Oh, we adventurous types like to try all sorts of things," said one of the women, a short, dark-tressed girl who looked to be about Cayley's age. "And we like the Chinaman's place. He always has a smile for us."

"We live close. We like to explore when not otherwise engaged, don't we girls?" Opal repositioned her hat on her head and readjusted her hatpin as she walked.

My goodness, thought Cayley. These must be the "new women" I hear so much about. "Where do you live?"

"Across from the church...on California Street. The one that says 'son, observe the time and fly from evil'," said Opal. Her friends giggled.

Cayley giggled too. "Oh, I thought that was all...if you'll pardon me...bordellos." The minute Cayley said it, she knew. She immediately stiffened, her cheeks a fiery shade of red. "Oh ...sorry. Didn't mean...."

Opal's eyes narrowed. "You want me to go back to the café and get my nickel?" said Opal. "The Chinaman didn't ask where it came from."

"Oh God, I've really put my boot in it, haven't I?" Cayley stopped on the street and the other women turned toward her. "I...I'm just a girl from south of the slot, and I don't mean offense to you. I moved out here on my own a few weeks ago—my husband didn't like me working down at the Blue Rooster on Market—I serve drinks there. Uh, just drinks. Serving drinks. I moved out to try to knock some sense into him, as if it would work..." Cayley felt herself babbling. Her face continued to burn.

"Take it easy, dearie," said Opal. "We won't contaminate you, if that's your worry."

"Oh no, please." Cayley brought her hand to her forehead. "I'm in no position to judge anyone, anyway. I've been judged enough myself, and learned the worth of that!"

"Well, that's in your favor, then," said Opal. "There's nothing worse than the nob's wives who hide their sneers behind their lace hankies, though they suspect we call their men by their Christian names. If you needed to know for sure, we do work the pleasure houses. And I spent all my bad feelings about it a long time ago, so I've got no more shame to waste. What do you think about that?" Opal put her hands on her hips.

Cayley waited for the Clay St. streetcar to rattle past before she replied; a sternly dressed nanny pulled one of her charges into the car as it rumbled up the roadway. "Better than staring at your shoes all day," she said.

"All right, then. We'll get along just fine. Shall we?" Opal turned towards the Washoe hotel. If Cayley expected the women to quietly shuffle along, she couldn't have been more wrong. Opal and the others called out greetings to people in the street, and loudly shared bits of personal news that would have made Cayley duck for cover if there were any. When they reached the front stoop of the Washoe House, Opal said, "We'll wait out here for you."

"Shouldn't you come inside the parlor where it's warm, at least?"

"I appreciate the kind thought—we all do—but once you set foot inside with the likes of us, you might not have a place to live, even in this garbage heap. We'll wait." Opal folded her arms across her chest and looked up and down the sidewalk. "Go on."

Cayley did as she was told, shamed by her relief at Opal's reprieve. When she returned to the parlor, she saw the back of the stout matron who ran the Washoe House, broom in hand in the doorway. "Scat," she was saying, "No need for the likes of you around this place. Get on with you!"

"With pleasure!" Cayley heard Opal's deep voice. "None of your louse-bitten tenants could afford to buy a friendly wink from the likes of us anyway." Cayley came up behind the woman and stood on her tiptoes to look over her shoulder. "And a jolly good day to you too, Missus." Opal caught Cayley's eye, touched the brim of her hat as she did before, and crossed the muddy street with her gaggle of friends, their expensive skirts swishing about their ankles.

Three days passed before Cayley once again ran into Opal at the Chinaman's café. "At least let me buy your breakfast plus what I owe you. I'm embarrassed about what happened. She had no right."

"There's a lot of ignorant people in the world. It used to bring me to tears sometimes, but now I try not to pay any mind."

"That's mighty forgiving of you. I can't say I'd be so generous."

"Why waste your spunk on things you can't change? I was like that woman once—probably still would be if my life had turned out different. And she'd be like me if she had to grow up stealing fruit off other people's trees to fill her stomach. Her old man likely owns that place, or she gets free board for running it, and she's content. She's lucky." The Chinaman brought two bowls of steaming soup and set them down on the table. The windows turned white with vapor as the fragrance of chicken broth and fresh cilantro wove into the air.

"So, you grew up poor?'

"Same old story. Just about all the girls tell it—not every one though. Sometimes we get rich girls out looking for a thrill. I grew up in the mining camps, met a few 'ladies' in the jail when I got caught stealing. Learned I could make decent money with my looks. I came here with one of the gals—she was a sweetheart. She's gone off now, but I stayed. What about you? Oh yeah—job at the bar, husband. You like what you do?"

Cayley manipulated her chopsticks to pull a thick noodle from the broth. "It's real nice—I guess I'm content, too, in a way. It's a lot more money than I made as a house servant. Though the husband is sure I...do what you do. I can't seem to convince him otherwise."

"They do get all possessive, don't they? So you just serve drinks, is that what you said?"

"That's all. I don't have to do anything I don't want to. I mean…this is a rude question, I suppose, but you can't blame me for being curious…what's it like for you?"

"Well, I gave up on marriage and a family a long time ago, if that's what you're thinking. It isn't romance, that's for sure! It's a quick business—and there are ways to make it quicker, if you know what I mean. No, I guess you don't. I like a few of the customers, and I can say no to whomever I want. The money is real good, though they—the owner Montrose and Madam Maude, who runs the place—take half of what I get at the door, which pays for my room there." Opal put a slim finger under the jet collar she wore and began to toy with it, sitting back in her chair. "It's not as bad as some—they get beat by their bosses. And the Chinese girls—that's the worst. They keep them like beeves for the slaughter." She was silent for a moment. "I'd like to save up enough money—leave town someday and start fresh someplace else. Someplace where I don't run into any of my customers." She patted the black beaded neckpiece and returned to her food. "I hear Seattle is nice."

"Maybe you could run your own boarding house."

Opal smiled, exposing yellowing teeth. "Yeah. And I wouldn't insult the working girls with a broom in my hand, don't you know. It's hard to save money though. Too many temptations." She ran her hand down the subtle shine of her mauve silk skirt. And I won't be young forever." Her smile faded. "This isn't all that I do, though. I work as an actress and singer when I can get a job. I was at the California Theater in "A Trip to Africa' last spring. I played Tessa, a young milliner. Did you see me?"

"I didn't have money for entertainments then," said Cayley. "But I bet you were wonderful." She looked down at her own skirt and picked off an invisible piece of lint. "When I was a kid, we used to put on little plays, my brothers and sisters. Oh, we'd sing and dance around like right fools. I forgot about that. We'd even charge the neighbors a penny to see our show." She laughed. "I guess they came out of kindness."

Opal smiled and looked down at her bowl, "What I do for a living—it's all about being an actress, isn't it? I love acting—on the stage. And singing. I wish I could do it all the time. But a girl's got to eat. We got a piano player at my house—he's playing that peachy new ragtime rhythm—can't sing to that though. Do you have music where you are?"

"Mr. Max just hired a man to play tunes people can sing along with—like 'Tavern in the Town." You come by and sing some time. And make sure to tell me when you get another part and I'll come see you. You'll save up that money, I know you will. Now you've got me inspired!" Cayley picked up her bowl and drank deeply to finish her soup, as she had seen the Chinese patrons do. When they had finished, the women stepped onto the street outside.

"I'll walk you part way back," said Opal. "I'm off to Sacramento Street to pick up my new dress. It's fine silk, the color of a mossy green river—those Chinese really make beautiful goods."

Cayley shook her head no, "It's out of your way. I need to run a few errands first, as it is." She was embarrassed, uncomfortable walking by Opal's side, as if the woman's sweet French perfume marked both of them. They kissed each other on the cheek and parted ways.

Cayley turned up the alley, planning on taking the short cut back to her room when a man who had been lounging against the wall pushed himself toward her. "Hello, pretty," he said.

Cayley kept her head down and walked rapidly past him. He grabbed at her arm. "Now wait just a minute. Not so fast. Come here and talk to me." He pulled her against him and began rubbing his lower half furiously against her skirt, in spite of her struggles.

"Get off me!" Cayley tried to elbow him in the face, but he pinned her arms to her waist and began moving his dirt-blackened free hand on the front of her jacket.

"Let go, you ass!" Opal's voice reached Cayley's ears at the same time she felt the man's head bob sideways from a blow. He loosened his grip, and Cayley bolted forward. She and the man

57

both turned toward Opal, him holding his ear. Opal opened her small beaded bag—probably what she had hit him with—and withdrew a pearl-handled derringer not much bigger than the palm of her hand. "Maybe you'd rather get friendly with this," she said, and leveled the derringer at his forehead. "Now git!" The man laughed nervously, backed down the alley, turned and walked away rapidly. Opal followed his progress with the gun; "When I saw you turning up that alley, I had a bad feeling. A lot of street girls work the alleys during the day—nasty business."

Cayley was shaking. "You'd think I'd know by now."

Opal shrugged. "Sometimes we gals have to learn the hard way. This town is full of desperate galoots. Might as well keep out of the alleys, especially at night. I'll walk you home." Cayley nodded, and put her arm through Opal's, holding on to the other woman tightly.

Chapter TEN

Cayley and Opal continued to meet at the Chinaman's café once or twice a week. They would sit with "the girls," and Cayley indulged her curiosity, shyly asking how each had ended up working as prostitutes in the city—stories they were eager to tell, since they seldom had anyone to listen but each other. Most were like her—not much schooling or any reason to aim high in life—but unlike her, they often came from brutal homes, or no home at all. It made her grateful for her ordinary childhood, poor as it was.

When the weather turned clear and cold and merchants began to put pine wreaths on their doors, Cayley celebrated Christmas with her brothers and sisters at her mother's flat. She was doubly glad to be among the noise and chaos of her big family, warmed by the joshing and roughhousing of the younger children. The only one who shied away from her was Michael. He wouldn't look her in the eye, which made her angry and ashamed at the same time—but any attempt at a conversation with him ended in silence. "It's like old times," her mother said gaily, trying to cover the gap, though Cayley noted that the neighbors turned their faces away from her when she stepped up to the door as well.

Later in the week, Opal invited Cayley and a few of the "girls" for dinner at Fior d'Italia, by the old church. Standing outside the restaurant with the rest of the women as their table was being prepared, Cayley kept looking about her; she couldn't help but wonder if passersby judged her to be a prostitute. She casually stepped back a little from the group and turned to examine the façade of the white church, only to lower her eyes to Opal's intense gaze. "Are you looking for angels or devils?" Opal asked. "Or maybe the cops?" Cayley felt her color rise. "You won't find any of those here, dearie." Opal smiled. "Just us chickens." She winked.

Cayley was aware of the turmoil that roiled around her heart and conscience. The church and everyone she knew looked down on these women; Opal and the others seemed to be decent, kind people—with more courage than most—and Cayley wanted to be comfortable with them. If she failed to do that, she was no better than Henry and his witless friends. But a lifetime of snickering and jokes about whores was hard to turn her mind against—and just as hard to relate to the girls she had come to know as ordinary souls, doing the best they could to get by. After all, didn't Jesus forgive Mary Magdalene? But then, he told her to go and sin no more. What sin was he referring to, exactly?

Once inside, the waiters doted on Opal, and cared not a whit about her profession. Cayley noted that in these modern times, money spoke very loud indeed. As the chief waiter refilled Opal's glass for the tenth time, she rose, her teal satin dress glowing in the candlelight, and made a toast to "All us gals what takes care of ourselves, everywhere." She sat down heavily in her chair and leaned over to Cayley: "It doesn't take an illusionist like—that new fellow, what's his name, Houdini?—to see you're glum. What is it?"

"Sorry, Oppie—I'm not to be spoiling your lovely party. I was thinking about Henry—my husband, or at least I think he's still my husband. I would know if he divorced me, wouldn't I? My ma's not heard a word."

"Ah, you'd know. Someone would tell you. If you want him to come around, maybe you should be first to make amends."

Cayley ran her fingers lightly up and down the side of her wine glass, and shrugged. Her eyes lingered on the greenery strung together on the rafters. *It's so pretty in here, and the food is delicious. I'd never even have stepped inside a place like this if my life had turned out the way it was going*, she thought. *Nice to not have to stretch every penny then clean up the mess everyone's left for me, like poor ma does. Especially after coming home from scrubbing someone else's kitchen.*

Opal leaned back and narrowed her eyes. "You need to distract yourself, dearie! Give your busy little head a project. Plan a party—not in your place, I mean at that saloon you work at—get your friend Ellen and that piano player to help you put on a show or something—a little comedy. We do it at the house all the time—different kind of show, though." She grinned, and Cayley blushed in spite of herself.

***

Darkness had set in early, and Mr. Max and Riley were standing near the cash register debating whether to go with the new electricity when it came in or keep the gas lamps.

Cayley leaned over the bar and put her hand over her friend's. "Ellen, listen to my idea."

"What is it this time?" Ellen laid the upper half of her body across the bar, eyes closed. "I'm beat-up."

"Why don't we—you and I—put on a little show here. We could dress up like Dorothy and Toto and look for the wizard, and pick out a scarecrow and lion and tinman from the patrons every night."

Ellen raised her head from the bar. "Jaysus." She rolled her eyes and put her head down again. "I suppose you want me to be the dog."

"You don't like it."

"Cay, darlin', it's just that—our patrons may not be interested in a children's story. They're more...they've got other things on their minds." She pushed herself upright on the bar and sighed deeply. "Riley—come wipe this down. It's sticky as molasses."

"Opal says it's a good way to get them to stay here longer, and give more of them a chance to appreciate us in a cash kind of way." Cayley stood up and put her hands on the rim of the bar. The wood was warm beneath her palms. "You know it's been kind of slow lately."

"Oh, I like the cash part well enough. But I believe your friend Opal's shows have very little to do with dogs. Or maybe not."

"Don't be rude. It would give us a chance to be more than just bar girls; even that famous Eye-talian ballet dancer Opal told me about—Taglioni, or something like that—had to start somewhere. It'll be fun. Come on, it's a good idea."

"What, the show, or cozying up to that woman? It's not safe to be around that sort. I'm talking about that knife man that's going after street girls in the Barbary, the one they call the West Coast Ripper. You read stories in the Bulletin."

"She's not in the Barbary, and it's safer to be around her than alone—I already told you about what happened in that alley. She's a decent gal. You aren't jealous, are you? You're still my dearest friend."

Ellen stood upright and rubbed the small of her back, blowing out a long breath and closing her eyes. "All right, all right. This show—we have to get a little more daring, you know. Dressing like a little black dog doesn't leave a lot of room for our womanly wiles to shine."

"So, what's your idea?"

"I'm too tired to hatch ideas."

Cayley stood on her tiptoes and whispered in Ellen's ear. "Too many nights out with that handsome gambler of yours. Handsome Bill."

"You're probably right. Now if it was Bill talking, he'd say we needed something fancy. Exotic, he would say."

"Exotic like what?"

"You know, like them Chinese girls with fans, or dancing harem girls...something like that. Not kids' stories or Irish dancing. Not ordinary."

"That might be fun. Not the Chinese part, but the harem girl thing. We could be dancing harem girls, what do you think?" Cayley moved her head from side to side on her neck.

"A purple veil would suit me very well, I'm sure. But I'm not going to dance around half-naked for nobody. It'll be tasteful or not at all. You need to talk to Max about this."

"Tasteful. Yeah, that's it. We're the classier sort of harem girls."

***

Cayley set up the event with Max, who had flyers printed reading "Mysterious Harem Girls from the Nile do the Dance of the Veils" in three different typefaces. They figured they could

62

get everything in place by early March. He suggested the girls tie shawls around themselves and drop them one by one down to a simple dress, showing a bit of bosom, ankle or arm; not much more than they revealed by wearing one of their fancy dresses, which put Ellen more at ease.

"Actresses do it all the time," said Cayley. "Opal tells me so, and she would know. There's Sarah Bernhardt on the stage. And that Duncan girl from Oakland, Dora. She wears them Greek-looking see-through dresses and goes flitting around—she teaches that new kind of free dance, and even plans on going to Europe, where the high-brows think it's hot stuff. You could do as well."

"Well, if it's for art," Ellen said sarcastically.

***

Cayley and Ellen got directions from Opal and went down to Little China to buy yards of sheer silk in different colors. Cayley found herself looking into the faces of the passersby to see if she could spot the Chinese man who had helped her carry Mr. Max to the bar.

"You're looking around like you've never seen yellow men before," said Ellen.

"It's all so…different," Cayley said, deciding to keep her search to herself. The two women had a high old time cutting and draping silks on each other, pretending to be modern dancers, arching their backs and touching their fingertips together. "Don't forget to point your toes," Cayley said. "It's more graceful."

"I must be putting on a little weight," said Ellen. "I seem awful out of breath these days. Not that they want to see us run around anyway."

Mr. Max kept the front area of the bar as it was, with tables for the customers, and set up the back of the room screened off with chairs arranged in rows like a theatre. "This way, we can charge 'em a nickel extra," he said. Cayley wasn't crazy about the idea, since she felt she deserved a bigger audience, but Max's practicality ruled.

On the day of the first performance, Cayley arrived in the late afternoon, and began to worry when Ellen didn't show up in time to dress. Max had to work the barroom himself. "Where do you think she is?" said Cayley. "She always shows up. This isn't like her at all."

Max shrugged his shoulders. "I'll say yes to that. But the show must go on, my dear, as I've already filled the seats and the natives is restless, as they say."

"Max...you don't think she backed out 'cause she's shy about showing herself off, do you? I'd feel awful if I pushed her too hard to do this."

"You can ask her yourself, probably tomorrow. As for now, scoot in the back and change. We'll work with what we've got."

Cayley put on her outfit and one of the cooks prepared to pound on pan lids behind a screen as the piano man played musical accompaniment. Both started to bang out a rhythm, and she emerged from the back door, the lower half of her face veiled. Her armpits grew damp, and her upper lip was wet with sweat; *Mother Mary, what am I doing,* she thought. *Too late to run for it now.* Pulling in a deep breath, she undulated onto the open area and prepared to peel off a scarf.

A drunken voice yelled, "I only see one harem girl. There's supposed to be girls. Where's the other girls?"

"Hey, that's Cayley" someone in the crowd shouted. "Show it off, Cayley." The men laughed and Cayley pulled aside her veil and stuck out her tongue. Then she turned around and wiggled her bottom at them, and they roared. The cook pounded on the pan lids, Cayley whirled around the room, dropping scarves on the laughing, hooting patrons, occasionally pinching one if he reached for her and shaking her finger at his naughty behavior. By the time she got to her final veil, the crowd was throwing money at her, begging her for more. She picked up the bills and coins, tucked them in the cleavage of her low-cut muslin shift, shook her finger at the crowd once more, and slipped out the back door. She heard the cheers and applause behind her and thought, *Bernhardt be damned. This is art if I ever!*

She changed her clothes and appeared on the barroom floor as if nothing happened, opening her eyes wide when a comment was made. "I don't know what you mean!" she said. And "The harem girl has gone home to her sultan." Everyone was calling her name, giving her big tips, and her laughter was heard over the din of the barroom all night long. When Ellen still didn't show by closing time, Cayley sat on the bar stool with her hands on either side of her face. "I don't like this at all," she said.

"Well, I believe I know where her aunt lives," said Mr. Max. "But maybe she was just sick tonight or something, and couldn't send word."

"She hasn't been feeling well," said Cayley. "That's true."

But Ellen didn't show up the next night, and Cayley danced alone.

***

By the third day, Cayley got the address of Ellen's aunt from Riley and walked to the far side of town near where Washerwoman's Cove used to be, before they filled it in. The house was a single-story affair of sun- and wind-bleached wood. Two cows on the side of the dusty road looked at her hopefully before she turned up the narrow path and knocked on the door.

The door opened a few inches. An elderly woman peered through the crack. "What do you want?"

"Does Ellen Leary live here? I'm a friend of Ellen's. I haven't seen her in a few days, and I was a little worried. Is she all right?"

"No, Miss Ellen Leary doesn't live here, at least not any more. And if you're a friend of hers, I want no business with you. You're right to worry about her, but it won't do no good."

"What do you mean? Do you know where she went? Did she go with someone?"

"No, and I don't care. She's trash, that's what. If she wasn't my sister's brat, I'd never have had anything to do with her."

Cayley's face flamed. "Look, woman. Ellen is a good and dear person, and you're the one who's trash if you're ignorant to that." The door slammed in her face.

As Cayley marched back up the dirt road, she couldn't help but think, *What if I caused her to run off, pressing her with my big ideas? I'd never forgive myself. Where can she be?*

Chapter ELEVEN
September 1891 – Two Years Later

At the behest of Lord Low, Sam began to go with Po Wen to each business negotiation whether his translating skills were needed or not.

"It is not necessary for you to follow me like a motherless puppy," Po Wen would exclaim with annoyance.

"I'm sorry to displease you," replied Sam with barely disguised pride. "But the *Ah Mah* requested that I accompany you."

The *Ah Mah* also sent him down to the docks to make sure the shipments arrived from China as promised, and to take charge of the delivery to various destinations, warehouses, or homes. Sometimes the shipments consisted of three-by-four-foot wooden crates filled with small ceramic containers of opium coated with a thin layer of paste ink; other times, of groups of young women, "relatives" of those already in Chinatown. These girls were, for the most part, big-footed peasants who came off the ship with open mouths, turning their heads this way and that.

Sam would steer them down the creaking long wharf toward the warehouse.

One Tuesday, Wo Sam carried the shipping papers to the dock, and waited as five women stumbled down the gangplank. The customs agent asked them questions through a translator: "You are the wife of Bo How?" "Show me the marriage documents." "You are the sister of Sai Ma?" "You are the wife of Lee Po Duck?" The girls would nod and produce documents proving that they were brides, or immediate family. Wo Sam knew that these girls were married on paper to husbands already here in Gold Mountain. When he identified himself as their escort, a moon-faced girl with thick bangs said, "Has my husband Bo How sent you? Why is he not here to meet me?"

"He has sent me. I will take you to where you will live." Wo Sam gave the reply he was taught.

"He must be doing very well to send a servant for me."

Wo Sam felt his stomach churn a little. Like many others, this girl did not know that she was one of many brides of Bo How, and that her real destination was a crib, a house of prostitution. Wo Sam took a deep breath, and steadied himself. These were merely uneducated peasants, and worthless women, at that. He needn't concern himself with their fates. He nodded in reply to her comment. "Let's go."

When the group reached the warehouse, they met the hardened women who supervised the cribs. The girls were looked over like livestock, their mouths and teeth inspected, arms and legs prodded to see if they were too fat or thin. The moon-faced girl protested, "My husband Bo How will see you are whipped for this!"

The wrinkled, gray-haired woman who had been inspecting her slapped her hard across the face, adding stinging tears to the girl's frightened countenance. "Shut up, cow," the old woman ordered, and pushed the girl roughly toward a waiting carriage.

Many times, Sam thought of returning to his original position of Yeung Lo scholar; then he remembered the money. There was no comparison. He would have his poke, the sum that would make him a rich man back in China, within six months by working for the tong; then he could leave all this behind.

***

As Wo Sam left the *Ah Mah's* house late one evening and strolled slowly down Waverly, he could hear the Mah Jong tiles clicking and shouts of anger or joy emanating from doorways along the alley. Why not? He had extra money, something he had little of as a scholar. He turned into a narrow doorway and made his way down to the basement. Card tables were set up in the far corner, and nearer the entrance, Mah Jong players clicked their tiles and gestured at each other. If the police came, the cards would disappear like smoke on a windy day and the room would hold nothing more than a friendly men's club sharing a traditional Chinese game, incomprehensible to foreigners. Sam stood in back of one of the Mah Jong players. He was too late to join—they had already begun their play—each still had their 13 tiles except for the man Sam stood behind, designated "East" with 14 tiles. He was the first to discard a tile, and the next player drew from the table, taking one of the four sets of 18 tiles that made up the "walls" on the table. Sam loved the game, the suits with carved pictures of bamboo, or circles, or characters: the four winds, three dragons, flowers and seasons. A lifetime played out on a table. But like a lifetime, it would take much too long for a player to gain *woo*, a complete hand of four sets plus a pair, or any of the other dozen winning combinations. No wonder foreigners were confused. *Too long to wait for good fortune.* Sam headed for the fan-tan tables.

Fan-tan was much simpler, and didn't take so long to win—or lose. Sam joined a group of eight men, and the dealer dealt the deck as Sam put his coin on the table with the others. With the odds so bad, he made sure he didn't stand on the dealer's left. The man who was there failed to lay a seven card on the table, and laid down a coin, instead. The next player laid down a seven of clubs. Sam had a six of clubs, and laid it down. The next player forfeited a coin. The circle continued to lay down coins or cards, depending. New suits were laid, and three of the players, including Sam, were within one card of cashing in when the man next to Sam laid down his final card and took the pot. Sam stayed in for two more deals, losing most of the cash in his pocket before he decided to go back to the room he was renting with his cousin in a men's residence hotel. They had moved there after Sam had quit the Yueng Lo company, and was asked to leave the *ui kun*.

At 2 a.m., Little China, particularly along Waverly and Spofford alleys, was filled with both men and women, white and Chinese. Wo Sam saw the moon-faced girl, the bride of Bo How, standing on the street with the older woman, who had a clawlike grip on her sleeve. The girl's face was vacant, her lips made up with bright red paint; she wore a yellow satin jacket, color of the *Ah Mah's* house. He kept his head down and hurried past. His memory flashed to the proud white whores he often saw in Little China at one of the restaurants where he collected protection money. He recalled his surprise at seeing the pale little housemaid among them, the one he had helped in the alley months ago—the girl who was as white as a porcelain statue of Quan Yin. He shook the memory out of his head.

As the crowds thinned, he realized that the footsteps behind him never faltered. He turned quickly to see a slight young man trailing behind. When the young man knew he had been spotted, he walked quickly up to Wo Sam.

"You are in the employ of Chee Wo Suey?" His earnest face disarmed Sam.

"What do you want?"

"I'm looking for someone. A girl. Named Wah Si. Very pretty. I believe that she is in one of your houses."

"I wouldn't know. I don't know the girls in the houses or their names."

"You would know this girl. She is not like the rest. She has golden lilies, not a peasant girl. You must know her." The young man seemed on the verge of tears.

"I don't know her. Please go away. I cannot help you."

"You must know her." The young man raised his voice, stepped in front of Sam and grasped the front of Sam's jacket.

Sam stopped, appalled at this rude behavior; he pulled the man's hands from his coat. "What's the matter with you! Are you crazy? I don't know her. I cannot help you. Leave me alone." He started to walk rapidly away. The young man followed him for a few steps, continuing his anxious pleas, but Sam didn't turn, and hurried up the street. After he rounded the corner, he checked to see if he was still being followed. The young man appeared to be gone; Sam continued to his room and his cousin's reassuring snores.

Chapter TWELVE

The next morning, Wo Sam mentioned the incident to Po Wen as they stood in the courtyard of the *Ah Mah's* house.

"He was looking for a woman with bound feet?" Po Wen tucked his hands into the sleeves of his heavy embroidered jacket.

"That's what he said. He called them golden lilies, the old-fashioned name."

"Imagine that," said Po Wen, and moved his hands farther up his sleeves until he clasped his forearms. The morning was cold and gray, so often the case in late spring.

"I thought he was crazy. I've never seen any but peasant girls in the brothels. Big-footed, silly farm girls who should be glad to get out of the wet fields and into a warm house."

Po Wen merely smiled without showing his teeth and nodded. "He said the girl's name, the crazy man, did he not?"

"Yes, I can't remember what it was, though. Wah something."

Po Wen nodded again. "Little China is becoming a dangerous place these days," he said. "What with all those who cannot control their desire for opium and such. Perhaps you need a bodyguard to accompany you on official business."

"A soldier, a *boo how doy*? No! No one is interested in me. He was just one crazy man."

"Still, I'm sure the *Ah Mah* would not like anything to happen to you, or to his business interests, either." At that moment, the *Ah Mah's* woman servant summoned them to his chamber.

Wo Sam loved to be in that room: the curved rosewood chairs, their deep red-brown polished to a high sheen, the fine silk paintings on the walls, the auspicious red brocade, color of luck. Round lamps covered with sheer ivory silk hung from the ceiling, pulled down by gold tassels to be lit. *When I return to China, I will have a room like this,* he thought. *My father will be proud of me, and my sister will have the dowry to marry a rich man. I shall have a noble wife. With golden lilies.*

"Sir," said Po Wen. "Young Sam has had a most interesting incident."

"It's nothing to bother *Ah Mah* about, a minor mishap." Wo Sam bowed deeply.

The *Ah Mah* leaned forward in his seat. "I'll judge that for myself. Po Wen always knows what interests me. Tell me what occurred."

Wo Sam reiterated the story.

"And this young man, what did he look like?" said *Ah Mah.*

"Slightly built, no facial hair. Rich clothes, though it looked like he had worn them too long."

The *Ah Mah* nodded and looked at Po Wen, then rubbed his chin with his left hand.

"The streets are so full of wretched types these days," said Po Wen. "From all classes. I suggest that we have one of the soldiers accompany Wo Sam, but he is resistant to the idea."

"Why is that? Why do you refuse the protection of Low Yet?" The *Ah Mah* looked coldly into Sam's eyes.

"I'm neither small nor weak, and I hold my own well," said Wo Sam. "This was unusual, sir, and I wouldn't trouble you to take one of your men to protect me as if I were a woman."

"These things are true," said Po Wen. "In fact, Wo Sam is very capable under ordinary circumstances. However, life is becoming so much more precarious these days. I have an idea that might solve the situation—make Wo Sam even more able to defend himself, and reassure Lord Low and myself that Wo Sam—our valuable asset—is well protected. One of our soldiers will teach Wo Sam to use a firearm, and he will carry one with him. To protect himself and others in his charge, you see. To render attackers useless."

The *Ah Mah* tapped his finger on his chin and nodded in the direction of Po Wen. "I see the advantages to your solution. Surely Wo Sam will agree to this, as it is to all our advantages."

Wo Sam was, in fact, rather excited about the prospect of learning to use a gun, and to carry one, though he doubted he would ever use it. Back in China, only Imperial forces were allowed firearms, but here in America.... "If it serves you best, *Ah Mah*, I will learn at once."

Ah Mah summoned his servant, and arrangements were made for Wo Sam to meet with one of the tong soldiers by the old brick fort where the bay opened to the sea. That evening, in the darkness, Wo Sam waited among the trees for the approach of a man wearing a traditional blue jacket and pants and a flat-brimmed western hat. The man was older than Wo Sam by several years, soft-spoken and quiet. He showed Wo Sam how to load a long-muzzled revolver with six bullets, and the men took turns firing at glass bottles they placed in front of a fire they had built several yards away. When they heard voices—someone must have reported the sound of the gun—they melted into the forest, but not before the nameless *boo how doy* handed the revolver and bullets to Wo Sam and told him to keep them hidden on his person under his jacket.

***

At first, Wo Sam only wore the gun when he ran errands for the *Ah Mah*, but within a few weeks, he began wearing it when he went to the gambling parlors in the evenings. He also adopted the western-style flat felt hat that many of the tong men wore. The gambling hall owners knew him by name now, and greeted him with sweet wine at the door and small bowls of delicacies.

Sam's cousin, Kim, asked him to put in a word for him to the *Ah Mah*, so that he too might enjoy an equally favored status. When Sam did say something to Po Wen, Kim was offered the position of soldier. Kim was not happy about this. "They kill each other, cousin. They fight in the streets," he said.

With a touch of impatience, Sam replied, "You wanted a better position. It's better than a dockworker. If I didn't speak English, I would never be where I am now. Be glad they offered you something at all." Wo Sam turned away from his cousin and hurried out the door to Waverly Place, and an evening in his favorite parlor.

Wo Kim trained as a soldier, a bodyguard assigned to the brothels to keep others from stealing or freeing the women kept there.

**

The late fall brought some of the best weather around San Francisco Bay; clear days and nights led to chilly evenings that heralded a rainy winter to come. Life continued much the same for Wo Sam. He escorted shipments from the docks to warehouses or the houses of prostitution that dotted the neighborhood. He collected money from businesses the tong "protected", though he did not see the pale little housemaid again. Every time he looked up and saw the words written on the Christian church, "—and flee from sin," he laughed, thinking of the number of white Christian men who stumbled out of the cribs down the street, saw the admonition, and hurried home to whatever was waiting there. Not that most of them were married. Prostitution was such a profitable business in San Francisco because men outnumbered women. Which is why, upon reflection, he thought it might be a good idea to carry a gun after all. Everyone knew the tongs were at war for territory, and it was getting worse every day. But he was favored in his tong and had little to worry about; a valuable asset, indeed.

Though Wo Sam was familiar with the back doors of several brothels thanks to the deliveries he made to the women who were in charge, he never ventured inside. One day, escorting a number of women to the crib in Spofford Alley, the *baomu*— "Mother Goose"—made him bring the large group inside. He got a look at what so many had already seen; the girls were much more attractive than he had imagined. It was daylight, and the crib wasn't open for business yet. The girls wore dresses the color of the rainbow rather than their work outfits of identical yellow brocade jackets. When he came in, the *baomu* locked the door behind him and dropped the key down the front of her shirt. Sandalwood incense perfumed the heavy, hazy air. When he turned to leave, the twittering chatter of the girls made him heady, like too much wine, and he reached for the wrong door. Inside, a young woman lay on a satin couch. All he really saw of her, before the *baomu* shrieked at him and steered him toward the exit door, were her tiny feet, encased in slippers of turquoise brocade.

After that, Sam's dreams were shadowy with images of the girl, and the young man who had followed him. *Was she the one he sought? Who was she?* Sam felt ripples of pleasure through his body when he awoke, the image of the girl on the couch still in front of him. Golden lilies were rumored to resemble a woman's female parts and were considered highly erotic, at least in the poetry he read. He tried to imagine the curvature of each tiny foot, the unnatural whiteness folded upon itself, and rubbed his hand over the hardness pushing against the seam of his bedding. Then he felt ashamed. If she was in a whorehouse, she must be a whore. He was determined to remain pure. But he continued to dream of the girl when both sleeping and awake, and finally struggled with ways to find out more about her. He couldn't ask Po Wen, and certainly not the *Ah Mah*. But maybe Kim knew someone who knew something.

"There is a girl in the house on Spofford—the one with the pink door called Conjugal Bliss."

"There are many girls at Conjugal Bliss," said Kim. He was definitely enjoying himself.

"There is only one like this."

"Has my cousin found his maiden—in a whorehouse?" Kim suppressed a laugh but his eyes were wet with amusement.

Wo Sam tried to look stern. "I'm curious, because I only caught a glimpse of her. Stop laughing, you fool, and listen. She has bound feet. Not like the others."

Kim now looked at him with one raised eyebrow. "You're crazy."

"No, I saw her myself. They kept her apart from the others. I only want to find out who she is."

Kim became serious. "I'm not so sure this is any of our business. If they keep her separately, there must be a reason that is not for our ears."

"What would that be?"

Kim turned away. "I've heard things, but it's dangerous for me to talk about them."

"Don't be so dramatic! The *Ah Mah* trusts me. He wouldn't mind if I knew, especially if it was tong business."

"Then why don't you ask him?"

"Don't be a dog's hind end."

"All right, all right. All I know is that sometimes if there's some kind of rivalry between the tongs, one tong will kidnap women from another, and make them into prostitutes to shame the other family. This is very serious stuff, and nothing to stick your nose into."

"So she could be a rival tong lord's family?" Visions of the slight young man in the alley came to Wo Sam. No wonder the *Ah Mah* wanted him to carry a gun. But the young man didn't seem like a soldier.

"Be wise and forget about it," said Kim. "These days, it pays to be like the three monkeys."

***

Wo Sam did manage to put it out of his mind, as the next few weeks were busy. He was at the docks every day, often escorting boxes of "ink" to the dingy opium parlors. The signs that announced them on the street were blatant: "Pipes Always Ready," or "Pipe And Fire In Easy Reach," or simply "Dreams"—but of course they were in Chinese characters, and the white police walked right past them. As part of his duties, Sam escorted the carrier from the docks into Little China, down a flight or two of stairs to the basement below. The sweet burnt smell assaulted his nostrils within seconds of entering the street door. Walls covered with peeling paint and layers of wallpaper supported the low, yellowed ceilings of the rooms. Couches lined up haphazardly, each with its own gas lamp on a small table. Men—and sometimes women—curled up in fetal positions on the couches. They often appeared to be asleep, or held long pipes, making a gurgling, sodden sound sucking on the burning black tar in the bowl. It was the only sound in the room. Wo Sam dropped off his shipment as quickly as he could, glad to see the narrow strip of sky in the alley when he emerged.

***

Kim had news. "I'm assigned to that crib, the one you mentioned, with the lilly-foot girl."

"Do you think you'll have a chance to see her?"

"It's a big house, and busy. But I would have to sneak around, because she's kept in a separate room. Sam, we both know that would be crazy. I'm not supposed to have anything to do with the merchandise, and neither are you. Don't entertain foolishness."

That night, Wo Sam could contain his curiosity no longer. He tried to think of some pretext to walk into the crib. At least he could try to get a better look at the girl. He decided not to warn Kim that he would come—Kim was such a worrier.

Wo Sam knocked on the door of the house, and the *baomu* opened the door a crack. "I have a message from Po Wen for the soldier Wo Kim. Let me in."

With a bored expression on her face, she nodded and opened the door for him. "He's in there," she said, and indicated the big room where the girls displayed themselves for potential customers. Kim was leaning over, whispering to one of the girls. They sat in groups of two or three, legs uncovered and crossed, long skirts slit and pushed aside. When Wo Sam entered, a few of them sat up and rearranged themselves, following him with their eyes. Others just stared off into space or continued with their conversations. Kim looked up, and didn't hide the surprise on his face. He walked over to Sam, who stood at the door, paralyzed.

"What are you doing here?" Kim whispered furiously.

"I thought maybe I could get in to talk to her, if she's here."

"That is a very bad joke. Leave quickly. You'll get us both in trouble."

Their frantic conversation was interrupted by a commotion at the front door. Next, they heard the *baomu* screaming for Kim to come help, and he was out of the door and down the hallway with Sam right behind. The *baomu* was on the floor, waving her arms and legs about like an overturned beetle. Doors had been flung open down the corridor. In one of them, the young man who had accosted Wo Sam on the street emerged with the girl on his back, her arms around his neck.

"Stop there," said Kim, pulling his pistol out of his pants.

"You'll hit the girl," said Sam. "*Ah Mah* will have us killed."

Kim fired in front of the young man's feet. The smell of cordite filled the narrow hallway.

The young man turned, lowering the girl to the floor and stood between her and the cousins. "Run," he said. She hobbled to the door.

"No," said Sam, as if that would stop her.

The slight young man ran toward the two, shouting and screaming, his arms waving overhead as if to appear bigger. Kim started to back up; the young man threw himself on top of Kim, causing him to drop the pistol as he fell back against Sam. The three men collapsed in a pile and the young man scrambled to push himself up. Sam grabbed the pistol and fired without aiming. The young man fell to the floor slowly, with unnatural grace. Sam was stunned. He and Kim both looked up at the empty doorway. Sam pushed himself up, and scrambled over the bleeding body to the open door. Fog blanketed the street; the girl was nowhere to be seen.

***

"I am at fault," Wo Sam stood, head bowed, before Po Wen. "Wo Kim tried to protect the girls and I shouldn't have been there."

"It is indeed your fault," said Po Wen sourly. "The daughter of the Hop Sing tong lord, a valuable prisoner and tool for profitable negotiations has escaped. And you have managed to murder the son of Wing Yee, one of our chief allies."

"I was only trying to do my job."

"You are a fool. However, I am in a merciful mood because you have saved our tong much money in the past. I will negotiate for you so that you do not have to be killed. But you must leave the area. Neither you nor your worthless cousin is safe here until negotiations have been completed. We will arrange passage for you to Virginia City, where you will work for our gambling operations. You will leave tomorrow. Go now and wait for word." Po Wen turned toward the *Ah Mah's* chamber.

Sam nodded and looked down at the carefully swept courtyard. Though he knew he was dismissed, he dared not raise his face, shamed by his tears should the servant see him. He heard voices murmuring in the nearby room, and listened hard to determine what his fate might be.

"How well this has worked out!" said the *Ah Mah*. "You are more clever than ever."

"In your service, Lord Low." Po Wen's voice was filled with barely disguised pride.

"It's a shame about the girl, but she served her purpose. Wing Yee's eldest son is now dispatched, and he has no one else to run his opium operation. Little China is now ours like a fat fish in a net."

"A shame also about the translator. He was quite useful. I said I would negotiate for his life."

The *Ah Mah* did not bother to hide his amused chuckle. "As soon as we destroy Wing Yee, there will be no need to negotiate, and we can bring him back. Hopefully, Wing Yee's tong is in such chaos that he won't be able to find those two so easily. But it doesn't matter."

"Not at all, Lord Low, not at all."

Chapter THIRTEEN

There had been no word from Ellen, and Cayley continued to pound on the rough-hewn door of Ellen's aunt every few weeks. Finally, the old woman refused to open, shouting, "She ain't here, I ain't heard nothing, leave me alone or I'll get the cops down on ya'."

As far as the search for Ellen was concerned, Cayley had reached a dead end; it took the sheen off her success at work. Since she began her dancing performances, the crowd had grown bigger and stayed longer at the Blue Rooster, much to the consternation of other bar owners on the cocktail circuit. Mr. Max bent easily to Cayley's request for more money, and she was able to move out of the Washoe and into the much fancier Hotel Pleasanton on the corner of Sutter and Jones.

Late at night, with the fresh white sheets tucked up to her chin, Cayley would let her hands and mind wander to the happier memories of her married life. In spite of the constant attention of men at the bar, she was lonely. She had been keeping to herself, only spending time with Opal, who came in to sing every once in a while. *Henry's no grand prize, but he's not the worst I've seen,* she thought. *When he was courting me, he treated me like a queen in front of his friends—and he wouldn't have put up such a fuss about me working at the Blue Roo if he didn't care. He's still my husband.* She'd move her hand around the cool empty space next to her on the bed. *All is not lost. It can't be.*

Cayley took to heart what Opal had said—that she would have to settle it with Henry to have any peace at all. She had high hopes they would make up, now that time had passed. *After all, he must miss me too. He's had plenty of time to mull over his own foolishness. We might even have something to talk about thanks to my books. I'm better dressed and can bring in more money—those are good things to have in a wife. We could still make a go of it, if he's willing. He might take me more serious now he knows I can be on my own. But I won't grovel. To him or anyone.*

One morning, as a brilliant and clear late October day dawned after a night's rain, she dressed in a tailored jacket and matching fine wool skirt of navy blue and asked the doorman at the hotel to summon a hack for her. *But what if he's gone and divorced me as he said he would?* She pushed the troubling thought aside and directed the driver to their old flat. She lifted her skirts and picked her way up the muddy steps, elbowing her way in the entry. As she knocked at her pale green door, a few paint flakes powdered down onto the floor. There was no answer. The door behind her opened, and Mrs. McClatchy peeked out. "Why, it's Mrs. Wallace, come to pay us a visit!"

"I've come to see Henry, Mrs. McClatchy. Is he not at home?"

"That I wouldn't know dear. He hasn't lived in that flat for near a year." Mrs. McClatchy grinned in a most unfriendly fashion.

Cayley took a deep breath to cover both her embarrassment and her anger at being an object of amusement. "Would you know where I could find him, then?" she said evenly.

"Word is he's in a boarding house on Howard with some of the other *bachelor* firemen."

Cayley got the address from the smug Mrs. McClatchy, and before leaving complimented her on clearing most of the stink of dirty diapers from the hallway—"such an improvement—though the smell of shite does cling to the walls here, don't it?"

She stepped up into the waiting hack and directed the driver to Howard Street. They clattered up to the boarding house, a plain wooden two-story building, slightly larger than the others leaning against it on both sides. Entering the parlor, she asked a man sitting in an armchair by the unlit woodstove to find Mr. Henry Wallace for her. He looked her up and down and disappeared. Moments later, Henry shambled down the stairs, obviously having been woken from a nap. He was unshaven, and half his shirt was hanging out. "Well if it ain't Cayley," he said, in a tone that let her know he expected her to show up sooner or later.

"Henry, you could have at least tried to keep in touch with my mother, to let me know where you were. I had to speak to that witch Moll McClatchy to find out."

The man sitting in the armchair returned, and brought a friend. They settled into the shabby parlor chairs, periodically rattling the pages of their newspapers as if they were really reading. Cayley stepped closer to Henry and lowered her voice, "We're still husband and wife, Henry." She looked at the blank faces of the newspapers held high against her. "Henry?"

"Wife?" Henry said loudly. "I have no wife. I had me a wife once, but she turned into a whore." He was declaiming loud enough for the entire first floor of the house to hear him. "Oh, excuse me," he said, "a HOO-ER!"

"Henry, for God's sake. What are you doing?" Cayley stamped her foot and looked hard into his face. "I swallowed my pride and came here to make up with you, you chowderhead."

"It's a little late for that, ain't it? You're the one who took off to be a fancy woman. Just look at you, dressed up like a rich man's dolly." He stuck his thumbs in his waistband and raised his chin.

Cayley saw the papers shift slightly, so Henry's witnesses could take in for themselves the authentic attire of a rich man's dolly. She whispered furiously, "Don't make more of it than it was. We were both crazy mad. Can't we talk like two people who were at least raised Christian? And don't you dare call me whore, again, Henry Wallace."

"Whore, whore, HOO-ER," sang Henry. "That's all I have to say to you, Missy, and I'm free as any bird. We're both free. Maybe I can come visit sometime when I have change to spare— though it weren't worth it when it was free, so I don't reckon much of a 'provement."

Cayley made a guttural exclamation of fury and turned on her heel. As she seated herself in the leather passenger seat of the hack, Henry ran out with the cigar box in his hand and thrust it at her. "I never spent your whorish money, neither—you'll need it." She grabbed the box from his hand and told the driver to head out. As the carriage pulled away, she heard him shout,

"When you're old and nobody wants you." In her fury, she took small comfort that Henry had water in his eyes when he was out of sight of his friends, and it wasn't from the mud spewing up from the carriage wheels. She hurriedly wiped away the wetness from her own cheeks with the back of her glove. *The damn fool. Throwing away his wife for pride. I don't need him. I don't need him at all.* She pinched at her nose to stop it from running. *This wasn't what was supposed to happen. Life is supposed to be better now there's finally money in hand. What's gone wrong?*

Chapter FOURTEEN

Cayley went straight to the Blue Rooster and poured herself a whiskey. By the time patrons were crowding into the bar, she was liquored up enough to forget to button the top of her red satin dress, leaving an inch of camisole puffing out over the rim.

"You're looking like a proud pouter pigeon tonight Miss Cayley." Rolifer's eyes wandered over her curves.

"I 'preciate that you're 'preciating my fine qualities," Cayley slurred with a dazzling smile. She stepped a little closer to him. "These treasures aren't for just anyone, y'know."

"Now there's a pity," said the attorney. "In this here free country we should argue the right of hard-working leaders of society to enjoy the finest the Blue Rooster has to offer." He removed his tall hat and ran the palm of his hand over the side of his balding head. He was sweating, his stiff collar just showing a bit of dampness.

Cayley sidled past him, rubbing her breasts against his arm. "I'll drink to that," she said thickly, "but first you'll have to get us both a whiskey." She sashayed over to the bar, holding up two fingers.

"Watch out there, young lady," said Riley, as he wiped glasses with a well-used rag. "You're whipping him to a fine froth. I'm surprised these upstanding members of our fair city don't jump you between the buffet and dance floor."

"Ah Riley. I blush at that terrible pun. These gentlemen love to think they're God's gift. What man doesn't?" She poured two glasses and watered her own. "At least he pays for my company, and he doesn't rub my face in the dirt. He can do that to his wife. And his servants."

"You probably see more of him than his wife does."

"Oh, lucky us, then." She screwed up her mouth scornfully, lifted the tray, and with her free hand pulled at her waist to expose a bit more cleavage. She winked at Riley and headed for the crowded floor, the twisted mouth replaced by her bright-beam smile.

"Where's our Red Rose Ellen?" bellowed one of the bowler hats from across the room.

"Ain't I too much for you already?" said Cayley, and the room erupted in laughter. "She's gone on to marry a man richer than any of you anyhow." She hoped it was true. She still had no word from Ellen, and nothing came from asking around. "But she said to tell you she misses you all, every one of you." Her voice sugar-coated every man in the room, and she blew a wide kiss with her free hand.

Cayley had heard the whispers—she knew that one crowd—including Rolifer—was betting on who would have her. *As if this lowly bar girl has no say in the matter,* she thought. *Worse than Henry! Thanks to him, half the town already thinks I'm in the business.* As she imagined taking one of the patrons as a lover, she shook her head and had a laugh. *I've made my bed, right or wrong. But I'll lie in it alone, thank you. Tainted by divorce or no, I still have my pride. I'm going to keep working here, stay out of trouble, and help out my family like I've been doing all along.* Her thoughts wandered to the responsibilities she'd taken on: three of the smaller children in her mother's house were in and out of fever, and the doctor cost plenty. She liked her job at the Blue Rooster, but she knew Max was squeezed out; the real money went to women like Opal who were the next destination of these men, in the houses a few blocks away, or maybe even Little China, for the more daring ones. Not the Barbary Coast, though—that was for sailors and the like, not gentlemen. And it was dangerous there, with all the talk of that slasher, the one they called the West Coast Ripper.

Even Opal is scared. I see how wore out she seems sometimes, though she always puts a bright face on it. I couldn't do what she does, giving herself to strangers, Cayley thought. *But I can still tease these silly men and have some fun. Especially Arnold Rolifer; him with his roaming hands when he thought he owned me.* She returned to Rolifer's side, squeezing against him. "Lord have mercy, it's so crowded in here!" Her eyes narrowed as she turned slightly away from him; *It don't mean nothing to me, and he deserves to be teased.* Looking over the rim of her glass, she said, "Tell me, Arnold, are those houses on California Street—the ones I hear so much about—are they as nice as they say?"

He looked at her with round eyes. "Wouldn't know."

She laughed and quickly touched her cheek to his, standing on tiptoe to reach, whispering, "You can tell me. I'll never be able to see for myself. I won't tell anyone." She took his free hand and placed it on the top of her breast. "Honest." His fingers twitched.

"Hey, Cayley," someone yelled from across the room. "Bring us a drink."

She looked at Rolifer and made a little roué with her mouth, but kept his hand on her breast. "Tell me later," she said. "Promise?" He nodded, and she felt his eyes follow her, but he left within the hour with two of his friends.

The next morning, her head felt like she had placed it between the jaws of a vice and turned the crank herself; she recalled her shameful behavior the night before with profound embarrassment. In a truly desperate mood, she prayed to the Virgin that Rolifer would remember little of what passed between them.

That night, however, he brought her a sparkling gold nugget on a black velvet ribbon, and tied it around her neck himself, saying, "Here's for my favorite girl." She fingered it all night, and kept glancing over at him, smiling like a cat full of canary, ashamed and elated at the power of her flirting. Every once in a while, she would walk close by him, pull his shoulder down and whisper in his ear, "What do they do in the fancy houses?" or "Am I really your favorite girl?"

When she asked that, he replied, "I said so," without hesitating, and she moved on, here and there, never spending too much time with him.

In the weeks that followed, Cayley continued to bait and leave Arnold Rolifer hanging. It was a way to amuse herself and a roundabout way to get back at Henry. After all, if she could get this fancy lawyer all lathered up, who needed a wooden-headed fireman? Every time she passed by and whispered to him, or rubbed against him, she could almost hear the sound of his friend's shoulders colliding as they rushed in to fill the vacuum and talk about her, saying it was only a matter of time. "She's asking for it," one of them whispered into his ear as she passed by. "What are you waiting for?"

***

A few days later, Cayley stood outside the alley door of the Blue Rooster before it opened, stealing a few moments of darkening sky before nightfall. The street always quieted down at this time; the sound of horses on the cobblestones faded into a dull clatter before the evening rush, and the whirring of cables for the Market Street line intensified. Most of those who rode the cars for work had already left for home. There was no fog on this lovely fall night, the finest time of year. It had rained the night before, the first of the winter rains, and the air was clear and clean with a touch of crispness. Though the streets were nearly devoid of plant life, the few maples planted in front of some of the better hotels were coloring up, the reds intensified by the new electric lights popping on as the sky darkened. The city was not yet so bright that you couldn't see a few stars on this moonless night. She walked to the front of the alley, hidden in darkness, and ran into Arnold Rolifer. He addressed her formally, touching the brim of his hat somewhat unsteadily, "Good evening, Mrs. Wallace."

"Mr. Rolifer." She gave him a little curtsy.

He walked toward her, and she could smell the alcohol on him, and noted his somewhat fussy, tipsy walk. "Out early tonight, Arnold?"

"Decided not to go home to dine," he said. "How fortunate I should run into you."

"Why is that Mr. Rolifer?"

He took her by the arm and backed her into the alley a few feet, though she resisted. "Now Arnold, what do you think you're doing?" she said, her voice rising in alarm.

He put both hands on her arms and pushed her against the damp wall. She could feel the cold stone biting through her thin dress. "Sweet Cayley," he said. "I must say it's been a mystery to me why you run so hot and cold with me. But now I've figured it out." He leaned against her, put his hands under her armpits and his thumbs over her breasts.

"Mr. Rolifer! I like you very much, but..."

"Oh stop with the coy act, you little tart!" He raised a hand to hold her chin steady. "You've been asking for this, and now you'll get it."

She struggled against him while he held his forearm over her upper chest and pulled up her skirts. "Arnold, stop this!"

He ignored her, and pulled at the front of his pants.

"Riley! Help!"

He clapped his hand over her mouth, a wicked smile on his face. "So you like to put up a little fight, do you?"

She struggled, freed her mouth, "Riley!"

At that moment, the dark parade of the Decency League reached the front of the alley and those closest to the street hesitated and began peering down the dimly lit passage. Rolifer froze, his eyes darting rapidly between Cayley and the curious onlookers.

She shook off his hand. "I won't say anything," she said. "Just get off me."

He stepped back and turned away from the street, rearranging himself and shielding his face from the ladies of the Decency League.

They stood in silence, not looking at each other as the group passed. Cayley straightened herself out, brushing the dirt from her dress and arms as best she could.

"I suppose I should thank you," he said, then cleared his throat. "Though I doubt anyone would believe the word of a bar girl." He ran his palm along the side of his head.

"I could have ruined you, and you know it. And I didn't. Don't you wonder why?" Cayley felt the fury rise. "Did you think I was worried about my reputation?"

He said nothing.

"I enjoy your attentions, Arnold, and I'm not fool enough to think I didn't bring this on myself. But I tell you this: if a man has me, it's when I say so, you understand?" Cayley spoke in a level, controlled tone, but her body was shaking. She had no idea where these words were coming from.

"Yes."

"Come in, and let me buy you a drink." She clutched his arm and they entered the Blue Rooster by the front door. "And how are the courts, today," said Cayley pleasantly, as she sat at the bar. She kept her hands under the edge so he couldn't see her tremors. "Can't complain," said Rolifer, still sweating a little, looking everywhere but at her face.

"I have to go help in the back," said Cayley, "but why don't you stay here and wait until we set up." She laid a tentative hand on his shoulder. The dirt from the wall clung to the side of it, and she withdrew it and wiped it on the side of her dress. "I'd like to dish you up some food—cook's outdone himself with a roast of beef you've got to have. Besides, you didn't have any dinner, and you've got to keep strong, don't you?"

Rolifer rubbed his forehead as if the motion would make sense of the evening so far. As she made her way into the kitchen, Rolifer slid off the stool and walked out the door. Cayley pulled herself a long glass of water and drank all of it, only stopping to gasp for breath between gulps.

Opal came in early that evening to sing a few tunes with the piano man. She always had the latest music thanks to her theater friends, and made the crowd laugh with "The Cat Came Back" and cry with her version of "Marguerite." When she sat down to have a drink before going off to work, Cayley told her what had happened with Rolifer. "It's my own fault. I've been teasing him worse than dangling a steak in front of a starving cur. Now maybe him and his crowd won't come back, and it'll be because of me."

"Oh Cayley, I know you're upset, but you've got to see this in a different way. God didn't make an open invitation to all men to do as they please when they please. There's no sin in being the kind of woman men want." Opal put her fists on her hips as though lecturing a naughty child. "God doesn't single out beautiful women for hell." She raised one hand and touched the back of her hair. "At least I hope not."

"But it all depends on what you do with it. I've not been taking responsibility. With Arnold *or* with Henry."

"My point exactly. You have to realize that you're holding all the cards, dearie. Do you know what I'm saying?"

Cayley nodded, then said, "Well, not exactly."

"Henry sounds like he either needs a different approach or he's a done deal, but this Rolifer is crazy for you, am I right?"

Cayley nodded. "It seems as if he is—not love, I mean. Lust."

Opal laughed. "Now *there's* a word! What I'm saying is that you can pretty much do anything you want. You can sleep with him or not. But I can see definite advantages to having him on your side, so to speak. This Rolifer is rich, right? He's the one who's running for city councilman?"

"Yes," Cayley answered suspiciously. "I don't like where this might be going."

"Now just a minute. When you were married to Henry, you shared a bed and your money too. If I was short some week, as a friend you'd lend me a little, wouldn't you? So, what's the difference with having this Rolifer as a friend? Someone who would be able to help you out if you needed it."

One of the men in the crowd came by, stood in front of Opal with his hat in both his hands; "You sing like a golden lark, Miss Boone." She turned her body toward him, "Better watch out or I'll give you a few singing lessons of your own, handsome." She winked; he smiled; his cheeks turned pink as a rose. He gulped twice, Adam's apple bobbing on his thin neck. With a silly smile pasted on his face, he nodded and headed for the door. Opal turned toward Cayley and looked hard into her eyes. "See what I mean?"

"If you're meaning a friend I share a bed with, Opal Boone, the difference is that he's got a wife, and I'm not her."

"And you probably never will be. But, Cayley, my dear, that doesn't seem to stop him from going after what he wants. And judging from that gold nugget around your neck, I'd say he's a very practical friend to have."

Cayley fingered the nugget then squeezed her hands together. "I don't know. I just wasn't raised that way."

"Oh Lord, what an argument! Neither was I, dearie. But we're not little children with Ma and Pa providing for us...if they ever did." Opal rose from the chair. "I got to go. Think about it. Just, whatever you do, be the boss—don't let him get the upper hand, ever. That's where the real danger lies, you hear me? That, and being foolish enough to fall in love."

When Cayley returned to her hotel room at 2 a.m. the next morning, she found Opal huddled miserably by the door, her dress torn and filthy. She was holding the side of her face. A ribbon of dried blood clung to her neck and spread onto the top of her pale satin dress, turning it rusty brown. "Can I stay here tonight? There's no power on God's green earth that will make me go back."

Chapter FIFTEEN

Opal wore Cayley's white silk robe wrapped tightly around her as she slumped forward in the upholstered chair next to the bed. "He nearly had me, but I give him the slip, along with my best fur-collar coat." Her hands shook around a steaming cup of tea Cayley brought up from the hotel bar. "I've been scared in my life, but this was the worst. Christ, what a night." She hesitantly touched the cheek where Cayley had dressed the wound.

Cayley perched on the edge of the bed and reached over to put a hand on Opal's shoulder. "So he started following you after you left the California Street house?"

She nodded. "After Madam Maude gave us the word about shutting down—damned Decency League! It's a wonder I saw him at all, upset as I was. Her and that Montrose want to take near everything we make in the new house on Morton. Montrose may own the place, but he still gives me the creeps, that oily bastard. When he gave us the take-it-or-work-the-Barbary speech, I raised my voice to him, and then he really made a ruckus. He was going to wallop me, so I stomped out and just walked. I wouldn't have seen anyone behind me at all if I didn't half-trip over my coat and stop for a minute."

"You're sure it was the Ripper? I thought he only worked the Barbary. Maybe it was Montrose coming after you."

"God, Cayley, you're as bad as the cops. I didn't ask for his calling card. The knife in his hand was real convincing."

"Easy, Oppie, I don't mean to disbelieve you. I guess I've been denying that this Ripper fella is real."

"Women have died out there. He's as real as it gets. Four girls slashed up now, they figure, and that's the ones they know about. It would've been five if I wasn't quick enough."

"Sorry. I'm so glad you're all right." Cayley went around behind Opal, and put both her arms around her. "You're still shaking. Shhh, shhh." She rocked her like a small child.

Opal relaxed within Cayley's embrace. "I'm sorry too. Sorry I barked at you. I was so scared."

Cayley nodded, but didn't move her arms. "I didn't want to think about this Ripper; 'cause…Ellen, see, I was afraid that's what might have happened to Ellen. That she didn't run off with her gambler, and maybe this guy…"

"We might never know. The man that grabbed me was small but real strong. It could have been Montrose, but how could he have followed me so quick? If I hadn't tore out of my coat and ran, he would have had me. The copper I spoke to at the station just gave me a look as if to say, 'well, what do you expect.' I mean, I couldn't say nothing to the police about what he looked like, 'cause he was all covered up, with a scarf on his face, and gloves and all."

"Well, you're safe now. You can stay here as long as you like. I appreciate the company."

"I'm going to miss that damned coat."

***

Opal moved her belongings—mostly fancy dresses and jackets—into a room next to Cayley's, and the two women began to take all their meals together. After a week, Opal's restlessness began to wear Cayley down.

"You can always come work at the bar," said Cayley. Opal fidgeted with her gloves and bag as they finished their lunch at the hotel café one afternoon.

Opal snorted, then shook her head. "I can't do that. First of all, I run into too many of my old customers at the Rooster—singing and showing myself off is one thing, but slinging drinks for pennies? And if I do any business there, Max would have both our hides, because the cops would be on him like flies on shite to ante up the boodle money. It's just the cost of doing business." Opal looked over the table at Cayley, "Oh, now I've gone and hurt your feelings, too. What a lovely day this is turning out to be." She leaned over and covered Cayley's hands with her own. "You're my dearest friend in the world, Cayley Wallace, and I'm ashamed of my attitude, but I'm used to making more money for less work, and that's a fact. I was damned disrespectful, and that isn't the way I think of you at all. I should mend my own stockings before pointing out holes in anyone else's. I need to find another house that doesn't take everything I earn."

"I don't get many insults for being too pure."

"Crap." Opal rolled her eyes. "I'm all shakes. I don't know what to do with myself."

"Stop apologizing. Let's figure this out. You said all the houses are taking a bigger cut, and they can get away with paying the younger girls less."

"There's no shortage of raw material. I haven't that much longer to work. I'm nearly 27. Fact is, I'm scared. I don't have enough money to move to Seattle, and I can't stay here long without working."

"There must be some place where the pay is fair." Cayley raised the white porcelain coffee cup to her lips. "Could you…work out of the hotel a little? On your own?"

"Wouldn't that be rich! How long do you think it would take the hotel dicks to throw me out on my keister and blackball me at every decent hotel in town? And maybe you with me! I'd lose what custom I do have if I went to a place that was less than topper. I'd start my own if I had the money. God knows, I can bring in the girls and I can bring the trade."

"How much would you need?"

"Oh Cayley, my darlin' friend." Opal raised her hand from the cup and laid it across her forehead. "I know you're trying to help. It would take thousands to set up a right proper house. First, you have to own it, and it has to be in a good neighborhood. That way, you can't get thrown out, and the neighbors are too polite to object—especially when they see that San Francisco's finest are regular callers. The Decency League would never pay a visit, as there're no yowling neighbors and no loud parties. This is a proper bawdy house. You've got to have the furnishings, and clothes for the girls—and the payoff money for the cops. Montrose likely put close to 80 grand into the California Street house."

"Oh Lord!" Cayley's eyes widened. "I'd never see that much money in ten lifetimes."

"Well, chances are good neither of us will. Don't worry, I'll think of something."

Cayley stood up and pulled the waist of her fitted jacket down. "Is there anyone you could borrow from? You have some rich customers, right?"

"It's the strangest thing," said Opal, remaining seated. "Men can't wait to get their hands all over me, but they get real shy when it comes to making a loan to a hooker."

***

Cayley hadn't laid eyes on Arnold Rolifer for weeks after their disastrous encounter, and she was beginning to think she'd seen the last of him when he showed up in the bar with his cronies one night, pointedly ignoring her.

She took a deep breath, and walked up to him. *I'm just going to keep my head, and make the best of this.* Cayley looked into his face without a hint of embarrassment. "Why Mr. Rolifer, I'm so glad to see you. I was afraid I'd only catch a glimpse of you at City Hall from now on. Congratulations on your win."

A smile flitted across his face, and he stepped away from his friends and leaned down toward her, whispering in her ear. "I had a bit too much cheer the other night. I hope it's forgiven and forgotten."

Cayley made her eyes wide and shrugged, "Don't know what you're referring to, Mr. Rolifer." She flashed him a big smile. "What can I get for you?"

Chapter SIXTEEN

Wo Sam and Wo Kim boarded the train after taking the ferry to Oakland. Chinese were directed to sit in one or two cars toward the rear of the train. A few Mexican families, their small parcels held tightly to their chests, sat among them. The rocking motion of the crowded train combined with body heat made both men doze periodically. Sam was in a somber mood, but Kim said, "Easy, cousin! Virginia City is home of the Comstock Lode, where all the silver comes from. It will be a rich town for us to grow our fortunes, wait and see."

"I don't think Lord Low is much interested in our welfare," said Sam. He sighed and shifted the bundle on his lap. Inside were his few possessions and a set of clothes wrapped around his revolver. "Who knows what we'll find there. All we have been told is that there are gambling operations we are to visit."

"If there is enough money to gamble, there must be enough for us, too."

"I think we're lucky we don't have to pay our own fares." Sam turned away from his cousin, hunched over his belongings and tried to sleep as the gentle hills surrounding the tracks softened and spread into acres of budding trees and farmland green with new growth. The flat countryside gradually gave way to the larger settlement of Sacramento, where many of the Mexicans and Chinese on the train departed, leaving considerably more room for the cousins to stretch out. The orderly terrain of farms and ranches erupted into larger hills, which seemed to double in size every few miles. Looking out the train window to the east, Sam caught sight of mighty peaks in the near distance. "Look Kim, even though it's not yet winter, there's snow on those tall mountains." He added excitedly, "Do you think we'll go through it?"

Kim joined Sam kneeling at the window; the wind, gusting with smoke and cinders from the engine blew their hair back. He looked at his older cousin. "It would be good to see snow," he said. "They say it never snows in San Francisco. See how lucky we are, then…in spite of the events of the past."

"You're so young to be a philosopher, little cousin." Sam smiled as he pulled on the back of Kim's long, unbraided hair.

The train pulled into the Sierras, the engine straining through a number of inclines. Granite cliffs with indentations just wide enough for the tracks dropped into canyons blue with pine. The air was clear and cold; both young men shivered but refused to close the window of the car all the way, in spite of loud complaints from the few remaining passengers. When snow appeared on the ground, they closed the window but continued to marvel at each long black tunnel blasted through the mountains.

"Chinese built this road," said an elderly man sitting behind Sam and Kim. "Chinese made these tunnels, too." As the train slowed for Truckee, Sam and Kim made to get out, to see the snow up close. The elderly man said, "This is not a good place to stop. They don't like Celestials here. Wait until Reno." The cousins shared their small supply of dried meat with the man, who told them that he had been one of the laborers when Central Pacific put the railroad through the mountains. "I was young then. I came to mine, but when the government started to tax us, I labored instead for the railroad." He looked out the window and the passing trees. "Many died here, in the blasts. I moved to Nevada. I like the desert." He smiled without opening his mouth. "It's very quiet."

"We're getting off in Reno," said Kim. "To take the train to Virginia City. Do you know it?"

The man's eyes crinkled at the corners. "To a couple of strong young men like yourselves, who have lived in San Francisco…" he grinned showing browned teeth with several gaps, "it may be too quiet."

Both Sam and Kim nodded wisely, and waved to their friend later as his train pulled out of the Reno station. "What do you suppose he meant?" said Kim to Sam as they boarded the small train bound for Virginia City.

Sam shrugged. "No tong wars, maybe. That would be a good thing."

The train bumped, ground and wound around a rough series of hills. It was much drier on this side of the mountains, though patchy snow still lay on the ground. The tortured route of the railway upset both men's stomachs. At last, the engine stopped in front of a small station among buildings that sprouted like square mushrooms out of the dun-colored earth. "Virginia City," the conductor called. The two young men stepped onto the platform. A gnarled miner sat on the ground not far from the tracks. His face was so dirty it wasn't possible to tell his race. "Excuse me," said Sam. "How far is the town?"

The miner looked up at him with a squint then pushed his felt hat back with his wrist. "'Bout fifteen feet, I reckon, give or take," and nodded toward the plank sidewalk on the other side of the street. The cousins looked at each other, then around them. Spreading towards the east was a vast flat plain almost devoid of plants. To the west were the mountains they had just traveled over. And in front of them was a town of not more than a handful of streets, nearly deserted. "If you're here for the mines, you're 'bout...let's see," said the miner, "'bout ten years too late. But if you got relatives here, you'll be wanting to go down Bull Run Alley, that way." He indicated the direction with his nod. "Got any whiskey on ya'?"

"Lord Low is very, very angry," said Sam.

Chapter SEVENTEEN

Sam and Kim were relieved to find a fairly large Chinese community within the withered town, and settled into their boarding house without difficulty. They were amazed to discover a number of women and children in the shops and laundry, descendants of earlier settlers who came before Chinese immigrants were kept out by the exclusion act of 1882. The Chinese population was almost a town in itself with its own cobblers, barbers, kitchens, herb shops, temples and gaming parlors. These businesses also served what was left of Virginia City.

Crumbling mansions on B Street, the fanciful churches, and several cemeteries remained, anchoring a dwindling population of individual miners who continued to eke out small amounts of silver from the blue clay hills that once made this the richest town in the west. The city was moribund—the mines, especially the great Comstock Lode, which had fueled the fortunes of so many company owners and the tumultuous ups and downs of the San Francisco Stock Exchange, had petered out years before. The large hotels that once held speculators and rich investors stood empty, as did the mansions that the owners had built for themselves. Now the town was populated by men who worked small claims, hoping to find a rich vein, or at least enough to scrape by. Many were Chinese, who were able to buy the used-up claims cheaply, and were willing to work hard to glean what they could. The Bucket of Blood, one of two saloons on C Street—the main street in town—still functioned as a meeting place for the motley assortment of men who ran their operations out of Virginia City. The row of wooden buildings with false fronts facing C Street still carried faded advertising messages painted on in decades past, along with nails that held remains of flyers advertising sporting events and entertainments in the town's heyday. The elderly passenger they had spoken to on the train was right: it was too quiet.

Within a few days, Sam and Kim had ingratiated themselves into the gambling dens in the basements of the former boomtown. In order to be as inconspicuous as possible while observing the operations of the gambling parlor owned by Lord Low, Sam became a dealer—an easy task for him, but much more difficult for Kim, who had little experience at the tables. What silver that was coaxed out of the hills or the money it was sold for often changed hands at the *fan-tan* and *pai-gow* tables that Sam dealt.

Since Kim didn't want to mine, he found work at the herbalist's store, gaining expertise quickly and taking over for the older man when needed. Part of his interest in the work involved the herbalist's unmarried daughter, a plain, kind woman ten years older than he.

Not many weeks had passed before Sam and Kim moved from a rented room into an old miner's cabin on the edge of town, the first time either of them had lived in a house of their own. The fifteen-foot-square wooden structure held together with pegs was sturdy enough to keep out the heat and some of the cold of the late fall days. A rusty metal stove heated the one-room interior when they were inside.

Winter brought isolation. Most of the residents who tolerated work in the heat of the desert summer found the cold another matter entirely—the town's population became sparse. The cousins awoke to a thin blanket of white one late December morning—the first they had seen since crossing the Sierras weeks before. Kim went out first, laughing and raising his eyebrows in amazement as he crunched around; he stomped his boots to break the crust. He gathered handfuls of snow, pressed them hard and threw them at his cousin, who waited sullenly by the cabin door, hugging himself for warmth. Finally, Sam leapt from the cabin, ran after Kim until he tackled him; they rolled around in the snow, laughing and rubbing cold stuff into each other's faces.

***

Kim discovered that he liked the diamond-bright cold and meditative calm of the desert, but Sam hated the bare hills and lack of trees and flowers. As they lay in their bunks at night,

Kim said, "It's beautiful to see the sky so clear at night. And I like the quiet—not like the city at all."

"That's just what I hate about it," said Sam. "Nothing is happening. Ever." He pulled his blanket over his face.

Sam continued to send dispatches to Lord Low, reporting on the take of the gambling operations, though he knew it was a sham, as the take was so small.

***

The gambling hall where Sam worked was almost deserted, except for a few older men who worked in the town. Kim stopped in to bring him a bowl of noodles from the local shop. "When are they going to send for us," Sam asked restlessly. He dealt out the cards, and two players put out their wagers in pennies. Sam rolled his eyes behind his hand.

"Little China has infected your blood worse than opium," said Kim. "In your memory, it's a perfect world. Don't you remember how it was?"

"At least I had face there," said his cousin. "Here, I deal to people who only have pennies to play with. The *Ah Mah* trusted me!"

"Keep your voice down!" said Kim. He whispered, "If the *Ah Mah* trusted you, he doesn't anymore—that's why we're both here. Why don't you get some new ambitions?"

But Sam remained disgruntled. Finally, he sent a message—against Kim's better judgment—to Po Wen to ask when they could return. Within two weeks, Po Wen's reply was delivered by a well-dressed young man. His jacket and pants were of fine silks and satins; he acted with utmost confidence as he delivered the words: "Po Wen says the danger has passed, but he regrets that he can no longer offer you your former position, as you are too visible. Other leaders in the community may take offense, which would be bad for the company, and bad for you."

"Who has taken my place?"

"Why, me, of course. With apologies," he bowed. "My uncle Po Wen has arranged for you and your cousin to stay here indefinitely in Virginia City if you so desire."

Sam steeled himself to keep his face placid, and nodded toward the young man. "Tell Po Wen that I understand perfectly, and I am grateful for his concern," he said. Back at the cabin, Sam paced the tiny splintered floor and unleashed his venom. "I was a faithful servant!"

"Sam, don't take it so hard. You could have been killed. Remember what happened—the *Ah Mah* did take care of us, after all. As for me, I like it here, and I intend to take up the *Ah Mah's* hospitality. Tell me what you think: I wish to speak to the herbalist for permission to make his daughter my bride."

"What about our villages? Going home to China?"

"I don't have the same obligations as you; my family is large. I have many brothers and sisters to care for my parents in their old age. If I start one family here, I could still start another back there when I return."

"But what about sending money home?"

Kim shook his head. "You are usually the practical one, cousin. There is no money to send back, not from this place. There's just enough to get along, if we lead quiet lives. As for the herbalist, he won't refuse—his daughter is almost too old to bear children. She will be a good and loyal wife. I want you to be here for my wedding. Why can't you settle down as well, and find a bride for yourself? We could raise families, and live near one another."

Sam covered his face with his hands. "Oh, cousin. I promised your parents I would watch over you. I have so many promises to keep."

Chapter EIGHTEEN

As the weeks and months passed, Opal, with little to do, became more withdrawn. Cayley was able to persuade her to come to the Blue Rooster to sing, which always lifted her spirits.

"You and that Rolifer seem to be mighty good pals these days, dearie," Opal noted one night after she finished her tunes.

"Who'd have thought?" Cayley passed by her table with an armload of drinks. "We've come to actually *like* each other."

"So why don't you take him as a lover?" Opal fixed her bright brown eyes on Cayley's face. "How long has it been since you had a man?"

Cayley jerked her head up and looked away. She could feel the color rising in her face, and wondered if she'd ever stop blushing like a schoolgirl whenever the subject of coupling came up. "I'll talk to you later, Oppie. Not now. Now's not a good time."

"Well then, I'll see you at the Pleasanton," Opal replied, and touched the brim of her hat with the old familiar gesture. After she had gone out the door, Arnold Rolifer appeared by Cayley's side.

"Well, Miss Cayley, do you have a kiss for me?" He seemed almost paternal since becoming a bigwig in the city government. Even his friends seemed to treat her with more respect.

All she could figure was that he had begun to defend her virtue; in case word got around of his "slip," he would have the appearance of a total gentlemen. *He is a politician, after all.* "Of course, Arnold my sweet." She reached up on tiptoes, put her hands on his shoulders and kissed him lightly on the cheek. Cayley genuinely liked him, especially since he had playfully begun to bring her into his conversations with others on the city government. She was under no illusions—she knew he considered her a pretty body and an empty, but entertaining, head—at first. "How did the ship of state steer today?"

Rolifer laughed. "You're a right smart little girl, Cayley."

Cayley found the best way to get anyone's attention was by repeating their words: using Rolifer's reference to "the city government of San Francisco, as the great Plato would have called it" would prove she was really listening. All the time." She flashed him a sunlit smile.

***

When Cayley returned to the hotel late that night, Opal wasn't in her room. Close to dawn, she was awakened by Opal pounding on her door, yelling her name. Cayley quickly drew her inside.

"What is the matter with you, Oppie? Are you drunk? You'll bring the hotel down on us."

"Drunk? Not likely, dearie. I'm in my own private world. It's the only place that'll have me."

"What are you talking about?" Cayley led her to a chair.

"I went down to Madam Maude's new place, and it seems I'm not wanted these days. Montrose was there. The stubby bastard had the starch to call me an old troublemaker. Troublemaker, yes, very flattering, But old? The little assface, midget pimp!"

"I'll get some coffee from downstairs and we'll sober you up."

"I'm not drunk, sweet Cayley—I've been down to the parlors, just to forget my troubles for an hour or two." Opal flapped her hands in the air like two confused seagulls, then plopped them into her lap as her head fell forward. With an effort, she raised it to look in the general direction of Cayley's face.

"Opium?" Cayley was horrified.

"Yezzzzz," said Opal, making horns on her forehead with her fingers, "Satan's smoke! Don't be such a schoolmarm. It's not the first time, and, things looking as they are, it won't be the last." Suddenly her face became stern, and then stunned; she crumpled into tears, falling forward and sobbing like a lost child.

Cayley fretted. "Oh, God in Heaven, Oppie. I don't know how to help you." She patted Opal's back as the woman continued to cry for a moment or two. "You're not the kind who gives up so easy, and I'm not going to let you. We'll figure something out." She helped Opal to her room, and into bed. She returned to her own room, sat in the chair facing the window and watched the sun climb down the façade of the building across the street. *That'll be me in a few years,* she thought. She pictured herself wrinkled and doubled over, creaking her way to a table at the Blue Rooster with a tray of drinks in her hand, trying to jolly up customers, standing on the edge of a group and laughing at jokes without a soul turning toward her. *Invisible. And I'll have less in my pockets than Opal does now. I think it may be high time to draw my friends closer—the ones that can do us all the most good.*

Chapter NINETEEN

Wo Sam was forced into the undignified role of go-between, normally reserved for a female matchmaker. He began negotiations for Kim's bride-to-be, bringing gifts of what few luxuries they possessed. After the herbalist and Wo Sam exchanged family credentials, and after extensive bargaining (which resulted in Wo Kim becoming an unpaid assistant to the herbalist for a period of three years as part of the bride price), the marriage was agreed upon. The two families waited an additional two weeks before a Feng Shui expert was able to travel to Virginia City from Sacramento, analyze the birth dates of the bride and groom, and consult the almanac for an auspicious day for the wedding. The decision was made to complete the ceremony at the beginning of the Chinese New Year, in February.

"I didn't know getting married would be so expensive, cousin," remarked Kim. "How will we come up with the dragon-and-phoenix cakes and tea?" He paced the floor of the small cabin, his arms crossed in front of him as if hugging himself. "My father-in-law understands that we have no poultry, sugar and wine, but we must at least have cakes and tea."

"The herbalist and his daughter have no family here, either. They are willing to forgo many of the formal preparations for marriage, especially since his daughter will be keeping house only for you and me. But the old man needs her too. I'm sure if we agree that you will go live in their home, there will be no problem with our lack of wealth. The herbalist is one of the most fortunate men in town, with a big house."

"I'm shamed at the thought of going to my wife's house as if I were the bride."

"We are not in China, Kim. We must adapt, especially if you wish to be married. You can bargain with the baker and tea merchant for their goods in exchange for future medicine from the herbalist's shop. You know the old man will welcome the suggestion of you becoming part of his household."

"Tell the herbalist to keep the dowry at his house then, if he agrees. This is most humiliating." Kim hung his head.

Wo Sam laughed and placed his hands on his cousin's shoulders. "I'm afraid many of our traditions will fall away here in America. We must keep what we can. But like water around a boulder, we will continue on our way."

Kim looked up with a wry smile. "So young to be a philosopher, cousin."

***

The day before the wedding, Kim chose the barber and the owner of the cafe to come with their mates along with Sam to carry the bridal bed up the stairs to their chamber in the herbalist's house. Both families brought gangs of their children, who sat upon the bed once it was placed. The children scrambled for dates, lotus seeds, peanuts and dried bits of fruit thrown on the bed to insure the fertility of the wedded couple. The bride was sequestered in another room, where she had been staying with a few of her women friends during the past week.

The next day, Kim dressed in a borrowed gown, red shoes and red silk sash. He and Sam lit a few precious sticks of fragrant incense at the makeshift family altar in the cabin. The altar, set on a shelf of the built-in sideboard, contained a single tintype of Kim's parents, a photograph of Sam's father and sister, and a few objects from home. The young men then stepped outside.

The din of firecrackers, loud gongs and drums marked the start of Kim's procession to the bride's home. He led the small group, walking with head up through the dirty snow, holding the hand of one of the barber's sons.

When they arrived at the herbalist's two-story yellow house, Kim's party was met by the bride's friends, who would not "surrender" her until satisfied by red packets of coins. Kim's party passed out the envelopes, amid much playful bargaining: "How can we let our friend marry a mere boy?" teased the tailor's wife. Her husband, handing her a red envelope with a few pennies in it declared, "A boy who is strong as a bull will give her many sons."

The herbalist invited the group inside. The bride, dressed in traditional red jacket, skirt and shoes, bowed to her father and to the ancestral altar, then sat to receive her husband-to-be. Her face was veiled in red silk. At the rear of her chair, a sieve to strain out evil and a metallic mirror to reflect truth were suspended for her protection.

The herbalist received Kim into the family by presenting him with a pair of chopsticks and two wine goblets wrapped in red paper.

More firecrackers were set off to frighten away evil spirits as the bride stepped outside onto a red mat. Following the old custom, a saddle was placed over the threshold, and she stepped back into the house over the saddle, murmuring the words for "saddle" and "tranquility," a play on words, as the names of the two sound the same in Cantonese—with this, she assured peace in her household. The tailor's wife laid rice in a bowl near her feet, to call in prosperity.

Kim stepped forward, raised the red scarf, and smiled into his bride's face. She led him to the family altar, where they paid homage to heaven and earth, and to their ancestors. She prepared tea and the two offered a cup with two red dates in it to her father. As he drank, Kim and his bride bowed to each other. They were now husband and wife.

Sam went outside, and began to beat loudly on a pan lid as the women in the group scurried into the kitchen to bring out the meal they had prepared for the wedding feast. During the celebration that followed, Sam drank and ate merrily with the rest of the party, but couldn't keep the thought of the cheerless, forlorn cabin he would inhabit by himself far from his mind. A light snow had begun to fall in the darkness as the party wound down, and Sam approached the door to return home, pulling his jacket collar up around his ears. He nearly collided with the café owner's middle son—who, deserting his post at the telegraph office—had run to the herbalist's home.

The boy apologized, almost out of breath. "Wo Sam!" he said excitedly, "it just came over the wire—one of the great leaders of Chinatown has been assassinated. Lord Low Yet is dead! Little China is in an uproar."

Sam held him firmly by the shoulder, preventing him from going inside. "Was it the white devils?"

"No. It is said that someone paid off his bodyguards to leave him alone in the barbershop, where he was shot. The funeral is already being planned. The biggest Chinatown has ever seen."

Wo Sam released the boy and tried to digest this news. He stepped inside the door, attempting to catch Kim's eye, but his young cousin, a big smile on his face, was surrounded by laughing well-wishers. Sam turned and made his way up the dim path to the cold cabin. The *Ah Mah* was dead. In an instant, everything had changed.

***

After three days, Kim visited Sam at the cabin.

"I'm going back to San Francisco." Sam leaned against the cabin wall, careful not to touch the bright orange sides of the metal stove.

"You don't intend something foolish? Like revenge on Po Wen? You might as well eat opium and die here, in the comfort of your own cabin."

"No, I'm not that foolhardy. Po Wen may or may not have had anything to do with the death of Low Yet, but either way he's a dangerous man. I'll keep far away from him. It's just that I am not made for the country."

"It's true that all you do is complain. But I will miss your complaints! You are the only blood kin I have here. What will you do?"

"I don't know. You're a married man now, with a business and a future. You don't need me to watch over you. Perhaps it is foolish of me to return—the tongs are still at war with one another, and I've insulted the Yeung Lo Company—they'll never hire me back as their scholar, and neither will anyone else. But I must make my poke and return to China, to my father and sister. What little I had left I lost at the tables."

"You could be a houseboy for the rich whites. You could keep their records, since you read the language and know their number symbols."

"The whites all hate us."

"No, the rich ones like us because they think we're meek and mild. And hard working," Kim grinned. "You would have to learn meekness, which wouldn't be a bad idea."

"That work is humiliating." Sam looked down at the worn-smooth floor in silence for a moment. He busied himself measuring out tealeaves from a tin container, putting them into a kettle of hot water atop the stove. "Where would I find such work, anyway?"

"You told me yourself that rich whites go for drinking to the bars on Market Street. You could always stop people and ask if they need house help—you speak English better than most of them, anyway. And there are the newspapers, where some advertise for workers."

"The last time I was on Market Street, I almost asked for a beating."

"Then stay here," Kim shrugged.

"How much can you lend me for train fare?"

Chapter TWENTY

"I'd like you to take me home this evening, if you would," said Cayley.

Rolifer's unhandsome mouth hung open slightly. "What?"

"Take me home. No strings on your part. You're a strong man," she teased, squeezing his upper arm through the wool of his suit. "A woman needs a strong friend to protect her these late nights. I go home at midnight. It would be nice if you'd be here."

Rolifer continued to look bewildered, but nodded, somewhat dumbly.

The evening went as usual. Cayley paid as much attention to Rolifer as she always did, but spread her regard out among the patrons, laughing louder than ever, persuading men to drink, eat and enjoy themselves. While moving between the tables, she replayed Opal's matter-of-fact instructions in her mind: the special ways to touch men, the business of how to protect herself from getting babies with a hollowed-out lemon half, how to check for disease. The thoughts made her stomach tighten, but she couldn't deny the thrill rippling down her back. *I'm going to do this,* she thought. *I'm really going to do this.* A memory swam up from her childhood: playing doctor with Freddy Reilly out by the church outhouse after catechism class—she clearly remembered the combination of forbidden touch, longing, and fear mixed with unsavory whiffs of the outhouse. A pang of disappointment roiled through her when Rolifer left with a bunch of his cohorts at around 9 o'clock. When he returned by himself at midnight, Cayley had just finished putting her coat around her shoulders. She felt weak-kneed and wild.

"I'm glad to see you, Arnold," she said.

"I'm not sure what I'm doing here. No funny business, young lady."

"Funny business?" said Cayley, and flashed him a smile. "What an idea. I'm afraid of that slasher fella. You can be my big, strong protector. C'mon." They stepped up into his gleaming carriage; Stilly, the mare that her brother Michael made such a fuss over, easily turned the rig around on Market and trotted along, making a right turn on Jones Street. Neither Cayley nor Rolifer spoke.

"I'd like you to come in," she said when they reached the door of her hotel. "There's something I want to talk to you about. Now I know it wouldn't look good for either of us to be seen together, so we'll go in separately. It's number 203." She put a finger to her lips, then reached up and let her lips linger on his a little longer than was friendly. She turned and walked into the brightly lit lobby.

Rolifer handed the reins of the horse to the livery boy. "How long will you be, sir?" he asked.

Rolifer stared into the etched glass doors that Cayley passed through. The shadows of the potted palms on either side of the opening were black against the glass. "I have no idea."

When Rolifer opened the door on the second-floor landing, he could see Cayley down the hall, waving him inside. The gaslights had been turned down low in the room, and a bottle of red wine and two glasses glinted on the table.

"Won't you have a drink, Arnold? On me, this time." Cayley tried to control her shaking by breathing deeply.

He sat down in the pale rose brocade armchair with his hat on his lap.

"Oh, let me take those things for you." She reached for his coat and hat and hung them on the tree by the door. "Would you like to loosen your collar a bit? It looks so…tight." She whispered the last word.

He nodded and she helped him widen the knot that held his stiff collar in place. She noted that he was far from young, and not a bit like Henry. The flesh of his neck hung over his collar, and once it was loose, she followed her urge to rub his neck gently. "It's like being in a prison collar," she said. "I didn't know it was so hard on a man. The collar, I mean." She blushed and looked away. *What an idiot.*

Arnold laughed and caught her wrists in his hands. "Now, what exactly am I doing here, Missy? I don't rightly understand what you want from me, so why don't you tell me."

Cayley sat down heavily on the bed and looked him in the eyes. She blushed a new shade of crimson, and shook her head, allowing a burst of embarrassed laughter to escape. "I'm seducing you, Arnold, can't ya' tell?" She laughed loud, then, a high, forced sound. "It seems like I'm out of practice."

"So now you want me to take you. Not like the other day. I don't suppose you've got some photographer outside just waiting to pop in at the right moment with one of them new boxy cameras, maybe make some money?"

Cayley's shock was genuine. "NO. Nothing like that." She took his hands in her own and spoke to him in a calm voice, focusing on his eyes from beneath her eyelashes. "Though I'd be lying if I said I didn't have my reasons for wanting you to like me."

"I already like you."

"And I like you too. It's that…oh, I don't even know. I feel like a fool." The hot tears gathered in her eyes; she put her head in her hands. He stepped over and sat beside her on the bed, his arm around her.

"There, there. You're just a girl, Cayley Wallace. Just a little girl with big ideas." He squeezed her to him and she put her head on his shoulder, her arms around his waist.

"It feels good to have a man hold me," she said. "It's been a long time since my husband and I shared a bed."

"I'd voice the same sentiment myself. Not with your husband, of course." He grinned.

Cayley looked up at him, and shook her head. "It shouldn't really be that way, should it? That's what they tell us in fairy tales, anyway."

"But that's the way it is."

In the warm circle of his arm, Cayley began to relax. The solidity of his body sent little pulses of electricity through her. She traced the buttons on his shirt, moving from one to the other. Slowly, she turned her face up to his. His mouth felt foreign, a poor fit for her own, used to kissing only one man. But Arnold slowed down, making the lips fit together, moving his tongue lightly across her lower lip, then the tip of her tongue. Blood surged through her body, her breath became more rapid. A slow, liquid sensation took over her limbs.

"Wait, wait," she said. She tried to reach behind herself to loosen the buttons of her dress.

"I'll do that."

She turned her back to him and closed her eyes, fighting down a moment of panic, remembering what happened in the alley. "I'm not a tart," she said.

He methodically unbuttoned the back of her dress. "No, I don't suppose you are."

The undone bodice of her dress released her breasts. She raised her arms and he pulled the garment over her head. She stood, unbuttoned her skirt, dropped it to the floor. Her nipples formed two hard points at the front of her shift. Neither of them moved for a moment; his hands came round her sides, covered

115

her breasts, and he pulled her back against him. They both gasped; he inhaled a mouthful of her hair, and coughed.

"Oh! Wait!" she leaned forward and took the pins out of her hair quickly, throwing them haphazardly in the direction of the wine bottle. He pulled her back against him, massaging her large breasts in his hands. She groaned and reached behind her, between his legs, and touched his stiffness with her fingertips.

He allowed her to turn and help him unbutton his shirt, remove his pants. His penis was hot in her hands—they were rabid to touch each other, his hand reaching for a breast, pinching, her bringing her face to his lap—what was that Opal said?—she couldn't remember, but she stroked and kissed. It didn't matter that his stomach was broad, and his flesh dimpled where she grasped it. He pushed her back, her petticoats flying up. He pressed them down, and searched for the slit of her drawers, opened it, pushed the folds aside, and leaned into her.

She was tight from disuse, but as wet as she had ever been. He began to move on her hard, and she met him with every stroke. Sometimes, he would pause to bend down to mouth one or the other of her breasts. "Jesus, you're as good as I thought you would be," he said. Suddenly, his member went limp, though he hadn't yet come. He made a noise of frustrated disgust, and rolled off her. They sat side by side in silence for a moment, both breathing heavily.

"I'm going," he said.

Cayley's mind raced. "Just stay for a little while, Arnold. Keep me company. Please." She held his hand, ignoring his downcast eyes. "I'm so lonely." She jumped up and poured him a glass of wine. "So what are you boys cooking up at City Hall?" she asked brightly. He started to talk about politics, what deals were made and why. While recounting a story of one-upmanship on his part, he even laughed, and she laughed with him. She put her hand on his leg, and moved it upwards until he stopped talking. He let her touch him lightly, and she paid attention to what seemed to please him and did it more. When he lay back on the bed, she swung her leg over him and slid down. In a minute or two, her legs wrapped tightly around him, she sensed herself near to a faint, and cried out as she felt him shoot inside her. She pulsed around him, squeezing him, drawing more of him in. She collapsed on the bed beside him.

They both lay, soundless, breathing heavily. He turned his face toward her and nodded twice, stroking the side of her face with the back of his hand. "Why are you crying?" he said.

"I don't rightly know," she said. But she did.

Chapter TWENTY-ONE

They stayed in bed, leaning against each other, finally falling asleep. Arnold woke to find her sitting next to the bed in a dressing gown. "Hello sleepyhead," she said.

"Good Christ, what time is it?" Rolifer searched frantically for his pocketwatch. "I have to go." He rushed about, pulling on clothing, tucking in his shirt, pushing his hair back with his hands while she observed him. When he went for the door, he turned to her, his mouth open.

"I'll see you at the Blue Rooster," she said, and blew him a kiss. He reached for his wallet and she stepped forward to stop him. "Don't do that. Don't do that to me. It's not like that." She turned away and bit her lips. *Real melodramatic; but I made my point.* He turned away and looked up and down the hallway before he made his way to the stairs.

It went real well; much better than I feared. She stood in the open doorway with her arms stiff at her sides, then turned and leaned against the door to shut out the world.

***

Arnold disappeared again for two weeks after their night together. Opal told her to be patient. "Sometimes they get the willies, and have to work out what they want," she said. "He'll be back. What man wouldn't, getting you for free?"

Cayley was surprised word hadn't gotten around the Blue Rooster, which meant that Arnold Rolifer hadn't told anyone he had slept with her. When she did see him again, looking sheepish and running the brim of his hat around and around in his hands, it was at the door of her hotel room. She unlocked the door and drew him inside.

After they became lovers, he would stop by late in the evening twice a week or more. Cayley spent as much time asking him about his work and rubbing his shoulders as she did making love with him. Money was never mentioned, though Rolifer often brought her a trinket or a fancy crystal bottle of perfume. As

118

spring began to soften the air, she threw open the windows to the unseasonable warmth one night, handed him a glass of wine and said, "I wish we could spend time together outside this hotel room. These four walls are closing in on us. Being with you is worth it and more, Arnold, but still sometimes…."

During the last weeks of July, Arnold surprised her with a special trip. He showed up in his carriage with one of his young male lackeys, and they rode all the way out to the Cliff House, always with the young man sitting between Cayley and Rolifer. She had never been there, and was curious to see how it looked since the schooner loaded with dynamite, the *Parallel*, ran aground on the rocks below a few years before and blew half of it up. "Oh, they patched it up," said Rolifer; "A new paint job, real water closets, and a new kitchen."

"I hear the cream of society dines there," said Cayley excitedly.

Rolifer grinned, "Not quite."

She saw for herself when they sat down to lunch—it was a mix of people, including tourists and a few unsavory types. But she couldn't have been more thrilled. When Rolifer came back that night by himself, she threw her arms around his neck and declared him the best fella she had ever known.

As the year wore on, she sometimes wouldn't see him for a week, then two. When he showed up, Cayley would test him: "Oh, you probably miss the hospitality at the bawdy houses, don't you?" He would demure, saying his work was taking him away more and more.

One night, as she complained to Opal about Rolifer's increasing absences, the other woman said sternly, "You didn't break rule number one and fall in love with this man, did you, Cay?"

"Well, no. Not exactly," Cayley replied. "I guess I just come to depend on him something regular. And since there isn't no one else…"

"This might be high time to take advantage of the man's connections. I'm saying this, because from what I know of men, they like to amuse themselves with variety if they have the means to do so. And Rolifer certainly does."

"Am I losing him?"

"As a lover, I think so. Men just don't have it in them to be faithful. If he's not on his way out the door now, it'll be soon, at least from what you say. And with him goes your best chance of keeping yourself off the streets. I know we haven't talked much about it, but do you think he'd be willing to back you in a business?"

"What kind of business? What do I know? How to rub tarnish off silver? My mother works her fingers raw with other people's mending. I suppose I could try to open a bar." Cayley put her hands over her mouth and shook her head no. "I don't know what to do. And I'm not so sure I can handle a business by myself, anyway."

"Well, there is one business you and I talked about before—one that I know how to run real well. It's more reliable than the Comstock Lode. What about him backing that pleasure house we talked about?"

Cayley gaped. Opal crossed her arms and looked her square in the eyes. "Don't panic on me. Hold on for a minute. With his money and my know-how, you and I would be set for life—and he would make a bundle, too. No more worries about being grey-haired beggars down in the Barbary. We could do this. It's possible—IF you've got the gumption to approach him. And it better be quick."

"I'd need more than just an idea—he'd laugh at me and say the 'pretty little head' thing."

"Then we'll figure out how much it's all going to cost. We'll find a place, and have it all down, in writing."

"That'll show him what pretty little heads can come up with."

"Cayley, you've got the power to save us both right now. I hope we can find a way to make it work."

Chapter TWENTY-TWO

Opal instructed Cayley on what to look for, but didn't want to take the chance on being identified while shopping for a house—it would drive the price up a ridiculous degree and might limit their choices. Cayley looked at three houses for sale downtown, and none of them were right. She needed a downstairs suitable for a bar, a large parlor and ballroom upstairs for parties, plus several rooms for the girls the next floor up. Everything was either too small or too large, or too hard to get around, or too expensive. She not only had to buy the house with as little as possible, but to furnish it in lavish style. She knew what she wanted—the things she had seen at Gumps but couldn't afford: carved and curved rosewood in the Belter style, ormulu chandeliers, ornate mirrors with gilding, and lots of deep, red velvet, a very sexy color. And she liked screens, too, the way the Chinese did them, with pictures made from bits of stone and shell. And brocade, red and gold. She'd have to go to Chinatown for that.

One autumn morning, the streets were dry and a little dusty from the lack of rain; the bells from the cable car sounded with bright clarity. The agent picked her up at the hotel and together they went to look at a three-story townhouse on O'Farrell, in the upper Tenderloin. The street was a good one—no other pleasure houses nearby, and a place where her best clients could be seen without embarrassment. There was a livery on the corner for client's carriages and horses, and no one would be the wiser. The brick facade on the house wasn't as pretty as she'd like, but the rooms were large and high-ceilinged, and the girls' rooms upstairs could be divided to make them smaller but still attractive enough for the best girls to want to stay there—and fit in more girls, too. This might do. When she hired the agent, Cayley told him she was purchasing the house for the Silver King Company as a lodging house for it's traveling representatives.

"They'll be plenty of them here, staying the night," she said. "There's a lot of travel among the company's directors, and they expect the best while away from home." They stood in the dusty vestibule of the house. Light poured through the naked windows across the parquet floors.

The agent, a wiry man with a short, gray brush of beard said, "This is mighty unusual, a woman doing the business part of it and all."

"Oh, they must approve my choices, that's for sure, but Mr. King trusts me, as I've been his assistant in the office for many years. And they like a woman's touch." Cayley smiled prettily and thrust her bosom forward.

"Is that so?" said the agent, his eyes dropping and holding as if weighted.

"Of course, being Mr. King's niece may have something to do with it, too. He likes to humor me, and doesn't like it if he feels people have dealt rough with me. You understand."

His eyes went back to her face.

"Since we'll be paying a large amount of cash initially, I expect that you'll want to improve the property to our satisfaction."

"And what would that be, exactly?"

"Well, I've only just seen the place, but a few of the things that would be necessary are,…" and she ticked off ten or twelve items. "Are you taking this down, Mr. Moore?"

Moore stood dumbfounded. "Miss, that's asking a lot for the sale of a house!"

"You're not interested? Very well." She smiled without showing her teeth and headed for the door.

"No, no, that's not what I mean," he stammered, hurrying after her. "I mean we will need to talk further."

"Oh yes, of course."

122

Chapter TWENTY-THREE

Later that week, as Rolifer lay spent on her bed, Cayley urged him to lean forward so she could puff up his pillow. She sighed deeply. "Arnold, we can't keep meeting here. A hotel room at the Pleasanton is no place for you. You deserve better."

"I suppose there's a better room for you in the Palace or Baldwin's. They're anonymous enough. Would that please you my dear?"

"I had something else in mind." She smiled coquettishly, and appeared to examine the ceiling.

"Such as?"

She rose from the bed and lifted an envelope from the side table, untying the ribbon that held it closed. "An investment property—something that would make you a considerable amount of money right away with no trouble to you at all."

"What thoughts have invaded your clever little head, my dear? It sounds like someone has sold you a get-rich-quick scheme."

"Actually, it's a very reliable business, especially in this town. I want to open a bordello—the best in town. Real quality."

He sat upright. Let out a single guffaw, then stared at her. "Are you serious? No, you can't be." He pulled his face into an accommodating grin.

"It's not a joke." Cayley leveled her blue gaze at him. "I want to open a bordello, and I want you to go in with me on it."

He sat hunched over the sheets and rubbed the side of his head with his hand. "Where did all this come from?" He looked around the room as if searching for clues. "Out of nowhere!"

"Arnold," Cayley said gently, but with humor in her voice, "you are a dear man, and lovely to bed down with, but we both realize that our time together is…well, it's not meant to last forever. I understand that. It would break my heart to lose your friendship, but it doesn't have to be that way. I'm offering you something wonderful; something that would make both of us happy. And rich."

"It's just, I thought, well, that you were above that sort of thing. Money was never an issue between us."

"Above that sort of thing. That's very sweet. Well, you're right, I am above that sort of thing." She held the packet in both hands and thrust it toward him. "I'm not asking payment for favors given. I never have, and I'm not now. I'm talking business with you, Arnold, pure and simple. I can make you money. Would that please you, my dear?"

"Cayley, you don't know anything about running a bawdy house. Do you?"

"Oh Arnold. I do a number of things well, handling money among them. But the thing I do best of all is please men." She laid a hand on his limp penis. "And I'm not talking strictly about sex, either. It's like any business. I can bring them in and keep them spending money, just like I do at the Blue Rooster. I'm not alone in this. My good friend Opal—whom you know—has had plenty of experience working in the best houses. She and I will bring in the prettiest girls, and we'll conjure up the most interesting entertainments. It'll be the finest men's club with special female attractions in town. We've already found the perfect house on O'Farrell."

He slid back down into bed.

"But Cayley..."

"Arnold," her face grew solemn, "You don't think my ambition in life is to remain at the Blue Rooster watering drinks until I'm so old and wrinkled I become a local joke, do you? I'll do this with you or without you, but I want you to profit from it too."

Rolifer pushed himself upright again and leaned toward her. "Listen here. Property costs a bundle in this town. There's no way I could come up with that kind of cash, much less have it attached to my name."

"You are so right, dear, as usual. But your friends would be happy to form a little syndicate with you in order to buy the property until I can buy you out, if that's what you want. Everybody benefits, and keeps their hands clean in the process. I'll be the 'front man,' so to speak. And you and I will have it written up, just between us, all nice and proper."

"I don't know."

"Look at me, dear heart." She laid the portfolio down on his lap, reached up and held his face in her two hands. His bristled sideburns puffed through her fingers, and she tenderly smoothed them down before speaking again. "I know this is a bit of a shock to you, but I've been working on it and planning for some time. Opal knows everything that needs to be done on the merchandise side, and I have years behind me running a bar and food service thanks to the Blue Rooster. This isn't some pipe dream. I know what I'm doing, and I'm willing to take full responsibility for it." She arranged herself next to him on the bed. "As for your reputation, and that of your friends—you can trust me completely. I've proven that time and again."

He put his hand over hers. A moment passed. He mumbled, "I can't agree to this just like that. I need to see some real numbers...to work my mind around it."

"Of course. You're a smart man and you expect to know what you're getting into. As for numbers, how about ten or twelve different, beautiful women, any time you'd want them. I'm not the jealous type, and it's always free for you." She winked. "Not for other investors though. We've got to make a profit, after all." She opened the portfolio in front of him. "Take a look at what we need for expenses. Here's the house mortgage, and furniture.... I figure I can buy at auctions to save us some money. You told me that each of your friends has favorite girls in the houses. We can offer a better cut, and a better place to live and work; the best place in town. Topper parties, beautiful women and full-strength liquor. And it's yours. With a hand-picked group of your friends, of course. You don't ever get your hands dirty. At the very least, you'll end up owning property on O'Farrell Street—but you can be darn sure I'm not going to run off with the money or cheat you. It's in my best interests to make you richer. Think about it."

Chapter TWENTY-FOUR - September 1892

Within six weeks, Arnold Rolifer had made up his mind and gathered a group of willing investors: the house became the property of the Silver King Syndicate, and in that name secured a tavern and rooming house license. Cayley discovered she had real flair when it came to creating a showplace she could call her own—as long as she didn't think too much about the real purpose of the "rooming house." She put carpenters and painters to work; the city's frequent booms and busts had made workers plentiful and cheap. Taking cues from the interior of the Rolifer home and Opal's advice, she kept the original wide entrance foyer on the first floor; stairs that led to the second floor blocked a view of the interior from the street. The original formal salon to the right of the stairs was kept as an office, walled off to face the house interior. She had walls torn down in the warren of small rooms in back of the house to put in a curved zinc-top bar and tables, backed by a kitchen. Plenty of natural light fell from the enlarged windows on either side of the front door and halfway down the interior, but as was the style, Cayley covered them in heavy drapes and depended on the new electric lights to illuminate the interior. A portion of the second floor above the office was made into a small private apartment with two bedrooms (each with its own door and wash basin) that Cayley and Opal shared. The remaining space became a parquet-floored ballroom, mirrored between floor-to-ceiling windows. Another stairway led up to the third floor, open to the ballroom, surrounded by a walkway and balustrade with doorways to twelve small rooms. The two women made several trips to auctions and Gumps to furnish each room lavishly, making sure the rooms were all papered with different colors and themes. Cayley even put in a Wizard of Oz room, done up like the Emerald City. But she didn't choose the beds. She would leave that up to the girls, with Opal's supervision, of course.

During the whirlwind process of setting up, Cayley's misgivings about the type of business she was getting into were pleasantly deflected by the fact she loved being in charge, making decisions, and handling large sums of money. *There's nothing like poverty to teach you to appreciate the almighty dollar,* she thought When it came to hiring servants and giving orders, she patterned herself on Mrs. Rolifer. *How funny is that? The leader of the Decency League as a model for the owner of a bordello.* In a touch all her own, Cayley had a local artist paint the ceilings in the office and ballroom with frolicking fauns and nymphs. She had seen examples in Harper's magazine and read that upper-class homes in Europe all had painted ceilings in the grand manner. *Class: that's what this place is all about. This is how I'm meant to live.* How the money would come in—well, she didn't dwell on that. She put the small library of books she had acquired over the past three years prominently on display in the office.

The girls arrived courtesy of Miss Opal Boone and the gentlemen of the Silver King Company, much to the fury of the other madams in town, particularly Madam Maude and Mr. Montrose, Opal's old employers. Their once-thriving business lost three girls to Cayley.

Ten girls made up their company, each as different as could be. Blondes, redheads, brunettes, one Negress, one Chinese girl, plump and thin. "Variety," said Opal, "that's what'll bring them in." Cayley was surprised: she had expected many of the girls to be harder, toughened by the street, yet some of them seemed almost innocent. She wasn't sure whether it was an act, but figured that as long as they did what they were hired for, everything would run smoothly.

While Cayley set up bar operations, Opal dealt directly with the girls. She paid them their nightly fees for a week while they got used to their new surroundings, chose the beds for their rooms, and prepared for the opening night party, a Saturday, two weeks after the new year's celebrations of 1893 had quieted down. Cayley had spent those last two weeks at the Blue Rooster working for half wages, which gladdened Mr. Max's heart, since he had a hard time replacing her. She whipped up excitement, impishly starting then denying rumors about what could be found at the House of Wallace; one rumor included a pair of tigers. Word traveled through the liveries and tobacconists: many potential clients relied on those sources for the latest news on the "sporting" parlors.

It was clear and frosty the evening of the official opening, but the temperature inside the House of Wallace was already rising. Opal had all the girls dress like brides, but with breasts and legs exposed. The serving staff prepared a wedding feast served with free drinks from the bar. Opal found actors to impersonate "father of the bride," "best man," "parson" and so on, and to give bawdy speeches which often included simulated sex acts among several members of the wedding party. One well-received combination was the bride giving "lip service" to the parson and best man at the same time while the father of the bride lined up the bent-over bridesmaids and tore off their skimpy undergarments before mounting them, one by one. Cayley's mood altered be-

128

tween merriment and profound embarrassment. *I better learn to look like this is a walk in the park or I'll ruin everything,* she thought. Opal wouldn't let anyone go upstairs with the blushing bride/s of his choice until her guest's appetites were good and whetted: more than two hours of mental foreplay, teasing, laughter, food and liquor. Much as she did at the Blue Rooster, Cayley wandered about the parlor rooms in great good humor, flattering the city's elite: a judge, the son of a railroad baron, and two real silver kings. Arnold Rolifer was there, beaming while his friends and associates, the rich and powerful men of San Francisco, clapped him on the back. Cayley made it quite clear that the house was his—including any woman or combination of women—he took a fancy to. It was a strange and sometimes uncomfortable transition for her; with the exception of Rolifer, she flirted with these men and nothing more—here, at the house named for her, she brought each man together with a young woman who would take him upstairs for sex—including her patron. She plastered a smile on her face; the men in the room looked at her with a new respect. She hoped.

The reality of the choices she had made in persuading Arnold Rolifer to back this pleasure house were just beginning to be made real for her. Her brain whirled. This was very different from the Blue Rooster, and she was in so deep that she either had to leave town and change her name or go forward. She looked at the sparkling crystal glasses, the velvet draperies, and fine wool suits of her guests. *I'm not going anywhere,* she thought. *Whatever it takes.* The party lasted until dawn, with guests trickling out into the quiet of the brightening streets.

Cayley had arranged for a stable boy to work the livery all night, so that carriages could be hooked up and made ready in a few minutes. A guest would emerge blearily from one of the upstairs rooms, and Cayley would fortify him with coffee while she sent a runner to wake the stable boy to bring the rig around. The House of Wallace was officially open for business, evenings only.

***

Cayley continued to favor Rolifer when he chose her, which he often did. She had thought to leave the sexual part of the business to the professionals. The girls knew it, however, and began acting cool towards her; she often caught them whispering and looking in her direction, then going silent and turning away from her when she approached them. Opal said, "What do you expect? They think you look down on them. They get enough of that on the street."

"Oppie, you know that's not true."

"It's not what I know that matters."

Most of the men who came to the house kept a distance from her, considering her Rolifer's "property." But little more than a month after the house opened, she was invited upstairs by a handsome up-and-coming politician she hadn't seen before. "Your patron is nowhere in sight," he whispered. "And I'm only one of many who've been longing for a taste of you." She shivered; as he began kissing her neck, her thoughts were jumbled. Going upstairs with him would be the final step over a line she avoided thinking about. A sexual act was all he wanted—and she was a young woman, and felt a physical need—she fought down panic and reasoned with herself: *I've only had one choice before, and it was always "no." How can I expect the girls to respect me if I hold myself above them? I chose to make Arnold my lover, and good came from that. I could choose "yes." I have a choice in this place that I've never had in my life. I can choose my own pleasure.* She took his hand and declared she was going upstairs loud enough for several of the girls to hear.

Once in her room, he pulled apart his breeches, roughly turned Cayley over, pushed her down face first on the bed and ripped her drawers to get to her. He entered her immediately, and with a few quick thrusts, it was over. He hurriedly rearranged his clothes, grinned triumphantly at her and left the room as she turned upright and eased herself down on the bed.

Alone, near tears, Cayley sat stiffly, hands on her thighs. Opal announced herself with a knock at the door: "How are you doing?" She let herself in.

130

"All right, I guess. I feel strange. Don't laugh."

Opal plopped down next to her on the bed and took one of her hands. "I'm not laughing. Did he hurt you?"

"No, not really. It wasn't like with my husband or Arnold, though. We didn't exchange a word. I feel...dirty."

Opal sighed. "It's like that more often than not. In the better class of place the girls are treated with more respect, but I guess this fella didn't get that message."

Cayley made a wry face.

Opal put her arm around her friend. "Happened to me at first, too. I couldn't help but hope one or the other of them would care about me. After all, I was giving my 'most precious gift' to them."

Cayley held her hand up to her face, and couldn't help but laugh. The tears squeezed out of her eyes.

"They just don't see it that way, darlin'." Opal held Cayley's shoulders firmly. "The minute he was done, his mind was on the deal he'll make tomorrow and the price of peas. They're not like us, where a little piece of our heart goes out to them. We're not proper women to them in this house—we're a means to an end. Desire without responsibility—that's what they're paying for—and he's going to pay. First thing, make sure that you send him a bill triple the usual, 'for professional services rendered by the proprietor.' He's probably downstairs now bragging on himself, and that will knock him down a peg or two. In the future, steer him to someone else. Be real careful about who you let in." Opal gave Cayley's shoulders a squeeze. "I mean in your heart and your twat both."

Cayley wiped the wet from her eyes with the back of her wrist. "I know all that, but still..."

Do you need to stay up here for a while? I'll get rid of your...client...downstairs."

"Yes. Give me a few minutes." Cayley stood up and straightened herself out as Opal went through the door. *So much for precious gifts...I have to learn to live with this,* she thought. *This is as much a business as trading horses. To every man that comes through this door, I'm a whore—a high-class whore, but nothing more than that—and I better get used to it.*

***

With Opal's guidance, the business ran smoothly. Unlike other fancy parlors that would charge a patron while they were in-house, Cayley sent bills to her client's men's clubs or offices at the end of the month: an invoice from the Silver King Company for business services rendered. No need to fear collection problems—failure to pay meant being barred from the door on a future visit, not only denying the visitor the obvious pleasures of the flesh inside, but also his place among the city's movers.

Within a few months, more money was rolling in than Cayley ever thought possible. She prudently paid Opal as much as she took herself, and plowed much of the money she made back into the business, paying off her loan to Rolifer's syndicate and raising the girl's incomes, while making sure they lived in a real home ("The best ones are so easy to steal. Believe me, I know!" said Opal). During the day, the girls would amuse themselves with needlework, and the halls began to fill with examples of their homilies, a popular one being "If every man was as true to his country as he is to his wife—God help the U.S.A."

Cayley was under no illusions about the social attitude toward her and the "girls." Though they were considered the best in town as prostitutes, miles above women who walked the street or filled the stable-like whorehouses of Chinatown, the women who were rich enough or fortunate to make marriages to men who could support them—respectable women—spat on them. For that reason, and for safety's sake—the Ripper was still about—Opal and Cayley encouraged the girls to go out in pairs. That was the beginning of the parade on Friday and Saturday nights.

"We'll send them out during the evening cocktail route down Market Street," said Opal.

"Dressed in the latest fashions from New York—topper way to show off the merchandise," Cayley agreed, and arranged for the girls to dress relatively modestly and walk arm in arm, faces turned up with sweet smiles. When a man tipped his hat to them, they handed out fancy lithographed calling cards with their names and the address of the O'Farrell house.

Within a few weeks, Cayley noticed that the evening streets, once filled exclusively with men, now held more women, also in pairs. But they weren't there to jeer—in fact, they discussed Cayley's girls' dresses and hats in detail, exclaiming over the fabric and tailoring. Though these respectable women wouldn't give her girls the time of day in most circumstances, they were eager to copy their beauty and style.

***

By the time Cayley had been open six months, she had learned a few other things—like how large a "donation" to the policeman's fund was necessary to keep her house free of raids. In fact, she enjoyed a good relationship with the police; Commissioner Reardon was a man, after all, and one of the few men she would take on as a client herself—his patronage was a direct benefit to the house, and she determined to never let any man get the upper hand again. She also learned to give the customer everything he wanted, then bill him plenty for it afterward, right down to the whiskey stains on the carpet.

This was made real for her the weekend she closed the house for a private party for the son of one of California's most famous men. The young man and his friends were so wild, they tore the velvet draperies from the windows—Cayley laughed and enjoyed the destruction mightily, but planned to send a whopping big bill to the father—with 25% added for good measure.

The Monday morning after the party, Cayley sat at the bar as her kitchen man Arturo—recommended by Mr. Max's Italian cook—brought out a steaming cup of coffee on a tray. "Looks like one of dem tornados in Ohio, where I come from," he said, indicating the torn curtains, playing cards scattered on the floor, and dribbling glasses on tables and on top of the piano.

"Looks like money in the bank to me," said Cayley, and winked at him. She dropped two lumps of sugar in her coffee and sipped it, squinting a little at the steam. She smiled, and looked out onto the alley off O'Farrell Street, visible in the dawn light through the half-down curtains.

A pretty brunette in a Japanese wrapper descended the stairs, and wandered sleepily toward her across the chaotic room.

"Coffee," she said.

"Arturo's in the kitchen," said Cayley.

"Annh." She shuffled toward the other room.

"Oh Angela."

She stopped and turned. "Yes, Mrs. Wallace?"

"Did you by any chance see Opal go out sometime last night? Or Toy?"

"No, Ma'am. I was much too busy. Those boys are cute, but they're full of pepper."

"That's fine, Angela. Go get your coffee." The woman continued on her way. Cayley poked her head in the kitchen as Angela poured herself a cup. "Miss Opal isn't back yet. We've got to get his place cleaned up for company tonight. Arturo—you're in charge for now. Make sure the maids take care of it."

"Yes, Mrs. Wallace."

Chapter TWENTY-FIVE

To celebrate their first anniversary in business, Cayley and Opal decided to have the girls stage a bawdy parody of Gilbert and Sullivan's *Mikado*. She picked one early afternoon to go with the dressmaker's apprentice to Chinatown to buy fabric for costumes. They stepped up into her carriage and rode up Dupont Street to Sing Hoy's where they made a selection from mountains of colorful silks and brocades. Cayley bought some pearl rope necklaces for herself. It was early evening when they were done, two hours before the house opened. "Let's go down Jackson Street on the way back."

The dressmaker's apprentice, a timid young German girl replied, "You mean the Barbary Coast? Isn't that dangerous?"

"Not while we're in the carriage. No one will grab you, Edna—I'll defend you with my whip!"

"If you say so, Mrs. Wallace. You're the driver." She slumped her shoulders and looked for all the world like a damp cat.

"It will be fine dear. I used to spend some time down here a while back—my first place by myself was here. I'd like to see if it's changed." Cayley turned the horses at the corner of Jackson, and they continued down the hill. The two- and three-story buildings of Chinatown gave way to one-story brick buildings jammed next to each other like crooked teeth. The streets were filled with merchant sailors and rough-looking types, women with dirty faces in tattered burlap dresses. Some stood in doorways and watched mutely as the fine carriage passed, others paid them no attention at all, intent on their own distress. The pot-holed streets were filled with debris and old horse droppings, ground into the roadway. Almost everyone was on foot except for a few mounted horsemen who looked at them long and hard as they passed.

Edna drew closer to Cayley, her eyes wide. "Lotta beggars here," she said.

"Well, it's not Nob Hill, is it," said Cayley, absently. "God, it is dreary." She returned to her own thoughts.

"Now there's a sad sight," said Edna. She pointed her chin toward a woman wrapped in gray rags holding out a small cooking pot in front of her with one hand while clutching a two-year-old toddler to her with the other.

"Half of them are fakes, maybe more," said Cayley.

The woman entreated passers-by, and a few dropped a coin in. When she saw the carriage, she ran up to it quickly, then gasped and ran in the other direction, carrying the child awkwardly under her arm. Cayley pulled the horses up tight and stood up in the rig. She wasn't sure, but she thought she glimpsed a face she thought she'd never see again. "Ellen? Ellen Leary. Come back here." She threw the reins to the startled dressmaker and leapt out.

Ellen continued to try to make the alley, but the weight of the child slowed her, and when Cayley reached her and put a hand on her back, Ellen's shoulders slumped. But she wouldn't turn around.

"I was worried sick about you, girl. Is this where you've been? Why didn't you tell me?" said Cayley.

Ellen turned, her face filled with pride and misery. She crumpled and started to sob without sound, leaning against Cayley as best she could with the wiggling and bawling baby in her arms.

'Why didn't you tell me?" asked Cayley. "I thought we were friends...."

"My aunt threw me out when she found I was pregnant and no husband in sight. She was just waiting for a reason, and that was it."

"So why didn't you come to the Blue Rooster? Max could've helped."

"Oh, just what he had in mind, a barmaid with a big belly, that would have really brought them in." She glanced up at Cayley. "And there's the shame of it."

"Well, what about me then? I would've helped you."

136

"Oh Cayley, you're my dear friend. But I thought Bill would take care of us if he only knew, and I followed him up to Sacramento, but he'd have nothing to do with me, saying that he wasn't sure the baby was his, and such. He gave me a little money, but I ended up back here; at least I know the place." She put her head down. "It's my own fault."

'Oh God, Ellen." Cayley put her arm firmly around the other woman's shoulders. "There's worse things in this world than having a baby out of wedlock."

"Not for me," Ellen sniffled. She put the struggling child on the ground. "My poor baby has no name in the church. What will become of her?"

"Well, she won't be begging on the streets for supper, and neither will you. You'll both come with me and my girl Edna in the carriage. You'll sleep in a bed tonight, and we'll see about tomorrow when the time comes." She led them back to the blue-lacquered carriage where Edna nervously held the reigns and was engaged in a one-sided conversation with a couple of sailors who had stopped alongside her. "Get off!" said Cayley to the young men who looked unsettled but reluctant to start anything with a woman who looked as well off as Cayley. "Edna, this is Mrs. Leary; she and her child will accompany us home." She squeezed the women into the carriage, turned down Sansome and returned to the house. "I'll have the livery boy take you home, Edna."

When Cayley got Ellen into the house, she filled a bath for her. "Your fleas are jumping on me, girl," she said gaily, and got a weak, embarrassed laugh from the other woman.

"Let me wash my daughter first," said Ellen. The exhausted child was making sullen noises. "Cayley, did you marry rich, or what?" Ellen took in the lush furnishings with a slack jaw and she tenderly ran a cloth over the malnourished child.

"Not exactly. I know the nature of where my money comes from will not sit well with you. But you've got to have a little patience with me, and I'm sure I can help you."

"What are you saying to me, Cay?"

"Well, flat out, this is a bordello, and I run it. Very well, I might add. We're very successful. Now shut up, and don't say a word. You'll stay here the night, and we'll find another place in short order if you're not comfortable, with the baby and all. We'll work things out."

"Cayley, how has this come about? Are you...I mean, do you...?"

"Have relations with men I'm not married to for money? Well," she pulled her lips into a tight line, "That's the gist of it. There are eleven women here, Ellen, and fallen or not, we're making a living—a good one—in a hard world. It's survival, when the only other direction for most of us would be the one you've taken. I'll leave it up to you whether it's a better choice or not."

"I've got no answer for you, Cayley. I'm sorry to see you come to this, though."

Cayley sighed and shook her head. "Well, I'm not sorry to see you come to a warm bath, decent food and a clean bed." Cayley brought out nightclothes from the carved mahogany armoire. "We'll talk more in the morning. That child is falling asleep in the tub. What's her name anyway?"

"Beatrice. After my grandmother."

"Beatrice—that's a beautiful name. You and Beatrice can stay here in my apartment; in fact, it's better if you don't venture out. Arturo will bring up some food. It'll be a little noisy tonight, but you'll get through fine. We'll pick up anything you have elsewhere tomorrow. Now I have to go to work." She threw her arms around the other woman. "I'm so glad I found you and you're all right."

***

It took one night for Cayley to conclude that the House of Wallace was no place for a child; Beatrice toddled around the upper floor just when one of the girls was on her way upstairs, and there was nothing more deflating for the average male than to see a baby when he was about to engage his lust. In the morning, Cayley moved them out into a room at the Pleasanton Hotel.

"In spite of your profession, Miss Cayley," Ellen said as she accepted a bundle of clean clothes and hung them in the armoire, "I'm mighty grateful to you for taking us in. I was at my ragged end, as you might have guessed. It's God's mercy that brought you flying down that filthy street in that lovely blue carriage."

"It's like no time has passed at all. And you have a beautiful child that blesses us both," said Cayley. She sat on the bed and ran her hand slowly over the bedspread. "I have an idea. I've been thinking I need a respite myself—so as I'm not in the business every hour of the day. What if I bought a home far away from O'Farrell Street roomy enough for the three of us? Would you move in there with me?"

"I can't take your charity forever." Ellen's face betrayed embarrassment.

"It's not charity. You'd be doing me a favor. I need to get away and be with someone who's more like family. It would be a safe place for me, and I've missed the sound of a child's laughter. Will you do that for me—as a friend?"

Within the month, she bought a well-proportioned two-story house on Green Street, Russian Hill, where the cemetery used to be. The old trees, just starting to bud fruit in the small orchard out back convinced her: it would be an ideal place for a child's swing. Ellen and Beatrice moved in. Russian Hill was far enough away from her place of business to preserve the illusion of a couple of respectable widowed sisters-in-law.

***

Back at the O'Farrell house, Cayley ran her daily check on provisions. "Have we got the ice we need?"

Arturo paused halfway to kitchen with a big box of grapes in his hands. "Yes, Mrs. Wallace. The icehouse delivered a big block this morning, and I broke it down into tubs. And the bar is overstocked, as Miss Opal asked."

"Good, good." Cayley fingered her hair absently.

"It'll be right fine, as usual Ma'am." Cayley's kitchen man bobbed his head at her.

139

"Thank you, Arturo." She wandered through the lavishly decorated rooms, looking for a smudge on a mirror here, dust on a chandelier there. Opal really did know how to run the place when she was around, but her absences were becoming more frequent; Cayley had a new set of worries about the woman who got her into "the business."

Chapter TWENTY-SIX

Cayley's blue carriage clattered into the Green Street portico, as it did every morning, arriving with the sun. She found Ellen on her knees in the parlor, tucking Beatrice's dolls into a chest. Ellen's long red hair fell loosely down her back, nearly obscuring the neat white shirtwaist she wore. She still shied away from the house on O'Farrell, but she double-checked the financial records each week for Cayley, cleaning up her hurried entries and balancing everything out, taking on one of her friend's many burdens. "I've got to do something to earn my keep," she told Cayley. "Cooking and cleaning this house isn't more than I'd do on my own."

Cayley entered the parlor, hurriedly untied her bonnet and threw it on the divan.

"What?" Ellen turned around to face her friend. "What's wrong?"

"I've just got a lot on my mind these days," said Cayley, hands on her hips. "Ice and booze and bills. I can't keep up the business end all by myself, I'm afraid. I've relied on Opal, and she's out of the house more every week. I'm worried."

"I'd be more concerned about that Ripper still on the loose."

"We're a long way from the Barbary Coast, but I agree, we DO need somebody to work the entryway, especially now that we've become well known. Too many uninvited guests. Arturo is a wizard in the kitchen, but he's about as threatening as a dormouse."

"Well, it's not only the Ripper. The Decency League is whipping up a fury against the pleasure houses. It's all over the papers. It's easy to stir up the crazies in this town. Remember those bands of hoodlums murdering the Chinese left and right when we were kids."

"The Decency League. My God, if Arnold's wife only knew!" Cayley rubbed her chin. "Speaking of Chinese, I was down visiting Max yesterday; he said a big, strapping Chinaman was in asking for a job. Apparently he was working here and there doing accounting, but he wanted something steady. Max was about to chase him off, but the fellow made such a good impression, what with his fine speaking and writing and all; he claimed to have met Max a few years ago—helped him out in some minor trouble or something. I wonder if that was the night I came to the Blue Rooster. He left an address, along with a list of jobs he could do. He said he knew how to handle a gun. Max gave the address and list to me, thinking I might need someone. Besides, he couldn't read half the words."

Ellen smiled and raised one eyebrow. "Dear old Max."

"I'm interested in this Chinaman for a couple of reasons. One, I'll need someone to help with the books and run the place, particularly since—and you, El, are the first to hear—I intend to open another house on O'Farrell by the end of the year—I've got the place picked out already. And second, I think Opal's sneaking off to Chinatown these days. It's bad for everybody concerned."

"She's taken to the pipe again?"

"I'm afraid so. I asked her about her absences, and she just laughed it off, which irritated me plenty. We aren't speaking to each other much these days, which makes running this business difficult at best. This Chinaman might get to the bottom of it. I'd send him around, find out where she goes."

"So you've never laid eyes on this fella yourself."

"No—but I've gotten to be a pretty good judge of people. Hell, he must be cracker-jack smart. I couldn't read half the words either."

"Won't hurt to look. Why don't you have Arturo get him. I'd feel better if I knew you had a little protection."

Chapter TWENTY-SEVEN

Wo Sam stood in the vestibule of the house on O'Farrell Street. His face betrayed no expression, but his eyes landed everywhere—on the heavy carved table, marble statues, Persian rug. An arrangement of fragrant white and yellow roses spilled out of a silver vase on the entryway table. *A very rich house indeed.* Outside, the quiet street and lushly landscaped entries indicated an upscale neighborhood; he congratulated himself on his good luck.

The small man with curly dark hair who had brought him from the boarding house appeared in the entryway. "Mrs. Wallace will see you now," he said. Sam followed him to the other side of the stairs, into a room lit by a series of windows from the street and a number of glowing stained-glass lamps. The room was as sumptuous as the entry hall, with deep green velvet upholstery, gold-flocked wallpaper, and paintings of landscapes on the walls between the windows. A tiny yellow-haired woman in a pale purple silk dress sat at a desk on the left side of the room. Though it had been years, he recognized her instantly.

She turned when Arturo and Wo Sam entered. "Thank you, Arturo." She extended her hand as a man would do, "Mr. Sam?"

"It's Mr. Wo, actually," he said shyly, and bowed when he took her hand.

"Sorry, I forgot—your last name is in the place where our first name is, isn't that right?"

"Yes Madam. That is correct."

"Well, I'm Mrs. Wallace; please sit down."

He looked around at the chairs behind him, and chose a loveseat from among them. Wo Sam's hair was cut short in the western style and he was dressed in a modest black suit that made him look like an undertaker. He held his hat in his hands.

"I understand you are looking for employment as a houseman, and that you are skilled with numbers—accounting. Is that true?"

"Yes Madam. I was brought here as a scholar—that is, a reader and writer of both English and Chinese figures—by the Yeung Lo Company in Little China."

"Why aren't you working for them now?"

"I quit their employ some time ago, and have been working recently as a card dealer in Virginia City. I returned to San Francisco a few months ago. I have been doing accounting for small businesses here, but nothing permanent."

"I see. So you have few references? No one I could talk to about your work?"

"Very few references, madam, I'm sorry to say."

Cayley raised her chin and looked at the Chinaman down through her lashes. Wo Sam noted how she fixed her gaze on him, as if sizing him up—or trying to make him squirm. *These English—they stare at you and believe they know you.* He did nothing, opaque as an onyx statue. "However, we met before," said Sam. "You and I."

"I thought so!" exclaimed Cayley. "That night at the Blue Rooster. You helped me walk Max back—right?"

"That is correct, Madam."

"Well, I wouldn't have recognized you—you've changed a bit, haven't you? The short hair and suit and all."

"I might say the same for you, Madam."

Cayley grinned. "I guess time has flown for both of us. I am a businesswoman now, Mr. Wo. My business is pleasure. Do you understand what I mean?"

"I can see that your business is very successful. Whatever pleasure you dispense must be of very good quality."

Cayley laughed. She narrowed her eyes at him, and said, with a devilish look on her face, "It's the best." She smiled. "I mean to say this is a whorehouse, Mr. Wo. A house of prostitution."

"I do understand, yes Madam." He answered calmly, keeping his eyes level and away from Cayley's face. He had heard of these elaborate whorehouses white men used. Sam thanked his quick wits for not exposing his surprise at this peculiar arrangement—not only the sumptuous surroundings, but this odd and composed little woman, so different from the timid houseservant he remembered.

"Not Madam, please. I prefer Mrs. Wallace."

"Mrs. Wallace. And you are the person who hires for the owners?"

"No, Mr. Wo. I am the owner. What do you think of that?"

"I think it is very fine." Sam continued to control his face. *This day is full of surprises.*

Cayley tapped a pencil rapidly on the desktop, rearranged the piles of papers on the desk, and then stood up. She walked the length of the room. "Are you quite familiar with Little China, Mr. Wo?"

"Yes, Mrs. Wallace. I know it well." Wo Sam's memory of the harsh sounds of Cantonese and the smells and sights of Little China filled him with such sudden longing that he felt his heart jump.

"If I were to ask you to find someone there, in an opium parlor, would you be able to do it?"

"I believe so." Sam calculated the risk of being seen in Little China by one of Po Wen's men, or someone from the tong of the boy he had shot to death. Though the *Ah Mah's* young son was the figurehead of Lee Wo Suey company, it was well known that Po Wen controlled the tong's interests, and had become a force to reckon with. Sam was sure Po Wen would find his presence in Little China inconvenient—and there was still a price on his head to revenge the killing.

"Well, Mr. Wo, I will hire you to perform a task. If you handle the situation well, I'll think about hiring you permanently for both your business skills and also your presence at the door to discourage uninvited guests. I will pay you very well. For this task, twenty in gold. If we make it permanent, we will discuss your duties and payment."

It was worth the risk. The chance for a permanent position rather than continuing to cast about for odd jobs made the offer attractive even though he was back working in whorehouses. Sam knew how to keep his head down, and if he moved quickly

145

in Little China, he would be hard to find. "I can start immediately."

"Good." Cayley described Opal and Toy, the young Chinese prostitute from the house who accompanied Opal on her forays. "They live and work here. They appear to leave early in the morning, but I'm never sure what days or how often. You'll stay here in the evenings and keep an eye out. Would that inconvenience your family?"

"I am not married, and my father and sister reside in China. I will return this evening." He rose and walked over toward her library of books. "I see you are a reader, Mrs. Wallace."

"Oh yes. It's a wonderful thing to disappear into a book when I have the time."

Sam selected *Around the World in 80 Days*. "Mr. Jules Verne. A fantastic thinker, don't you agree? Though I doubt he has ever traveled to Hong Kong or San Francisco, judging from his limited descriptions in this book."

Cayley couldn't help from smiling. "I've never seen it snow in San Francisco, that's for sure. But it's the tales of exotic places that I love, true or not. I've never been anywhere but this town my whole life, and it interests me to read about different parts of the world. I doubt I'll ever see them myself. Are you from China, Mr. Wo?"

"I am, Mrs. Wallace. I have also spent time in the British holding of Hong Kong."

"Well, that explains your accent. Perhaps, if we have the opportunity someday, you can tell me about China."

"I hope that comes to pass, Mrs. Wallace. Meanwhile, I'll start work on my assignment." Sam bowed to her, replaced his hat and walked himself out of the front door of the O'Farrell house.

Though he knew he could follow the two women from the house to wherever they were going, he now had a purpose to support his desire to once again enter Chinatown—if he were going to take the chance of being spotted anyway, he should at least have an idea of what the settlement was like these days. He returned to his room, changed clothes, and walked to DuPont *Gai*. Once there, he began moving under the shadows of the awnings, staying anonymous among the crowds of Chinese, pulling up the collar of his blue laborer's jacket to hide his short hair. Turning up a narrow alley, he stopped by the door of an old opium den he once delivered to; when a stranger came out, he said, "Have you seen a white woman, very pretty, with dark brown hair, dressed fine in the American style. A Chinese girl comes with her."

"How do I know if they are pretty or not," said the man at the door. "These white girls, they all look the same to me." He looked vaguely annoyed. "Why are you asking?"

"Chee Wo Suey is looking for them," growled Sam, using the name of his old tong's company. Fear was a great motivator in the alleys of Little China. It would also help those with whom he spoke to forget his face if anyone asked. The man paled.

"They do not come here," he said. "But many white girls go to the Palace of Lotus Dreams on Waverly. A lot of white people there."

"You are telling the truth?" Sam touched the side of his pants where his firearm lay snug against his waist.

The other man nodded vigorously. "I would not invite trouble from Chee Wo Suey."

"Don't tell anyone I was here," said Sam, and turned on his heel, pleased with himself and his tough tong enforcer act. The white woman, Mrs. Wallace, was willing to pay a good salary. He would be able to return to China in less than two years with more money than he could make elsewhere—if only he could find these opium-addled whores. He made his way down DuPont *Gai*, keeping his head low to blend in with the grandmothers and their shopping bags. It had been so long since he walked the streets of Little China; on his return from Virginia City, he had found a boarding house near the south docks that would take anyone without question, providing an opportunity to move about the white sections of the city and avoid being spotted by the wrong people. He would be all right if he wasn't caught, and he wouldn't be caught if he were careful. The smells and sounds around him slowed his walk. He stepped into an herb shop, explained the trouble he had been having with his teeth, and let the shopkeeper feel his pulses. The man then measured out several roots and other unidentifiable dried ingredients, ground them in a mortar, and funneled the mixture into a paper package. Wo Sam paid and tucked the package into his pants next to his gun. He went up one of the side streets and decided to duck into the temple. *I could use a little mercy from heaven right now,* he thought. *And this place is safe enough.* The doorway on the street was an ordinary one—it might have led to apartments. The entry opened into a dark room lit by smoking candles; two fierce foo dog statues guarded the entrance. The air was hazy with incense. Light flickered off a thousand gilded surfaces, dancing on the gentle face and slender form of a statue of Quan Yin, one delicate hand extended outward in benevolence. Sam removed his shoes before stepping inside, lit three sticks of incense, and dropped a few coins into the plate set for that purpose. He planted the incense into the gilded ceramic pot of sand at Quan Yin's feet, and knelt to pray for good luck. A Taoist priest was reading in the corner by the light of an oil lamp. Sam approached him, and waited until the man looked up at him.

"Would you throw my joss?" Sam asked. The priest nodded, rose, left the room and returned with a cylindrical container filled with thin strips of bamboo on which were written Chinese characters.

"Is your question prepared?" he asked Sam, and Sam nodded. The priest put his hand over the top of the container and prayed, shaking the container up and down. Then he removed his hand, and three sticks fell out. "You have a love of reading and the quiet arts," said the priest. "But you also have a restless spirit, which will cause you trouble. I see that you have a very powerful friend. It's not someone you know well, but you will. The judgment is success, by crossing many rivers."

Sam paid the priest, and left relieved. Though he was mystified by the identity of the "powerful friend," the answers were often allegorical rather than practical. He smiled to himself; he wouldn't be crossing rivers, but he would be crossing the streets of San Francisco, which were even more treacherous.

Sam made his way to Waverly Place, to the Palace of Lotus Dreams. He descended the narrow stairway two flights down—he could smell rotting meat from the restaurant garbage bins above on the stairwell, which mixed nauseatingly with the sweet smell of burnt opium. The den was a labyrinth of spaces separated by rough cloth curtains hung from bamboo rods. The low ceiling was cracked with years of neglect, but this was a fine den: each private space had its own bed, table and lamp. It took him a few minutes to find the attendant, a wasted little woman whose child-sized hand pushed a pipe at him. Disgusted, he waved it aside.

"I'm looking for two women. A white woman with dark brown hair and a Chinese woman—they would come here together. Do you know of them?"

She looked at him incredulously. "Do you think I inspect everyone who comes here? This is the place where you forget who you are and who you see!" Her cackling laugh echoed in the stairwell.

Sam lowered his voice and leaned down near her ear in what he hoped was his best threatening manner. "Chee Wo Suey wants to know."

"Why would Chee Wo Suey send you to ask who comes here? After all, they own this place, or did you forget that, soldier?" She looked at him with amusement.

"Of course I know that, old woman," Sam said. He berated himself for his overconfidence. He should have waited until a "customer" came out rather than asking the proprietor. He began to sweat under his jacket and his voice went up in pitch. "Po Wen does not deal personally with these matters." He saw a new respect in her suspicious eyes at the mention of Po Wen. "It is of great importance that I find the white visitor and her companion as soon as possible."

"Well, they aren't here now," said the woman. "I have seen two like those you mention. They do not come on a regular day, though. Usually, they are here very early in the morning. Sometimes they make me open the door, but it doesn't matter. They pay very well, those two." Her eyes narrowed. "If you pay me now, I will send a runner to the house of Chee Wo Suey when I see them again."

Sam rubbed his hand on the back of his neck. "No, I must speak to them personally, and escort them myself. I am under direct orders from Po Wen. I will have my own runner give me the message." He took the stairs two at a time and gulped down the somewhat cleaner air of the street, pleased with himself over his quick thinking.

That evening, Wo Sam reported back to Mrs. Wallace. "Are you sure it's them?" she said. "I'm almost sorry to hear it."

"I'm not sure, Mrs. Wallace. The woman said she had seen two as I described them, but it's not uncommon for white people to go to these opium parlors."

Cayley sighed. "I know, I know. I'll take whiskey, myself." She drew in her breath and stared across the room. "Well, I thought at first that they had a man on the side, a private client, which would have been bad for business—my business, anyway. One of them having a boyfriend was out, because they always went together. But either of those things is better than this. You'll have to keep an eye on them, watching for when they slip out," she said. "I can't do it myself."

Chapter TWENTY-EIGHT

Wo Sam remained at the house every evening, greeting callers at the door and patrolling the hallways as unobtrusively as possible. Early one Thursday morning, fighting off sleep, he saw Opal go to the kitchen in her undergarments and silk wrapper, followed a few minutes later by Toy. He went outside. Across the nearly deserted street, he saw a slight figure dressed in men's clothing dart toward the alley opening and disappear into the shadows. He thought to report this to Mrs. Wallace—it was the second time he had seen such a person watching the front of the house. Sam crossed the street himself and hid behind a trimmed hedge. Within a few minutes, both women emerged from the alleyway covered in cloaks. He followed them as they rapidly walked the blocks to Little China, and made straight for the opium house on Waverly. He checked to be sure the street was empty before he descended the stairs. The old woman saw him coming and quickly disappeared.

The Chinese girl, Toy, sat in a chair by the door, looking bored and miserable. Opal had already disappeared into the maze of rooms. Sam grasped Toy's arm tightly and leaned over to speak to her. The girl was visibly frightened.

"Mrs. Wallace has asked me to come get you," he said, and held on tight as she tried to twist out of his grasp.

"Oh please don't tell Mrs. Wallace," half-wailed, half-whispered the girl. "I don't come here for myself; Opal makes me. She will pay you well to forget you saw us."

"I'll think about it. Take me to her," he said. She leapt up and began walking down the narrow passageway between the beds. She hesitated at several stalls, then chose one and drew back the curtain to reveal Opal, still dressed in her thin wrap. She was curled up on a filthy mattress, knees to her chest. The pipe she was holding had fallen onto the table, where a lamp flickered. A fog of burnt opium filled the air. Her eyes were closed, but she opened them slowly when she sensed people next to her. She focused on Sam. "I'm not ready for more yet," she said.

"You must come with me," said Sam.

"I said—" she expelled a damp breath, then put her head down on her arm. "No."

Wo Sam reached down and jerked her upright. She was limp. "Ow! That hurts," she said, and began to giggle.

"You, help me," he nodded toward Toy. Sam threw Opal's coat around her shoulders; Toy went round to the other side of the bed, and together they half-dragged, half-carried Opal up the narrow staircase to the street. While still within the boundaries of Chinatown, passersby averted their eyes from the Chinese man and woman pulling and pushing a staggering white woman down the street. It had begun to drizzle lightly, and the smell of earth and manure filled Sam's nostrils. Once out of the Chinese sector, they would have to be even more careful, so he tried to look ahead and choose empty streets to get back to O'Farrell. It was still early enough in the morning so that passersby were few, limited to delivery wagons and carousers heading home after a lively night of drinking and gambling. Just as they reached the intersection of Grant and Sutter, a policeman rounded the corner fifteen feet in front of them. His beefy red face bulged out on one side with a healthy hunk of chaw, and he was about to tip his hat to Opal when he slowed his walk, suspicious. Wo Sam and Toy looked at each other and both dropped back behind the tall white woman while keeping a hand under each elbow. Opal was weaving dangerously.

"Oh, ve'y long night, almost home, Missy!" said Sam. "Hello Off-cer! Ve'y long night, go home now!" He started bowing and nodding, smiling almost painfully.

"Must get Missy home," said Toy, bobbing, bowing, never looking the man in the eye.

"Ma'am," said the policeman, taking off his hat and looking at Opal as they passed. She stopped, swayed, turned her body so that she could focus on who had spoken to her, then snorted loudly.

"Almost home, Missy," said Sam. The copper shook his head and continued past them. Sam and Toy rushed the remaining few blocks to the house, got Opal inside the door, and locked it behind them. Cayley was standing next to the stairs, her arms folded across her chest.

"Put her to bed." Cayley's lips were a razor-straight line. "I'll be waiting for you down here."

Toy and Sam returned from upstairs, and Sam bowed and turned to leave. To his back, Cayley said, "I expect to learn all about China, Mr. Wo." Though he didn't turn around, he nodded slightly, and left the hallway with a grin he didn't attempt to hide.

Chapter TWENTY-NINE

Toy crept into the office, eyes downcast. "I should have told you."

"Yes, you should have," said Cayley. "Tell me now."

"She started out slow a few months ago. We did it together the first few times, but then I stopped. She didn't. She said it helps her sleep. She makes me take her there."

"You could have said no. You could have come to me."

"I was afraid. She was becoming more and more crazy. She said nobody wants her anymore. I was afraid she would tell you that it was my fault."

"It is your fault, in a way."

"I don't want to go back to work in Chinatown. Please Mrs. Wallace!" Toy pleaded. "You don't know what it's like there." Tears glistened in her black eyes.

"I have some idea. Well, now it's all out in the open. You say you don't smoke opium anymore."

"No."

"You know Mr. Wo will find out the truth."

"Yes."

"All right. Don't worry. When Opal comes around, we'll get to the bottom of this."

***

Early that evening, Opal sat in the office with a cup of strong tea, facing Cayley.

"Liquor is one thing, being a drunk is another. Opium is in a class by itself, and you know it."

"You sound like my mother, which is why I left," said Opal. "You are not my mother."

"Toy said you have a hard time sleeping."

"I do."

"Work not agree with you?"

Opal rolled her eyes. "Funny you should ask that question, considering you're the one who was so lily-white to begin with.

154

The money's all right. I'm just not seeing near as much of it as I used to."

"You make what I do and keep all your own tips when you have a john. You know I depend on you to run this business."

"Well, working for you makes me YOUR whore, doesn't it?"

"What are you saying to me, Opal Boone?" Cayley's face grew hot. "I'm trying to make things right here, and you're not helping."

"I'm saying what you're saying—this business wouldn't exist without me, but a fat lot of good that does me. I still own nothing—it's not the House of Wallace and Boone, is it?"

"I'm the one the loan hangs on. Did you forget that? You could walk out the door tomorrow, and you'd be free as a bird."

"With about as much as a bird carries." Opal's pretty face soured.

Cayley folded her arms under her chest. "It's not my fault you smoke it all up and spend it on clothes. You're the one who said you wanted to save up to get out of the business."

Opal looked up defiantly. "You think you're so smart, just because you got the old man to lend you the money. You'd still be watering drinks if it wasn't for me."

Cayley inhaled; her thoughts careered about in her brain. She covered her face with her hands and suddenly felt very tired. She lowered her hands and shook her head from side to side, then shrugged her shoulders. "All true," she said. "All true."

"No matter what I do, I've got nothing to show for it," Opal whispered in a childlike voice. She looked down quickly at her cup. Her hair curtained her face. "God help me. I've tried to put money aside, I really have. There are fewer and fewer men coming in that want me. Don't get me wrong, Cayley." She rubbed her eyes with the back of her hand. "I feel used up, is what it is."

"Oppie, you've been a good friend, and, as you say, this house wouldn't exist without you. But we both know the road you're taking leads nowhere. You've got two choices. For both our sakes, you've got to straighten up or make a new life for yourself. I'll be honest with you. This has been going on a while, and I don't have much faith that you'll become a perfect angel."

Opal's face hardened as she raised her eyes to Cayley. "So it's the street. Where have I heard this before?"

"I didn't say that." Cayley stood, and began to pace. "Seeing you on the street would be the shame of my life." She turned toward the other woman. "I'll not throw you out, but I will make you an offer—a business offer."

Opal looked more alert, and began to follow Cayley with her eyes.

"You're a smart woman, Oppie. Most of the time." Cayley turned the corners of her mouth down. "You've advised me well, and you run a hell of a house, when you're on top of it. I'm willing to stake you in your own house."

Opal turned toward Cayley, swinging her legs around on the green velvet sofa. "What's the catch?"

Cayley smiled. "You'll pay me off with interest, of course; after that, a percentage of the gross. I planned on another house here, but you and I need a little space between us. We're like two women in the same kitchen. I'll set you up in Santa Rosa, maybe, or Sonoma—no that's too small. Or down in San Jose. Close enough so I can help you out if you need it."

"And keep an eye on me."

"Yes, indeed, my dear old friend. And if you make a botch of it—go back to the pipe, or throw yourself away on some fool of a man, I won't have to watch it. You'll have no one to fall back on but yourself."

Opal put her elbows on her knees, her chin in her hands. "Why are you doing this for me?"

"I think you'll make a go of it. Call it a gamble that has a good chance of paying off." Cayley leaned on the table between them. "And you're my friend, God help us both."

"What about Toy? I'll tell you right now that she only took me in and translated. She was getting high at first, but then she stopped. She's all right."

"I'll deal with her separately," said Cayley. "We'll see.

Chapter THIRTY

Wo Sam settled into the routine of the house quickly, taking up residence in one of the upstairs apartments once used by Opal and Cayley. He worked hard to control his sense of isolation, feeling more alone than ever in a house of women—whores, no less. How strange that fate would lead him in a circle—or more of a spiral, since the whores he was hired to protect were, except one Chinese girl, all English. He counted the Mexican and Negress among the "others" along with his milk-white employer. His world and homeland seemed more distant than ever, barely kept alive through correspondence with cousin Kim in Virginia City, and his books. Kim had wasted no time in starting a family—a son already! The last of the irregular letters he received from his sister in China told of increased fighting in the villages near their home, and he worried for his father and her.

Among the pleasures he counted, he found Mrs. Wallace to be a formidable boss and businesswoman who did not shy away from difficult decisions. Yet, she managed to remain very feminine. He could not help but notice how adept she was at flattering her patrons to get what she wanted, and how he was considered their equal in the application of her charms. He shared her hunger for books and ideas, and enjoyed the times she had drawn him into discussion. She sincerely respected his education and intelligence—more so than any white man for whom he had worked. He also noted her firm grip on the profits of her business while caring about those who worked for her. This was most evident in the way she handled Opal. A house was found in San Jose, purchased quickly, and Opal took up residence there immediately to supervise refurbishing and decorating. Though the house wasn't as grand as O'Farrell, Opal seemed content.

He was sitting at the bar downstairs, reading, when Cayley came up behind him.

"Look at that, would you!" She indicated the long string of Chinese characters on the page in front of him. "Tell me what it says."

157

He moved the book over to her as she sat next to him. "It's a poem by Su Tung Po; it was written nearly a thousand years ago. You'll like it. It's called 'Painted Flower.'" He began reading in a soft voice, tracing the characters with his fingers:

In the soft East Wind
Rising moonbeams float
On mingled mist and incense.
The moon spies on us
Over the edge of the balcony.
The girl I have hired
Falls asleep. Pensively
I hold up a gilded candle
And look long at her painted beauty.

A slight smile sprang to Cayley's lips as she turned away. "That's beautiful. He's talking about a prostitute, isn't he? 'The girl I have hired….'"

"In China, they were called courtesans. They were very beautiful and accomplished—music, poetry, the arts—and often had a patron who kept them."

"He sounds like he was in love with her."

"Some think it was written about a woman who became his long-time lover."

"I think that only happens in fairy tales—and poetry. Here, it's all business. Speaking of which, will you sit in when Opal comes later to hear what she has to say about the new place?" Cayley looked down shyly. "And if you don't mind, could you copy out that poem for me? You can borrow anything you'd like from my library—as usual."

***

"It's coming along well. The carpenters and furniture are the easy part," Opal unpinned her hat and set it on one of the gilt chairs in the office. It reminded Sam of a large white bird roosting on the slim-legged chair. She remained standing.

"How's the search for girls?" Cayley held up a bottle and a glass. Opal nodded, and Cayley poured them both a drink. Sam held his hand up. "Whiskey not agree with you?" He shook his head no. "Well, I'm glad someone around here keeps a clear head." She glanced up at Opal, and gave her a wry smile.

"It's easy enough to find the houses—just getting to the girls is the tough part. There's lots of Chinese down there, but I can't get through to talk to them. Can't speak the lingo anyway."

"Well, that's easy enough. I can spare Sam for a few days—he can get through for you."

"Much appreciated, Sam." Opal nodded in his direction and held her glass up to him. "No hard feelings."

"So, how's the rest of it. You know…" Cayley looked out the window as she said this.

"I've been too busy to be fooling around. And I'm sure Sam won't be a bad influence." Opal threw her head back and laughed, some of her old fire returning.

"I think this is going to be a good investment," said Cayley. "But you're responsible if it goes under—so says the contract."

"You always bring up the unpleasant parts, Cayley. But yes, I haven't forgotten. It's my intention to blow that little town out of the water—maybe even give you a run for your money"

"That's the spirit! You're a helluva woman, Opal Boone."

The two women eyed each other for a moment then clanked their glasses together so hard whiskey spilled on their satin skirts and over the fine wool of the closely knotted rug.

Chapter THIRTY-ONE

Cayley dropped Opal off at the ferry building and turned the horse back to Green Street. Ellen and Beatrice were out in the garden in back of the house, sitting in the shade of the maple trees on the iron bench. The dappled shadows of the long afternoon moved across their faces as Ellen wiped the child's mouth free of cookie crumbs. A tea set balanced on a small table nearby.

Cayley plopped down on an ornate white-painted chair and clapped her hands together. "Come sit with Aunt Cayley, Miss Bea." She held out her arms and the little girl toddled over and allowed herself to be picked up. She pulled a lock of Cayley's blond curls out and promptly stuck it in her mouth. Cayley let out a delighted giggle, which caused the child to smile and gurgle happily. "What a blessing to have you here," Cayley said, feasting on the bright eyes and pink cheeks of the little girl. "The money is grand and all that." She turned to Ellen. "I've been able to buy a lot of happiness in spite of what they say. But this…" She stroked the child's head, causing Beatrice to nestle against her, thumb in mouth. "This is the best it can be."

"Do you ever think of getting out of the business? Having a normal life?" Ellen stood up to get another cup for Cayley, but the newly hired housekeeper, Manuela, was already out the door with fresh cup in hand. She set it on the tea tray, poured and handed it to Cayley, who nodded her thanks.

"A little late for that." Cayley sipped carefully out of the cup as Beatrice bounced on her knees. "You know how it is. When you're young, you make choices that seem like the best thing at the time. Life's a long hallway with doors that open onto other hallways. Once you choose one door, it leads you away. It seems you can't find your way back. I've built a house of cards based on money, and now I can't touch any of the cards or it will all fall down."

Beatrice began to chant "horsey, horsey" as she continued to bounce, and Cayley handed Ellen her cup and saucer before it was knocked to the ground.

"Only one regret, really…no little ones of my own." Cayley petted the child's hair and hugged her tight. "Grrr, bear hugs for my little bean. I won't eat you up though, 'cause mommy and I would miss you sooo much!" Beatrice wiggled around to kiss Cayley on the cheek, broke free and lurched toward Ellen.

"This child has enough mothers for any three people. And you've just added another one." Ellen nodded in the direction of the kitchen.

"Why shouldn't we give her what we never had; we have the desire and the means. It doesn't hurt anyone to be loved. And she's likely the only child I'll have the chance to spoil."

"That's what I'm worried about," said Ellen, drawing the child's hair back from her damp forehead. "There is too much of a good thing, Cayley; and I know how you can be."

Cayley put her hand to her breast in mock horror. "Do you mean to say I'm *de trop*?"

Ellen rolled her eyes. "I don't know those fancy words, but if it means 'too much' and sometimes foolhardy, you probably are dee trow."

"*De trop* bought us this safe haven, and a comfortable life. And it's going to provide our little girl with the best of everything. What could be bad about that?"

"Why are you single? Why do you live alone?
Have you no baby? Have you no home?"
—"After the Ball" Charles K. Harris, 1892

BOOK II: Daughters and Sisters

Chapter THIRTY-TWO – Six Years Later
Beatrice

Journal of Miss Beatrice Leary, 9 years of age, September 1899

I have started this very private journal because ~~Sam~~ Mr. Wo, Aunt Cayley's houseman, said it was a good way to learn how to write stories, and I love stories. I told him how much I liked it when he read to me, and he brought me a special little book of my own to write my secrets in for my ninth birthday yesterday. He said it was good practice to remember how people talk to each other and write it down, plus all my own thoughts, and that is what I have tried to do.

I'll start at the beginning. We have always lived in the big house—my mother, Aunt Cayley, my nanny Miss Lipp, and the housekeeper who also cooks, Manuela. My mommy is very beautiful, and her hair is red, like mine, only redder. Aunt Cayley doesn't look like us at all—she's a tiny lady, with yellow hair and big bosoms. I have asked Miss Lipp why two sisters look so different, but she says that isn't so unusual, all of her brothers and sisters look different from her, and she's the only one in her family that's black Irish. But she's not black at all; she's just got black hair and blue eyes. Anyway, she said, they aren't really sisters, my mother and Aunt Cayley, they're what are called sisters-in-law, because Aunt Cayley married mommy's brother, and then he died. That's why Aunt Cayley's mother and sisters come around, but they're not part of our family. I think mommy doesn't really like them very much, because she always finds some reason to not be in the room when they come calling. She says Auntie Cayley is too soft hearted, which sounds like a good thing but isn't. I love Aunt Cayley, and I guess they do too.

My mother and Aunt Cayley are both widows. That means they were married but their husbands died. My father was one of those husbands but I never knew him because he died before I was born. I've never even seen a picture of him, because mommy doesn't have any. He was very handsome, she said, but he hated sitting still for a picture. So do I. It takes forever, and you can't move at all. I know this because mommy took me to a picture studio and we had our picture taken together, all dressed up, with this painting of trees behind us. It was very boring.

Miss Lipp and I spend most of the day together, because mommy and Aunt Cayley don't get up much before teatime. Miss Lipp says they are very social, which is why they go out every night, all dressed up like princesses.

One night, after I kissed them goodbye and they went out the door to the carriage, I said to Miss Lipp, I want to be very social myself when I grow up.

163

Well, she said, I hope you won't be as social as them two.

That made me mad. I said I want to be just like them.

And she said, All right then, little tyke, and shook her head like she was laughing inside.

What happens when you are social? I said.

We were in my room, and she asked me to pick up my dolls and put them in the trunk for the night so they can sleep in peace. She picked up one of the dolls, my favorite with the shiny dark brown hair, and she held her under her arm and danced her around my bed and said, Well, you'll go to balls a lot, and laughed out loud this time.

Are balls fun? I said, as they must be, since she was laughing.

Oh yes, she said. You dance a lot, with many handsome men. And some not so handsome, but very charming. And because you're so beautiful, like your mother and your auntie, the men will want to give you nice gifts.

Oh, presents!

Yes, presents.

Are balls where you meet your sweetheart? Maybe mommy is trying to meet a new sweetheart.

She pressed her lips to one side, sat down on the bed, and laid the doll across her lap. I don't know if your mother, or your aunt, for that matter, are looking for sweethearts.

Why, are they still in love with their husbands? I hugged myself when I said this, because it was SOOO romantic.

I would think so. That, and they don't really need to marry, do they, since they're already nicely set for money. I wouldn't mind that.

Do you want money or do you want a sweetheart?

Oh, I suppose I'd like both. And you, Beatrice, do you want a sweetheart?

Yes, I do. I want a handsome prince, like in the Cinderella story. Or Snow White.

164

Well, first, you'll have to be presented at your cotillion. Every young lady of means attends a cotillion. (cotillion was very hard to spell. I had to look it up in the dictionary twice).

What's that?

It's a ball, where young ladies of society who are 16 years old wear lovely white dresses and they're introduced to all the proper people. You'll want a beau who's as well off as you are, of course.

I have to wait until I'm 16?

I'm afraid so.

I went to bed after Miss Lipp read me part of my Oz story, and dreamed about a beautiful fluffy white gown. The next day at tea, I sat on mommy's lap even though I'm getting big, and told her about the cotillion—I couldn't remember the name of it, but I talked about the white dress, and meeting all the proper people—and mommy got tears in her eyes and crossed herself like she always does when she's worried about something. What's the matter, are you thinking about daddy? I said. Tell me about your cotillion, and how you met daddy.

Some other time, Bean (which is what she always calls me), and gave me a big squeeze. Aunt Cayley was sitting across from us, and she had one of the teacups with violets on it halfway to her mouth, and she just stopped and said, Beatrice sweetheart. Miss Lipp was talking to you about this? And I nodded yes. She looked at mother, and mommy said, Will you have a word with her, or will I?

I'll do it, said Aunt Cayley, and a little later, I saw her talking to Miss Lipp in the hall in a low voice, and Miss Lipp with her head down, saying Yessum, and I'm sorry, ma'am.

I wondered what Miss Lipp was being punished for. Maybe she wasn't supposed to spoil the surprise about the ball, but I felt bad that she got in trouble.

Miss Lipp didn't talk about cotillions any more after that, or balls, either. I didn't ask, because I didn't want her to get in trouble again. But I remembered what she said, and I only had seven more birthdays to go.

There, I finished one story.

Miss Lipp and Mr. Wo and I drive downtown in the carriage sometimes, especially when it's time for me to have a new outfit. When the weather gets cold, we go to the City of Paris. They have a huge tree at Christmastime, and rows and rows of counters with many beautiful things. The people there are very nice to us, at least to Miss Lipp and me. ~~Sam~~ Mr. Wo waits out in the carriage because he says we would have more fun without him. I can pick out a new coat with fur on it, and a hat to match, and a muffler if I want, but mostly I think they are disgusting, like holding onto a dead cat or something. No, not that terrible. But sometimes the inside gets sticky from candy I'm eating, and it's always sticky after that.

When we ride in the carriage, I see boys and girls on the streets, and their clothes are torn and dirty, and the cloth looks very rough. Their faces are dirty, too, and their hands. Sometimes they run alongside the carriage with their hands up, begging for a penny, which I think is very rude. Why do they do that? I asked Miss Lipp. Haven't they been taught any manners? She said it was because not all children were as lucky as me, to have enough to eat every day. Then I felt bad for them, but mostly, I felt happy we were rich and that I didn't have to wear dirty clothes and beg. But I wondered where the other children like me are, and why I never see any.

That's kind of short, but I think it's another story.

Chapter THIRTY-THREE

"Ellen, this business won't run without you. If you hadn't stepped in when Opal left, where would I be? Especially now that I opened the Golden Door. I can't run two houses by myself."

"I appreciate that, Cay. And you've always been a good friend to me." Ellen toyed with a fold in her skirt, sighing heavily. "Sam can take care of everything twice as well as I can, and he's completely devoted to you."

"Please tell me you'll change your mind."

"Can you blame me for wanting to get Bean away from this? She's getting older." Behind the tall redhead, the potted ferns in the hallway glowed in the low afternoon light. The colors from the stained-glass panels on either side of the door smeared against the hallway wall.

"Ellen, I'll give you a loan if you really want it. But if you stay, I'll raise your salary, and you can save up the money you need. You won't owe me anything. It's not just the business—you and Bean are family. The only real family I have." Cayley looked up into the other woman's eyes, pleading.

Ellen led Cayley to the red velvet cassocks in front of the divan, then sat across from her, taking her hands in her own. "Bean's getting too old to school at home, and it's personal, too. I've got to stop going to the houses, even though I'm only there part of the night—every once in a while, one of your liquored-up "clients" puts his hands all over me; it makes my skin crawl. I can't laugh it off like you. You're in the paper nearly every day with your escapades. If my name gets in the papers, they'll not make a fine point between someone who runs the business and a prostitute. Us living here makes it worse. I can't continue to keep Bean isolated from other children; if she were in school around here, they would be so cruel to her if they found out."

Cayley withdrew her hands from Ellen's, covered her mouth with one, her forehead creased in concern.

"She still talks about that damned cotillion," said Ellen.

167

"And moving away will make that disappear?"

"I've got to get Bean out of the city. I want to put her in Holy Cross, up north. It's far enough away that they don't know who I am—or who you are. When she's old enough, we can go back east to my cousin's in New York; Bean'll have a chance to meet someone decent, get married, have a family. I don't want her to make the same stupid mistakes as me. If I had a business of my own, a little dressmaker's shop…I could put enough away so by the time she's in high school, all this would be behind us."

"I guess that means me too."

"Cayley, don't you think about the future? I have to—I've got a child. Maybe you can grow old running brothels, but I've got nothing beyond my job here. You know where I'd be if you didn't come along."

They sat for a moment, their thoughts disturbed only by the ticking of the gilded shepherdess clock on the mantel. Cayley left the room and returned with a silver tea service and two thin porcelain cups on matching saucers. She poured for both of them, adding an extra lump of sugar to Ellen's. "You don't have to leave. I'll pay for Bean's schooling at Holy Cross. Like you said, it's far enough away. When she's ready for high school, then you could make your move." Cayley sat and brought the cup to her lips. "A business might fail—not because of anything you did—but if that happened, you'd be worse off, not better. You could work at the houses during the day and leave before things got started in the evening. If you had a business of your own, you'd be there all the time—it would be worse for the child, not better. If you're willing to wait a year or two, I would have some time to get used to the idea. It tears my heart out to lose her; I love her like my own. But we'd see her every week."

"Cayley, that's just the point. We live in your house. I work for you. I want to get out, and I'll take my chances. I would have told you sooner, but I knew you'd disapprove. Can't you understand?"

"Ellen…" Cayley stood up, bumping against the table with the tea service; the silverware rattled, threatening to fall over onto the carpet. "I hear what you're saying, but there must be some other solution. Whether it's a year or ten years, she's going to find out."

Ellen also stood up. "No, she won't!" she said fiercely. "I can protect her."

"But El, you said yourself: Every newspaperman in this town knows who I am. I'm not intending to retire in a few years. She'll come back from the east, and I'll be here, an old bag in fox fur and egret feathers. What do you think she'll make of that?"

Ellen put her hands in front of her face. "I don't know, I don't know," she said from behind them. "I can only worry about what's happening now, and I've got to do something. Please, Cayley!"

"Oh jaysus." Cayley stepped forward and put her arms around Ellen. "We're in this boat together, adrift on a hell of a sea." The women stood together for a moment. Cayley stepped back. "I'll make you a deal. If you'll stay with me for one more year, I'll buy a place up near Holy Cross right away, and you can be there a few days a week. The child can go to school, and you'll both be out of the city, at least part of the time. You can still run the business for me, but she won't know a thing about it. Does that suit you?"

Ellen bit her lips into a thin line. "Do I have a choice?"

"Don't you care for me at all, Ellen Leary?" Cayley put her hands on her hips and shook her head. "I'm trying to do the right thing by all of us."

"Cay, I'm grateful, and I love you like a true sister. But you're hardly alone. You have Wo Sam. The plain fact is if I have to make a choice between you and my child, there is no choice."

"Sam? He's an employee—he doesn't care a whit about me."

"If you think that, you're more blind than I thought."

Cayley twisted her mouth and looked hard at her friend. "Take my deal. You can earn money and get what you want at the same time. This Holy Cross," said Cayley. "Are the nuns mean? I won't have my girl with any mean nuns."

Ellen shook her head tiredly. "There's no going against you once your mind's made up. There never was."

***

Before the last-of-1900 Old Year's party at the House of Wallace was in full swing, Cayley sat at her desk with her head in her hands. She raised her face as Sam walked into the office. "Here's your book," she said, handing him a copy of "The Scarlet Letter." "I admire Hester Prine's courage, but why is it that the ideal woman protects the man, even though he's a cad like Chillingworth or a weak fish like Dimmesdale? Even in 'Around the World in 80 Days,' the female, Aouda, was this little soft creature that went along with everything. Where're the women with spunk?"

"I thought *you* were writing that book," said Sam, taking the tome from her. "Neither Hawthorne or Verne are particularly up with the times. Are you all right?"

"Yeah. Ellen wants out—and I can't say I blame her. She'll hang on for another year. I hope. Meanwhile, there's this business to juggle. I hope you don't have plans to go back to China on the next boat. That would be the capper."

"I have no immediate plans." He smiled, avoiding her eyes. "I've copied out something for you—you'll like it." He handed her a small slip of paper and left the room.

The New Year's party was attended by ten college students from Yale, nine of whom were very good friends of the local labor boss's son. Girls were shrieking with laughter, and as usual, drapes were being pulled off the windows. Cayley's barmen were spending a great deal of time dashing over to sweep up broken glass before someone fell face-first in it. The girls were on vomit duty—that is, if the boy they were with had to let loose, they were in charge of getting him to the plumbing in time, cleaning him up, and keeping him from poisoning himself. Cayley sailed through it all, with an occasional conspiratorial wink

170

to Wo Sam, thanks to a small piece of parchment tucked into her bosom:

> "The Last Day of the Year"
> The year about to end
> Is like a snake creeping in a field.
> You have no sooner seen it
> Than it has half disappeared.
> It is gone and its trouble is gone with it
> —Su Tung Po

The next morning, after the last boy was pumped with coffee and driven back to his hotel, Cayley surveyed the damage and began taking notes. Sam walked over to her and took the paper and pencil out of her hands. "I'll do that for you Cayley. You could join Ellen at home, and I'll report back with the figures later. By the way..." he held the end of the pencil to his lower lip. "That man was watching the house again last night."

"Probably some working stiff dreaming big." Cayley stifled a yawn. She looked over at Sam. "You don't think it's the Ripper, do you?"

"He has been here several times. Just something to note."

"It could be Mr. Montrose from across town. Trying to see why our business is doing so well, and his is doing so poorly. Maybe that fool IS the ripper." Cayley smiled, but a chill raised the flesh on her arms.

Chapter THIRTY-FOUR
April 1901

Journal of Miss Beatrice Leary, ALMOST 11 years of age, April 1901

The first few months of school were miserable, especially starting in the middle of the year. Getting ready for it was great fun, with the new clothes and all. Mother's right, I do learn more here. The religion is a bit dreary, but I like the girls I'm with very much. And of course, I've been home to the city four times already. Sam comes for me in a carriage, and we ferry across the bay, which is great fun—oh, I'm overusing that phrase, I must be more careful about that.

Mother and Aunt have bought a little cottage here, as many of the good families do, and that way, we have a home away from home—and they come here so I don't have to travel all the time. Mother visits three days every week, and Aunt comes for a few days every month—I wish she'd come more often, but she has to stay in the city to run the family hotels. I miss the Green Street house sometimes, but the new house in San Rafael is lovely, especially with Manuela here all the time; during Christmastime I had the run of it and my friends came over to spend the night several times.

I really don't mind traveling back to San Francisco, especially with Sam. He said I don't have to call him Mr. Wo anymore. He's very entertaining; he tells me stories about his village on the big river in China, and about his sister, Wo Li, who's just a little older than me. He speaks English terribly well, and is so very polite. The other girls are impressed that we have such a smart and clever Chinese houseman (he really hates it when he's called that, so I don't say it around him). Many of the other girls are as well off as my family, but their dowdy old Irish stablemen come for them, smelling of horse sweat and manure. Sam, on the other hand, always wears a neat suit and smells like bay rum, which I like. From the name, though, shouldn't bay rum smell like fish and liquor?

The ferry is fun, too. The seats are covered with red velvet and the wood is trimmed with gilt. People are always very festive, since many are traveling on holiday to Marin County. Sam told me that one of the ferries ran into a ship, and people drowned in the bay. However, he said not to worry; because of the accident, the captains are a lot more careful.

Anyway, about the girls: Alma Rolifer is my best friend here, and her parents are terribly important. Her father has recently been elected to the state Senate! Her mother isn't social— she doesn't seem to attend the balls that my mother and aunt do, as they haven't crossed paths. Alma asked her mother about Mrs. Leary and Mrs. Pearson-Leary (that's Aunt Cayley's married last name, which she uses socially, of course), but she doesn't know them. Mrs. Rolifer is very concerned about the lack of moral fiber in San Francisco and is quite involved with the Decency League, which is against the consumption of alcohol and the existence of houses of easy virtue. Alma says she's actually relieved to be away from her mother's "bible-thumping" as she calls it. "Besides," she says, "Everyone knows the whores are the most fashionable women in the city." I can't believe she uses the "W" word, but I think it's just to shock me.

I said, "How can that be? The whole idea is totally disgusting," but she just laughed and said, "You're such a CHILD, Beatrice." She's almost two years older, but sometimes she thinks she's a lot smarter than she really is.

I can't be too mad at Alma, though, because she really was very good to me when I first came to Holy Cross. She was assigned to be my "big sister" and show me around—all the new girls have one, but we also liked each other right away. We came from the same kinds of families, and the same kind of house. Alma said she was glad she got me, because some poor girls come to the school, and she didn't want to have to spend time with one of those. "It's not that they're dreadful or anything, they're actually quite nice. It's just that we have nothing in common," is what she said. I think Alma has a good soul. That's what her name means; isn't that lovely?

The campus is very beautiful here, with big trees and large buildings, and plenty of space all around, like a park. The weather is much better here too, than in San Francisco. Of course, we have to spend part of the day in the prayer chapel, but I miss mass on Sundays at least half the time because mother is visiting. Alma and I and some of the other girls make chapel a little less unpleasant by passing notes, and the nuns haven't caught us yet.

Alma says her mother and the other members of the Decency League are planning a big demonstration, and the newspaper will be there to write about it. Imagine! Alma says her mother finds people who seek publicity to be quite dreadful, but this is a good cause, and others must know that the Decency League exists. I must remember to tell Mother about the Decency League—I'm sure she'll want to be part of something so socially important.

I'll finish this story later—I'm just so busy now with all the things I have to do for school, and my friends.

Chapter THIRTY-FIVE

"The Decency League—that bunch of rotted apples. They march through the streets, and there's not a soul here for a week. Well, two days anyway. Sharp thorns in my side, is what they are. As if those society dames weren't bad enough, I still have to deal with Madame Maude and that bastard Montrose. I despise that woman," said Cayley, making her hands into claws. "Maude never misses an opportunity to copy something I've done and claim it as her own. I staged the Mikado, she had the Pirates of Penzance. We had a Mardi Gras night, she had an Easter Egg Hunt. God!" Cayley paced with her hands on her hips, staring out the window of the office. Wo Sam sat quietly at the other end of the room.

"You've been angry at Madame Maude and Montrose for many years," he said. "But competition creates opportunities."

Cayley wore a pained expression. "Sam, save the philosophy; I need ideas. I wish she'd come up with something original, so I could copy HER for a change!" Cayley turned and faced the seated figure. "We started the Saturday night parade on Market, then her girls were down there. We take the front row at the theater, and her girls are right behind us." She picked up her cup of steaming coffee and brought it to her lips. "It's confusing the customers, for Christ's sake!"

Sam hid his smile behind his hand.

"You're laughing, I know you are," Cayley said. "If it's so funny, why don't you come up with a way for me to top her once and for all. Then I'll shut up."

"Horses will grow wings before you run out of words."

Cayley threw her head back, studied the mural of dancing fauns and nymphs painted on the ceiling. "No, I'm serious, Sam. You've got a good way of maneuvering people, figuring things out, like that." She looked at him. "You've handled problems here with the girls, and come up with business ideas that have put us ahead. You read books and are swell to talk to; our conversations are not peppered with stupid sexual jokes, for which I am so, so grateful. Hell, you've even got me loving poetry! Beatrice thinks the world of you. Everybody comes out smiling." She pointed one finger at her Cheshire cat grin. "You're the brains here, Wo Sam. Think of something."

A few days later, Sam met with Cayley in her office and they spoke for an hour, his voice a calm monotone, hers rising and falling.

"Remember the poem you asked me to copy for you—the "Painted Flower?" said Sam.

"Of course I do. I keep it here when business becomes too much for me." Cayley gestured to her desk. "It reminds me that the whole world doesn't think of women like us as trash."

"When we spoke about it, I mentioned that courtesans were proficient in the arts: music, painting, poetry…"

"Yes, I remember."

"And think of Hester Prynne and the way she defied the village when they scorned her? Perhaps it's time for you and your girls to show the city how refined you can be."

***

Cayley announced to the girls that they would not be attending the theater that week, or the next, though she would purchase the seats as she always did. Everyone was to order a spectacular new dress with hat. On the third week, the girls from both houses dressed in the new clothes and waited in carriages outside the city's elite opera house until the overture started. Then they walked down the aisle just as the lights began to dim. Cayley was in front, and moved with a stately grace that belied her small stature. The dusty rose ostrich plumes of her hat nodded to people in the boxes, and a hundred pairs of opera glasses fixed on the girls as they paraded slowly down the middle aisle to their seats in the front, one after another. The soprano knew better than to try to upstage the new celebrities; she signaled to the orchestra leader to hold her introduction until Cayley and the girls settled into place.

The next day's newspapers were full of the incident, and Cayley's antics made the front page, along with information on

176

upcoming elections and gossip about corruption throughout the city. Cayley, savoring her notoriety, turned hopefully to the social columns and saw not her own name, but a familiar one. "Did you see who made the paper this week," she said, leaning over toward Ellen with the open pages. Arturo was rattling dishes in the kitchen behind them.

"Yes. I saw his name in there. Like a bad penny."

"I wonder how long he's been back in town."

"Don't know, don't care." Ellen furiously brushed sugar crystals off her skirt.

"Not going to contact him, then."

"What's the point? I can't imagine he'd be any more receptive now than he was years ago, either as a husband or a father."

"Well, you know where he is—just in case you want to blackmail him." Cayley smiled wickedly.

***

Cayley and company's operatic exploits were knocked out of the paper the following week, when the Decency League staged a march that included a burning cross down Morton Street.

"I hope they don't hurt themselves," said Cayley. "Dried up old sticks."

"Did you see the crowd that followed after them?" said Ellen.

"They didn't look particularly religious to me. Come to think of it, maybe we should try that."

"My point precisely, Cay. The rabble in this town is always looking for some bandwagon to jump on, and the Decency League may be a joke to most, but to others it's a handy excuse."

"You worry too much. Don't forget, thanks to the Policeman's Benevolent Society, we've got the full weight of the law behind us—as long as I continue to line their retirement fund with golden pillows."

"I'm glad Sam's around, though. He makes the girls feel safer—he's always watching out for us."

"A lucky find, that one."

177

"If it weren't for Max, we'd never have known about him. See, it was fate."

"Fate, indeed. Here." Cayley held the paper up and pointed to a figure next to the burning cross. "Did you get a look at Mrs. Rolifer? It's no wonder we entertain her husband regularly."

"That's mean." But Ellen laughed along with Cayley in spite of herself.

Cayley folded the paper and pushed it to one side of the table. "Let's hope fate's kind to both her and me, and she doesn't find out."

Chapter THIRTY- SIX

Wo Sam awoke one Monday morning to a persistent rapping on the door below his window at the O'Farrell house. He stuck his head out, surprised to find his cousin, Kim, looking up at him. After they embraced and went to the kitchen for a meal, Kim shared his news. "I'm sorry to go against your wishes and come to your place of business, but I have heard a rumor from one of Po Wen's messengers. Your sister, Wo Li is here in Little China in the house of Wing Yee. She is being held as a hostage—they plan to turn her out as a prostitute."

"How has this happened? I thought the Wing tong was disbanded?"

"Old Wing Yee lives on, and though his power has diminished greatly, his anger still burns over the death of his son—and at the man who shot him in the house of Conjugal Bliss."

"But how did they bring my sister here?"

"Po Wen believes that agents of Wing Tong persuaded her that you had sent for her. They probably arranged passage in the usual way—she has a close family member here, already." Kim indicated Sam with his palm.

"Can Po Wen help me get her out?"

"I'm sure Po Wen arranged for me to hear this rumor and bring it to you. But he cannot help, or involve the Chee Gong...for political reasons, of course."

"He was good to warn me. And you are good to come to me straight away."

Kim refused to stay longer, citing the need to get supplies for his shop in Virginia City, and return speedily home to his wife, son and daughter. They embraced once again and made plans to see each other before the year was out.

After Kim left, Sam wondered if the rumor was true, or merely a way to find where Sam was keeping himself—after all, Kim came straight to him.

Chapter THIRTY-SEVEN
Wo Li/Lilly

Wo Li was locked behind the heavy red door; the only source of air and light in the room came from the slats above it. They—whoever "they" were—had already brought in a tray of food: rice with a little meat on top, and tea. She had passed out the chamber pot. On her brief and hurried journey to this room, she had seen that this house was richer than her own, but she was a prisoner here and didn't know why. When she asked for her brother, the answer was that Wo Sam would be here "soon enough." Something was terribly wrong. This was no better than the warring factions back home. But she learned to think quickly to evade the worst there, even escaping from the soldiers who had killed her father. She would use what she had learned to free herself here, too. First, she needed an ally.

When she stood on a low table, one of the few sticks of furniture in the room, she could see through the top of the door; louvered slats allowed her a view of the leaf-littered courtyard beyond. Several times a day, Li saw a young girl with bound feet probably around 15—only a little younger than Li herself—go by on the arm of her servant, or by herself. Her hair was carefully molded into a classic style, and she wore rich silks in bright colors. On the third day, Li made the sound of a dove through the slats as the girl passed by alone. She hesitated, and looked around at the eaves of the courtyard for the bird, then moved on. The next day, when Li again cooed like a dove, the girl, alone, moved hesitantly toward the red door.

"Come closer," Li said.

"Who is there?" said the girl. "Is it you, nurse Sai? Playing tricks on me?"

I am...uh..." Wo Li thought quickly—she must be a personage that would impress the young girl—royalty, perhaps? "I am Princess Li, from the Golden Temple," whispered Li.

From behind the door, the girl was silent. Then, "Nurse Sai, stop that at once!" she said in an imperious voice.

"I am not Nurse Sai. I am Princess Li from the Golden Temple. I have come all the way from the Pearl River to help your family."

"Show yourself."

"I cannot. No one must lay eyes upon me or they will shrivel and turn into a..." Li looked across the room at the framework of the walls "... a stalk of bamboo."

"Stop this at once," said the girl. "I am not a child you must fool with silly fairy tales. Who are you, and what are you doing in my house?"

"Please believe me. I can speak to no one else, favored daughter. My words are only for you."

The girl again was silent. Li could hear her leaning over, scratching her ankle. "What do you want to tell me," she said.

Li smiled. Perhaps this child would help her get out and find her brother. "There is a curse on our houses. I am here to remove it, and when I do, I'll be able to return to my own family and walk out in the world once again. But I need help, and I have been told in a dream that you are the one to help me."

"Tell me about this dream." The chair next to the door creaked as she sat in it.

"Please whisper to me when we speak. Part of my curse is that my voice is so loud that I make a hurricane when I speak normally, and other's voices are also so loud that they hurt my head." Li pressed her lips together, hoping the girl would stay.

"The dream—" the girl whispered.

"In my dream I saw a cloud the color of sunset descend to the ground, and you stood upon it. A dragon swirled around your head, and in your hand were two objects, which you held out to

181

me. The sound of doves filled the air. When I woke up, I was here. I promptly locked the door so no one would hurt themselves, and I have been waiting for you."

"How did you know it was me outside the door?"

"I saw you in the dream ..." and Li described the girl, down to her tiny feet. "I even heard your voice, sweet and strong. I knew you would come to the sound of doves."

The chair creaked as the girl swung her legs back and forth. Li heard motion in the front hallway, and the voice of the girl's nurse. "Favored daughter!" Li commanded. "You must not tell anyone we spoke, not even nurse Sai. If you do, I will drop through the floor into the earth, and must stay there until I dream again. And the curse will remain on our families."

"What is the curse?" said the girl.

Li could hear footsteps growing closer. "Tomorrow, at this time, I will tell you. Remember your silence!"

Li listened to the crunch of gravel under Nurse Sai's feet as she stepped into the courtyard. "Mei Mei, where are you?"

"Here, nurse Sai," said the girl, and she slid off the chair and padded toward the nurse. They continued into another room.

The next afternoon, the girl came to the red door. "Are you there Princess Li?" she whispered.

Li, who had been dozing next to the wall, jerked awake. "I am here. So you are a princess too, Mei Mei."

"No, nurse Sai just calls me that, silly."

"You look like a princess from ancient times, with your tiny feet."

"Don't you have tiny feet?"

"Oh no. My father is a great warlord of China, and also a scholar. He said that women should be able to walk freely, like men, without the help of servants, and that prosperous people like us should set an example."

"That can't be true! How can peasants know you are not one of them?"

"By our house and our deeds. But it is my deeds that brought this curse to me."

182

"What did you do?" The girl's whispery breath was inches away from the keyhole in the door.

"When I was walking about the town, an old woman who was carrying two heavy buckets on a pole across her shoulders asked for my help, and I refused, since she was dirty and ragged. I could have told one of my servants to help her, but even they turned up their noses at her. I passed her the next day, and she asked for my help again, and I pushed her away. The third day, it happened again. She cursed me for my selfishness. She said I must teach another princess how to be merciful before the curse would lift. So here I am, but you could not be that princess, because you are far too kind. Do you have a sister?"

"No. Only two brothers. My eldest brother is dead, killed by a soldier of Chee Wo Suey. I'm not supposed to know that. What will happen if the curse is not lifted?"

Li felt a chill through her thin jacket. Didn't her brother, Wo Sam, write that he had become an employee of Chee Wo Suey? She suddenly had a very bad feeling about why she was being held. She drew in her breath and made her voice even, "You are the princess I am here for, then."

"But I'm not a real princess."

"Yes you are. That's why I woke up here in your house."

The young girl thought about this, and remained quiet when nurse Sai called to take her away.

The next day, the girl was once again at the door. "You didn't tell me about the curse."

"First tell me. You never go outside without someone, do you?"

"No. Nurse Sai, or one of father's men is always with me." She paused. " I don't go outside much at all. I think I would be frightened."

"When the curse is removed, you will no longer be frightened."

"Is that the curse?"

Li could almost see the girl's hesitation through the door. "Without fear, you can take the time to look at the leaves on the trees, or walk among all the people and look at them, and go anywhere you please."

"Why would I want to do that?"

Li tapped her long fingers on her forehead. "That's not the curse. It's much, much worse. Name what you fear most in the world."

Mei Mei was silent for a moment. "Being alone, I think. Without family. Or no, maybe being poor."

Li pushed away the thought of her father, caught and killed months before by one of the warring factions near her home, and her missing brother, Wo Sam. "That is the curse," she said. "To be alone and without means."

"We must remove it at once." Mei Mei sounded breathless. "What must I do to save my family?"

"You must bring me two objects. They are not hard to find. Will you do that?"

"What are the objects?"

"I can only tell you about them one at a time. Do your kitchen servants keep chickens?

"Yes, of course."

"The first is a black rooster feather. Just one feather. You must push it under the door. Can you bring me that?"

The girl said nothing, but Li heard her slip off the chair and make her way across the gravel of the courtyard. After what seemed like an eternity, the girl's delicate step returned, coming right up to the door.

"What are you doing there?" said nurse Sai. "Your father said you aren't to play by that door."

"I'm not doing anything, foolish old nurse," said Mei Mei. "I was only taking a pebble out of my shoe." A single iridescent black feather slipped under the door. Li heard her straighten up. "Why am I not supposed to be by this door?"

"No explanation is necessary," said nurse Sai. She came round and steered the girl away. "Your father has said so."

Chapter THIRTY-EIGHT

"What's bothering you?" said Cayley. "You look like you've been kicked in the head by an ornery mule."

"It's nothing, Mrs. Wallace. Family business," Sam looked down at the floor, unable to keep the anxiety out of his face.

"Mrs. Wallace? You've gone all formal on me, Sam. Something I can help you with?"

"I don't think so, no, but thank you for your concern."

By the next afternoon, Sam had formulated and discarded a number of plans to get his sister out of the heavily guarded home of old Wing Yee. It was easy enough to find out the truth of Kim's rumor. A trap, of course; they expected him to come for his sister. Sam was aware he meant less than nothing to Po Wen, but his death at the hands of another tong would humiliate Chee Wo Suey, now controlled by Po Wen; that was why he was warned. Po Wen, of course, expected him to ignore the plight of a worthless woman such as his sister.

Cayley stood in the hallway, newly papered in a subtle stripe overlaid with a pattern of full-blown roses. She held a sheaf of bills in her left hand. "I think you better tell me what's on your mind, Sam. Things are beginning to pile up, and I don't like the idea of being found half-dressed under a landslide of unpaid bills."

"I'm so sorry, Cayley. I'm concerned about my sister, who is in a bad situation."

"Does she need money, is that it?"

"No. Not at all."

"Well, that's a surprise," said Cayley, fanning herself with the bills. "Everybody needs money these days." Sam blinked rapidly several times. "I'm sorry, Sam. This looks to be more serious than I thought. What's the problem?"

Wo Sam took a deep breath. He knew how clever this white woman could be, but could he trust her? What other option did he have? "Some years ago, I offended a member of the Chinese community, and he has never forgiven me. It is quite a serious matter. This man has lured my innocent sister from China, and is now holding her prisoner in his house. I believe it is his intention to make her a prostitute if he hasn't already. I don't mean to offend you, but this would be a most definite humiliation for my family, and would make my sister unmarriageable. He is holding her because he wishes to lure me in order to do us harm." He ran his fingers along the immaculate collar of his shirt. "I don't know what to do."

"And there's no talking to this fellow?"

"Wing Yee? Most certainly not."

"What did you do to offend him, if I may ask?"

"I'd rather not say."

Cayley grunted a confirmation. "That bad?"

Wo Sam nodded. "It wasn't intentional, but the harm I caused has brought great misfortune. I cannot allow my sister to suffer because of it, but..." He glanced up at her briefly then returned his eyes to the floor at her feet.

"So, your sister's being held in Chinatown?"

"Yes, on Spofford Alley. Wing Yee's house is heavily guarded. He is a very powerful man." Wo Sam expelled a frustrated breath, shook his head. "But this should not be a concern of yours. *Ai Yah!*" He rubbed his fingers across his eyes.

Cayley moved out of the patch of sunlight that streamed through an opening in the silvery gray draperies of the saloon behind her. "By God, I hate to get involved with problems I didn't make, since I seem to make so many of my own." She screwed up her mouth and looked at Sam's averted face. She put her hand on his shoulder. "You've been a faithful friend, Sam, and I'm going to help as best I can. Do you know who Donaldina Cameron is?"

"From the church—the white woman who takes in the Chinese prostitutes."

"That's her. The crusader from the Presbyterian mission."

Sam nodded.

"Not that I have much to do with her, or she with me. My girls are here because they want to be. But she's got connections. She might be just the person to get your sister out of there."

Chapter THIRTY-NINE

Eight days passed before Mei Mei whispered, "Are you there, princess Li?"

Li had been dozing on and off. She saved some of her drinking water to wash in, a little every day, but her clothes smelled foul. She had been here, by her calculations, nearly three weeks. Food had dwindled to a small bowl of rice a day. Hope of escape dimmed as her mind became more confused. She roused herself, wondering if she were still dreaming.

"I thought you had gone away."

"I wouldn't let you sink back into the earth," the girl's whispery voice barely penetrated the heavy door.

"You really do have a kind heart," said Li, and put her cheek against the cool wood.

"Nurse Sai is watching me all the time. I finally gave her a gift of wine from my father's cellar, and she drank it at the noon meal. She will sleep well."

"You are a clever girl."

"I'm here for the second task."

Li put her hand against the door, steadying herself from the wave of dizziness that swept over her. "The second task."

"Yes, to remove the curse. The second task."

Li blinked several times, and nearly nodded off, her head moving against the door.

"Are you all right," Mei Mei asked, her voice alarmed.

"I grow very weak," said Li. "but you can help me. For your second task, you must bring me a wooden flute."

There was silence from the other side. "How will I give this to you?" said the girl. "It won't fit under the door."

"Then you must find the key and open the door," whispered Li. "You can leave the flute just inside. I promise I will not show myself to you."

"What will happen when the tasks are completed? Will you go back to your golden palace?"

Li pinched her cheek to stay alert. "I must leave, yes. I do not belong here."

Mei Mei put her own hand on the door. "Then maybe I shouldn't complete the second task," she said.

Li sat upright. "If you don't," she said, "I will sink into the earth, and both our families will be destroyed. You must help me!" She tried, and failed, to keep desperation out of her voice.

The two girls sat in silence for a moment. "Either way," said Mei Mei, "I'll lose you."

Li said nothing. After a little while, she heard Mei Mei rise and make her way slowly across the courtyard.

Chapter FORTY

"Well, I'd never thought I'd see the likes of you here, Cayley Wallace!" Donaldina Cameron's voice boomed out into the plain brick meeting room of the mission house. "You'd be right welcome, as a reformed woman."

Cayley, rolled her eyes. "Reformed from what, Miss Cameron? Making a living?"

The two women stood eye to eye. Cayley had "dressed down" for the occasion, in a dark blue mutton-sleeved jacket and skirt. She was wearing (for her) a prim little hat of straw with fruit on it instead of her usual egret feathers. Donaldina Cameron, in a severe black dress buttoned to the throat, seemed too big for her clothes, as if she were about to burst through. Cayley took in the embroidered hanging on the wall; in spite of its subject matter—a lamb holding a cross—the fine quality indicated that it was done by some of the "rescued" Chinese girls.

"So why, may I ask, are you visiting our lovely mission house?" Miss Cameron's Scots-tinged accent turned lovely into "luflee." "If repentance be not on your mind."

"Though we're at odds when it comes to the necessity of my business, Miss Cameron, I've always respected what you've done for those poor Chinese girls. I'm here to ask for your help."

Donaldina rolled her eyes heavenward and put her hands together on her bosom. "Here's another proof of the power of prayer!" she boomed theatrically.

"Oh for Christ's sake!" said Cayley. Donaldina raised one eyebrow.

"I'll get to the point. My houseman, Wo Sam, claims his sister is being held against her will in Wing Yee's house on Spofford; they plan to turn the girl out in a crib against her will if they haven't already. He's sure it's a trap to lure him in, and he's desperate to do something. He doesn't want to lose her, and I don't want to lose him. Can you help us?"

"Wing Yee, eh? I hear another tong murdered his boy, next in line for headman a while back. I don't suppose your 'house-man' had anything to do with that."

"I didn't ask for details. He claims it was an accident, what-ever got him into this mess."

"Well, the important thing is that there's an innocent girl involved. Here's what I can and can't do. I can have my people check into the truth of this story—and I will, make no mistake. Because what I can't do is interfere with these people's personal business unless it involves women in the cribs that don't want to be there, you see."

"I understand."

"I'll send a messenger around as soon as I know some-thing."

"Thank you, Donaldina."

"You're a decent sort, Cayley Wallace. Why not come to the mission and help me out."

"I thank you, Miss Cameron. But I have my hands full al-ready." Cayley spun around and fled from the brick building.

Two days later, Cayley again stood on the steps of the Pres-byterian mission.

"She's there all right, and heavily guarded. Your man was telling the truth," said Miss Cameron.

"Of course he is."

"You might want to know why Wing Yee would like his head on a platter."

"None of my business."

"So it isn't. I plan to bring in two or three rough police boys, and march in there myself, which I'll do gladly for the love of God." Donaldina took a breath and looked at the floor as she said, "I've heard plenty about your generous nature. Have you thought about a contribution that would help us to continue our good work?"

"You may be surprised to find that I have, Miss Cameron. I'm all for women having a few choices in life. Will a hundred brighten up this place?"

Donaldina rubbed her chin and her eyes twinkled. "I expected a woman such as you to be twice as generous."

Cayley's mouth fell open in mock disbelief. "You're not a crusader, you're a blackmailer!"

Donaldina Cameron leaned toward Cayley until her face was three inches away: "We could do a lot of brightening with two hundred."

Cayley squinted, and refused to back away. "When I see her and Wo Sam tells me she's all right."

"Done. He must be some houseman."

"He's a friend. A good and loyal friend," said Cayley, and realized, perhaps for the first time, just how much of a friend he was. *How many others would I put my pride aside for?*

Donaldina looked at Cayley with new respect. "Good woman," she said. "The girl should be in your hands within the week. Oh, and Mrs. Wallace…"

"Yes, Miss Cameron?"

"If I find out that this is some sort of trick and you've put this girl to work on the street, I'll come personally to your house and tear it—and you—down to the ground."

Chapter FORTY-ONE

Li held the bits of dried rice that she used to count the days in one hand and ran her fingertips over their smooth surfaces. She had fallen on them the other day, scattering them, and couldn't remember how long she'd been locked in this room. She had not spoken to Mei Mei in a while—several days at least. She didn't know how long they intended to keep feeding her, or what their plans were, but she sensed her captor's impatience. The guards now openly taunted her about her brother's cowardice, and how little he cared for her. His behavior was no surprise to her however—he always preferred words to action.

The room was very cold. She sat tucked into her body, covered by the now-ragged pants and jacket she had changed into before the ship docked and she was brought to this place. Occasionally she would hear movement in the courtyard, and get up to peer out the slats. Once or twice, she saw Mei Mei, who never looked her way. She fell asleep again. It was a good way to ward off hunger, the restless growling of her stomach. Half asleep, she heard Mei Mei's footfall coming toward her, crunching lightly in short steps across the courtyard; a horrendous crash brought her fully awake. Her heart jumped in terror. Shouts erupted from the direction of the entryway, and the loud voice of a woman, yelling her name and other words in English she couldn't make out. "Here" she cried in her dialect, then in Cantonese, then wondered if she shouldn't. "Here, here, here!" What could she lose? Her heart was pounding out of her chest.

The crashing came toward her. A heavy object pounded against the door, and Li leapt back as the door splintered into dozens of red-lacquered pieces. A Chinese man stood in the doorway. "Wo Li?" he asked. She nodded, and tried to stand, shaky. He took her under the arm, and brought her out into the courtyard where a white woman grabbed her by both shoulders and looked into her eyes. Just beyond the woman stood Mei Mei, a bamboo flute in her hand, her mouth hanging open. Li focused on the girl, ignoring the white woman, who then spun her around, put her arm firmly around her shoulders, and marched her out the front steps into daylight so dazzling that Li's eyes ran with tears.

Chapter FORTY-TWO - 1903

Journal of Miss Beatrice Leary, October 1903

Alma and I have been planning our coming-out parties. Of course, she'll be ahead of me, as she's older, and of course Alma's party isn't for a year, but I'm sure mother will let me go to the ball. Right now I'm concerning myself with learning my catechism, as I'm preparing for my confirmation. That's almost like a coming-out party—at least we get to wear white dresses, like brides.

Catechism is SO boring. We memorize answers to questions, then we must all stand before Father O'Hanlon while he asks us silly things like "What is a Catholic?" Alma is very daring—when I ask her that question, she says things like "Someone who fondles beads instead of wearing them, has bad knees from kneeling all the time, eats fish on Friday and chokes on bones." I don't think Father would appreciate that answer. Alma comes over to spend the night away from the school quite a lot—she has her own room here in our little house, and I helped her pick out the colors for it. I tend not to like the pale purple-gray that Aunt Cayley favors—Alma and I both prefer something more modern, like a heavenly blue.

Well, picking a dress is interesting. Sam is coming for me now, and mother and I will go to the dressmaker. I must remember to tell her that Father O'Hanlon wants to talk to her as soon as possible—something about the confirmation (at first I thought I was about to get in trouble for passing notes, but Sister Carmel said it wasn't anything I had done, that I was blameless, which certainly isn't true—but I'm still glad she doesn't know).

A week later, mother came to school with me, gave me a kiss, and went off to the priest's office while Sam waited in the carriage. Her face was pale and tight, and she twisted her gloves in her hands. Something odd is going on. The nuns who teach the morning classes—Sister Carmel and Sister Maria—are both looking at me strangely, like they pity me. I wonder if there's something wrong with me, though I feel fine. Perhaps I have the cholera, which so many people in San Francisco have, though it's mostly in the poor quarters where there is so much dirt. Perhaps one of the ferries brought someone with cholera from the city here. Can you get cholera from another person? It could happen.

Sister Maria, with a sad look on her face, said, "Beatrice, where is Mexico on the map?" I had to say, "Excuse me?" which I hate to do, because Sister Maria is Mexican, and sometimes we all have trouble understanding what she says (though we have quite a bit of fun imitating her during meals when she's not around). Anyway, she asked me again, and I pointed it out. Then Sam was at the door.

"Pardon me, please. I must speak with Miss Beatrice Leary," he said to Sister Maria. I went to the front of the room, and he drew me out to the hallway by the hand. My mother was waiting out there. She had been crying, it was easy to see. Her face was all red and splotchy, and her gloves were twisted into a ball. She squatted down and gave me a hug. I knew it. I was dying.

"Darling, Bean," she said, "Mother wants you to know that we are taking you out of Holy Cross and putting you into another school as soon as possible."

"What? NO! I want to stay here." Then I asked her, "Am I sick, Mama?"

"Sick?" My mother looked puzzled for a moment. "Do you feel ill?" She held her hand up to my forehead.

"Oh no. But there must be something wrong with me. Isn't there? Do I have the cholera? Is that why I'm being taken away?"

"Oh dear." She wrapped both arms around me and pulled me into her, so that I knocked her hat aside a little. "No, you're not ill. Not at all. It's nothing to do with you." Her face grew hard. "I've just finished talking to that great Christian, Father O'Hanlon. I've decided that this school isn't good enough for you."

"But my friends. Alma...I don't want to go. I WON"T."

"I know dear. It isn't easy right now. But you'll like the new place better, I promise, and you'll make wonderful friends there too. We'll come for you on Thursday, so you must be packed and ready. Make your good-byes." She stood up, and I started to cry. "I'm so sorry," she said, and put her hand on my cheek. "I wouldn't do this at all unless I absolutely had to." She looked at me with love in her eyes and I knew it was true. I would be brave for her.

"All right, Mama. I'll be ready on Thursday morning." I was still very angry, though I pretended it was all right.

She smiled and nodded. When she walked away, I could see that Sam was holding her under one arm and that she wobbled a little. "Mama," I called after her, and she turned around. I ran to her. "You're not sick, are you?" I held onto her skirt with both hands. She smiled and shook her head. "Not at all, sweetheart. Everything is going to be fine." And she turned and was gone. These adults can be so stupid and difficult.

***

Alma and I both cried. After I left Holy Cross, I stayed at the Green Street house for a week, which was terribly boring. Then Sam and mother took me to my new school across the bay to the little town of Berkeley. Though I missed Alma terribly (oh no, I just wrote "terribly" twice!), I did like this new school better, as it wasn't Catholic, and mother told me that it was a private school for gifted children. The classes had both boys and girls, which was also different, and very interesting. I had not been around boys my age at all before. Of course, the boys and girls slept in separate dormitories, but the girls here spent a lot more time talking about boys than answering the question, 'What is a Catholic?' Definitely more interesting. And I was still writing to Alma, so it wasn't as bad as it could have been.

Except for the religion part, we study the same things as in Holy Cross, but only a few of the girls are planning on coming out. Many students are on scholarship (which means their families don't have enough money to pay the tuition), and the more well-off girls are in a tight little group that doesn't seem the least interested in letting me join. So I ended up with two friends, both daughters of merchants. Frances's father owns three livery stables, and Donna's parents are greengrocers. I hadn't really known anyone whose parents worked in the common trades before, and it was very interesting to hear what their lives were like.

I still spend every other weekend with Mother and Aunt Cayley in the city. They've sold the house in Marin, as they don't need it any more, but Auntie says property is like gold and she's kept some land up there. I don't care if I ever see the place again. Mother and Aunt plan to buy some property up on the hill above the Berkeley school. They've already hired a woman architect to design the new house. Women can do anything these days. Next, the vote! Mother expects that the house will be competed in January. We decided to name the new house Century House in honor of the millennium, though 1901 was all of two years ago. Aunt Cayley said it was to be in honor of all the bad things that might have happened but didn't.

Chapter FORTY-THREE – New Year's Eve 1903

The party was going to be a big one, but it wasn't going to start until 1 a.m., because a lot of Cayley's clients would be out celebrating the New Year with their wives at private parties. Then they would drop them off, and come to the houses on O'Farrell to see the New Year in with style—the top tier of the city's movers at the House of Wallace, and the rest at the Golden Door. Style was what the House of Wallace was all about.

The food was exquisite. The usual roasted pigs and sides of beef, accompanied by lovely mounds of duchesse potatoes golden with melted cheddar, three soups, three salads, and the best champagne from the cellar. Lilly (Wo Li preferred the Americanized version) and the helpers had set the table with Cayley's best silver, in the Versailles pattern dripping with entwined roses and garlands. The china was French Limoges, in her favorite color, mauve ("Just like the Czarina," she said). Sam set out the party favors: Cayley planned to appreciate each of her guests with a tiny gold crown set with pearls, made by Shreve, the local society jeweler. The girls were in a festive mood. Toy wore red silk for good luck; the rest of the girls were dressed in gowns of silver or tissue of gold.

"It's flashy, but good for the new year," said Cayley. "Is Ellen here yet?"

"No," said Sam. "But the ferries must be crowded coming across the bay, and she'll have to hire a hack to come up here. Has my sister done all her tasks?"

"Of course she has," said Cayley, somewhat annoyed. "Sam, you've got to stop chewing on that girl or one of these days she's going to turn around and bite back."

"She's a Chinese woman, and it's her duty to obey me until she marries…" he said. "…now that our father has passed on and I lead the family."

"All the time you spend here, and you still go on like that. I don't understand it," said Cayley. She moved a fork in a place setting then replaced it in the original position.

Just then, Ellen swept through the door in a floor-length cape and hood of black satin. Her cheeks were flushed red with the cold.

"How's Miss Beanie?" said Cayley.

"God, don't ever call her that to her face. She'd scour us both! She's excited—about the party with her friends, and all. Thanks for doing without me for the set-up."

"I'm glad one of us could be there with her."

"The house looks gorgeous!" Ellen said happily, noting the silver satin streamers winding down from the chandeliers. She walked over beside Cayley.

"You seem unusually happy tonight yourself," said Cayley.

"A new year ... a new life."

"Oh if it were only so," said Cayley. "But I'm happy with the one I've got, so I won't be making any changes." She smiled at her.

"Sam, what needs to be done?" Ellen opened her palms, arms out.

"Only for you to dress," said Sam. "If you need to."

"Christ, I better check on the champagne." Cayley left the room.

"Sam, I've got a secret. Can you keep a secret?" Ellen grinned and put her arm through his elbow. "Oh, of course you can. I've just got to tell someone, and it's neither the time nor place to speak to Cayley."

"I'm honored," said Wo Sam. "But if it affects Cayley, of course I'll have to inform her."

"Oh Sam." Ellen rolled her eyes. "Loyal to the last. I'll 'inform' her myself—later, if you don't mind. I'm giving Cayley my notice tonight."

Sam leaned away from the woman. "I've expected this for some time. So it's come."

"Bean is getting so big. She's a young lady now, and she's thinking of the things a young lady wants—a beau, a coming-out party. None of that's going to happen while I'm still here."

"Cayley won't take this well."

200

"Oh sure she will. We made a deal for a year and I stayed for three. I've saved up enough money so that we can start over back east. I've already written my cousin, and she's expecting us. I told Bean tonight—you know how young girls are. She'll miss her friends, but she's excited about New York. As far as I'm concerned, it'll be a wonder to be somewhere people haven't heard of Cayley Wallace."

Sam shyly took Ellen's hands in his. "I am very happy for you and Miss Beatrice," he said. "She's a fine young lady and deserves a good life. I will miss you both."

"Maybe you can come with us."

"That's a very generous offer." He hesitated for a moment, looking toward the kitchen as if Cayley left a trail of glitter behind her. "I have a secret too."

Ellen withdrew her hands and pulled Sam into the hall and down into a pair of parlor chairs, leaning toward him. "Go on."

"I've also saved enough money to begin a new life. I've always intended to go home to China a rich man, and now I can do that. I fear for my sister here, too—we are still vulnerable, and she will be much better off in a traditional life. I would not have considered this during the uprisings, but my money can protect us in China. Speaking to you has helped me make up my mind."

"This is going to be tough on Cay."

"I'm only a man who works for her." His voice became softer. "It's not the same as losing someone she loves." He glanced up at her for a few seconds. "Like you and your daughter."

"Oh Sam," she said, and laid a gloved palm on his cheek.

Cayley came striding into the room. "Jaysus, I still get the nerves before an important party. What are you two confabbing about?"

Ellen turned toward her. "We're deciding which one of us is going to dress in diapers as the New Year."

"And I suppose I'm to be dressed as the old year, eh?" Cayley laughed. Well, tonight I feel like the old century, that's for sure. Let's get this theatrical production underway!"

Cayley's guests began arriving in groups of one or two, and each was plied with champagne; most were already well-lubricated, but gentlemen knew how to hold their liquor, and the House of Wallace was a safe place to let loose. The girls sat on either side of each man, their plump pale arms draped around the stiff collars and evening jackets of their guests. A few had even opted to go upstairs before the party began. "If I hear one more man say he wants to start the New Year with a bang!" Cayley whispered to Ellen, though she laughed as if it was the world's most original joke every time she heard it. Sam walked back and forth between the houses, making sure everything was running smoothly. Cayley disappeared upstairs later in the evening, taking on one of her old favorites, Abe, the downtown labor boss. The quartet in the ballroom stopped playing at around three o'clock and the party quieted down earlier than expected—the house was silent before four a.m., a paean to the amount of partying the guests had done the night before.

Sam laid himself out in a couch behind a screen near the front door, to make sure he had gotten every guest out; he was first to hear the clamor when dawn light reached into the dim recesses of the hallway. He roused himself, washed his face quickly in the kitchen and went outside to find a milk delivery wagon stopped just beyond the narrow alley next to the house. Three people stood talking animatedly, standing around in a circle near the entrance. Two were policeman; a fourth man—another policeman—came out of the alley. Sam thought about waking Cayley, then decided to find out for himself what the problem was.

He shuffled up toward the policemen. "Wha' matta' here?" he said. Years of experience had taught him that the best defense with dumb cops was to be a dumb Chinaman. One of the police turned around, saw who was talking, and turned back toward the alley. When Sam reached the group, the policeman who had turned around spun toward him and said, "I don't think this is any of your business, son." Then he had second thoughts, and said, "What are you doing around here anyway, this time of the morning?"

"I houseboy here, numbah one houseboy!" said Sam, thumping his chest. The cops undoubtedly knew that the house was Cayley's; Sam figured he had better align himself quickly with a known evil rather than an unknown one.

The cop looked at his compatriots and said, "Well then, you might know who this girl is," and nodded up the alley. Sam froze. He moved on leaden feet toward the alley entrance and looked down the narrow passage. In a swirl of ice blue satin, with white satin trim around the shoulders, Ellen lay in an awkward sleep, with her legs pressed under her, as if she had fallen backward suddenly. Sam moved toward her. Her eyes were open, and her lips and skin had taken on a bluish cast. Around her neck, just above the jet necklace with the jet–and-diamond cross, a neat, red line bled her life out into the ground beneath her. Sam felt if all the air had moved out of his lungs, and he was unable to speak; his mouth worked, but no sound came out. He fell against the dirty brick wall, holding himself up with both hands pressed hard against it.

"Speak up, boy," said one of the policemen.

Sam turned his head suddenly toward the man who spoke, his vision blurred by held-back tears. "I'll get Mrs. Wallace," he said.

He didn't bother to knock. Cayley lay across her ornate bed, the rumpled sheet pulled haphazardly over her naked, slumbering body. He touched her shoulder. "It's Ellen," he whispered. With an annoyed look, she pulled her eyes open, and, on seeing his face, sat bolt upright, threw off the sheets and pulled on a silk robe. They stumbled down the stairs. He pulled her out to the alley by one hand while she held her wrapper closed with the other. They moved as if their feet were made of logs. When Cayley saw Ellen, she fell to her knees next to her, her fingers touching Ellen's hair, the necklace, the stained shoulders of her dress. Her hands landed lightly, quickly, like a manic butterfly. She shook her head, murmuring, "No, no, no, no" so softly it almost wasn't a sound. Before two policemen pulled her upright, she

203

closed her hand around the thing that Ellen held, the knit glove, funny shaped with a thumb and two big fingers instead of four, like it was made for an animal with a cloven hoof.

***

Cayley held up well that morning, or appeared to. Sam could see she moved like a life-size French mechanical doll. Her face waxen, she sat among the chaotic remains of the party of the night before. The smell of liquor in unwashed glasses turned his stomach. The girls upstairs whispered fearfully among themselves.

Cayley repeated to the questioning officers that Ellen was her business manager, she had no enemies, the last time she saw her was before 2 a.m. She refused to name her party guests. "It was none of them, I'm sure of it," she said. "It was that rabble that follows the Decency League around. She was always afraid of them." She shivered, and Sam closed a blanket around her shoulders, saying, in his normal cultivated voice, "Gentlemen, that's quite enough. Now get out."

The officer in charge looked up at him with a sneer, but then his face straightened. He was well aware that this woman was a friend of the police chief. After the police trundled into the street, Cayley spoke in the same vague, mechanical manner: "We'll send her to Santini's, Sam. It's the best place in town. We'll do it right, with a mass and everything."

"I'll take care of it," he said, his hand remaining on her shoulder. "When are you going to tell Beatrice?"

She sighed deeply, hung her head, stood up and grabbed two bottles of whiskey off the bar shelf. "In a couple of days—before the funeral. Not today."

"I'll get the carriage and take you home. Then I'll come back to calm the girls."

Cayley nodded. She shook her head as if suddenly waking up and looked at him. "Sam, what would I do without you? What would I ever do?" She folded herself against him.

He rewrapped the blanket around her, put his arm around her shoulders, and guided her to the carriage. They rode in silence through the streets emerging from the morning fog, the city now wide awake with cries of produce peddlers and the rattle of carts filled with milk jugs. At the house on Green Street, Cayley grabbed the rail and pulled herself up the stairs, two bottles in her free hand. "We'll let Bean believe all is right with the world for another day or two," she said without turning around. She closed the door behind her. Wo Sam quietly made his way up the stairs and slumped down outside her door. He listened to her wail for nearly an hour. After she quieted down, he went downstairs, found a pen and piece of writing paper, and recalled as best he could a poem by Mei Yao Ch'en he'd read years before:

Who says that the dead do not think of us;
Whenever I travel, she goes with me.
She was uneasy when I was on a journey.
She always wanted to accompany me.
While I dream, everything is as it used to be.
When I wake up, I am stabbed with sorrow.
The living are often parted and never meet again.
The dead are together as pure souls.

He left the poem on the small table in the hallway, wrapped the pain in his heart in the list of tasks that lay ahead and returned to the O'Farrell houses.

Chapter FORTY-FOUR

Two days later, Sam picked up Beatrice at school in a rented hack. "There's been an accident," he said, avoiding her eyes. "Aunt Cayley will answer your questions." The other girls flowed around them on their way to class as they stood on the steps in front of the dormitory.

"What? Is it mother? Has she been hurt?"

"Aunt Cayley will answer your questions."

"Sam?" Beatrice shivered with a sudden chill. "What's wrong?"

He directed her toward the carriage as she looked questioningly at him. The pink in her pale cheeks hardened into red dots. He helped her up then came around the side. He turned toward her in the carriage and smoothed her curly red hair behind her shoulder. "You must be very brave," he said. "Your mother has been in an accident. Everything will be all right."

"What happened?"

"Aunt Cayley will..."

"I know, I know. All right." She sat, rigid and sullen, as the ferry pulled across the churning waters of the bay, busy with boats of all sizes scurrying about like waterbugs. As they pulled into San Francisco, the clock tower on the ferry building read 10 a.m. Sam had left the blue carriage in a nearby livery stable, and he put his hand under her elbow as they made their way along

206

the busy waterfront street. The smell of oiled rope and leather mingled with mildew and the sharp, salty odor of the bay. In front of the ferry building, newsboys yelled out the morning headlines: "Ripper still at large; more on the latest victim!"

"Oh dear," said Beatrice. "Those poor women. Mrs. Rolifer was right—the bawdy houses are bad for everyone." Sam remained silent, his eyes fixed ahead. "Look, here's a picture of of...." Beatrice stood transfixed.

"Paper, lady?" said the scruffy newsboy, as he thrust the newspaper in her face. Sam tried to push the paper away, but Beatrice held him off with one of her hands. She took it from the newsboy's hands with the tips of her fingers, delicately, as if it were a basket of eggs.

"That's a nickel, lady. A nickel. Hey!" The boy's dirty face took on an indignant cast.

Sam dug in his pocket and flipped the boy a nickel. He put his arm around Beatrice's shoulders. She was looking at a familiar picture—it was her and her mother, taken at the photographer's studio when she was eight. The painted trees formed a dark mass behind them in contrast to their still, white faces. The caption under it read: "Red Rose Ellen, notorious prostitute, is buried today." Her legs went out from under her, and Sam held her up and kept her moving toward the carriage barn. When they reached it, he sat her down on a dusty bench and nodded to the man to bring out the rig.

"What IS this?" she asked. "What exactly is this?" She held the crumpled paper out to him.

"It's a mistake," said Sam. "The newspaper has made a mistake with the picture."

"Are you telling the truth? What's happened to my mother?"

"She was hit by a delivery wagon while crossing the street," Sam said, ashamed at having to tell the lie he rehearsed with Cayley just that morning. "Aunt Cayley wants to talk to you."

"Sam? Is my mother alive or dead?"

"Aunt Cayley will straighten everything out, I promise."

"No," she said, and hit him once, hard, in the chest with both fists. "Tell me now."

"I promised Cayley I would bring you home first, Beatrice. Please help me honor that promise."

She saw the pain and pleading in his eyes, and allowed him to help her into the carriage, but kept the newspaper crumpled in her hands. They covered the distance to the house on Green Street in silence, the rhythm of the horse's hooves on the pavement the only sound either of them heard. Sam pulled the carriage around the driveway under the portico and Beatrice got out herself, her legs nearly collapsing when she hit the cobblestones that lined the ground. She marched into the house, shoving the door open wide, not waiting for Sam. He hurried in behind her and stood in the archway. Cayley was sitting in the front parlor her hands folded in her lap, a cup of cold tea in front of her. Her face was pale and drawn, and she didn't turn when Beatrice came into the room.

"What's going on?" Beatrice demanded. "Where's mother?" Her face crumpled and she started to shake, gasping for breath.

Cayley jumped up, tears streaming down her face, and went to embrace the girl. They held on to each other for a long moment, until Cayley held the girl out at arm's length. "Oh God, poor Bean. Poor all of us."

"Auntie Cay, what happened?"

Cayley composed her face and looked deeply into the girl's eyes. "Your mother was crossing the street downtown on New Year's Day when a runaway carriage struck her. She was knocked to the curb and hit her head. It was over instantly. There was no pain," said Cayley. "She's gone."

"Oh God," Beatrice wailed, and collapsed into Cayley's arms again. Cayley held the girl, patting her back.

"We have her down at Santini's Mortuary. There'll be a mass said for her on Sunday. We'll bury her today. I'm sorry to have waited to tell you, but I...just couldn't. I'll bring you a cup of tea. It will strengthen you."

"This isn't really happening. I can't believe it." The girl was gasping for breath.

"Neither can I." Cayley put a supportive arm around the girl's shoulders. "But don't worry dear, everything will be all right. I'll take care of you." She kissed her forehead. "Sit down. Do you want anything to eat?" Beatrice shook her head no, and sat in the space Cayley had vacated, on the white brocade couch.

Cayley walked out into the hallway, and glanced at Sam, who was standing with his hat in his hands. She nodded, and veered off toward the kitchen. Sam went into the parlor, to find Beatrice unwadding the newspaper, reading the story that ran with the picture. Her eyes widened briefly and he turned toward the kitchen.

"She's got the paper with Ellen's picture on the front, with a headline saying she's a prostitute," he told Cayley.

"Great God almighty, that's all we need right now," said Cayley. "What does it say?"

"I don't know."

Cayley sighed and stared at the floor. "We'll deal with it. We have to." She turned with the tray in her hands. Sam started to follow her. "No, stay here. I'll do it—woman to woman."

"Are you going to stick with the story?"

"As long as I can. It depends what's in the article."

***

Cayley made her way back to the drawing room to find Beatrice breathing quickly, staring out the window with the newspaper open in her hands.

"You lied to me."

Cayley said nothing as she set the tray down on the table.

"It says here that the body of Red Rose Ellen was found in the alley next to the house on O'Farrell Street owned by 'the notorious madam Cayley Wallace.' I didn't know you owned a house on O'Farrell Street."

"That's the boarding house. The saloon. You knew about that. She was probably on her way to check on the books."

"In the middle of the night? The newspaper says it's a house of prostitution."

"The newspapers will say anything to sell a few copies."

"But this is horrible. Look at this!" Beatrice's voice rose, and she thrust the picture of Ellen in front of Cayley's face. "They're saying my mother was a prostitute, and that she was murdered outside your house of prostitution. What are we going to do?"

"We'll do something. But not right now. Right now, we have to give your mother a proper burial. That's what we have to think about." Cayley struggled to keep her voice level. "We'll deal with this foolishness later."

"We should sue. We could sue, couldn't we?"

"Tomorrow, sweetheart. We'll worry about it tomorrow. One day won't make a difference."

"It will to me. How can they say those things about my mother. And you!"

Cayley sat down on the couch next to Beatrice, and took both of her hands in her own. "I'm sorry you had to see that paper. I would have taken care of it myself, and you never would have known otherwise. We'll straighten it out, Bean, I promise. Now I want you to wash your face. You can wear one of my hats with a veil. Let's go do what must be done."

Cayley accompanied the thirteen-year-old Beatrice, who stood stiffly, her shoulders encircled by Cayley's arm. They walked behind the casket together. Sam and Arturo managed to fend off the newspapermen who tried to shoulder in next to the two women as they walked behind the black coach, white plumes streaming in the light breeze. The casket was covered with gardenias, and the sweet fragrance was almost overpowering, carried on the wind down lower Green St., mixing with the food smells from the Italian restaurants and delicatessens in the surrounding blocks. The funeral hall was full, and the group included Cayley's girls, whom Sam warned away from contacting Cayley while Beatrice was with her. Cayley saw a familiar face in the crowd—older, beardless, and still handsome—Ellen's lover, Beatrice's father: Bill Duarte. She caught his eye then turned her back to him. After a brief procession, the entourage mounted carriages and made their way to the Presidio, where, by special permission usually granted only to the city's notables, Ellen was buried.

When they finally arrived home in the late afternoon, Beatrice pleaded exhaustion, and went to her room. Cayley was relieved. She desperately needed time to think, to push aside the overweening numbness, despair and puzzlement she felt. The glove in Ellen's hand was knitted by Cayley's own mother. It belonged to her brother Michael. Arnold Rolifer said Michael had left their employ a few years ago to work in a commercial livery; her mother had lost touch with him.

Before Cayley could go upstairs, she heard the sound of men's voices at the door. Sam came into the parlor. "Bill Duarte is here. He's very insistent, says he's an old friend of yours and Miss Ellen's. Do you want to see him, or should I keep everyone away?"

Cayley dropped her jaw in disbelief. "Bring the son-of-a-bitch in," she said. "And keep an eye on Bean—make sure she stays in her room."

Sam looked at her quizzically then brought the other man into the front parlor.

"I'm here to pay my respects," Duarte said.

"You're a few years too late for that." Cayley held her arms crossed in front of her like a shield.

"Don't judge me so hard," he said. "I tried to get in touch with her many times, but she wouldn't have any of it."

"She never mentioned anything to me," Cayley said coolly.

"Why would she?"

Cayley spit out the words: "Well, dear, we were close friends. But friendship requires responsibility and I know where you stand on that."

"If you're such good friends, then you knew she made sure I couldn't come near my daughter. That was my daughter, at the funeral, wasn't it?" Bill's eyes narrowed.

"Why should you care?"

"Why shouldn't I? I never married or had any children to call my own. I've spent a lifetime building up a good business and finally getting to a place in life where men look up to me, and I want to do right by my girl."

"Ellen said you denied you were the father."

He looked miserably at the rim of the hat in his hand. "I wasn't sure. No, that's not true. I was sure. You're right. I didn't want the responsibility. I came back a few years later, but Ellen said she was good and done with me." He looked up at Cayley, his eyes creased with concern. "And now she's gone. What's going to happen to the girl?"

"She's my responsibility. Beatrice doesn't know anything about you, and it's better that way. Unless you insist on telling her she's your bastard…if you really think that's in her best interests." Cayley's voice was sarcastic.

"Living with whores is better?"

Cayley calmly lifted a cup of cold tea and saucer from the side table and threw it at him. He dodged it easily and it fell against the fern behind him, hitting the floor with a ringing sound.

"She's led a completely sheltered life. I can take care of her like a princess—I've got the means, and money can buy a lot of things—and a lot of silence. We don't need you."

Duarte looked behind him at the broken cup on the floor. "You and I don't have to be enemies. I'm doing all right financially. Beatrice is a young lady now—what, fourteen? I can help out with school, or whatever. I want to. I let Ellen down…." He rubbed the back of his neck.

Cayley sighed and put her hands on her waist, rolled her shoulders forward tiredly. "She'll be fourteen in September. It's been a long, rough day. If you want to help, we'll talk later. Right now, I don't want you anywhere near that girl. She doesn't need the sudden appearance of some man who claims to be her long-lost father." She looked hard into his eyes. "We told her you were dead. And as far as I'm concerned, Bill, you are."

He nodded. "I'll be back."

212

Chapter FORTY-FIVE

Journal of Miss B. Belle Leary, June 1, 1904

I'm amazed at how badly things can turn out, and how quickly it can happen. On that day, the day I found out about mother—all I could think of were the horrible things they said about her. Clearing her name seemed like the one thing I could do for her. Early the next morning after the funeral, I snuck downstairs when the household was quiet and slipped out the door. I walked downtown until I was able to catch a cable car, asked one or two people the address of the Examiner offices, and made my way to the newspaper building. I couldn't wait to clear up that shameful blot on my family name. When I was ushered into the pressroom, I announced, "I'm Miss Beatrice Leary, and I demand a retraction!" They led me to the city editor's desk, where I held my head up proudly and once again demanded a retraction. "It's shameful and insulting that you would associate my family with such activities," I said.

"And who might you be, dear?" asked Mr. Forbush, the city editor, a slight man with a foxy look.

"I'm the daughter of Ellen Leary—the woman whom you've wrongly characterized as a prostitute in yesterday's paper. We've just buried my mother." I stopped speaking for a moment, and took great deep breaths so as not to lose what little self-control I had. "How dare you! My family will sue you to the full extent of the law." I raised my chin a notch higher. Oh, I was so sure of myself and my noble purpose. "But first, it will go easier on you if you print an immediate apology."

An older reporter, overhearing the conversation from his desk nearby, sidled up to me. "Mr. Forbush?" he said. "Let me get this young woman's information. This is quite a story here."

Forbush and the older man exchanged glances. "Go ahead," he said. "Find out what we need."

"Come this way, young lady. Your name is...?"

"Miss Beatrice Leary. And you are?"

"Mr. Ambrose Bierce. Perhaps you've read my byline?"

"I don't read the papers Mr. Bierce. I attend school in the East Bay, and anyway, mother says they're full of sensationalism. Which certainly appears to be the case."

"So you're Ellen Leary's daughter! There was a child in the picture. Was that you? I don't think anyone knew she had a daughter for sure."

"Why would anyone need to know?"

"No reason, I guess. Please, sit down here, Miss Leary. May I get you a cup of coffee?"

"No thank you, I prefer tea. Let's get this over with, shall we? I'm quite exhausted."

"I can imagine. So, what exactly would you like us to say?"

"Well, my Aunt Cayley—Mrs. Catherine Pearson-Leary— whom you've implied to be the owner of a house of prostitution...my God, could you be more scandalous?" My anger nearly overwhelmed me. The heat surged in my body, making my collar damp.

"Yes, sorry, apparently the wrong information," said Bierce. He seemed so nice.

"I should say so. Well, my aunt, who owned the boarding house on O'Farrell Street along with my mother, said my mother was..." I had to stop, as the tears started to come. Bierce pulled out a rumpled handkerchief, and I took it and dabbed at my eyes. "My mother was fatally injured by a runaway carriage. How could you have been so wrong?"

"I don't know how such a mistake was made, Miss Leary. I personally will try to trace the source of this misinformation, and set all wrongs to right."

"Oh thank you, Mr. Bierce. Just talking to you has been such a relief. My aunt was going to take care of this, but I simply couldn't wait to clear up this dishonor around my mother's good name. If you'll see me to the door." Once on the street, Mr. Bierce summoned a hack for me, and waved as I drove away, still dabbing delicately at my nose with his handkerchief. I burned it later.

I slipped unnoticed into the house and went up to my room, passing the day quietly by myself. The next day, I eagerly awaited the morning papers.

When I heard the newsboy's call on the corner, I hurriedly dressed and ran out to buy a copy, past the inquiries of Auntie Cay who was just sitting down to breakfast in her dressing gown. I handed over a nickel for a copy and scanned the front page for a story, finding with no trouble the picture of my mother and myself among the columns. The headline read, "Slain Prostitute's Daughter Speaks Out." The column went on to detail Red Rose Ellen's "secret" life, the discovery of a daughter completely innocent of her mother's line of work, and the daughter's relationship with the infamous madam Cayley Wallace. I was so stunned I stood in the street, unable to walk back to the house right away. The newsboy thought to ask if I was all right; when I didn't answer, he shrugged his shoulders and continued down the street to hawk his papers.

I put one foot in front of the other and made my way back to the house clutching the newspaper. I opened the front door, walked into the dining room and laid the paper carefully over Cayley's plate of eggs and bacon; the grease stain spread from the plate beneath.

"What's this?" said Aunt Cay. "More nonsense from the press?"

"I went down there yesterday after the funeral. I told them I wanted a retraction."

Aunt Cay read the headlines and her eyes whipped through the article. "Oh Christ girl, why didn't you listen to me? I would've taken care of this."

I knew then it was true. "No more lies. Tell me."

Cayley pushed the paper away and looked down at her plate. "Your mother was dearer to me than anyone I've ever known," she said. "She was my closest friend, and one of the best people born on this earth. I curse those who tear down her memory with every punishment hell has to offer."

"That's not an answer."

215

Aunt Cay pushed her plate away and put her head in her hands. "Beatrice, you are not going to like what I have to say. I wish it were different. I didn't want you to find out this way."

"It's true, isn't it?"

"Some of it is true."

"Well, WHAT?"

"I AM a madam. The house on O'Farrell IS a house of prostitution. A damned good one, too."

I couldn't breathe for a moment. "That's disgusting! How can this be? All these years! If I had only known!"

"If you had only known, what? What would you have done?"

She was right. I turned left and right, brought my hands up, palms open. "I don't know! What about my mother?"

"She was NOT a prostitute and she never approved of it. Your mother and I met many years ago. We both worked down at a bar on Market. I didn't marry her brother—far as I know, she didn't have one. She was raised by her aunt—dead many years now, the mean old crone. She threw your mother out."

"Is everything I've ever known a lie? Why did she throw my mother out?"

Aunt Cay looked up at me, her face beginning to redden. "Get hold of yourself, girl. Your mother is still the same person she was two days ago." She was shouting at me, and I was shouting back. She said, "You have no right to condemn her for trying to do the best she could by you, and that she always did."

"She was a...a prostitute, wasn't she? I'm the product of some foul coupling with a stranger, aren't I?" I felt filthy and I was shouting and crying at the same time. It really seemed the only explanation. I was so ashamed.

Cayley said, "Try to keep the drama to a minimum, Bean." Hearing my mother's name for me calmed me down a little. "Your mother loved your father. She knew him a long time, but he disappeared when he found out she was pregnant. He was not a good man, but it hardly matters. He's been dead for years. The aunt wouldn't have her in the house, 'dishonored' and all. I found her on the streets, begging, with you just a babe in her arms. God save us all. I was already in the business. I asked her to come help me run it; she always had a sharp head for figures. She didn't work on the floor—I mean, it was strictly business. She wasn't one of the girls."

"The Examiner seems to think she was."

"The Examiner is wrong."

"Is it possible to prove they're wrong?" I had a tiny bit of hope that maybe this nightmare could be made right somehow.

After a moment of silence, Aunt Cayley sighed and said, "No." She traced the pattern of the tablecloth with her fingers. "Even if the Examiner prints a retraction—and they'll bend over backwards when I'm done with them, believe me—there will be doubt." She looked up at me. "Because I am who I am."

"How do I know you're telling me the truth about all this? After all, how can I trust you? You and your dirty business."

"You don't. You can't. Though I can't think of why I'd make up such a story, can you?"

"And both of you lied to me all these years."

Aunt Cay stood up suddenly and the chair behind her fell backwards, chopping a bit of plaster molding off the wall. "Well, I can think of why I'd make up THAT story you foolish girl. Your mother wanted to protect you. And herself, and me."

I was angry, and in no mood to give in to this woman who wasn't even related to me. "Was I supposed to be lied to forever?"

"She was going to take you away and leave all this behind. She told me the night she was...the night she was taken from us. You never would have known if this terrible thing hadn't happened. If you consider that 'lied to forever', I suppose the answer would be yes. I wish to hell it had happened that way."

We stood there and stared at each other. "Me too," I said and started to cry once again, covering my face with one hand. Aunt Cay made her way around the table and put her arms around me, but I shrugged them off, ran out of the room and up the stairs.

I avoided Cayley the next few days, and asked if I could return to school. Sam took me later that week.

"You lied to me too," I told him.

"Yes, I did." We stood at the ferry railing. Seagulls followed after the wake of the boat, looking for food churned up in the waves. "You are very young, with a lot of things to learn about the world. It's not what it looks like much of the time."

"What's that supposed to mean? That people you trust will lie to you?"

"Life is far from perfect. People must be judged not only on what they do, but why they do it."

"I don't want to hear it."

"I understand you're only concerned for yourself right now. Perhaps as time goes on, you'll once again be concerned with others. Like your Aunt Cayley."

"She's not my aunt. She's a prostitute that gave my mother a job to keep us off the street. I suppose I should be grateful. Ha!"

Sam shook his head, and kept his eyes on the white trail of foam. "It's more complicated than that. Your mother didn't have any way to support you, and Mrs. Wallace was very kind to you both. She helped you the only way she could."

"I'm ashamed and embarrassed. This on top of my mother's death is all too much. What if they know at school?"

"Even if they don't, someday, someone will know. What will you say to them then?"

"I don't know. What can I possibly say?"

"You can tell the truth. That you loved your mother very much, and that she loved you and gave you everything." We stood in silence and listened to the birds cry out as the ferry approached the dock. "She was a good woman. And Mrs. Wallace is also a good woman." Black smoke from the smokestack hung low over the boat as it slowed.

I stayed at school and didn't go back to San Francisco for a month. When I did, I asked to see Cayley. We met in the drawing room like strangers.

"I've done a lot of thinking," I said. Cayley nodded. "I've got no future here. Everybody knows who I am, who my mother was, and who you are." It was hard to get the words out, but I knew I had to.

"Bean…"

"Don't call me that. I want to go to school back east. New York. My mother's cousin is there. She was expecting us. I don't have any family here anymore. Will you send me?"

Aunt Cayley seemed to have difficulty breathing. "Sweetheart, you don't really want to leave, do you?" She turned away from me, and I thought she was starting to cry.

"That's what I just said."

Now I knew she was crying, and it made me feel good to imagine the tears rolling down her cheeks.

"Bean…Beatrice…I, well, I never had a child that lived, myself. I had a baby once, a little baby boy. He died before he was one and it broke my heart. You…you sort of became my baby, living here in this house. And your mother let me love you like you were my very own. Please don't throw away all the good things we have here."

"I want to leave as soon as possible," I said.

My mother provided for me very well financially. In March, I boarded a train bound for the east coast. My mother's cousin found a boarding school for rich and proper young ladies in Manhattan. The leave-taking at the station was brief and frantic. Cayley scurried about, clucking and fussing, Sam manhandled a mountain of luggage, and I barely tolerated either of them. When the train was ready to pull out of the station, the two of them waved at me beneath my window. I heard Sam say, "It's better this way." Cayley looked tired, and he took her by the arm as he had my mother, so many years ago at Holy Cross, and steadied her on their way back to the carriage as the train pulled away.

I have to make a new life for myself here in New York, and forget about the past. And I will."

Chapter FORTY-SIX

"Maybe this…" Cayley lifted her hands to take in the heavy bottle-green velvet draperies, the ormolu candelabra, the dancing fauns on the ceiling, "was all a big mistake. Some huge devil's bargain that's come to beat me into the ground." She let her coat drop carelessly on the floor, as if trying to shed her skin along with Beatrice's coldness at the station. "Like that Faust fella."

"You're just tired," said Sam. "You've had a lot to deal with. We all have."

"I'm falling apart, Sam." She collapsed against him and circled her arms around his chest. He stood not more than an inch taller than her; she had never touched him so intimately before. He patted her awkwardly as she sobbed; his arms wrapped protectively around her back and he was shocked and gladdened at how good it felt. He reluctantly released her when she collected herself and opened her bag to retrieve a handkerchief.

Cayley went to the desk and sat down. "It's worse than you think."

Sam shook his head as if to clear it. "That's hard to believe."

She looked at him for a long moment. "I know who the Ripper is."

"Cayley, you need to rest. A lot has happened. Opal can come up and take over for a month or so."

"Sam, listen to me. I'm not hysterical. I'm not the hysterical type. But this couldn't be worse. You've been my right hand through good and bad times and you've got to stick by me now." She withdrew a key from one of the desk cubbyholes, unlocked the second drawer, and took out a bloodstained glove. "This belongs to my brother. I'd know it anywhere. My mother made it."

Sam looked puzzled.

"It was in Ellen's hand."

He gasped and covered his mouth with his fingers. "Are you sure? Is there any other way she would have had it?"

"I couldn't be more sure. But what can I do about it? I've got to stop him, but I don't know where he is."

"So we find him. Then we decide what to do. There may be some reasonable explanation—it doesn't mean that he…did anything to Ellen, or that he's the Ripper. We can't jump to conclusions."

"I appreciate the 'we' in this more than you'll ever know."

Sam put his head down and smiled.

"As for taking some time off, work is what I need." Cayley stood up and looked out the window to the bustle of the street outside. "Thank God I've got something to keep me busy. Besides, we've got to hold it together for the girls." She looked over at him, the worry lines creasing her forehead. "What would happen to them if we lost it all?"

***

Bill Duarte dropped by a few days later with a cash-filled envelope for Beatrice's schooling. Cayley thought about refusing the money, but her practicality ruled.

"I'm going to keep coming back," he said.

"Like a bad penny—that's what Ellen said about you." Cayley stood with her hands on her hips in the entry hall.

"Won't you even let me in to have a drink?"

Cayley turned her head toward the bar. "We're not open yet."

"All right then, come out with me and have some dinner. I want to convince you that my heart's in the right place."

Wo Sam came in the front door at that moment, and caught Cayley's eye. She dismissed Bill with a wave, "Some other time," and joined Sam in the office.

"Any luck?"

"Nothing so far. If he's working in a commercial livery, it'll be easier, but there's no guarantee that he's working at all. I'll keep at it."

"Thanks, Sam. You're the best." She reached over and patted him on the shoulder. "I've been thinking—the house on Green seems so empty now. How do you feel about Lilly moving

221

in with me? It'll get her away from O'Farrell and I know you'd like that."

"That would be excellent, Cayley."

"We're family now."

Sam nodded. "I'll keep searching for Michael."

***

True to his word, Bill showed up the following Tuesday and for several weeks after that, cash and dinner invitation at the ready. "You're mighty persistent," Cayley told him as she flicked the envelope from his hand.

"It's the secret of my success. Persistence has made me a rich man." He smiled without showing his teeth. His finely textured dark gray suit spoke to his wealth. "It's also healed a lot of old wounds, and that's my intention, Mrs. Wallace. If you come out to dinner with me, you'll have an opportunity to hear the excellent apology I've prepared for the cruel thing I said to you after the funeral."

"Saints be praised. A man who apologizes. Give it to me now."

"It's meant to be said over a bottle of fine champagne at the Old Poodle Dog. Won't feel right otherwise." He fixed his pale eyes on hers, unblinking.

Cayley grimaced and shook her finger at Bill Duarte, "I thought I heard it all, but you're the topper."

"Let me try to make it up to you." He took a step toward her and reached for her fingers with his right hand; she didn't resist. "Go get your wrap. Let's try to live a little in these awful times," he said quietly. "We'll drink to the memory of a fine woman we both loved—though you were better to her than I could ever claim. I'm ashamed of myself, and that's no lie. Help me? Please?"

They left in his sleek carriage and clattered down Market to the restaurant. Upstairs in one of the curtained private booths, Cayley managed to consume not one, but four bottles of champagne. "You're paying, right?" She grinned at him and raised her glass. "Still waiting for that apology."

Bill got down unsteadily on one knee. "Madam...I mean Mrs. Wallace," They both were giggling. "I was an ass. I raise my glass...."

"Oh, poetry!"

"I'm a man of many talents. I raise my glass...to the best piece of ass... and the most clever girl...in the entire world."

"Oh, hokum. And how would you know anyway—clever, yes, but the other..." Cayley examined one of the rings on her hand. "That wasn't exactly an apology."

"You're a hard one, Cayley Wallace." He steadied himself by holding on to the table. "I'm sorry that I said 'living with whores'. I deserve to be hit with that cup, and would have, if your aim was as good as your business sense."

"I'll show you aim," she said, and poured a glass of champagne over his head. He tipped his face back, opened his mouth, and let the golden liquid pour into and over him. Then he looked her in the eye from under his smooth brow. Feeling foolish, she grabbed a napkin and dabbed at his face and suit. He held both her wrists and drew her down to him on the floor, pressing his mouth to hers, delivering a gulp of champagne and a passionate, enthralling kiss.

***

"He's like Napoleon," she told Sam. "He's going to conquer the world."

"He's a rascal. I don't trust him." Sam planted his hands on his waist.

"Don't be jealous. He can't replace you. He doesn't even want to. He's got plenty of ambition of his own—he came up from nothing, like me, and he's going to the top. Money, respect, power—he's going to have it all."

"Have you forgotten what he did to Miss Ellen?" Sam couldn't keep the sullenness out of his voice.

She turned to him, her hands on the edge of the desk. "We've discussed it, Bill and I. We're both suffering her loss, but she's gone. We've got to go on. And we have a daughter to think of."

223

Sam's face became stern. "The night we met, you said, 'that's no way to treat someone who helped you.' Do you remember that? I thought, 'this might be a person of substance!' But such a person wouldn't dismiss the life of a good friend in such a way. And what about the search for Michael? Do you still want me to continue, or do you no longer care?"

"Sam, what is this? Of course I care. Nothing has changed. Ellen was the closest friend I had in the world! As for Michael, we have to get to him before the police do. It would kill my mother. I don't know what I'm going to do, but I've got to do something. And I will. I will."

"You're right," Sam looked away from her face. "Nothing has changed."

***

Cayley began to fill the O'Farrell house with busts and paintings of Napoleon, and even bought a bed that supposedly once belonged to him, a huge carved gilt affair. She stopped taking clients and kept a painted miniature portrait of Bill by her bed at home. She saw him three or four times a week, their time together a wild flurry of drink and dance and money thrown around like candy at a parade. He never hesitated taking her to the finest places in town, demanding the best service and goods for her.

One afternoon as they sat in one of the Old Poodle Dog's private rooms on the third floor, served by a parade of waiters, Chef Calixte Lalanne came in with a special bottle of champagne Bill had ordered for her. "It's the best in the house," Chef Lalanne said. "For the king and queen of 'Frisco—not even the mayor would dare order this!"

"We deserve it," Bill told her as the Chef poured the golden liquid into cut crystal flutes. "We're no different from any of these nobs—they got their money by skullduggery too. Someday, Mrs. Wallace…" he kissed her on her flushed cheek, "we'll be more than backstreet royalty. We'll own this town. Maybe even this state."

224

Chapter FORTY-SEVEN

Lilly was forbidden to leave the Green Street house when her brother or Mrs. Wallace weren't there. It wasn't distrust—it was for her safety. She continued to help at the O'Farrell houses, and drew a salary from Mrs. Wallace—the first money she had ever earned. However, as the days dragged on in the quiet house, her longing for her home in China became intense. She missed the ordinary things there: her garden with the familiar vegetables, so different from the rich food Mrs. Wallace served; and the sound of her dialect spoken in greeting as she passed through the village on her way to the market.

She picked up English quickly with the help of Wo Sam, and was able to persuade Mrs. Wallace's housekeeper, Manuela, to take her along to the open-air produce market downtown. The next step was to get her to prepare vegetables more simply, atop steamed rice. Her brother Sam appreciated the traditional dishes when he came for dinner, and even Mrs. Wallace enjoyed her soups. "Back in the days when I first started out, I used to have this for breakfast every morning," she said. "Different noodles, though—but delicious."

"I could find the missing ingredients in Chinatown, Mrs. Wallace."

Cayley looked up from her bowl and glanced over at Sam.

"Still too risky," he grunted.

Lilly sighed. It had been nearly a year since she was rescued from the house of Wing Yee. Though she often went along with her brother to help set up for Cayley's parties, she was used to running her father's house and needed something to do she could call her own. As she sat picking at yet another embroidery, her thoughts wandered to the girl who was willing to help her escape: the little princess with the tiny feet. She was brave, even though she thought she was playing at a fairy tale. Lilly wondered what Mei Mei thought of her now, after Wing Yee's home was invaded and ruined by white devils. The girl had watched Lilly emerge from her room not as a mythic being, but as a ragged, disheveled, ordinary peasant. Lilly was just as much a prisoner here, though the circumstances were more pleasant. She was grateful to both her brother and his employer, but was of two minds: though she loved many things about America, she didn't feel she was part of it; nor was she able to be among other Chinese. She made plans to leave the house early in the morning before Mrs. Wallace returned from the O'Farrell house. It was just a matter of convincing the housekeeper that she could attend the market on her own if she hired a hack that would wait for her. She was very good at convincing people. And Chinatown wasn't far from the market.

***

Lilly left the carriage and walked quickly to a nearby hotel, ducking into the toilet. She held her breath as she shed her western skirt and jacket and donned a blue cloth jacket and domed cap. Her hair was already neatly braided down her back and she wore trousers beneath her wide taffeta skirt. She stuffed her western clothes into one of her market baskets and hurried to Stockton *Gai*. It was intoxicating to be among so many voices, the ornate pitches of several dialects, but mostly Cantonese. The produce stalls on the street were overflowing with bitter melon, bok choy, peaches and other foods grown in small gardens. She chose a number of things, and went inside the shops for packages of dried noodles and tea. Her baskets full to overflowing, she slowed as she passed a tailor shop, fine silks blazing in the windows. She came to a full stop when she looked inside the doorway and saw Mei Mei fingering a bolt of sky-colored silk. Behind her, nurse Sai haggled with the shop owner. Lilly's heart began pounding like festival drums. She entered the shop, her bulging baskets at her side. "Do you know me, Mei Mei?" she whispered to the girl.

Mei Mei looked up, startled, and was about to shout when Lilly said, "I've come back from the golden temple to see you." Mei Mei's mouth hung open.

Nurse Sai came charging from the back. "Get away you dirty boy! Don't bother your betters." She began to swat at Lilly, who turned and ran, her baskets flying out on either side. Lilly's hat, a prim little straw tucked on top of her skirt in one of the baskets, tumbled out onto the floor. Mei Mei stooped to pick it up and stuffed it beneath her jacket.

Lilly walked quickly to the borders of Chinatown, pinned up her braid, and changed back into her western dress, minus her hat. She felt exhilarated, a strange warmth spreading over her. *I have someone here,* she thought. *Someone of my own.*

Chapter FORTY-EIGHT
January 1905

"You and I are a good team, Cayley," said Bill lazily. "With your money and brains, and my money and brains, we could run this town." He stretched his body out full length in the gilded bed.

"I've got connections too, don't forget. It's not just money that's opened a few doors." She pulled on the velvet rope and asked Arturo to bring more champagne. It was a few days after the New Year, and Cayley was in a mood to celebrate. Beatrice was doing well in school and seemed fairly happy, though she communicated little to Cayley. It had been a year since Sam and she stood in the alley over Ellen's lifeless body; after the thrilling first few months of her love affair with Bill, memories of her friend invaded her quiet moments and filled her with guilt. The Ripper—if indeed it was Michael, and Cayley was beginning to have doubts—hadn't surfaced since Ellen's death. After all, Ellen knew her family—perhaps she had gotten the glove some other way. She buried the blood-stained glove in the bottom of her wardrobe at home—that way, she didn't have to make any decision at all. Sam was unable to locate Michael; perhaps he had left town for good. Cayley tired of mulling over an unsolvable problem.

"It looks like our Bean is going to apply to Women's Medical College in Philadelphia," said Cayley. "Imagine our little girl, a medical doctor. Isn't that a laugh!"

"Our girl sure has big ideas. What's THAT going to cost me?" said Bill

"Are you going to start complaining? It was your idea to pay for half her support, and so you should."

He took a linen cloth along with the bottle from Arturo and proceeded to uncork it, spilling a little onto his sheet-covered lap. "She thinks it's her mother's money."

"It should have been her mother's money. You owe them both and I'll never let you forget it." Cayley put an arm around his neck and kissed the side of his face.

"I'm not complaining." He poured glasses for both of them. "It's just that district elections are coming up, and if I want to get in, my money has to go to the votes. What am I supposed to do?"

Cayley set her glass down, lay back on her satin pillow and toyed with a strand of her hair, inspecting it closely. "You and I could really be a team. Then you'd have more money than you'd need and you could be a real father to our girl."

He raised himself on one elbow and put his glass on the side table. "Cayley, not again."

Cayley's jaw tightened, ready for battle. "Cayley, not again," she mimicked. "What's wrong with wanting to make it legal. Every woman wants it. You sleep with me every night."

"Half the city has slept with you."

She picked up her champagne glass from the bedside table and threw it in his face. "Get out! I'm tired of your mean jokes."

He pulled a towel off the end of the bed and calmly wiped himself off. They sat there for a few moments in silence. Cayley was rigid with anger.

"I'm sorry. You know I love you, Cayley. My mouth gets to talking before I think, sometimes."

"I'll say. You got a nerve trying to shame me. Your money's dirtier than mine and you know it. At least when it's spent here, they get their money's worth."

"I sell the pleasure of possibility. It's certainly not as pretty as a rosy bosom, but some men find it even more attractive. Take your man Sam. If I didn't pull him out of a gambling debt here and there, he wouldn't have a pot to piss in."

"Call it what you like, but you're trying to change the subject again."

"What difference could marriage possibly make to us?"

Cayley leaned back against the pillows. "Why don't you say what you really think? It might mess up your chances to be a big-time politician, being married to a whore and all."

"Since we're being so honest, why don't we talk about what you really want? You want to follow me up that ladder and meet the social set in the front parlors rather than the back stairs."

She laughed mirthlessly. "I won't deny it. The money is great, but a little respect would be mighty nice. There's plenty of others around, but it's you I'm after, you beardless fool." She crawled across the bed on her hands and knees, breasts pressing against her fine lawn gown. "And you can't deny that my money would speed you up that ladder." She came up behind him and put her arms around his shoulders. "Wouldn't it?"

He patted her hand. "You're quite a gal, Cayley. I don't think there's another like you."

"Then you better get while the gettin's good."

"How long is that going to be?"

"It might be over by the time I get back from New York in the spring." said Cayley. "Long train trips are famous for giving a gal time to think."

"So you're still determined to visit Beatrice. Then maybe I should come along and keep your brain occupied—among other things." He reached behind her and patted her rump.

She jumped up on both knees. "Bill, you mean it? You'll come along?"

"I can take a little time off before I begin greasing palms from the Ferry Building to the beach."

Cayley threw her arms around his neck and covered his face with kisses. "You're the best man I've ever known, Bill Duarte."

Chapter FORTY-NINE

The evening after Cayley and Bill left on their trip east, Sam and Lilly stood in the kitchen of the Green Street house as she leaned against the washtub full of soapy, lukewarm water.

"These dishes are not as clean as Mrs. Wallace likes."

"Then clean them yourself."

"Don't speak to me in such a manner. It isn't fitting."

"You have no right to order me around. You can't even keep enough money to pay your own way back to China, much less mine. Why don't you find yourself a wife to abuse?"

"I am your elder brother!"

"Yes, you are! End of argument." She sighed deeply, elbows bent, the backs of her palms on the edge of the sink. "It is hard to be here among the whites. I wish I could be with our people, and enjoy a feast in a restaurant surrounded by family and friends."

Sam hung his head. "I wish that too, little sister. Gold Mountain has not been kind to us."

"Well," she smiled ruefully at him, "at least you kept me out of the cribs."

"And there are many men looking for a smart, clean wife to keep their homes and bear children. We will make you a good marriage in spite of everything that's happened."

Lilly looked away from him; she had managed to keep her secrets well. Not only about what the soldiers had done to her after they killed her father, but also about her friend. Her brother would not have been happy about either of those things.

After her first brief foray into Chinatown, Lilly began to visit often in the early mornings dressed as a young boy. She was amazed at her own courage—or perhaps it was need—when she found the house of Wing Yee and kept watch for the girl, who would always leave with her nurse or one of the soldiers. Now that Mei Mei was a little older, her guardians were not as vigilant, and Lilly was able to slip her a note or trade brief words with her. During one of these exchanges Mei Mei gave her a

231

message asking for a meeting late in the evening, not far from the house of Wing Yee. It was easy for Lilly to slip out then, since Mrs. Wallace's housekeeper was a heavy sleeper who snored like roaring tigers and no one would be home before late morning. When she arrived at the arranged meeting place, no one was there. She feared a trap. Then she saw a small figure walking down the street, hunched over like an old woman leaning on a cane. Clever Mei Mei!

"How did you get out by yourself?" whispered Lilly.

"My brother used a passageway in the wall—he showed me before he died. I never had a need for it until now."

"Should we stay here or go someplace else?"

"I can't walk very far," said the girl looking down at her feet. "Useless."

Lilly bent down to touch the tiny embroidered slippers. "Does it hurt?"

"Not anymore. But it starts to hurt if I walk too far."

"Then I'll carry you." Lilly turned around and hoisted the smaller girl on her back while Mei Mei let out a delighted giggle. "Let's go to the park by the big white church." Lilly shifted the girl's weight, feeling the length of Mei Mei's body and small breasts pressing on her back. She suddenly felt warm.

"Won't that be dangerous?"

Lilly grinned, made braver by Mei's timidity. "Let's do it anyway."

They hurried down the streets, across Columbus Avenue. To passersby, they looked like a boy and his sister—or a young servant and his mistress—making their way home. Though the restaurants around the park were bright with lights, they chose to sit among the shadows on the edge of the greenery. They put their arms around each other's waists.

"I miss China," whispered Lilly.

"I've never been there," said Mei Mei. "What's it like?"

"It's hot in the summer, and the air is wet—not like here. The mist comes up off the ground, and it's very green. Everything grows there. We had a peach tree in our yard. Its mate was in the yard next door and my father said that every year they would renew their vows and bear fruit like golden suns."

"Is your father still in China?"

"He's dead." Lilly shook her head. "There was a war…"

"There's a war here, too," said Mei.

The girls held each other closer and leaned together. "These foolish men and their wars," said Lilly. "I don't think I'll ever get married, no matter what my brother says."

"But don't you want to have children? Who will take care of you when you're old?"

"I don't know. Maybe YOUR children will take care of me!" Lilly tickled the girl beneath her ribs, making her squirm and giggle. Lilly suppressed the urge to hug the younger girl tightly to her.

"Well, if you're not getting married, I'm not getting married either!" said Mei Mei, breathlessly.

"About our brothers…" said Lilly.

"I know," whispered Mei. "Don't say anything else."

They sat in silence for a while, then giggled as a group of merrymakers left a restaurant across the street; several were singing loudly off-key.

"Are there many girls like me," Mei indicated her feet, "in China?"

"There are a few. Only wealthy families practice foot binding. Some are speaking out against it." Lilly and Mei stared at the younger girl's feet. "Would you show me? I've never really seen how it's done, though I've heard that bones in the foot are broken. Is that true?"

Mei Mei nodded solemnly. She hesitated for a moment, then brought one tiny foot up on her opposite thigh and removed her embroidered shoe. The foot and lower part of her leg were tightly wrapped in a long white cloth bandage. "I have to clean and rewrap my feet every night," she said. She began to unwind the bandage, slowly. "We're only supposed to do this in front of our husbands."

Lilly put her hands over the girl's. "Then you shouldn't."

They sat for a moment, hands together Then Mei nodded and rewrapped her foot. "This doesn't mean we aren't friends, does it?" she said anxiously.

"Of course not. Even best friends don't have to share everything."

"Are we best friends?"

"I guess we are." Lilly smiled down at the girl.

They both grew sleepy after an hour more of sharing their lives, and Mei Mei partially walked and was partially carried back to her street, where she lightly kissed Lilly good-bye on the lips. Lilly stood for a few moments with her hand pressed to her mouth before turning back to her home.

Chapter FIFTY

"I'm all a-twitter to see Bean! It's been so long. More than a year!" Cayley beamed as the train rumbled out of Sacramento station after taking on water and coal for the next leg of the journey.

"Well, she doesn't make the effort to come to us, does she?" Bill had his back to Cayley as he struggled to move the stuck-tight window in their first-class compartment. The window shrieked open, and he adjusted it to let in a small stream of air.

"She's busy with school. But she seems very happy there. New York is so lovely this time of year. Of course I'll take her shopping, and perhaps the three of us can see some sights. I hear that new reservoir is really something!"

"Cayley," Bill leaned over and lowered his voice, "She still may be sore about the whole thing with her mother. And your profession. You know that."

Cayley stopped jabbering, and said in a serious and somewhat hurt voice, "Not after so long. It's been ages. She's just a self-absorbed young girl."

"I'm just trying to prepare you, is all—just in case."

"Well thank you for thinking of me, darlin'," Cayley dimpled at him and sat back in the plush first-class seat as the train rocked and rumbled into the Sierras.

***

A week later, the couple settled into their suite in the 23rd storey of the sparkling new Peninsula Hotel. Cayley read the message from Beatrice that waited for her: "Bill, she's coming here with an escort this afternoon! See, I told you she wanted to see me. How do I get room service on this thing?" She pointed to the upright telephone, which sported a set of holes with numbers next to them on the shaft. It sat on a small dark wood stand inlaid with pale parquetry in a scroll design.

Bill patted Cayley on the shoulder. "I don't know what the numbers are for. Pick it up and I'll bet the operator will answer—just like home. New York isn't that far ahead of us."

"This is so exciting—and so wonderful to be here with you—and me and Bean together."

Cayley discovered a list of number combinations on a printed sheet in the small drawer under the telephone; she and Bill took turns dialing to reach various hotel services, and ordered tea for Beatrice's arrival.

At four o'clock, a knock brought Cayley to her feet. "Oh, you're a young lady now!" she said when Beatrice swept in the door. "And so sophisticated! A real corker!" Cayley hugged the girl with both arms, and Beatrice responded limply. "This is my chaperone Mrs. Main, my Aunt Catherine and..."

"Oh I'm so excited, I forgot my manners. This is my fiancé, Mr. Duarte." Bill flinched, then smiled and shook hands with the girl and woman.

"I'm sure I wrote you about him, dear." Cayley began to fuss with the teapot, indicating for the women to sit in the brocade chairs around the low table. "I'm so glad we're here at last. We ladies can do some shopping in the next few days, and then perhaps you'll take Mr. Duarte and me around to meet your friends, and we'll see some sights; that new Hippodrome Theater, maybe?" Cayley poured tea into the china cups and held out the sugar bowl. "How do you take it, now that you're so grown up?"

"Aunt Cay, I'm really sorry, but you're here during final tests, and I'm afraid I can't take any time off at all. I have to do very well, of course, to get into Women's Medical College. You understand."

Cayley's face fell. "Yes, I understand, of course," she turned away, and put her teacup down. "I suppose I should have checked on this before we scheduled this trip. It's so hard to get away from the business and all."

"The hotel business—very demanding," said Beatrice quickly to Mrs. Main. "I've told them all about your hotels, Aunt Cayley."

Cayley nodded. "Of course you have, Bean. Of course you have."

"Bean, what a cute nickname! But how do you come by that?" said Mrs. Main.

"It's from my first name, which I never use anymore," said Beatrice. "Everyone here calls me Belle, Aunt Cayley. I prefer that."

"There are a lot of changes in the last couple of years, aren't there?" said Cayley. "I suppose I'm not as up with the times as I should be."

"Well." Beatrice Belle put down her teacup. "It's been delightful visiting with you. I do have to get back to my dorm for dinner—I promised. Congratulations on your engagement." She spoke with little enthusiasm. "Do enjoy your stay here, and I'll try to drop by again before you leave. When is that?"

"I'm not sure—but only a day or so. I doubt if you'll be able to arrange it, since you're so busy."

"You're right about that! It's a pity. Lovely to see you again, however. Well, we're off. Mrs. Main?" They picked up their hats and coats, applied hatpins, buttoned themselves up and hurried through the door as if caught up in a whirlwind.

"Charming girl," Bill said tartly. "Too bad all she got from her mother was her looks."

Cayley looked disheartened and flopped down on one of the brocade chairs. "Crap. Miss Belle can certainly hold a grudge."

Bill walked over to Cayley and stroked her shoulder. "I'm sorry, Cayley. That wasn't a very good show at all."

"We spoiled her, and now I pay the price. She wants nothing to do with the street garbage that raised her."

"Don't be so hard on yourself. She's not even grateful for the money that keeps her in fine flowered hats and tailored clothes and good schools. Someday, she'll be out on her own, and she'll think twice, believe me." He pulled Cayley up from the chair and gathered her into his arms. She leaned against him, exhausted.

Looking up into his fine-boned face, she said, "You're a good man, Bill Duarte. And thank you for not fainting when I called you my fiancé. I had to explain us being in the same hotel room in a hurry, and even that's a little racy for Miss Belle's social set."

"You're a paragon of sin, Mrs. Wallace."

"Thank you, Mr. Duarte."

***

Cayley and Bill did a little shopping and sightseeing in the city, but left after a few days. Cayley's mood darkened further as the train neared Broad Street Station in Philadelphia. "Let's get off here and at least see what hole our money is going to be poured into," she said. "Besides, I always wanted to see Philadelphia."

They took a trolley from the station into town, and booked rooms at the elegant Bellevue-Stratford Hotel. Bill hired a hack to take them to the campus of the Women's Medical College, where Cayley informed the office personnel that their daughter was about to enter school there and as dutiful parents, they wanted to look around. One of the male secretaries offered to show them the campus, and took them on a tour. Young women in shirtwaists and skirts were rushing about, talking, arms full of books. When they returned to the hotel, Bill commented, "Don't be so downhearted. She'll be happy here. You've got nothing to worry about, Cay."

"Aw, Bill, it isn't that. I thought by seeing the place I'd have something more in common with her, but it didn't work like that. I've got to get used to the fact that she's got a life completely separate and I have no part in it. Nobody in this world really gives a damn whether I live or die."

"What about me?"

"Yeah, what about you? You're great company, Bill, and I love you dearly, but you don't love me so much. Something better comes along and you'll be gone like yesterday's news."

238

"Don't get mad at me because the girl's put on airs."

Cayley sat down on the bed and dropped her elbows to her knees, her hands around the back of her neck.

"You're a good woman, Cayley Wallace." Bill stood in front of her for a few moments, than sat beside her and began to rub her back. "You didn't have to stick by that girl, but you did. You're as loyal as they come, and you're not the kind to back away from an unsavory job to get what you want. You'd make a good wife for a man who works both sides of the law." He placed his hand on her waist. "You want to get married?" he said softly. "We'll get married."

Cayley didn't raise her head. "There's something wrong with my hearing. I thought you just said we'll get married."

"That's what I said. Just because Bean doesn't know what a treasure you are doesn't mean I don't."

Cayley brought her head up, and her eyes were red. She looked at him sternly. "This isn't one of your nasty jokes, is it?"

He laughed. "No. I would like you to be Mrs. Duarte. If you want."

Cayley threw her arms around him. "I want," she said. "I want!"

They got a marriage license at city hall the next day. "Where can we find a justice of the peace?" Cayley asked the clerk. "I don't know how long his bout of insanity will last," she added in a stage whisper. Bill threw his head back with a laugh and shrugged his shoulders at the obviously bored clerk.

"Oh, they don't do weddings here," said the little man, his expression not unlike that of a very tired basset hound. "You have to go out and find a minister. Or if you're Quakers, you can just do your vows yourself. Congratulations. Next."

As they walked out of the courtyard of the building, Cayley said, "Forget the minister. I'm afraid if I wait half an hour more, you'll disappear. I just became a Quaker. I, Cayley, take you Bill, as my lawful wedded husband."

Bill turned toward her. "Cay, are you sure about this? It may not be legal—do you really want to give me such an open door?"

"Couldn't be more sure. Now you say it." She put her arms around his waist. "Say it."

"I, Bill, take you Cayley, as my lawful wedded wife."

"Please kiss the bride. I don't even need a ring to know you really love me."

"Oh, you'll get a ring out of me, if I know anything about you…Mrs. Duarte."

***

On the train back to San Francisco, Bill told her, "If you love me, and you want the best for both of us, you'll keep this marriage quiet for a while; just until after the election. My cronies are a bunch of reform-party men, and it would look mighty bad."

"Of course, sweetheart." Cayley promised, and kept the promise for five months, financing Bill's campaign payoffs. After he was elected, she started her own campaign, and he finally agreed to a church wedding in San Francisco.

Since no Catholic church would welcome a divorced woman, Cayley reserved Episcopal Grace Church, and sent engraved invitations to every customer that ever stepped inside either of her houses—with their wives, of course. "All the big names will be there," she told Bill. "It'll be the perfect opportunity for us to meet them out in the light of day, because they'll all want to congratulate the groom." She planned the reception at the nearby Fairmont Hotel, even though it wasn't quite finished. "It would have been better at Baldwin's, if it hadn't burnt down."

"Aw, Cayley, are you sure this is wise?"

"Well, why not?"

"I just don't want you to be disappointed. The kind of people you're chasing after think more of appearances than you want to believe."

"If you can get elected running a bunch of gambling halls, I can get married, whore or not. San Francisco's a wide-open town. Hell, I know everybody who's anybody."

On the big day, the cathedral was full of invited and uninvited guests. The newspaper, in a rare moment of courtesy and

240

respect, published news about the wedding using Cayley's maiden name.

The reception, however, was a different story. The wedding party moved to the Fairmont, and the still-in-progress hotel dining room was decorated with an abundance of white roses. A staff of 20 servers waited at attention by the dais. As Cayley and Bill took their seats at the table, fewer than 30 guests filtered into the large ballroom. The attendees, mostly Bill's business associates, brought regrets from their wives. The few women who did come appeared confused, as though they expected someone else to be sitting at the wedding table on the raised stage. The staff hurriedly moved tables out of the room and consolidated the guests who did show up—including Cayley's sister Mary, several younger siblings and their mother, all dressed in the fashionable garb Cayley had provided. *They look like paid mourners at a funeral,* she thought. The room seemed vast and empty. Cayley held her head up and moved to the floor for the waltz of the bride and groom. *Who do I think I am, Venus on the half-shell?* She looped the train of her ivory satin gown over her wrist. *As if the social register would suddenly forget what I do for a living.* She smiled at Bill and arched her back as he swung her into a spin. *Screw them all.* After they had shared and served the enormous cake, she quietly told the servers to give the remainder away to whoever wanted it. Much as it stung, she had achieved her purpose, to be the lawful wedded wife to an up-and-coming politician in the City of San Francisco. She may not get respect now, but it was coming. It had to come.

When they returned to the Green St. house, Sam was waiting.

Bill went upstairs to the bedroom to change. "Well Sam, you didn't miss much," Cayley said. "The reception felt like a wake for a leper."

"I'm very sorry it didn't please you, Mrs. Duarte." Sam's face was impassive.

Cayley's eyebrows flew up. "What the hell? What's this Mrs. Duarte stuff? My name's still Cayley."

"As you wish, Cayley."

"Sam, come on. Nothing is going to change, except that Bill has made an honest woman out of me." She laughed richly. "In a manner of speaking."

"It's really none of my business. I'm here to drop off the month's numbers, and I'll be on my way." Sam turned briskly, picked up his homburg from the hall table and shut the door behind him.

Chapter FIFTY-ONE - January 1906

Lilly waited until she heard snoring from the housekeeper's room down the hall. She took out a bundle of Sam's old clothes from her bureau and dressed in them; she braided her hair into a queue. Silently, she slipped into the night, and began the long dark walk down Russian Hill to Chinatown. When she reached the bottom of the hill, among the silent houses not far from the house of Wing Yee, she called out like a dove, and a small figure hobbled toward her. They embraced a long time in silence.

"I almost couldn't get away tonight," said Mei Mei. "Even without nurse Sai hanging around, there are guards everywhere. Father's health is failing, and I don't know what will happen when he dies."

"I'm glad you convinced him that you were too old for a nurse, at least!" said Lilly, kissing the girl on the lips. "Is elder brother still trying to arrange a marriage for you? He'll take over the family."

"They are already fighting among themselves. Elder brother is negotiating to get a better deal on the dowry. His greed is shameful."

"This doesn't surprise me. I worry for you."

"I'll run away when father dies. I have no life here. The husband they have chosen for me is more like a grandfather."

Lilly saw the lamps from the street reflected in the girl's bright eyes. "You can come live with me."

"Your brother would not have it. He is the same as my brothers. Besides," she said wanly, "I'm valuable to them as a prospective bride. I can never be on my own."

Li nodded. They wrapped their arms tightly around each other for warmth and comfort.

"We could live by ourselves, if we had the money," said Mei Mei. "My father has money."

"What are you saying?"

"My father has gold coins in his chests, and many pieces of jade."

243

"Are you saying you would steal this?" Lilly held the girl away from her.

"When he dies, I'll see none of it. It will become the property of my eldest brother. He will sell me to the highest bidder as a wife. Probably not even a first wife."

"You'd make an excellent second wife."

"Lilly!"

"Your grandfather-husband wouldn't bother you much."

"I don't want any husband at all. I want..." she cuddled up against Lilly. "I must do it soon. When father dies, my brothers will tear the house to pieces. I will bring the gold to you. And then we can run away."

Lilly stroked the younger girl's head. "And where will we run?"

"I don't know. But you'll know, when the time comes. Maybe we can disappear into the ground and wait for the next dream."

They made their way to a curb surrounded by scruffy bushes and sat. Lilly held the girl and gazed into the smoky dark bay. "I cannot live without you," she said. "But this is dangerous talk. They can kill us. It's not a fairy tale."

"I want to show you something." Mei Mei reached down, removed her shoe, and began unwrapping the bindings.

Lilly put her hand over the other girl's. "Wait! I don't understand. What are you doing?"

Mei put her head on the other girl's shoulder. She continued to undo the wrappings; the bindings fell like a long white peel on the ground until her foot was exposed, bent in two, like the root of an exotic flower. Lilly touched the foot tentatively with her fingers, exploring the tiny misshapen toes.

"You are the husband I choose," said Mei Mei. "Now do you understand?"

Lilly looked at her from beneath her lashes. "It's wrong to feel this way about another girl."

"I don't care if it's wrong. I want to be with you. I want to go to the markets with you, and live every day with you. I want to feel you next to me in bed."

Lilly pulled her hands away from the girl and wrapped them around her own waist. "It's wrong to think such things!"

Mei Mei's face crumpled. "If you don't want to be with me..."

Lilly quickly put her arms around the girl and held her close, "No, that's not it at all." She kissed the girl's hair, her forehead, cheek and lips. The heat rose from between her legs. "You're so young," she whispered.

"You are my life," replied Mei Mei, in the same low voice. "Without you, there is no reason to breathe." She held Lilly's face between her hands. "If you love me, you can save my life. Is that wrong?"

***

The next week, a sack of coins and jade bumped against Mei Mei's leg when she hobbled from her house to their meeting place. Lilly carried Mei on her back through the darkened alleys of Little China. The main thoroughfares were hung with red silk lanterns and strings of firecrackers for the upcoming Chinese New Year. The girls climbed slowly up the hill, resting frequently until they arrived at the Green Street house. They slept together in Lilly's narrow bed and woke at dawn the next morning, shy with each other in the morning light. Mei covered Lilly's face with soft kisses, and their shyness turned to touching. "There," whispered Lilly, as Mei Mei explored her body with her mouth and fingertips. "And there." She never imagined such pleasure existed. She stopped the other girl and began her own explorations, moving the palm of her hand over the younger girl's firm breasts, belly, and thighs, thrilled at Mei's undulating movements and the soft sighs that escaped from her mouth. When they heard Sam come in from his duties at the O'Farrell Street house downstairs, Lilly reluctantly drew herself away from her partner after several kisses, and told her to wait. She put on a wrap, went downstairs, and told him who was in her room.

"Are you crazy? They'll kill us all!" The white of his eyes showed in fear. "They'll think we kidnapped her."

"Only if they find us, and they haven't found us yet."

Sam began to pace frantically across the parlor floor. "We have to tell Cayley."

Lilly grasped the elbow of his jacket. "She'll help us."

"She's not an idiot."

"No, but she's friends with the white police, and because of her, they'll protect us."

Sam looked at his sister as if she had lost her mind. "You think you've got this all figured out, don't you? You have no idea who you're dealing with!"

She looked up at her brother. "You've just given me an idea."

Sam placed both hands on his forehead as if to keep it from exploding. "*Ai yah*!"

"Listen, just listen. Mei Mei says her brothers are already tearing the house apart looking for their father's treasure, which of course we have. Her father is dying, or is already dead."

"A fine filial family."

"What if we—we would use a made-up name—claim to kidnap her and demand a ransom. One of two things would happen—they come up with the money and want her back, or they don't, and wash their hands of the whole thing. Since we have the money, the odds are in our favor, are they not, brother?"

"Wouldn't they want her for her value?"

"I think she is of little importance to them right now. Don't forget, they're also battling for control of the tong. And they're looking for the money."

Sam stopped pacing and turned toward his sister. "Couldn't we just send her back?"

Lilly looked at him indignantly. "She's staying here. With me." She pulled her long hair behind her and wove it behind her head. "I love her. And she loves me."

Sam's jaw dropped. "Where did you get such a stupid Western notion? Love has nothing to do with anything."

246

"Love has kept you around Cayley all this time!"

He turned away from her. "You don't know what you're saying."

"Yes, I do. We could have left for China a long time ago, but when she returned from New York married to that Bill, you gambled away all the money. Don't you think I have eyes?"

Sam leaned his palms against the back of the loveseat and hung his head. "That has nothing to do with our present problem little sister." He turned toward her. "What if we use your plan and they pay for her—what then?"

"Then we pretend to kill her. We'll take on a new name. We'll become a new family, and move to another town."

"There IS no other town! She'll never be able to show her face in Little China again. How can you spit on our ancestors; dishonor our father's name? How can you be anyone other than Wo Li?"

"Look, that only matters if you want to go back to China. I want to stay here, and I'll make up a new name. I like Lilly Long. It sounds like an American stage actress."

"I thought you wanted to be with Chinese people. Now you want to be an American."

"I want to be both. Look at what Cayley can do here, all the freedom she has."

"That's different. She's a...a prostitute. A white prostitute in a white city."

"So! She's a rich prostitute! And when she wants to go somewhere, she does! She doesn't have to wait for permission."

"So you won't go home to China. Even if you bring that girl with you."

Lilly shook her head no, smiled at her brother, and put her hand on his shoulder. "Maybe you should forget about China." She paused and turned half away from him, facing the wall. "It's not like you remember. Our floor was dirt, and we were lucky to get one egg a day and enough rice to eat. The war took everything, even the few clothes we had—they would have taken our chickens, too, if I didn't hide them in a pit. They found them eventually. The famine was terrible. Even as a prisoner, I ate

247

more here. The only thing I regret is that our father is dead—but with the new American laws, we could not bring him, anyway. What we had is gone." She turned toward him and said gently, "This dream you have of going home a rich man and marrying well, a girl with tiny feet like Mei Mei," she shook her head, "It's all gone, brother. In rags, like everything else."

Sam sat, head bowed. Then he stood up and got a glass of water from the pump bucket and drank it down.

Lilly clasped her hands together as if in prayer. "You're still afraid of the Wing Yee tong."

"Yes."

"If I could find a way to make them back off you, would you think about settling here?"

"Impossible."

"Which, shaking the tong or staying here?"

"Getting rid of Wing Yee."

"I just haven't put my mind to it yet." Their conversation was interrupted by the sound of the front door. Bill and Cayley walked in and shook off the cold. They were arguing. Lilly and Sam looked at each other. "I'll go," she said.

Chapter FIFTY-TWO

"Mr. and Mrs. Duarte. May I get you anything?" Lilly spoke from the doorway to the sitting room.

Cayley looked cross, arms folded against her chest. "I'll take a whiskey."

"Of course you'll take a whiskey," said Bill. "When wouldn't you?"

Cayley looked at him with vitriol. "I might take tea if I had better company."

"Look, I've got a lot of places I have to be. Let's not get into that again."

"I feel like my money's flying away without me; this campaign and that pay-off. Why don't you take me anyplace like you used to? Are you ashamed of me?" Cayley wrapped her arms around herself.

"I'll get that whiskey," said Lilly. "Mr. Duarte?" He shook his head no.

Lilly went to the bar and poured a glass. The two kept silent until she had brought the drink and was already on her way to the kitchen.

"I want to go the Greenway Ball." Cayley downed a mouthful from her glass.

"Jesus, Cayley, pick something easy, why don't you. You know that's the big society event." Bill peeled off his soft black leather gloves and held them in one hand.

"You're going, aren't you?"

"Strictly business."

"My foot! You'll be all over those society women, drooling and flattering."

"I told you, it's business. I have to cozy up to people in power, and you know it. Those women are all shriveled prunes, anyway—I come home to a nice juicy pineapple."

"Well, this pineapple wants to go to the Greenway Ball."

Bill put his head in his hands while Cayley downed the whiskey in a couple of gulps and headed for the bar for a refill. "Cayley," he wailed. "Be reasonable."

She whirled around and almost spilled the remains of the drink on her pink silk evening dress. "I'm reasonable when I give you an open bank account to go about your business, but not when I ask for what most wives take for granted." She raised the glass in a toast to him "How about it...Lord and Master?"

Sam appeared in the doorway. "Cayley? May I speak to you a moment? It's important."

"Christ, what now?" She put her glass down on the bar. "You can speak in front of Bill. You know that."

Sam acknowledged Bill with an embarrassed nod. "My sister has done something foolish. She has agreed to house a runaway girl from the home of Wing Yee."

Cayley leaned her back against the bar and squinted one eye. "That name sounds familiar. Isn't that where...?"

"Yes. The family we have had difficulties with in the past. Apparently, she made friends with this girl. What is worse, the girl has stolen a large sum of money from the house." Sam put his hand briefly over his eyes. "She is here, in Wo Li's quarters."

"Oh wonderful." Cayley looked at Bill.

Lilly stepped into the parlor from the hallway. "I have a plan, Mrs. Wallace. Please listen." She recounted her ideas.

"You're putting your brother in a hell of a bind, Lilly. I don't like that." She looked at Sam, his miserable expression hadn't changed.

"The house of Wing Yee is collapsing. Mei has brought most of their fortune with her. There might be a way to buy Sam's freedom from their vengeance using their own money." Lilly put her hands together. "Please, Mrs. Duarte."

"Buy them off? If money would do it, I could do it myself without risking your necks." Cayley looked skeptical.

"Mei Mei's absence will only add to their troubles, making them weaker. It is to our advantage to keep her here. Please, Mrs. Duarte; you rescued me from a terrible situation, and now you

250

could do it for another Chinese girl who would be forced into marriage."

Cayley looked to Bill. "You're the do-gooder," he said. "It has a nice twist to it. Especially if I don't have to pay for it."

"All right. She can stay. Find out what's up with Wing Yee. If you can get Sam off the hook, it'll be worth it. But if this girl is more trouble than she's worth, she goes. Understand?" Cayley reached around behind her for her glass.

Chapter FIFTY-THREE

Bill told the coachman to pull over at the entrance of the garden court and asked him to wait, just a moment, as other revelers trotted past to the main entrance of the Palace. Polished brass harness tracings gleamed in the bright electric lights—the Palace hotel was the biggest place in town to have a state-of-the-art lighting system. Cayley watched from behind the carriage curtain as one fancy trap after another arrived. Ladies were helped down from the carriage steps, gracefully pulling aside their skirts and adjusting their bustles behind them. The gowns were spangled with sewn sequins, bits of lace, pearls and rhinestones, and the ladies carried fans of ostrich feathers, painted silk and lace. Everyone, men and women alike, wore masks decorated with feathers and jewels. The ball started at 8 o'clock, and nearly everyone arrived fashionably late, after 9 p.m., including Cayley and Bill. He left the carriage for a few minutes, then returned and led her, not in the main entrance as she expected, but up a series of stairs to the side until they were about to enter a balcony overlooking the ballroom.

The lights went out; then flickered back on again as Cayley and Bill entered the balcony. Cayley caught wisps of conversation about the reliability of the newfangled electronics. Gradually, through whispers and glances, nearly everyone on the main floor took notice of the couple standing in the balcony. "Isn't that Cayley Wallace, the Madam?" she heard someone say. "And her husband, Bill Duarte, the poor man, tricked into marrying her by some device. Surely she didn't claim to be pregnant!" Cayley held her anger in check and kept her face forward like a queen surveying her realm.

The ballroom below was decorated in gold and cream. The balconies were hung with garlands of pine and laurel, dotted with gold and cream silk roses wound with satin ribbons. Below, the celebrants began to drift to the buffet tables laden with meat and drink, greeting each other with kisses on both cheeks as if they hadn't seen each other the day before at the Widows and

Orphans Committee meeting or in Golden Gate Park on a Sunday drive.

After a few moments, Bill patted Cayley on the shoulder. "Don't move, I'll be right back," he said, and left her to go downstairs. She watched as he entered the ballroom below, heartily pounded the backs of several men and kissed the hands of their wives in a manner most continental. No one looked up to her on the balcony. *Should I go down there,* she thought. *No, Bill must have some reason for this—a grand entrance or something. I'll wait a few more minutes.* Cayley's confusion and fury increased by the minute; after nearly an hour, Bill returned to her side and held his finger to his lips in a signal for silence. At 10:15, the lights dimmed once again, and Bill ushered her down the stairs and back to their carriage.

"You could at least have danced with me," Cayley said. Her flushed face burned in the darkness of the compartment as it rocked over the rough street.

"I took you, didn't I? Are you never satisfied, woman?"

"I'd be satisfied if my own husband treated me with respect. How could you do that to me?"

He pulled the carriage over to the side of the street and put the reins down. "I'm sorry if I handled it badly. I really needed to talk to those people, and let's face it, you're a distraction: a beautiful, famous distraction. You saw how everyone looked up to the balcony when we made our appearance. If you came down to the floor everyone in the place would have been looking at you, and not listening to me. Next year, we'll do it differently. All right?"

"Don't think I'll fall for that."

The next day, the society page dutifully reported the presence of Mrs. This and Mrs. That, but no mention of Mrs. William Duarte. Cayley took out a large advertisement space in the next day's paper: "Lost, one large diamond brooch, in the Palace on the night of the Greenway Ball. Reward. Please contact Mrs. William Duarte, etc."

Chapter FIFTY-FOUR

Mei Mei had been in the Green Street house twelve days; a week had passed since the Greenway Ball. Lilly and Cayley were setting up for the evening in the main O'Farrell house when Sam came in and made an announcement: "I have decided that Mei Mei should be my bride."

Both of the women looked at him in amazement. Cayley had been leaning over the table arranging flowers on the buffet. She straightened up and looked at Lilly across the room. "What brought this on, Sam," she said.

"It is time for me to marry. She's an acceptable wife for me."

"I'm not sure that's such a good idea, Sam." Cayley looked uncomfortably over at Lilly.

"Why not? I'm sure she would be glad to truly be part of our family." Sam was sweating, and he held his face stiffly. This was a difficult decision for him, and he had reasoned it out thoroughly. It really was his only option.

"Lilly, perhaps you two need to talk." Cayley nodded toward the office.

Lilly led the way in, and turned around. She fussed with her hair and avoided his eyes. "This is embarrassing."

Sam said nothing.

"You know that Mei Mei and I are very close."

"Like sisters. That's why this would be the right thing to do."

"More than sisters, Sam. We're more like—married. To each other."

Sam's face betrayed nothing, but the muscles in his jaw worked.

"We're both your sisters, you see? Please don't be upset. Don't be disappointed. Please." She moved toward him and put her hands on his arms. "You are very dear to both of us."

Sam stepped back and her arms dropped to her sides. He turned around and walked out of the office into Cayley's anxious gaze.

"Oh for God's sake, Sam," Cayley told him. "Some of the girls in the house are like that. Men do it too."

"I'm aware of that, Mrs. Duarte," said Sam, evenly. "I'm also aware that marriage is a sacred duty, though my sister does not seem to think so."

"Anywhere you can get love in this world, Sam, you just got to go after it." He walked past her without another word. "Don't go all formal on me. Sam…" she said to his retreating back. Cayley rolled an idea around in her mind: maybe there was a way to get him together with one of Donaldina Cameron's adopted "daughters." They were the only eligible women in Chinatown, regardless of their pasts. *He's a smart, sweet, good man—even though he's a little strait-laced—and he deserves someone who can love him,* she thought as she turned to other tasks at hand. *Toy might be good—but he'd never go for somebody still in the business. Too bad he's Chinese. A lot of women would go for a good solid fellow like him.*

Chapter FIFTY-FIVE
April 1906

"Well, what did you and the girls think of the great Caruso?" asked Bill. He was sitting at the bar in the O'Farrell house, his hat and overcoat in his lap.

"He sings like an angel. You should have come," replied Cayley.

"You know I hate that screeching. The Tivoli—that's the place for me."

"But it's a real event—him coming here puts San Francisco on the map. Besides, your hoity-toity friends were all there. Where are you off to, tonight?" She hoisted herself up backward onto one of the stools at the bar and signaled for a whiskey.

"I'll make the circuit of the gambling clubs. Do some of the cash-and-carry, so that nobody is overloaded—the usual. I'll see you at home in the morning. Expecting a busy evening?"

"It always is after we display ourselves at the opera. That combination of screeching and low-cut Paris gowns gets 'em horny as horses in stud."

Bill laughed. "Those friends of mine could certainly take a lesson or two on business from you, Cay."

"I'll open a school. What do you think? Me as a teacher of proper salesmanship."

She raised her chin and made as if she held a pointer to a blackboard. "Of course, we'll have demonstrations of various positions. Bring in a dog or two. They like their dogs."

Bill shook his head, put an arm around her neck and kissed her on the cheek. Then he turned on his heel and was out the door.

***

The main O'Farrell house was packed to the rafters around midnight, but many of the guests had left by 2 o'clock. The ones who remained were too sodden or lazy to make it home. Sam snoozed behind the folding screen at the door, ready to jump up should anyone need a carriage from the livery on the corner. Cayley escorted one of her guests to the front door, arm in arm.

"You, Chinaman! My carriage and make it quick!" he slurred. Sam appeared from behind the screen, and his face reddened. He didn't move.

Cayley reached up on her tiptoes and tapped her closed fan on the right side of the man's neck; she whispered loudly into his left ear, "Isn't it embarrassing when you forget a man's name? It's Mr. Wo, silly. I know you'll remember that from now on." She nipped his ear. He wobbled and she placed his hand on the side table to keep him upright. Her eyes met Sam's; she flicked open her fan and backed away, saying, "Excuse me, gentlemen. My other guests."

An hour later, the house became quiet. Cayley waltzed up to Sam. "I'm dead on my feet and dizzy from too much champagne and not enough food. I have to lie down a while upstairs before I head home. What about you?"

"I'll stay down here and wait for Lilly. It's a strange night. The last time I went for a carriage, the liveryman said, 'These nags have been kicking up a fuss all night—you'd think a wolf be on the prowl.'" Sam imitated the liveryman's Irish country accent perfectly, and made her laugh.

"You look pretty restless yourself." Cayley began to unpin her hair. "You worried about your sister?"

Earlier that night, Lilly had gone to Little China to buy Sam's freedom from the Wing Yee tong. Their desire for revenge for the death of their son was negotiable in light of their sudden poverty. They agreed to Sam's "offering."

Their "kidnapping" scheme had appeared to work. It had been more than a month since Mei Mei's brother refused to pay the price for her return; Lilly sent a pair of Mei Mei's slippers, stained with some of her monthly blood, and hoped that was the end of it. With any luck, they would believe her dead or sold as a slave. The two girls had taken lodgings on Telegraph Hill, and Mei's money supported them amply. Since neither Sam nor Mei were able to show their faces in front of Wing Yee tong members, Lilly volunteered to go to Little China in her boyish disguise to deliver the money to an intermediary.

"I should have gone myself. She saw it as a kind of revenge against them, but it's foolish. Lilly is sure they won't recognize her, since no other members of the family have laid eyes on her before—but what if that nurse is there? Or if one of the tong soldiers recognizes her? Yes, I worry. No one should suffer for my mistakes, least of all my sister."

Cayley brought her arms down and laid a handful of pins on the table that had supported her guest earlier. Her hair, loose in back, cascaded in a river of yellow-white curls down her back. She put her hand on his arm, and he didn't pull away. "She'll be all right. We have to believe that." She squeezed his arm, and the starch went out of his posture for a moment. "You're a good man, Wo Sam. Mistakes and all." She dropped her hand, and they stood for a moment, heads nearly touching. In a voice barely above a whisper she said, "Sam? You've always been good to me. Loyal, kind, helpful. Treated me with respect. Affection, even. Is it just because I pay you?"

With a sharp intake of breath, Sam looked straight ahead. "No."

Cayley gave a brief nod, turned and went up to the second-floor apartment. Lilly—and her brother—were on her mind, even as the house settled into a quiet, low-lit serenity.

***

A little after 5 a.m., Cayley was dreaming of goldfish eating out of her hand. The goldfish began to make a peculiar sound, like the roar of an oncoming train. Seconds later, her body slammed against the wall, and rolled onto the carpet. The room bucked like a wild horse, and the bed banged on the floor like a giant hammer—she could hear it, but she couldn't see it. *This is not a nightmare.* Dust and plaster chips rained down from the ceiling, and the air quickly became so thick she started to cough. The bed moved toward her like a beast intent on smashing her into pulp, and she tried to push it away. *Why won't this stop?* Suddenly, it did. As she started to rise, the shaking began again.

258

An enormous crash was followed by repeated waves of breaking glass. *The chandelier. The ballroom mirrors. My God, an earthquake! A big one.* And behind it all, the roar. She struggled to get onto her hands and knees, to get away from the bed, but it was worse than the worst drunk she had ever had—all her strength drained away. It was like trying to hold the reins of a runaway carriage; all she could do was hang on. The marble busts from Italy jumped off the tables like they had springs under them, bouncing and chipping across the floor, providing another hazard. One of her Napoleon busts hit her in the side of the face, knocking her backwards. *Why won't it stop?*

Then, it was over. An erie silence fell over the house. The black air was thick with dust, still rising from the walls; a piece of the ceiling rosette fell onto the bed and hit the floor with a clatter. The wailing began. It rose, an unholy symphony, from rooms up the stairs to the left and right of her. She struggled to her feet, winded. Her jaw hurt, and she touched it with her fingertips. She felt around for her dressing gown, gave up, and made her way to the door. The house started to shake again, and Cayley was knocked to her feet. It sounded as if the walls were exploding: nails shrieked as they pulled out of wood, pipes severed with a hollow metallic clang. Then silence. Cayley pulled herself up on the doorjamb. Several of the girls and a few clients were staggering down from the third-floor rooms. Cayley saw that the rail of the stairs leading to the lower floor was missing. She held a hand up, and tried to say "Be careful," but it came out garbled because she couldn't open her mouth very wide. She waved her hand in the air, hoping they would see it in the dusty gloom. The wailing turned into words. "Help me! Somebody, help!"

Cayley pulled herself up the stairs and felt along the wall until she came to an open doorway. Gas hissed out of the unlit vents. *That has to be turned off. How do I turn that off?* She moved toward the sound, felt around, and touched the wet face of one of her girls. "It's on top of my leg," she said. Cayley felt down the girl's body. Part of the wall had come down on the girl. A warped shout escaped Cayley's throat, "Hey! Anybody!" Another woman joined her from the hallway. "I'll try to lift, you pull her out," Cayley tried to say. The other woman understood, and together, they got the girl free. Moving her was a different story. Someone in the hallway had found a candle, and held it in the doorway. "We've got to get out of here," he said. He was wearing long-johns, and his hair stuck up in points. Cayley knew him, but his name was lost in the rubble.

"Stairs," she said. "Gas off." He looked at her, puzzled. She gave up, and she and the other woman dragged the injured girl to the doorway. Others were already making their way, staggering like drunks down the side of the staircase that looked more solid. It creaked with every step. The groans coming from a room a few doors on the other side of the balcony had grown fainter. She took the elbow of the man with the candle as he started down the stairs and tugged at him to go in that direction, but he jerked his elbow away and continued down the staircase. She turned to go herself.

Cayley stumbled over debris—oil paintings and broken glass, overturned tables with shattered marble tops, water from broken vases and the slimy stems of flowers. She listened at the first doorway. Silence. She called out, "Where are you?" and heard a groaning response from up the hall. Cayley stumbled forward, calling out for help over her shoulder. One of the girls turned from the stairs and followed Cayley up the broken passage. The room the sound was coming from was a shambles, illuminated by faint moonlight from where a portion of the wall had broken away. Cayley saw a pale leg sticking out from under a pile of rubble, and began to move away pieces. The other woman helped her, until Cayley bent down and put her hand around the ankle, "She's gone," Cayley mumbled. Another groan came from the rubble in front of them, and the two women piled pieces of plaster and torn bedclothes behind them as fast as they could. Another piece of the wall gave way, and the whole house shook again. Cayley and the other woman froze, both gasping in terror. As soon at the building stopped swaying, they started again. They uncovered a hand, poised as if to summon them into the pile. "It's Poppy," said the other woman, and shook her head. They continued to dig, but came across the rafter from the ceiling, which they were unable to lift together. The other woman reached down and tested Poppy's pulse. "It's barely there," she looked up at Cayley. The wall across from them fell away with a whisper, followed by billowing clouds of dust. The beam they had tried to lift followed the wall down, and both women jumped back. Where the pile of wood and mortar lay was now nothing but a cloud of luminous dust. They edged out the door, and hurried down the hall clinging to the walls. They held hands, going single file down the remaining stairs to the floor below. It was covered with shattered crystal, and Cayley cut her feet. "Where's Sam?" she called out. Women and men were rushing about the lower floor in chaos. "Stop!" she said. "Where's Sam?" All movement stopped.

"We've got to get outside," someone said.

"Union Square," said another voice. "Carry what you can." One or two women were laughing hysterically, or perhaps they were crying. Someone was reciting, "Hail Mary, full of grace, the Lord is with thee."

"Go," Cayley said. "Does anybody know where the gas mains are for this building?"

"I turned them off, Cay."

"Sam! Thank goodness you're here! Are you all right?"

He held a candle up to her. "What happened to your face?"

Cayley shrugged. "Napoleon slugged me." She laughed oddly. "We should get out of here. I need to check on the other house. And home. I hope your sister and everyone else is all right." she looked toward the shattered stairs. "We lost Poppy. And...others. I don't know who."

"My sister..." he said. "I must try to find her."

"Of course."

She pulled his ear to her face and whispered, "We need to get the safe from the office. Take the money and wrap it in the piano shawl. Then put it in one of the birdcages." Cayley thought about going upstairs and getting the dress and hat she had worn to the opera that night—they were new, and absolutely stunning.

261

"Idiot," she said out loud, and contented herself with looking for her evening cloak in the closet downstairs. Sam came up beside her with the birdcage in both hands, and they headed out the door.

"I was outside—couldn't sleep," Sam said. "I've seen these things before, but nothing like this." He looked straight ahead, and spoke in a rush. "There was a sound like the roar of the ocean, and I looked up O'Farrell Street. The whole street was moving in waves. The buildings looked like they were dancing. Like crooked teeth in a mouth. The church bells were all ringing."

"Maybe it's judgment day," said Cayley. They moved along the street, surrounded by hundreds of others in various states of dress and undress. A pink dawn, nearly obscured by rising dust, made the surroundings even more surreal. One woman sat on the curb and toyed with a pair of shoes. Several people had wagons or wheeled carts loaded with plates, silver knives and forks, luggage, lamps, pictures—all manner of precious, worthless objects. The people they saw were talking in low, monotonous tones, babbling, trying to make sense of what had just happened. Bricks and masonry continued to fall on the sidewalk. Calls for help came from various buildings, largely ignored by the passersby but for a few good Samaritans that tried to move rubble much too large for one or two people. Cayley stopped to help one woman who pleaded with them to find her children. Sam set down the birdcage, but kept an eye on it while the three of them leveraged a piece of wall. A table with one crushed leg hid two small children who huddled under it. The mother cried with relief and threw her arms around her young ones. Cayley and Sam continued up the street to the other bordello on O'Farrell that Cayley had opened: The Golden Door.

The chimneys had caved in, and the place was deserted, but the building was more intact than the main house. "You'll come with me to Union Square?" she asked him.

"Yes, then I must go on."

Cayley nodded, then put her head on his shoulder. "Thank you for staying with me this long."

"I wouldn't leave you," he said, and looked away.

In front of them, two men carried a large painting of a nude out of a building, and a woman in a nightgown carried a baby upside down by its legs.

Union Square was rapidly filling up with all manner of refugees. Several of Cayley's girls were there, and she sat near them. Sam handed her the birdcage, nodded his goodbye, and ran north in the direction of Chinatown. The injured girl had been carried to the square on a tablecloth by two of the girls and one of the clients. She was pale and moaned miserably. Cayley looked around for some kind of medical help, and saw the St. Francis Hotel was still open. She dashed across Powell Street, but once inside was told the house doctor was already in the square, treating as many as he could. On her way out, she passed the restaurant, where, as if in a freakish dream, she saw Enrico Caruso sitting down to an enormous breakfast of several eggs, a mound of bacon, and toast.

The smoke from the first fires spiraled above Market Street a few blocks to the south. "The fire department will handle it," she reassured the girls. "We've got the best one anywhere, and the best pumpers too." As the minutes wore on, the smoke became giant licking flames, and the crowd grew more silent.

"Why aren't they stopping those fires?" a woman nearby asked.

Another man, whose face was a vacant as the buildings surrounding the square stared straight ahead and said, "There's no water. The mains is broke, I'll bet." He rubbed furiously at the side of his face. "I hear a wall fell on Sullivan."

"The Fire Chief?" Cayley said.

The man didn't answer her.

It was difficult to tell how much time had passed. Small tremors rippled through the ground, some a few minutes apart, others longer. The fire spread rapidly, its progress marked by a pall of thick black smoke. It was moving toward the slot, Market Street, only a few blocks from Union Square. To the east, the fire seemed to curve around—it had crossed the slot and was now burning in the produce market by the Ferry building.

"We've got to get out of here," said Cayley. "We've got to get to higher ground to see what's going on."

One of the girls protested, then another. All their belongings were still in the O'Farrell houses.

"It's still shaking, and now we've got the fire to worry about. You know how this city can burn," said Cayley. "I won't stop you, but it's a fool who'll trade her life for a few trinkets."

"It's all I got," said one. "And I worked hard for it, too." A few of the other girls nodded.

"I locked up," she said. She handed a set of keys to the girl who spoke. "Those who are coming with me, let's go. Who's going to help me with Selma here?" She indicated the girl on the makeshift stretcher. "And somebody help me carry this damn birdcage."

They joined a great migration coming up from south of the slot—people carrying bathtubs, rugs, furniture, bedding. The babble and blankness had been replaced by terror verging on panic. *Oh Lord, what will happen if people give in to the worst side of themselves?* Cayley led the way up Powell to the top of Nob Hill, her arms around the heavy birdcage. They passed a horse that looked alive, but was buried to the neck in rubble, its eyes dull. The few girls remaining with her struggled to carry the injured girl in the sling.

"They won't let this burn down," Cayley said, nodding toward the mansions of Huntington, Crocker, and other showplaces on the hill. The women, covered with frozen sweat, shivered in their dirt-stained bedclothes. With the other survivors, they turned and watched the insatiable fire leap from building to building on the north side of Market Street up toward the financial district and the piers.

Chapter FIFTY-SIX

Sam zigzagged on Post, Stockton and Bush to Dupont and hurried up the main street into Little China. He had no idea where to find his sister, only the strong feeling that because of his weakness she was in danger once again. He vowed to find her, dead or alive. The city-within-a-city was filled with people milling about with belongings on their backs. Crib girls and workers, children and soldiers pushed against one another on the narrow streets. Many buildings were damaged; domes had collapsed and roof tiles had fallen onto the ground, sliding dangerously beneath the feet of the jostling crowd. He headed for Portsmouth Square. As he turned down Clay Street, the crowd surged back against him. They were backing away from a huge tawny bull, blood-stained and bawling in fear and pain. People parted before the terrified animal in panic. A man threw a machete at the beast and it clove deep into the bull's side with a great gush of blood. The animal staggered; Sam ran beyond him to Washington Street, pushed past the deserted telephone exchange to the park. The encounter with the bull was a mystical experience; Sam's mind reeled: *The world is supported on the backs of four bulls, and one of them is dying; that's why the world is shaking apart.* Sam stopped running and bent over, catching his breath and easing the sharp stitch in his side. He heard a pistol firing and looked across the park, where a uniformed policeman had shot down the still-staggering bull.

Chapter FIFTY-SEVEN

From the top of Nob Hill, Cayley could hear the explosions from the city below. "They're dynamiting buildings so the fire won't jump," she explained. "I used to be married to a fireman. I'm sure he's down there now, doing his best." A wave of emotion rushed over her, memories of the life she once had, a home, a baby. Then she remembered she had a husband now, and wondered where he was. If he was down on the Barbary Coast in one of his gambling places and had managed to stay out of the way of a falling building, he was probably all right. It was still far from the fire at this point. *Bill is a survivor, if he's anything at all. He's all right. I know he's all right.*

"They's got doctors in the hotel there," said a man passing by when he saw the girl on the makeshift stretcher.

"Thanks friend," said Cayley.

He tipped his hat, like a gentleman.

Cayley and two girls struggled with the injured woman on the tablecloth, finally getting her into the main lobby of the Fairmont. Desperate, disheveled people milled in the pillared great room. "Some of the hospitals have collapsed," said a weary man who came up to them. "There's nowhere to take her. I can bandage her, but that's about it."

"I'd be grateful," said Cayley.

"You might as well leave her here, then," said the man, indicating the ballroom. "I'll get to her as soon as I can." Cayley opened the white carved door, and a stench assaulted her nostrils. The floor was filled with people: bleeding, dying, dead in their own excrement. They set Selma down; she was very pale and appeared to be asleep, though she was still breathing. Cayley put her hands in front of her own broken face, and willed herself not to cry. Her jaw was very tender, but the swelling had gone down a little. The other girls who were still with her were in various states of exhaustion. All were still in their underwear, torn and smudged with dirt and blood. The contrast between the elegant red plush surroundings, gold-trimmed mirrors and chandeliers of

266

the hotel and the shocked mob that shuffled about the corridors would have been funny, if only.

"We'll walk to my house," she said to the girls. "It's not far. God willing, it's still standing. My husband might be there."

"I can't go any farther," said one of her followers.

"And I can't argue with you," said Cayley. "Stay here with Selma and keep an eye on her."

They crossed Nob Hill into the valley and climbed Russian Hill to Green Street. Smoke flowed and eddied everywhere, low over the city like a black storm; the air was thick and hard to breathe. Time seemed to slow down; it was hard to tell if it was day or night. On top of Russian Hill, they turned and looked out. From Gough Street and Golden Gate to the west all the way to the bay, and from Townsend below the slot north almost to the border of Chinatown—the most heavily populated area of San Francisco—a wind-whipped holocaust flared against billowing smoke. Fire bells rang everywhere, and the sudden sharp crack of dynamite rose above the roar of the fire. A group of soldiers from the Presidio passed them, heading downtown. Cayley and her companions continued to her house, which appeared little touched by the quake except for a few items off the walls and shattered china. She passed the wide-eyed cook cowering on the lowest of the stairs. "Manuela?" The woman woke out of her trance at the sound of Cayley's voice. "Why don't you lie down?" Cayley helped the woman to the divan in the living room, then went to the cupboard, opened two jars of peaches, and gave them to the girls to eat with silver spoons.

"It's like eating sunlight," one of them said as she hungrily scooped the velvety fruit into her mouth. Her eyes focused somewhere in the distance.

Chapter FIFTY-EIGHT

Sam searched frantically around Portsmouth Square with no luck. The streets were beginning to fill with armed soldiers and worse, with armed civilians. He tried to make his way back to Union Square, but the fire was already moving toward him. As he passed a haberdasher's shop on Kearny, a tailor Cayley sometimes used emerged with his arms full of clothing and a sewing machine. A soldier ran up to him and demanded that he stop. The man panicked and ran, and the soldier dropped him with a single shot. "Looters are to be shot on sight!" shouted the soldier as he looked in Sam's direction. Sam turned and walked back toward Chinatown, careful not to run. Once again, he shouldered his way to Portsmouth Square. It was now laid with dozens of bodies covered with sheets, and police surrounded what looked to be a group of prisoners from the nearby hall of justice. The prisoners were ordered to dig and fill the shallow, unmarked graves.

Sam began zigzagging in the streets and alleys of Chinatown. He called his sister's name, but the din swallowed his voice. At the corner of Clay and Kearney Streets, Sam saw a group of soldiers emptying a tin of black powder on the floor of the drugstore. They warned passersby to stand clear, and detonated the powder. It exploded with such force that the floor above the drugstore sent flaming bedding across the street. It settled on the roof of a building that had escaped the fire until then. Within a minute, the roof exploded into a gigantic curtain of yellow flames.

Chapter FIFTY-NINE

Cayley and the others slept a little as the day wore on, and drank as much of the liquid from other preserves as they could find. "You know what I can't stop thinking about," she told them. "That damned fancy fireplace in the Golden Door. I paid a fortune for that, all the way from Paris, France. It's probably melted to ingots right now."

"Maybe not. Maybe the fire missed the house. I hope so," said Spanish Sally. "I'm thinking about a few things I'm going to miss myself."

"Let's see what we can get out of there. Thomas Shane was still in his livery when we passed by," said Cayley. "I'm going to find out what he'll change me for a cart and two men. I'll be cursed if I'll let this God-damn shake-up and fire knock me down for the count. I want my bed, too! Who's going with me?"

"I will," said Sally. "Let's get a look at the real action!"

"That's my girl," said Cayley.

Thomas wanted a shameful amount of money, five times his normal fee; Cayley chastised him for his greed, though she knew it was merely birdseed in her golden cage. And it would be worth it, IF the fire hadn't taken the houses yet. It was a gamble. Since Bill hadn't come home, he might have gone down to the houses, and she'd find him there. Cayley and Sally rode in the back of the buckboard with Thomas and his boy driving against the crowd into town. The houses looked much as they had left them, though the fire had already passed City Hall and moved relentlessly toward them. Cayley pushed down thoughts of the bodies that still lay upstairs under the rubble. This had to be done. The dust had settled. It was surprisingly easy to see, thanks to the buildings that blazed a few blocks away. They got belongings and Cayley's Napoleon bed minus the mattress out of the O'Farrell house. The bed tore half the lower staircase out of the wall as they pushed it down to the first floor. Cayley took the fact that it held together on the way down as a good sign. They were able to pry off the gold-plated mantle from the fireplace at the Golden Door. The city police, rather than the army or the volunteers, patrolled the area and recognized Cayley at once, sparing her the fate of looters who were still being shot without question. The foursome, with Cayley and Sally perched precariously on the bed, clattered back toward the hill, away from the main part of the fire. It was evening—roughly 14 hours since the first 'quake—when they passed Delmonico's Restaurant on O'Farrell, Cayley looked up and saw smoke and sparks raining down from the roof. Through the windows, a group of soldiers were lounging inside drinking from fancy crystal stemware. She figured that the soldiers had lit the range, and the chimney was broken—fire had ignited the inside walls and roof. They stopped the cart and shouted at the soldiers until several came out with their guns to find out what the problem was. When they rushed back into the restaurant to alert their comrades, Thomas started up the cart again and drove away toward safety. Within minutes, the fire was beyond control, sweeping up O'Farrell behind them. They turned north, up Hyde, to home.

With her load of recovered treasures rattling in the back, Cayley felt a tiny victory over the despair that was settling on her shoulders. Her fear was beginning to coalesce into a single question: *Where? Where was Bill? And Sam and Lilly and Mei?*

Chapter SIXTY

Except for the scurrying rats, Little China had emptied out like a cloth sack. The fire was beginning to sweep north, carried by blasts of hot wind that accompanied and drove it like a herd of monstrous horses. Sam continued east, though the Barbary Coast section with its saloons and sleazy whorehouses to the piers. Here, at least, the fire pumps and crews were able to do their work, siphoning water from the bay and continually spraying the docks, wharves and buildings along East Street. To the south, Sam glimpsed the outline of the Ferry Building with its tall clock still standing. He ran along the pier, and cut in at Green Street. He realized the fire was advancing through the financial section toward him and wanted to give himself some room to move farther north if he had to. By the time he reached Montgomery, though, the fire seemed farther away, and he zig-zagged toward Telegraph Hill and the small apartment his sister and Mei Mei rented on the Filbert Steps. *A strange place,* Sam thought, *full of whites who called themselves bohemians; but they welcomed two Chinese women, so that was something.* He climbed the steps to the top of the hill. The ache in his belly reminded him he hadn't eaten all day. He turned to watch the dark drama play out. The heavy smoke that hung over the city reflected the flames in a strange way. The evening sky was a shifting panorama of lavender, orange and red. It could almost be beautiful. He sighed, and went to the apartment, which appeared to be untouched. At the bell, Lilly answered the door, and stepped out to hug him. They held each other for a long moment. "I've been looking for you," said Sam. "I put you in danger."

She held him away from her. "I'm all right," she said firmly, and drew him inside. "I met with the intermediary last night, and gave him half the money. Then this happened." She waved her hand in the air. "I tried to go by the O'Farrell house but it was crazy down there. I came straight home. I'm so glad to see you're all right, too."

Sam blinked rapidly. "Cursed smoke!" He wiped his face with one wrist. "I looked for you in Little China. I was afraid you were still there. That they had you again."

She put her hands on his cheeks and smiled into his eyes. "I'm all right," she said firmly. "And we're unhurt. No water though, but a little food...no rice." She shrugged.

"The fire is moving fast," he said. "Little China is burning. We can probably stay here for the night, but tomorrow morning we've got to get out."

Chapter SIXTY-ONE

On the way to the Green Street house, Cayley, Sally, Thomas and his boy passed a parade of people heading west. "We're going to Golden Gate Park," a man said, his arm around his pregnant wife. "They're setting up a camp for us there. There'll be food and water."

"And an emergency hospital," said the woman. "We were going to the Mechanics Pavilion, but the fire's taken it already."

"Well, let's avoid camping out in the park if we can," Cayley told Sally. "I think the house will be all right if we stay outside. I've got plenty of supplies." When they arrived home, Bill was there, throwing dried sausage, cheese and bread into a saddlebag. Cayley ran to him and threw her arms around the back of his shoulders. "I was so worried," she said. "It's been all day, and I didn't know where you were. My imagination made the worst of it!"

"I'm all right, Cayley. Nowhere near any danger. But I got to go now."

"Why?"

"There's a committee forming to make decisions about the refugees and the soldiers, and food and all. You must have heard some of the soldiers are running wild. The committee will be made up of the most important men in town; Abe Ruef and Mayor Schmitz are there. It's my big chance to make something happen where people can see me."

"I thought Ruef and Schmitz are laying low because of the graft investigation."

"City politics are temporarily put aside."

"But what about us—and the house?"

"You'll be fine, Cayley. You're always fine. I don't think you're in any danger up here from the fire, but you should know that there are plans to destroy the houses on the north side of Van Ness with cannon if the fires move west up the hills. The dynamite is all gone. Tonight will tell. If you think you're in some danger, go to the park, or the presidio. The park is probably better, if you can make it. That's where the food and water is going. I'll meet you there when I can."

"But Bill," she held on to his arm.

"Cayley, I've got to go now." He gave her a quick peck on the cheek and was out the door. The girls in the room turned away, suddenly preoccupied with everything but Cayley's face.

"Let's start deciding what's to be brought if we have to move to the park. Just in case," said Sally, and they all began to arrange little bundles. A few, like Cayley, slept in the house. Others took bedding out to the yard, away from the buildings.

Chapter SIXTY-TWO

On Thursday morning, the day after the first shocks, Sam, Lilly and Mei Mei walked to the summit of Russian Hill and faced south, toward Nob Hill, where the grand mansions of the wealthiest men in town were already burning. First, the Hopkins' place and Leland Stanford's next door, then Collis Huntington's, then the Crocker house. The fire was not only moving up the hill, but down, flashing brightly from the Barbary Coast gin mills at the foot of Telegraph Hill. The air was filled with floating ash and flying cinders. The smoldering remains of San Francisco were in a peculiar twilight. Below Market Street, new fires were eating what was left of the mission district. The fires on Nob Hill had moved north toward Russian Hill.

"The city is being erased," said Lilly. "By fire and wind." Yet another aftershock rippled through the earth beneath their feet.

People were streaming out of the neighborhood, carrying what they could, and heading west. Just over the crest of Russian Hill on Taylor Street, before the ground dropped off to a steep precipice, the three Chinese watched as an elderly man climbed to the roof of his house. In his hand, he held an American flag on a pole. He fixed a holder and unfurled the flag. Three times he dipped the flag, then left it in the holder to fly in the hot updrafts from the fire advancing up the hill as he fled on foot. Within minutes, as they were about to turn back and follow the exodus to the park, they were treated to an extraordinary sight. A company of soldiers ran up the hill toward the house. Though the roof was already beginning to catch in places from the burning debris in the air, they threw handfuls of mud on the smoldering house. Others rushed inside and brought out soda water siphons, and sprayed where they could. One by one, the surrounding houses caught and blazed, but the house of the flag stood alone.

Long before the drama played out, Sam and the two girls snatched up their belongings and followed their neighbors. The little group stopped by the Green Street house, and found no one

275

there. Heading up Green Street toward Van Ness, the repeated firing of large artillery guns became louder.

Chapter SIXTY-THREE

Thirty hours had passed since the first earthquake; so many shocks rumbled the earth that people were almost numb to them. In Golden Gate Park, Cayley, Manuela, and the three women who accompanied them were standing in line, waiting for blankets and a plate of beans. Soldiers were building wood huts, and putting up tents in the meadow. Groups were gathered in prayer here and there, and they had encountered at least one religious type who was loudly proclaiming that the earthquake and fire was God's revenge on a high-living town. For once, Cayley was glad she and the girls were unrecognizable—dirty, tired and disheveled. The park was filled with milling bodies. She recognized Mrs. Rolifer in the line ahead of her, in about the same shape as everyone else. A woman worked her way down the line, showing a tintype of a little girl.

"Please, Mrs., have you seen my Annie? They say she was in our house when it fell—I was setting up my market stall, you see—but I know she's all right."

"You poor thing," said Cayley. "Of course she's all right. A mother knows these things." Cayley examined the picture of the child closely. "Oh, by the Virgin, I wish I'd seen her, but I haven't. I'm so sorry."

The man standing in front of Cayley looked over her shoulder at the picture. "A lot of people from south of the slot and Little Italy is gone to the ferry building, and then on to Oakland. I hear they're setting up a place for lost children there."

"In Oakland, you say?" said the woman hopefully.

"But you can't get down to the ferry building now," said the man. "There's crazy soldiers everywhere shooting and stealing what they can."

The woman looked frantic and hurried off, clutching her oval tintype. Cayley followed her with her eyes and spotted Bill across the grounds 40 feet away. She shouted out his name and ran after him. He wheeled his horse about when he saw her. "I see you're all right, my girl," he said.

"Bill, can you get someone down to the Ferry building? Is it still standing?"

"It is, but it's not likely anyone can get through now. It's gotten pretty dangerous down there." He patted the holster strapped to his thigh. "You see I'm taking you with me wherever I go." She recognized the old Army Colt 45 he ordinarily kept in the drawer at home. For his birthday last year, she had sent it to Tiffany; they engraved the grip and barrel with both their names and laid in gold and silver. She presented it to him to "celebrate the end of his rough-and-tumble ways."

"Here's your chance to be a real hero." She told the story of the woman and her missing daughter, and pointed her out in the crowd. The woman continued to hold the picture up to anyone who would look. "Is it true that there's a place in Oakland for missing children?"

"That's where it is."

"Will you take her?"

Bill's face soured. "I've got bigger things to do than to escort one woman to a place where her child might not even be."

"Bill! You know what it's like to lose a child. I don't ask much of you."

At this, he laughed. "Always the joker," he said. "All right. Wish us both luck." Cayley smiled for the first time in two days, then remembered the bruise on her cheek and shut her mouth quickly.

"We'll go around the north end of the fire, over the hills, since most of the Mission is gone," said Bill. "I can check what's going on then. I'll look in on the Green Street house."

He galloped off to talk to the woman, pulled her behind him, and set off northeast.

Chapter SIXTY-FOUR

A few blocks up Green Street, Sam saw Bill riding toward them, a silent woman clinging tightly to his back. The sound of dynamite being set off grew louder behind them.

"I thought the mayor put an end to that!" said Bill as they came up even with the little crew.

"To what, sir?" said Lilly.

"The dynamiting. I thought they were out of dynamite anyway. It's done more harm than good. Mother of God!"

"What is it, Mister?" The woman riding with Bill was clearly alarmed. She sat upright, ready to jump off and run.

"One moment," said Bill, dismounting by throwing his leg over the horse's head; he lifted the woman off the horse.

"The fools have blown the fire across Green—there's nothing to stop them." He ran to the dynamiting crew a block away, and exchanged heated words with the headman while houses erupted in flames on both sides of the street. He gestured toward a house—his own—on the south side of the street and shook his fist at the man. Then he turned back toward Sam and the women, lifted the woman astride once more, and set off. "I told those fools about the cisterns—at least there's some water around here. We better get ahead of this fire now, while we still can," he said. He looked back at the dynamite crew and Green Street. "Let's hope we have a house to come home to."

"Oh, I am sorry, sir," the woman said, breathless from the jouncing of the horse and the intense wind. The fire leapt from rooftop to rooftop to the east of them. "I can't thank you enough for helping me. I'll pray for you every night."

"I could use your prayers." Bill nodded to the Chinese man. "Chinese are being sent to the Presidio. But Cayley's in Golden Gate Park. All right?" The small group murmured assent, and began to move in the opposite direction as Bill spurred his horse toward Chestnut Street. On the deserted avenues, an uneasy kingdom of loose dogs and cats, chickens and rats of every color ran helter-skelter. The stench of burned and rotting flesh made

Sam cup his hand over his face periodically, but since it made their progress slower, he just took deep breaths and held them for as long as he could. The women followed his example.

Both the park and the presidio were several miles away, in different directions. The presidio was closer, but over several hills, difficult to walk with bound feet. Sam and Lilly took turns helping or carrying Mei Mei as they went down the more level streets toward Golden Gate Park. Mei Mei laid her cheek against Sam's back and her arms around his neck, even as her feet bled into his dusty coat. Her weight made him stronger. It was a peculiar family—two women who loved each other, and a man who was brother to them both—but it was family enough for him. He was determined to keep it.

The fire was raging to the south, and the wind was gusting into their faces. Everywhere, soldiers and sworn-in deputies were patrolling in couples or groups with bayoneted rifles. More than once, they saw uniformed men coming out of homes or shops, their arms full of precious objects.

"I thought they were supposed to be protecting us," said Mei Mei.

"They're not in their right minds," said Sam. "They'd shoot me if I opened my mouth. And you too."

Mei Mei buried her face in his back.

When they reached Van Ness, they saw that homes across the broad avenue were being shelled and brought down in the hope of keeping the fire from crossing the road. Firemen, worn past the point of exhaustion, fought off the fire from the buildings on the west side of the avenue.

The three were careful to avoid groups of wandering army personnel. From this perspective, Sam saw the fire had already breached the holding line, near the big cathedral of St. Mary's. Nothing could stop it now.

In one of the yards, Sam found a wheelbarrow in a gardener's cottage, and he and his sister took turns pushing Mei Mei in front of them on the ash-littered pavement. They arrived in the park after sundown.

"Chinese, over there," said a guard, and gestured with a nod of his head. Sam looked at Lilly. "We are with a white family here," Sam said to the guard. "We are their servants, and we became separated."

"Don't know how you expect to find 'em." The man scratched his generous beard. "Go over with the Chinese 'til morning."

"Yes sir," said Sam. As soon as they were past the guard, Lilly whispered, "We can't go over there. It's too dangerous."

"I know. We'll just have to find a space and wait until daylight." They settled in under one of the tall eucalyptus trees and huddled together for warmth. Sam turned the wheelbarrow on its side to shield them from the wind and prying eyes.

The next morning, Friday, Sam and Lilly took turns looking over the park. "They could have moved on to the Presidio," said Lilly. "And I don't think we can make it much farther."

"I'll look in the food lines," said Sam, and went to the longest one.

"No Chinee in this line," growled one man.

"The Chinese line is over there," a woman said.

"Thankee, thankee, but I lookee for my mistress!" said Sam. He added, "dirty dog asses" in Cantonese with a big smile.

"Lookee no further," said Cayley. "Jaysus, am I glad to see you." She put her hands on the shoulders of the Chinese man, then shook her head and embraced him, much to the curiosity of the crowd. They pulled apart. "I'm a mess," she said.

He laughed. "Strange time to worry about your looks."

She shook her head with a woeful smile. "Is everybody OK?"

"Lilly and Mei Mei are with me. We spent the night over there, under a tree." He indicated the grove some distance away. "They wanted us to go to the Chinese section, but of course ... "

"You'll move into our tent, and you'll get into this line to get some food for everyone." She turned to her right and left. "Anybody object to that?" The crowd remained silent; one person grumbled a few feet behind, and Cayley gave him her most fierce look. "What's that?" she said. No answer. "As long as you drop that pidgin crap," she added to Sam under her breath.

"No problem, Mrs...." Sam held his eyebrows up, wondering what she was calling herself in this situation.

"Yup," she said. "The Smith family, together again. Except for Bill, who's off on a mission of mercy."

"We passed him near the Green Street house yesterday. He was fine." Sam decided not to say anything about the dynamiting or the woman. Like everyone else who worked in the O'Farrell houses, Sam had heard rumors about Bill's philandering. Who knows; even Bill might be capable of more than anyone expects.

In late afternoon, a pair of trumpet players marched through the park, announcing on the mayor's authority that the fire was almost contained. A shudder of relief rippled through the crowd.

Old City Hall at Larkin St., June 1906

"Life's a very funny proposition after all:
Imagination, jealousy, hypocrisy and law.
Three meals a day, a whole lot to say;
When you haven't got the coin,
You're always in the way."
—George M. Cohen, recorded 1911

BOOK III
Life in the New City

Chapter SIXTY-FIVE - May 1906

The fires finally ran out of fuel by Saturday evening; the entire central city, the most populous area, had been completely destroyed except for an odd house or street that remained untouched. On Sunday, a rainstorm brought on by the intense heat of the fires cleared the air.

In the week that followed, Cayley, Sam, Manuela and the girls continued to live in the tents, making timid forays into the ruins to find what was left of their lives. Both the O'Farrell houses had burned to the ground.

At first, soldiers scoured the camps looking for Chinese to send to the Presidio. Cayley repeatedly battled to keep Sam and the girls with her. When the harassment stopped abruptly, rumors circulated that the dowager empress of China objected to bad treatment of Chinese, and backed her statements by sending money to rebuild Chinatown around a new consulate in the middle of the old area. Plans to ship the entire Chinese population south of town were scrapped.

Miraculously, the house on Green survived the fire with some damage, but largely intact. It was on the shore of a sea of destruction. As soon as they were able, Cayley's makeshift family moved back into the house, but continued to cook and sleep outside. The Napoleon bed was set up in the backyard; no one bothered to wipe the grime off it. Everything in the house smelled of smoke, but the ocean breezes broke up the pall that had hung over the city for many days after the last of the embers had burned out.

Food and goods were pouring in from all over the world. By the end of the week following the shaker, 150 relief stations doled out bread, canned meat, coffee and potatoes for little or no cost. Cayley's girls went to the nearest one, in Pacific Heights, and waited in line for hours. In early May, grocery shops began to sell food again; it was priced astronomically high; cash from the "golden bird" kept everyone fed. The biggest problem was getting fresh water, but the Green Street house had an old well—Sam pried off the boards nailed over it—that provided enough to cook, if not clean. Within a few weeks, the broken mains south of the city were repaired, making much of the city habitable.

Both Cayley and Manuela had family south of Market, the first area to burn. Neither had seen any relatives camped in the park among the thousands of people milling about the tents and food lines. A trip to the burned-out blocks below the slot revealed nothing. Cayley hoped their families had survived and found work clearing the rubble—the city was paying $2.50 a day for labor, an outrageously good salary. The word in the camps was that nearly 250,000 had been left homeless: Cayley and Sam saw dozens of families on the streets in shacks cobbled together from rubble.

Rumors of sickness were common—most feared a recurrence of the bubonic plague that broke out in the city a few years before. It wasn't hard to see why; the streets were littered with dead animals, including horses that had been used to clear the rubble. They lay fallen from exhaustion, left to rot while others took their place.

Cayley had never seen so many automobiles on the streets. They were a more reliable way to get around and deliver goods and water after the fire, and didn't require feeding and care. Even Bill—who was seldom seen, only stopping by Green Street periodically to pick up fresh clothing—was using one. "I have to take care of a city," he said, and Cayley let him go with a nod, too tired and anxious to argue. She was restless and bored, and so were her girls.

Cayley sat at the kitchen table with two of her employees over teacups holding dabs of whiskey. "Sally, I've got an idea. All those plate lunch sales by ladies' social groups—we could do that."

"And what'll we call our ladies' social group, Mrs. Wallace? Hooker's Hot Table?"

"What a brilliant idea, Sally! We'll have the most popular plate lunch service in town! 'Dine here and be fully satisfied!'"

Sally rolled her eyes. "I wouldn't put it past you."

"It's our chance to help out the city a little, keep ourselves busy, and polish up our image at the same time." Cayley took a sip from the teacup. "Bill is doing his part rebuilding, we should too."

Sally looked at the other girl. "What do you think, Iris? Ready to be a short-order cook?"

Iris smiled broadly, her teeth white against her dark skin. "I already done plenty of short orders. And I know how to flap a jack or two."

"I knew I could count on you." Cayley smiled mischievously above the flowered rim of her cup.

Within two weeks, Cayley had an open-air stand set up on Fillmore Street, which was proving to be the new commercial area now that the downtown was gone. Every shop and storefront was flying an American flag. She charged as little as possible for the meals the girls served, and they always dressed to the nines (outfitted by Cayley's bountiful closet) as they stood behind the planks that served as tables. Behind them, an open fire provided the heat to make coffee and set a griddle. Iris held to her promise and made the best flapjacks in town, served with syrup tinged with whiskey. The "Get-it-Hot Palace," as Cayley expected, had as many gentlemen callers as they could handle.

Chapter SIXTY-SIX

Sam scavenged what he could from the docks. As he brought in a 20-pound sack of flour and laid it across the kitchen table, he said to Cayley, "I've heard some of the girls complaining that Mei Mei doesn't do enough of the work."

"Well, it's true. They are, and she doesn't. Her bound feet are hardly an excuse considering all we've been through."

"I know. I'll speak to her. There must be something she can do, other than sleep all day."

"There's not too much any of us can do, really. I think that's the problem. We all need to get back to making some real money. We're just living from meal to meal here, then going to bed at dusk." Cayley looked thoughtful. "The O'Farrell houses are gone, but I still own land here and property in Berkeley—that's intact. It would be stupid to sell it now, though." She pinched the skin between her eyes with her forefinger and thumb. "I've got to get up and running again. I'll talk to Bill. He should be able to get us some start-up money."

Sam nodded but didn't look her in the eye. From the girls, he heard rumors about Bill and a society girlfriend. He couldn't find the words to tell her. "I'll speak to Mei Mei," he said.

Sam went to the room where Lilly and Mei Mei were staying, and scratched at the door until Mei told him to come in. She was alone in the room, her knees drawn up to her chest as she sat on the blankets that served as a bed on the floor. He opened his mouth to speak without looking directly at her. She interrupted and told him to sit down.

"I never thanked you properly for your help when we were running from the fire," she said.

"It was my duty."

"I think you are a very good man, Wo Sam."

Sam said nothing, but experienced a flush of warmth at the compliment.

"I've been thinking," continued Mei Mei. "You're right. Maybe we should be married."

Sam looked up suddenly, his mouth open.

Mei's laughter bounced off the walls of the narrow room. "Yes, I mean you and I." She looked down at the blankets, and began to trace one of the woven designs with her finger. "I haven't talked to Lilly about this, but I would like to have children, and so would she. You would be a good father. And who better than you?"

Sam failed to shut his mouth during this entire short speech. She reached over and gently closed it with two fingers applied to the bottom of his chin. "It's not the love match that seems so important to the whites, but it would be a good match for us—for the three of us."

Sam shook himself out of his shocked state. "But you wouldn't be a true wife to me, would you? You do not care for me that way."

"I wouldn't be in your bed every night, no. Sometimes, at the right time to grow a baby." At this, she blushed. "But I would keep your house for you. We both would." She looked up at him from under her lashes. "And I know you don't love me either. But many fine marriages are built on respect."

"Lilly would never agree to this."

"Why not? She loves you."

"She scorns me all the time."

Mei Mei nodded, a piquant expression on her face. "That's just her way with you. I'll soften her up. Why don't you think about it, and we'll talk again." He nodded. "What was it you wanted to talk to me about?"

"Oh!" Sam covered his face with one long, slim hand. "Mrs. Duarte has requested that you participate in more of the household chores."

"Is it Mrs. Wallace or the other girls?"

Sam moved his head in a complicated pattern from side to side, indicating both yes and no.

"Of course," said Mei. "They will never forget that we are Chinese in a white world. And we must never forget that we are Chinese." She reached over and covered his hand with her own.

Chapter SIXTY-SEVEN - February 1907

"Why can't you get me the money? You've got plenty of rich cronies." Cayley crossed her arms under her breasts, her brows joined together in a determined line. They stood in the dining room, where they had just finished coffee. Outside, a heavy winter rain pelted the mullioned windows. He had spent the night, but did nothing more than pat her hand when she leaned against him in the big bed.

"It's different now and you know it. Most of the men on the committee have joined up with the Decency League, including your old pal Rolifer. They don't want to risk being tied to a whorehouse, now that Mayor Schmitz has gone down. Ruef will be next, mark my words."

"Look, Bill, I got a payout from Aetna Insurance, but it's not enough. It costs a fortune to build now because everyone is buying up materials as fast as they can. It's almost like the city is going up overnight. There's plenty of money to be made in what I'm offering. There always has been, always will be."

He leaned against the wall covered by a mural of Vesuvius erupting over Pompeii. Black dust from the ceiling had darkened parts of it during the earthquake, dimming its bright colors. "Cay," he turned the dining room chair around and sat down on it backwards. "Have you ever thought of going legitimate—a tavern, or shop, or something like that? How about that little plate lunch place you had for a while?"

"Are you crazy? Why would I want to go into a hardscrabble work-a-day life now of all times?"

"It's just that...," he ran his hand over the top of the chair as though polishing it.

"You don't want to be associated with a whore either, am I right?"

Bill signed heavily and put his forehead on the top rim of the chair back. "We've been over and over this." He looked up. "My political career is just as important to me as making money is to you. Why can't you give in on this?"

289

"Why can't we do both? We did before. You weren't so ashamed of me then."

"Do you think I'm making up what's happening in the city? Look around you, girl!" He got up and swung the chair around, banging it against the table. "The fire changed everything, and everyone."

"The world will always need accommodating women."

"Yes, maybe, and I could use one too. Why are you always against me?"

"I'm not against you, Bill." She leaned forward and held one of his hands with both her own, looked up into his eyes. "I love you. I love you more than anything. But you're asking me to give up everything I worked hard for. I have people to watch over, too. What would I do, as a little shopkeeper, or behind a bar? Don't you see what a step down that would be for me? Don't ask me to back into the shadows just to make you look good."

He edged away from her, and her hands fell to her sides. "Same old story, eh?" He smoothed the back of his head with his palm. "How many times have we come to this?"

"Bill, be reasonable. We can work it out."

"No, Cayley, we can't." He squeezed the back of his neck with his fingers, suddenly awkward. The lit candles in the chandelier above the table glinted on the rings of his left hand. He blurted the words out so quickly she almost didn't understand what he said: "I want a divorce."

She stood for a moment in silence, and he almost spoke again, but she exclaimed, "No! Don't say that. Don't ask that of me…. Bill, please." She touched his sleeve. "I love you. You're all I got."

He turned to leave the room, and she caught up with him, forcing her hand into his. "We'll find some way to work it out, I know we will."

He turned to her, his hand slack against hers. "No, we won't," he said, avoiding her eyes. "We aren't going to do this anymore." He went up the stairs, his voice receding with each step: "I'm done old girl. Nothing to talk about." She could hear the sound of drawers opening, his footsteps returning down the stairs. He didn't turn around as he made his way to the front door. "Good-bye Cay."

She ran out after him as he pulled himself up into the driver's seat of his REO runabout and placed his case on the passenger seat without looking her way again. The rain had turned to a drizzle. After she lost sight of him, she returned to the house to find Sam standing in the hallway.

"Mr. Duarte has gone?"

"None of your business," said Cayley, and took the steps two at a time up to her room.

Chapter SIXTY-EIGHT

"She still has pictures of him next to the bed," said Lilly. "It's makes my skin creep." She and Mei Mei had stayed on in the house with Cayley after the new "smaller, more modern 'resort'" was built. The insurance plus the sale of one of Cayley's properties paid for a less grand version of the O'Farrell house among the big hotels downtown.

"He's not coming back. Everyone knows he has someone else." Sam sat across from his sister in the parlor of the Green Street house. He had loosened his collar and crossed his legs with one foot on the other knee.

"*She* doesn't."

"She won't believe it. She thinks as long as she's married to him, he still belongs to her. But he'll find a way to break free."

"Are you sure he's not coming back? They've had fights in the past and have always gotten together again."

"He's not coming back," said Sam fiercely.

His sister nodded. "Poor Sam. You're mooning over Cayley Wallace, and that's no secret either." She watched his face.

"I am not," he said, uncrossing his legs. "I'm loyal. And don't use so much American slang."

Lilly sighed and shook her head. "Speaking of marriage..."

Sam drew in a sharp breath.

"I didn't speak to Mei for two days when she suggested it. You know what I'm talking about."

Sam nodded. "I thought she had forgotten about it. Just a girl's whim."

"Mei's always been a clever girl. She made such a sensible argument I'm surprised I didn't come up with it myself. We get children, and if her brothers—receiving the joyous news that she's still alive—are still bent on revenge, they're less likely to murder the father of their own blood. Nobody is going to question a household with a spinster sister. We could live in the new Chinatown, Sam. Among our own."

"There's only one problem."

292

Lilly sighed. "It's not what you planned."

"She made it clear she would not be a real wife to me."

"There would be affection though. We have time. Mei's still young. Don't forget—this was your idea. We'll be waiting for you if..." The knocker thumped against the entry door. She stood up, "I'll get it."

"Is Cayley home?" It was Cay's younger sister, Mary. The tiny girl stood rigidly, clutching her gray shawl tightly around her.

"No, she's not," said Lilly. "She's down at the business, but should be home soon. Please come in and wait. She'll be glad to see you, as she's had no word since the fire and was worried." She looked around for a cab and saw none. "Did you walk all the way up here?"

The girl nodded and began twisting the ends of her wrap in her damp hands. "Well, perhaps I shouldn't stay," she said. "My ma told me to come here to see if there was any extra Cay could spare. We've gone to Oakland, you see, and I guess we'll be setting up there now. But we ain't got much, and no work, now that the clean-up is done."

"It won't be long. And if you have to go, Sam can take you down to the Ferry Building. Come in and have something to eat."

The girl's eyes reflected gratitude, and she was led into the kitchen where Sam sat. He greeted her and offered her a seat, but didn't get up himself.

"Mary says the family is in Oakland, now," said Lilly, fixing the girl a plate of cold meat and rice.

"And how is everyone?" Sam held one side of his face in his palm. "Did everyone make it out all right?"

"Oh, we all did, just ahead of the fire. It moved so fast," she chewed enthusiastically, bits of food falling from her mouth as she spoke. "We lost most everything, of course. Not that there was much to lose." She wiped her mouth on the back of her hand before remembering that Lilly had handed her a napkin. She glanced at the two Chinese, a little embarrassed as she touched the cloth to her lips. They sat in silence for a moment.

"We had a nice surprise, though, when we got off the ferry and were looking for a place to stay."

"And what would that be?" Sam retained his bored expression.

"It was Michael, my brother, who we hadn't seen for the longest time! For years, even, and him alive or dead, we didn't have a clue. You know, the one with the...." She pressed her fingers together to make two fingers instead of four. "He was down at the dock looking to pick up passengers with his own horse and cart. We're able to stay with them—him and his little wife. It's mighty crowded, so we're looking to get out on our own. Which is why I'm here. Cayley's always helped us out in the past."

Sam's face became more alert. "You're staying with Michael?"

"Oh yes. He got a loan from a friend a few years back and made his own business, he did. We were as surprised as anyone, I tell you—him with his affliction and all. And he's got himself a wife, too." Mary covered her mouth with her hand. "I don't want to say much to shame his happiness, but she's a little simple, if you know what I mean." She raised her eyebrows and took a sip of tea from the delicate cup in front of her. "But very sweet. Very sweet."

"That's news I'm sure Mrs. Wallace will want to hear, Mary," said Sam. "I believe I hear her trap coming up the street, now. Why don't you tell me where Michael's place is, so she can stay in touch with you?"

Mary gave him a description, and within a few minutes, Cayley came into the kitchen, stripping off her gloves. She was genuinely glad to see her sister, and gave a meaningful glance to Sam when Mary shared the news about Michael. They loaded the girl up with food and coins, and Sam took her down to the Ferry Building to wait for the next boat across the bay. When he returned, he went straight to Cayley.

"What are you going to do?"

"I guess it's time for a family visit," she said. "I've been dreading this, but I have to find out. If he did do…those terrible things, something must be done." She focused on Sam's eyes and he quickly looked away. "If it was your sister, what would you do?"

He raised his palms and shook his head. "At the very least, I would prevent her from doing any more harm. By whatever means."

"Yes. Now he has someone depending on him, too. Mother of God!" She rubbed her fingers across her forehead. "The shaking never seems to stop around here."

Chapter SIXTY-NINE

Cayley and Sam stood on the deck of the Bay City. She held her hat on with one hand; gusts of wind buffeted the hull. As they approached the dock, squat buildings on the misty Oakland shore became more defined. "There's no guarantee he'll tell me the truth," she said.

"So why are you going?

"I honest-to-God don't know, Sam. Maybe it's because I want to do the right thing as much as possible. I owe it to Ellen to do my best."

He squeezed her gloved hand briefly. "We both do."

They hired a carriage and drove east to the far edge of town, past the cheerfully painted Victorians that clustered beyond the harbor docks. With some difficulty, they found the rough un-painted structure that housed Cayley's family among the shanties perched on low hills. In the dusty yard two of the younger children were chasing a skinny dog, tugging at a rag in his mouth; it appeared to be a doll, or what was left of one. They squealed when Cayley stepped into the yard and led her to the door, each taking a hand. Sam followed behind.

"Auntie Cay" was ushered into the house. It looked like a waiting room; a member of her family hovered over every horizontal surface. Most stood up to greet her. Cayley took in the surroundings: a single white-washed room with a wood-burning stove and mismatched chairs centered on the left side, a cookstove, table and benches to the right. Pots and pans were hung neatly around the cookstove, and a simple hutch held brownware. A hallway across from the entry door led to one or two other rooms used for sleeping. As the older children touched Cayley's hand or curtseyed respectfully, her mother introduced her to Michael's wife, who promptly apologized for the modest surroundings. "Michael's off making a living, with such a large family to take care of these days," she said in response to Cayley's question. Her eyes held fast to the floor.

Cayley took tea, and insisted Sam sit down with her. Two siblings made space for them at the table.

"It's a blessing to see you alive and well, daughter." Cayley's mother stood over her and pressed her hands together. "It looks like you've recovered at least part of your fortune." She looked out the window. "That's a very nice carriage."

"It's rented," said Cayley, flatly.

"Mmmm, oh yes, of course." Her mother fingered the pleats on her faded calico skirt.

Cayley addressed Michael's wife. "How nice that Michael was able to start his own business—and now a family, too." She pushed her mug toward the edge of the table to avoid being splashed as Michael's wife poured a thin stream from a blue tin teapot.

The wife straightened up and proudly patted her swollen belly after replacing the pot on the stove. "I'm mighty proud of him, I am. And he's real good to me, too. I often think of myself as a very lucky girl."

"I'm sure he's the lucky one," said Cayley. "When do you expect him home?"

"Oh, he comes in when work is done, whenever that is. He…"

"He works so hard, does our Michael," Cayley's mother stepped in front of the pregnant girl. "But of course, it's hard to support so many…"

Michael's wife shut her mouth with a snap. As she stepped around her mother-in-law back to the table, she folded her arms and said, "I'm sure your ma and her brood will be much relieved to have their own place again, Mrs. Duarte."

Cayley leaned toward her mother and held out her hand. Her mother took it. "Rest easy, mother. I'll help you out as I've always done. But I need to talk to Michael, first."

Cayley's mother rubbed her chin with the other reddened hand. "Why would that be?"

"Private business. I think I'll sit outside. It's a lovely day. Sam?"

He nodded, stood up, and they both left the house and went to sit atop the cracked leather seats of the rented trap. They were dozing as the sun turned the western sky apricot and blue; Michael's cart rumbled to a stop in front of the house. He dismounted warily.

"So there you are," said Cayley. "You disappeared on us."

He didn't look at her as he lifted the yoke from his horse and pulled the harness. "I have to walk him out back, sister. You can come with me if you like."

"I'll do that." Sam began to follow Cayley out of the carriage, but she put a hand on his arm. "It's all right. I'll yell if I need you." She walked a few feet behind the horse as Michael led him around the house to a crude shed. He proceeded to brush the animal down after scooping out a bucket of oats from a jute bag and pouring it in the trough. Cayley leaned against one of the shed's supports. "Ellen Leary," she said.

"Who?"

"Don't 'who' me. I found your glove in her hand. Her dead hand."

Michael moved away from her to the other side of the horse, brushing vigorously.

"Say something, Michael."

"I've not a word to say."

Cayley was around the animal with her hands on her brother's powerful shoulders in an instant. Before he had time to think, she whirled him around and slapped him as hard as she could. Tears sprang into his eyes, and he shook his head back and forth. "I had nothing to do with it. She was a friend to me. I would never do anything like that."

"I've never heard anything about this friendship. How do you explain that?"

Michael shrugged his shoulders and looked away. "I…I…"

"You what?"

Michael bit his lips together. "She was the one that lent me the money for this place. That's why I was there with her. She

298

told me she was going to help me." He nodded. "That's it—she told me to meet her there."

Cayley turned her face and squinted one eye at him. "So when did all this 'friendship' take place, that I wouldn't have knowledge of it?"

"Oh, here and there." Michael's eyes darted about. The horse shifted from side to side, annoyed at the interruption of his brush-down. He bumped against Michael, who lurched forward, then quickly drew himself back. "Just once in a while. We met at the old house south of the slot when she came there once. She felt sorry for me."

Cayley stepped back. "That isn't the kind of thing she'd keep from me."

"I don't know why she didn't tell you."

"That still doesn't explain why your glove was in her hand on the night she died."

Michael's mouth worked, but no sound came out. Then he whispered, "Please don't talk about that. I ain't sure at all what happened. I was just about to leave with the sack of money she was to give me when this fella stepped into the alley. She wasn't happy to see him, and she grabbed my hand, but I run off. He scared me, that fella."

"Cowardly little shite. I don't believe you. I think you had something to do with this, and I always have. I'm turning you in, and giving that glove as proof."

"NO, sister, no! What would happen to my wife and child if they took me away!" Michael's eyes flew wide with terror. "All right. I lied. She wasn't giving me the money. I found out about the girl—that daughter of hers—when I worked hauling for the school she went to. I watched them when your friend came to visit, and I realized the girl didn't know about your whorehouses. I figured I could get a little money if I threatened to tell her. So I did. I ain't proud of it, but what else was I to do? I surely didn't have nothing to do with killing her. She was the goose with the golden egg, you see?"

"The goose was about to fly out of town."

A cloud of confusion passed over Michael's face. "She didn't say nothing to me."

"What happened in the alley?"

"It was like I said. She give me the sack with the money, and this tall slim fella walks into the alley. The light was behind him, so I couldn't see his face, but he saw me, all right. She says, 'What are YOU doing here?' She knew this fella and wasn't happy to see him. 'I still don't want to talk to you,' she says. He didn't make a sound, just kept coming. I bent down to get the bag, and she grabs my hand hard, like to keep me there—that really scared me, and I ran out as fast as my legs would carry me. That's how she got the glove, I guess. When I read in the papers that the Ripper got her, I figured it was that fella. Like I said, I didn't get a look at him, but he saw me plenty good. So I high-tailed it out of town and stayed in Oakland. I was too scared to do anything else. It would be me next, you see." Michael touched his hands together, clasping them as best he could. "Please, sister. I ain't the best, but I'm no murderer. I'll pay the money back, if you'll take it little by little." He looked up from the ground to his sister's face, but she was no longer focused on him. Her vision had become diffused; her mind was somewhere else.

"She was a good woman. It weren't right, all that happened to her, including what I done. Please, I'm begging you…"

Cayley continued to stare into the far distance, her lips moving in some silent litany.

"Think of my little family, here. Sister? Are you hearing me?"

She turned her attention to him suddenly. He was shaking. "Give the money to mother." She pivoted on her heel and walked toward the carriage. "I'll hear if you don't," she said without looking back.

Chapter SEVENTY

"You're sure?" Sam shook the reins to get the reluctant gelding to move down the street.

"I know him as well as I know myself. He didn't do it."

"Then who…?"

"He didn't recognize the man that came in the alley, but Ellen did. 'A tall slim fella' is all he said. It could have been anyone."

Sam turned his attention to the horse as he steered him into the increasingly busy streets near the ferry landing. Oakland had built up quite a bit with all the refugees moving there after the fire.

"I know what you're thinking," Cayley said.

"I'm not thinking." Sam kept his eyes straight ahead.

"You're thinking it might have been Bill. That's impossible. It's the job of the police now, as far as I'm concerned." Cayley pulled her thin shawl tighter around her and busied herself staring at the shop windows and saloon doorways that increased in number the nearer they drew to the harbor. A pall of greasy, fishy smoke hung over the docks, as if someone was burning garbage left from the oystermen. Both covered their mouths with handkerchiefs to draw cleaner breaths, and neither spoke. The odor of creosote used to patch the planks of the dock made her head ache, and she rubbed her temples until the skin turned dark. They boarded the creaking boat, stumbling aboard with the few who had made late departures visiting friends or working. The trip to Green Street was made with minimal interaction, little more than simple questions and answers. Sam returned by himself downtown to the business.

Cayley sat at her dressing table and picked up the mother-of-pearl-backed hairbrush. She began to pull the bristles through her tight curls, pulling the coils into fine waves. With each stroke she tried to drive the image of Bill's face from her mind. *He couldn't have anything to do with it. What possible reason would he have to do such a thing? Perhaps there was a struggle, and it was an accident. Bill couldn't be the Ripper.* She pulled her hair to the back of her neck and bound it up, plunging the pins deep into her scalp as if to make outlets for evil thoughts to escape. *But he was always shaming me and my business, then pretending he was sorry.* She stood up and turned toward the armoire, selecting a red satin gown with jet beads sewn into the bodice. *Opal said it was a short fella that came after her, really strong, and that's not Bill—more like Michael. But it couldn't be.* She pulled her corset laces tighter, then sat down on the bed next to the empty dress. Out loud, she said, "I can't reason this out." She covered her face with her hands. *I'm gloomy, with Ellen so much on my mind. I need to be around a little gaiety.* She pushed the thoughts away, finished dressing and rang for a hack to take her downtown. Sam would bring her back in the morning.

As she stepped down from the carriage, she noted with satisfaction that her newest sporting parlor was as elegantly furnished as in her pre-earthquake days. Two man-sized concrete urns on either side of the large brass double door were nearly hidden by cascading flowers and ferns. The house was smaller, more intimate. The bar was less like a saloon, more like a private club; the girls were fewer—since the fire, many top girls had fled the city and those that stayed were in demand. *It's quality over quantity,* Cayley thought. *Though I remember the days when it was both.* She drew a deep breath, pasted a smile on her face, and swaggered down the alley towards the back door of the kitchen. Cayley heard voices and stooped beneath the kitchen window, hoping to get an earful of what the girls were talking about these days.

Three voices floated over the kitchen sill: Spanish Sally from the old days, and two new girls Opal had brought up from San Jose.

"Well, it's best if you keep close about what you saw, for her sake." That was Sally.

"How come SHE don't know?"

"Doesn't", said Sally. "She DOESN'T, not don't."

Cayley heard the girl groan, then assume an exaggerated upper-class British accent: "I do not grasp how Mrs. Duarte remains IGNORANT to the fact that her dear husband is FUCKING Miss Jeanne Norton, the elegant society notable."

The other girl stifling laughter, chimed in: "Well YES, my dear. He is escorting Miss Norton about town in the most obvious way, though, of course, the society pages properly do not mention their COUPLING as he is married to the prominent society whore, Mrs. Cayley Wallace Duarte!" The two women shrieked with laughter, and even Sally added a guffaw or two.

Cayley felt her face redden in anger and shame. She crept out from under the window and collected herself as she made her way back down the narrow alley to the front door. Lightheaded, she placed her right hand against one of the urns to steady herself. Sam saw her through the front window. He opened the door and stepped out, putting a hand beneath her elbow.

"Are you all right, Cayley?"

She looked up at him, her blue eyes wide as a child's. "I don't...think so."

"Come inside."

"No, I need to walk. Walk with me, Sam."

He stepped up and pulled the front door closed, then returned to her side. They began to walk, rounding the corner to a steep hill. She grasped his elbow and leaned forward. When they reached the street at the top of the hill, she pressed her side, breathing heavily. "Damned stays," she said.

"What is it?"

"You know what stays are."

He squinted at her. "Cayley?"

She took a deep breath. "You'll tell me the truth if it's really important, won't you Sam?"

"Only if it's really important."

"My God, you're making a joke. It truly is a new day!"

"What?"

"Bill. Is it true he's left me for Jeanne Norton?"

Sam took in a deep breath. "I've heard that. I have no idea as to the truth."

She looked at the ground a few feet in front of her. A dandelion had grown, lived, and died in a crack in the sidewalk. "Well, that would explain a lot. How long have you heard this rumor?"

"Since before the fire. I didn't give it much credit. But I still hear it, so there's likely something to it. I'm sorry." He raised his arm to put around her, and then let it drop to his side like an empty sleeve.

Cayley raised her eyes to the lights of the city. "Well, I guess it wasn't your place—or the girls either—to tell me."

"How do you tell someone something like that?"

She shrugged. "Bill's finally stepped up in the world. It's easy to see why he's pushing so hard for a divorce—so he can marry her and have his passel of frilly little brats!" Her face hardened, eyes narrowed. She was trying very hard not to cry. "He sure doesn't need me any more, that lousy sponge."

"Cayley...." Sam's hands flapped around helplessly.

"Just shut up. I know I'm only a wallet to him, or you, or anyone else. That's what you hang around for, isn't it? Your pay at the end of the week?"

Sam gripped her arms above the elbows and brought his face even with hers. "Now you're insulting me. I won't allow you to say these things about me or yourself. Bill Duarte may not be the best man in this city, but a lot of people care about you, me included. I could have left a long time ago."

"Why didn't you?"

The words tumbled out of his mouth before Sam realized it: "I love you, you foolish woman."

Cayley's mouth hung open. "Oh Sam. Don't do this. Don't do this now."

Sam said nothing, but continued looking at her. His face turned an alarming shade of ashy gray.

Cayley's smile flickered on and off. "You're just trying to distract me, aren't you? Trying to shock me into thinking of something else." She shook his hands off her arms. "Well, you succeeded." She turned him to the side, took his arm, and made her way cautiously down the hill, taking tiny steps so as not to stumble. "Sam," she said, and shook her head, "Let's go to work and forget this ever happened."

Though Cayley greeted her guests as she always did that night, she avoided joking around with her girls. One by one they approached Sam to find out what the problem was. Sam himself was more withdrawn than usual; even the customers felt the cheerlessness in the house and left early.

Sam drove Cayley home to Green Street in the early hours of the morning. Only the sound of the carriage wheels against the paving stones could be heard in the pre-dawn light. He cleared his throat. "About what I said earlier..."

"Sam," she stopped him. "I've got a cheating husband on my mind, and it's taking up all my attention right now. If you said something to me earlier, I don't even remember it. I'm sorry, I just wasn't listening.'

"Thank you," he whispered.

Cayley tossed restlessly in her big Napoleon bed that night, after she had turned down the pictures of Bill on the nightstand one by one. Memories intruded on each other—the times he didn't show up when he said he would, the smell of lavender on his shirt; there were a million signs, and she ignored every one. Her rage blossomed and bloomed like a rose gone wild: instead of flowers opening into fragrant color, they shrunk and darkened. The thorns grew enormous, sharp and hard.

Chapter SEVENTY-ONE

"I made a mistake. I said too much. I'm a fool." In the privacy of their own rooms, Sam sat with his sister on the floor in front of a small table holding a pale green vase and two tiny flowers.

"Oh Sam. What did she say?" Lilly reached over and touched his shoulder.

"She said she didn't hear me. She was very kind. Of course we both know nothing could ever happen between us. I don't know what came over me."

"It's not evil to care about someone, and to tell them so. Look at me and Mei Mei." She stood up, came around the table, leaned into his back, and put her arms around his shoulders. "I'm glad you said something. She takes you for granted too much."

Sam's hunched shoulders relaxed under his sister's steady embrace. He sighed deeply. "But things will change now. We'll feel awkward around one another. I've ruined everything."

"It's about time things changed. You've saved money, and we have some too. Maybe it's time we all thought about having a life of our own, away from this crazy white world." Lilly stood up and gathered her long hair behind her ears.

"Still, I'm afraid for her. She's taken the news of her husband's faithlessness very hard, even though he hasn't lived with her for some months."

Lilly stamped her foot. Sam could hear the exasperation in her voice: "Stop thinking about her and start thinking about yourself! She's not the first woman to love a scoundrel, and she won't be the last."

"But she is the same as you and me. She cannot help who she loves."

Lilly stepped forward and leaned her hip against his shoulder. They both looked outside the window at the dappled shadows made by the wind-rustled trees in the back yard. "What about Mei-Mei's proposal?"

Sam raised his hands to his face. "I don't want to talk about it now."

"The only thing missing from our home is the sound of children's laughter."

Sam stood up abruptly, nearly knocking his sister over. "Is there anyone who doesn't want something from me? Devotion without anything in return seems to be the order of the day. What is wrong with you women?" He grabbed up his jacket and marched downstairs.

Chapter SEVENTY-TWO

I need to find out what's going on before I make myself crazy. I need to settle this. Cayley pushed the empty bottle away from her on the table and made her way unsteadily upstairs to her bedroom. She knelt and pulled the heavy lower drawer of the mahogany hutch toward her. Hands scrabbled through the collection of leather belts, money clips, folded handkerchiefs and bits of paper. She pulled out a packet, scraps of poems Wo Sam had given her over the years, tied with a pale blue ribbon. She cast it aside. The stained glove she buried in the drawer so long ago wasn't among the drawer's contents, though she barely noted it. Another packet contained love notes Bill had written to her, usually thanking her for a "campaign donation" or some trinket she had bought him. She lifted a heavy old-fashioned pistol out of the back of the drawer. The engraved handle of Bill's old Colt felt smooth and cool—she held it to her forehead for a moment before she examined it. It was a plain old Army 45 when Bill first showed it to her. She had Tiffany put her name on one side and Bill's on the other, entwined in an ivy vine. He wore it during the fire; he didn't bother to take it with him when he left. *I'll bet that's when he started up with her—when he was so busy saving the city. I just have to find out for myself, that's all. I'll ask him. I'll make him tell me and remind him I'm nobody's fool. That's what I'll do.*

Cayley finished dressing and put the love notes and revolver in a carpetbag—it was too long and heavy to fit into her reticule. She breezed past Sam in the entryway, not looking him in the eye. "Be back later. Tonight," she said, halfway out the door.

Sam followed her out to the porch. "Shall I take you somewhere, Cay?" he called to her retreating back. She shook her head "no" and walked quickly down Jackson, keeping her eyes open for a hansom to flag down.

She ordered the driver to Bill's office in the temporary city hall on Market Street. After the earthquake and fire, the old city hall was a mess; damaged parts of the building were taken down,

308

though several of the city offices still used it—but not Bill. She sat in the cab, humming snatches of the "Pineapple Rag" to herself, petting the carpetbag as if it were a cat while never taking her eyes off the building. Bill emerged from the door, pulling his dark coat over his shoulders and running his thumb and forefinger over the ends of his pale moustache. She hated that moustache. A couple of his cronies were with him and he was talking and laughing as they walked toward the carriage barn and disappeared into the darkness. One by one, their traps or autos emerged, and Cayley instructed the cabbie to follow Bill's red REO as she drew her veil down over her face.

Bill's auto coughed, whirred, and headed for the park.

She followed a block away, and dropped farther behind as the traffic thinned on the edge of the city. It wasn't difficult to keep up—she was concerned the cabbies' horse would outrun Bill's automobile. He passed through the park and kept going. They were well out of town now, and Cayley guessed his destination was probably not the Cliff House—more likely the Trocadero. Bill pulled up to the rustic two-story main cottage and stepped out as the stableman hopped into the driver's seat. She had the cabbie drive beyond the entrance and instructed him to leave. She would be returning with her husband, and that was that. She walked up the gravel road, hard-packed by the wheels of the elite "sportsmen" who used this place as their special hideaway. This was where all those Decency folks—including her old crony Rolifer—found Abe Ruef hiding out after his graft trial; they threw him in jail. So much for loyalty.

Cayley felt like a little girl playing hide-and-seek as she moved from bush to tree. Bill was walking toward one of the cabins in the back, removing his hat to smooth his hair, taking his time. He stopped to light a thin cigar, and take a couple of puffs. At that moment, the cabin door opened, and Jeanne Norton's well-groomed, hatless head popped out. "Billy," she hissed. "Get in here!"

Bill laughed, tossed the cigar on the ground and spit after it. Jeanne stepped out on the porch and looked around to see if they were watched, then ran to him as gracefully as a ballerina. He embraced and kissed her, cupping her smooth young face in his hand.

Cayley began to shake. Her heart dropped to her toes. Tears burned her eyes, escaped, and she blinked them back. "No," she said. "No, no, no, no." Bill turned at the first sound and stood in front of the girl.

"Ah, Cay," he said. "What are you doing? You of all people should know better."

Cayley stepped forward until she was in front of the tree that had shielded her. Her face was a mask of pain, her mouth open, eyes pleading.

"Now don't look like that," said Bill. "It's not like I haven't tried to let you down easy."

Cayley said nothing, shaking her head side to side, eyes on the ground. "Bill." She said it so softly the wind almost stole it from her lips.

The girl grasped Bill's arm. "Is that her?" she said.

"Hush," answered Bill. "Go inside now."

"Make her go away."

"I said hush."

"You, go away," said the girl. "Leave us alone."

Cayley looked up, her eyes harder, and focused on the girl. Bill moved in front of her again. "She's got nothing to do with it Cay."

"She's got everything to do with it. Your little high-class piece. No wonder you wanted to get rid of me." Cayley made a sound somewhere between a sob and the whine of an injured animal. "You're my husband, Bill. You're mine, don't you remember?" She tried to keep from grimacing. *If I can only talk sense to him.* She forced her mouth into a slight smile, though her eyes were wild with the storm raging behind them. "All we been through…."

Bill softened his voice as though he were gentling a horse. "Cayley, sweet, we had our time. These are different times now. We're different people. I tried to tell you. I'm telling you now. We're done, you see? Done."

Reason fled. "No! No, we're not." She was shouting. "You're not thinking clear. That little fancy bit has turned your head, but you'll see, you'll see. Come home with me where you belong."

Bill looked behind him at the girl's upturned face. His expression was somewhere between exasperation and pleading. "Go in. Now. I'll be there," he said in a low voice.

Jeanne pushed herself back from Bill and stepped beside him. "I'm not afraid of you. You're a crazy old whore and Bill told me how you tricked him into marrying you. Everybody knows it. He'll be free of you soon enough!"

Cayley looked stunned. "What? What did you say?"

"You heard me." The girl stepped back and looked down. "Now go away." She backed away two more steps, her eyes lowered. "Just go away."

"Bill, tell me this isn't so." Cayley set the carpetbag down and moved toward him, made to grasp his lapels, but he took her hands in his and brought his face in front of hers.

"This is neither the time nor place, Cay." He squeezed her hands until her nails bit into the flesh of her palms. "You're right. Go on home and I'll come in a little while and we'll talk it over. I promise."

"That's what you told her, isn't it? My God!" Cayley jerked her hands away and staggered backwards, head bobbing as if it were held on with string. "What you told them all. Could you shame me more? Could you grind me down any harder? Don't you remember all I done for you...?" Blood was buzzing bright crimson in her brain as she reached down and began tearing at the mouth of the carpetbag, fumbling inside for the love notes; she found the handle of the 45 and pulled the metal piece back with her thumb, just as he had taught her. She drew out the weapon slowly and aimed it. The sound of the trees in the wind, the birds calling to one another disappeared; she was surrounded by silence. "Did you ever love me? Did you?" Her voice was barely above a whisper.

"Jesus Christ, Cayley! What are you doing?" Bill glanced back at the girl then at Cayley. "Put it away. We'll work it out,

311

Cay, don't do anything crazy." He turned his face sideways, "Get inside" he screamed at the girl and she quickly backed away, stumbling over the edge of the cabin steps and falling backward on the porch, her skirts flying up like a pile of rags in a windstorm.

Cayley brought the gun up to eye level. "I don't believe you," she said, closed her eyes, and fired. Bill, stepping sideways to aid the girl, crumpled onto the ground. As Cayley walked away, the girl's screams ripped the air again and again. *Sounds like seagulls,* Cayley thought. *Like seagulls on Ocean Beach.*

Chapter SEVENTY-THREE

The man from the front desk of the Trocadero held tightly onto Cayley's arm until the police came. It didn't hurt, and she didn't resist. She watched the commotion as if from a cloud. A doctor, who arrived just before the police officer, attended to Bill. Jeanne Norton had disappeared. The officer was someone she vaguely recognized—he picked up payoffs from the new house every once in a while. He was very polite, didn't handcuff her, and allowed her to walk to the carriage in front of him. He had picked up the carpetbag from where she had dropped it, placing the gun inside. "This yours, Ma'am?" he asked, and she nodded and smiled dreamily. They rode through the park into town, pulling up to the make-shift Hall of Justice.

"This used to be where the Tivoli was, wasn't it?" Cayley spoke as if in a dream. "We all used to dress up and come down here to see the show."

The officer looked at her curiously. "That's right, Ma'am," he said. He took her arm and escorted her inside, where she was booked for assault with a deadly weapon. "No need for the paddy wagon," said the officer. "I'll take her down myself." He helped the docile woman into the carriage again, and they made their way to Anna Lane, to the temporary city prison. She was escorted to an empty cell, next to another full of street prostitutes and women hauled in for public drunkenness.

"Is there anything I can get for you, Ma'am...to make you more comfortable?" The arresting officer inquired before he shut and locked the heavy iron door. The women in the next cell mocked his offer, calling out to him, "We can make you more comfortable, sonny. Just open this door!"

"Oh, no, thank you," said Cayley. As he turned to go, she stood up. "Officer?"

"Yes Ma'am?"

"Is my husband all right? I hope he's not hurt. We're always getting into spats, I'm sorry to say."

The policeman squeezed his hands together and shuffled his feet from side to side. "That I don't rightly know, Ma'am."

Cayley nodded and sat down on the bench again. She heard her name murmured from the next cell. Finally, one of the inmates, a woman with dusty hair hanging limply on her shoulders asked, "Ain't you Cayley Wallace? THE Cayley Wallace?"

Cayley raised her head without moving her body. "Why yes I am," she said in a sweet voice. "Very pleased to meet you." The women in the next cell crowded against the bars, starring solemnly at her.

"What you doin' in here?" asked one of them. "I thought you was above the law."

Cayley didn't answer. She turned her face away and began to hum the Pineapple Rag.

**

Within the hour, the policeman returned. Cayley hadn't moved from her position on the bench, hands folded in her lap. "Your husband is at City Hospital, Ma'am," he said. "He's badly wounded, but it looks like he'll pull through. He pressed charges against you." He looked at his shoes. "I'm sorry. It looks like you'll have to stay here. Is there someone I should notify?"

Cayley looked bewildered, and then appeared to wake for a moment from her hazy dream. "Wo Sam. He's the one." She gave the officer the phone numbers of her home on Green Street and her sporting house.

**

Sam walked into the prison just after a metal plate of unidentifiable food was handed into the cell. The jailor was reluctant to open the cell door to let the Chinese man enter until Cayley insisted.

"What have you done?" His face was lined with worry as he sat on the bench beside her.

"It's just one of our spats," she told Sam. "He'll come to his senses soon enough and stop all this foolishness."

Sam was adamant. "Cayley, you asked me to tell you the truth when it's really important, so listen to me now. Bill has hired the best lawyer in town. He means to bring you down, whatever it takes. You must defend yourself."

Cayley covered her face with her hands and whispered, "I was crazy angry. I wasn't aiming at anyone, Sam. Bill stepped into the shot, plain and simple. What can I defend?"

"What came over you? You could have killed them. And for what!"

"I don't know. I don't know! I was so angry. I wanted to teach him a lesson. The things she said to me…. I wanted to hurt them. I know it doesn't make any sense." She shrugged her shoulders. "I went a little crazy. A lot crazy."

Sam had never seen her look so tired. "I'll only say this once. He got what he deserved. It's too bad that you were the one to do it."

She looked up and their gaze locked for a few seconds. "And now I'll get what I deserve," she said quietly.

"I'm hiring a good lawyer for you—Jackson, if I can get him."

"Ah, one of our customers."

"I'll have a hard time talking him into it, but he'll do it. Nobody likes to lose, and it looks like this is a case no one can win. I'll tell him he'll see his name in the papers a lot. He'll go for that. How are they treating you in here?"

"They're as good as they can be. I have my own cell, whoopee." She smiled at him. "And lots of company. Don't waste your pity, Sam. I was meant for a bad end."

"Don't. Don't." He leaned toward her and put his arms around her. She collapsed into him, curling into a ball against his chest. "Don't you stop fighting now," he whispered to the top of her head.

Chapter SEVENTY-FOUR

Sam returned to stay at the Green Street house. Manuela cooked and cleaned as though Cayley was still in residence. In the days that followed, Sam continued to run the business, which seemed to be more popular now that Cayley was notorious. He had expected things to slow down, but with the onslaught of curious customers willing to pay top dollar, he gave some thought to selling the new bordello.

He came every day to the prison, and sat across from Cayley in a room set aside for that purpose on the lower floor. It was as grim as the cell, with chipped cream-colored walls painted over many times. The scuffed table between them made it difficult to speak low. Cayley had taken to wearing simple frocks without stays, since bathing was only possible one day a week. Sam cleared his throat and looked away. "What do you want to do about the business? If we sell it, the money could be put to good use for your defense."

"You could run the house as well as me." She sat with her knees drawn into her chest.

"That will work for a while," he said. "But soon they'll be calling it 'the Chinaman's place' instead of the House of Wallace—and clients won't want to pay top dollar any more. Let's face it—you were the reason a lot of them came."

"We had some good times, didn't we?" Cayley leaned forward and smiled wanly at him. "All that doesn't seem to matter much anymore. You decide. You're a smart fella."

"If we're going to sell, we better do it while the price is still high. What about approaching Montrose?"

Cayley put her arms over her head like a small child. "Oh God, have we come to this? I hate that slime."

"He has the money, and he knows the business." Sam turned slightly to face her. "The longer we wait, the less the business is worth. And Beatrice is still in medical school. We have to consider that."

Cayley kept her arms over her head and sighed deeply. "It wouldn't hurt to make a few inquiries. Go to Opal first. Just don't embarrass me too much," she said softly.

"I would never do that to you. Don't worry—I'll get every cent it's worth and more."

She raised her eyes, and held him steady with her gaze. "You know, Sam, I've had plenty of time to think in here. My head is clear for the first time in years. Even a real fool like me can see what kind of man you are. I'm only sorry I had to land in jail to appreciate it."

He smiled a tic of a smile, and nodded. "About time." He reached into a vest pocket, palmed a slip of paper to her, stood up and walked away.

In her cell, Cayley read:

….Yet I never weary of watching for you on the road.
Each day I go out at the City Gate
With a flask of wine, lest you should come thirsty.
Oh that I could shrink the surface of the World,
So that suddenly I might find you standing at my side!
—Wang Chien

Chapter SEVENTY-FIVE

Sam paused between the thirty-foot-high columns support-
ing the gilded dome of the Hibernia Bank on the corner of Jones
and McAllister. After patting down his pocket to make sure he
had what he needed—a note from Cayley authorizing the contin-
uance of Beatrice's monthly check from her personal account—
he strode into the ornate marble and gilt lobby to the manager's
desk. The man barely gave Sam a glance as he stamped the
transaction, then walked over to one of the cages and handed it
to a clerk. Sam overheard the two talking.

"Her cash is still good," said the manager.

Sam's eyes moved over the ornate plasterwork of the cof-
fered ceiling.

The clerk glanced over at Sam. "Still and all, I wouldn't
give a nickel or a half-dime for her chances. I hear she has a big
church-going family." The clerk shook his head from side-to-
side causing his wire-rimmed spectacles to slide down his nose,
"maybe they'll come forward for her." He pushed up his glasses
with a thumb, and the manager returned to his desk.

"Tell your mistress it's done," he said, looking up at Sam.

That afternoon, Wo Sam met his sister at the door of the
Green Street house, drew her inside and sat across from her on
the white brocade sofa in the parlor.

"Li, listen. Maybe we can get Beatrice to write to Cayley—
it might make a difference."

"Have you been in the sun too long? I thought she hated her
auntie."

"I'm going to tell her the truth about the money." He rearranged himself on the red ottoman to face his sister squarely.

"Do you think knowing a whorehouse paid for her school
and fancy dresses will make her feel affection? You might as
well ask her to come testify to Cayley's good character." Li
pulled down the edge of her Western-style jacket and fixed her
eyes on the bronze statue of a ballerina on the sideboard. "This
place could use a good dusting."

318

"That's not a bad idea. The testimony, I mean. She's going to study to be a doctor, which is highly respected by these whites. Her word will be important."

Lilly sighed and dropped her shoulders in exasperation. "That was a joke, elder brother. How do you think she's going to feel about being identified as Ellen Leary's daughter?"

"She doesn't have to be. All she has to say is that she was an orphan and Cayley supported her all the way through school."

"What if the newspapers find out? She might not want to take the chance."

"Help me persuade her. You're the clever one."

Lilly sat elbow-to-knee, one hand propping her chin. "It's finally happened. You've lost your mind."

Chapter SEVENTY-SIX

The envelope came in the morning post; it sat on the tray near the door. A gust of wind followed Beatrice into the foyer and blew the contents of the tray to the floor. Exasperated, she continued to her room, removed her coat and hat, set down an armload of books, and returned to the foyer. As she picked up the contents of the tray, she examined the handwriting; her name—B. Leary—and address were neatly printed in large letters clear across the front. The writing was familiar; she touched upon a memory hollowed by age, spiced with the vague scent of bay rum. She pressed her lips together, carefully slit the top with the opener next to the tray and began to read:

"Dear Miss Bean…"

Chapter SEVENTY-SEVEN

The day after Sam posted the letter, he attended Cayley's arraignment at the temporary courthouse on McAllister Street. As he sat in the back of the room, Cayley was called before the bench by name, attorney Jackson by her side. "Catherine Pearson Wallace Duarte, please hold up your right hand," the court clerk instructed. She did so.

Sam recognized the judge, a fatherly man, as a former client of the house on O'Farrell—his tastes ran to the darker-skinned girls. Cayley always made a point to spoil him; he was one of the early investors and a great pal of Rolifer's. The judge slumped forward over his podium like a hungry raven eyeing a potential meal; the clerk read out the charge: "You, Catherine Pearson Wallace Duarte, stand accused by one William Duarte, for the crime of aggravated assault with a firearm with intent to kill the aforesaid William Duarte on May 15th 1908 in San Francisco, California, causing grave bodily harm. This is an indictment against you for pre-meditated assault with a deadly weapon. If convicted, you will serve a term of not less than fifteen years in the state penitentiary for women. Do you understand the charge against you?"

"Yes, your honor," said Cayley softly.

"Please speak up, Mrs. Duarte," said the court clerk, who looked more like a boy than a man, with his slicked-back hair, snappy bow tie and crisp collar. The typewriter behind him clacked loudly in the wood-paneled room.

Cayley repeated her words with more force.

"How say you, Catherine Duarte, guilty or not guilty?" The clerk continued.

Jackson stepped forward and put his hand on Cayley's shoulder. "My client pleads not guilty due to mitigating circumstances, your honor. We request a trial by jury."

The judge nodded. "As you wish," he said tiredly.

"We request that Mrs. Duarte be free while waiting for the trial date, your honor," Jackson said. "She is not a flight risk."

The judge shook his head. "I can't grant that, considering Mrs. Duarte's…. No."

"The plea will be recorded, and a court date for criminal trial by jury will be set," said the clerk. "Mrs. Duarte, you will be held in city jail until such date."

The judge caught Cayley's eye for a brief second, then turned his face away, impassive.

True friends will be rare as rubies, thought Sam. His lip curled in disgust as he left the courtroom.

Chapter SEVENTY-EIGHT

"Dear Sam:

I was certainly taken aback by the situation in which Cayley finds herself. It's very disturbing. I'm not at all surprised she has been the source of my living. I ignored what was in front of my face for a long time, but simple mathematics proved me wrong.

She has been writing to me these many years. At first, I didn't answer out of childish anger, then I found myself shamed by her simple honesty and desire to be as truthful as possible to make up for lies of the past. She never criticized me for not writing back: her letters were always full of good cheer and encouragement. With every one I received, I felt more and more guilty that I had pushed her aside. I was much relieved when you and most of her "girls" made it through the earthquake and fire. She carried on considerably about "her Bill," the man she married. It must have been unbearably painful for her to learn of his betrayal. I haven't heard from her in some time.

I felt great relief when reading your letter. I've thought many times of trying to bridge the troubles of the past years but could not find the words.

The other interns and I work in the charity hospital here in Philadelphia. I have seen so many desperately poor women—women I used to think were so different from me—beaten down by factory work, cruel husbands, or the effort of trying to feed themselves and their children by selling their own bodies. Some of the youngest ones and many older women are ravaged by the French disease—none invited this terrible sickness and most never willingly chose the life that brought it. I couldn't treat these people without admitting that the only reason I was a physician rather than a patient was Cayley's generosity to my mother and me. I have been, at times, filled with shame for the cruel way I acted toward her. Those I treat would be my equals if they had my advantages. Cayley might have made different choices, as well.

I hardly know what to say to her after all these years, but I would consider myself less of a Christian if I didn't at least send her a short note of some sort. I will do my best.

As to traveling to San Francisco to testify to Cayley's character, I'm sure you'll understand that's quite impossible. I cannot leave school and my responsibilities in the wards. I don't know if it will make a difference, but I will send a letter to the court if you provide the address. I'm terribly sorry to see both you and Cayley in such a difficult circumstance. Strange how things turn out, isn't it?

Your friend,
Belle Beatrice Leary"

Chapter SEVENTY-NINE

"Sam, look, it's a letter from Bean!" Cayley shoved the note to him across the table with two fingers. "She says she's heard through mutual friends about my predicament." She looked mischievously at him under her lashes; the thinness of her face made the gesture seem exaggerated. "Now who do you suppose that could be?" She reached across the table and squeezed his hand hard for a few seconds, causing the guard who was watching them to step forward. Cayley withdrew her hand quickly. "She says she's doing well in medical school and it was the right choice for her, and she thanks me for all I've done for her. See?" She pointed to the note, then clasped her hands together and bit her lips, giving him a moment to read it. "It makes it almost worth being in jail." She smiled and raised her eyebrows. "Almost. Silly me, such a fuss over a little note!" She swiped at the corners of her eyes with the hem of her sleeve. "I'll write to her right away. Sam?"

"Cayley?"

"I'm so grateful I can hardly see straight." Tenderness softened the deepening lines in her face.

***

"I'll buy it, no matter how long it takes. San Jose is growing like a spring pig thanks to the fire, and the business is growing with it." Opal sat like a man with one ankle on the opposite knee. Her striped bloomers inched up to reveal a length of dark stocking above her boot. "She stuck by me when I was down and I'll do the same for her." She swirled the red wine in her glass. "I'd as soon cut off my own toe than see Montrose take over the place." She aimed the rim of the glass at Sam and squinted one of her eyes. "I always thought he was the one that came after me with the knife, 'cause I sassed him. He's the Ripper, I'm sure of it." She took a sip. "You tell Cayley we'll do it fair and square."

"I'm greatly relieved to hear you say that, Miss Opal," said Sam. "Now let's go and do what we have to do." He helped her into the carriage and they clattered at a moderate clip from the Green Street house down to McAllister.

Gawkers filled the courtroom, making the warm air seem even closer. The wood paneling on the walls looked powdery dry in the shafts of light that penetrated from the few high windows. Opal wedged herself beside Sam in the gallery. "That's her mother down there, isn't it?" said Opal.

"And a few of her brothers and sisters," said Sam. "I'm surprised they came, considering there won't be a handout."

Opal leaned away from him and brought the corner of her mouth up in a wry smile. "You're sounding a little bitter, Mr. Wo. 'Course I know what you're talking about as I recall a few family visits to the old O'Farrell house myself."

"I asked her mother to testify to her character, and she refused. What kind of person does that?"

The gavel brought their conversation to a halt.

Bill Duarte, pale and obviously weak, sat next to his attorney. The man was one of Bill's big-shot friends from city hall, short in stature, with a jutting jaw covered by a salt-and-pepper beard. He jumped up as if spring-loaded to make his opening statement. "Your honor," he declaimed, "Cayley Wallace Duarte is a notorious dipsomaniac who, for a decade, has run several houses of ill repute. She's routinely given to rages and emotional outbursts of all kinds." The man turned toward the jury and raised his eyebrows, thumbs wrapped around the edges of his jacket. "I will prove beyond all doubt that she has mistreated and abused my client for years, forcing him to marry her under the most false of circumstances. AND,..." he paused for dramatic effect, sweeping his hand over the courtroom, "I will also prove that she knowingly and willfully intended to murder my client in order to bury her own dark secrets and secure his wealth for her own use."

"What the hell is he talking about?" Opal hissed. Sam shook his head.

When the prosecutor sat down, Cayley's man Jackson stood up. The contrast in appearance couldn't have been more evident.

326

Jackson was tall, clear-eyed, and several years younger than his opponent. *The Examiner will write about his looks,* thought Sam.

Jackson held up both hands, palms up, and addressed the jury quizzically. "Who in the world is my opponent talking about? It can't be my client. Catherine Duarte, married to Bill Duarte for nearly five years now." He turned and indicated Cayley with one of his hands. "Cayley—that's what her family and friends call her—is just like you, ladies and gentlemen of the jury. She was a hard-working house servant, and did what she had to do not only to feed herself and her large Irish family, but also her husband. If it weren't for her, he'd still be running two-penny gambling games instead of trying to run City Hall!" The courtroom erupted in laughter. "Her only crime is that she loved too well, and not wisely. Driven to madness by her husband's faithlessness, his blatant affair with another woman…well, in one single moment, she lost her reason. Does she regret it? Oh yes! But should she bear penalty for a crime she was forced to commit? Who really IS the victim here? I tell, you, ladies and gentlemen," he turned to face the jury once again, and put his hands together prayerfully, "you WILL find mercy in your hearts to understand and forgive this sad and dejected woman who has—painfully—lost the only thing she truly cared about—the love of her husband." He bowed and sat down.

Opal and Sam leaned back slightly and looked at each other, impressed.

The prosecuting attorney began his case. He called a neighbor who lived down the street from Cayley's new sporting house and began questioning him. The neighbor asserted that Mrs. Duarte's "boarding house" only seemed to have women in it, and that "gentlemen callers" were there all hours of the night, especially on weekends, when "a regular free-for-all" took place. He added, "I don't think much of it was free, if you know what I mean." The crowd in the courtroom tittered.

Jackson cross-examined the neighbor: "Are you aware there are many boarding houses that cater exclusively to women?" to which the man had to answer "yes." "And, since Mrs. Duarte doesn't live on the premises, perhaps her boarders make their own rules about who comes to call and when; could that be true?"

"But I seen her there all the time! All dressed up fancy. Everybody in town knows…"

Jackson held up his hand and stopped the man with a hard stare. "This court is not interested in your opinion, or that of "everybody in town", either. Your job is to answer the question as put forth, thank you. That's all, your honor."

The prosecutor called up a few more witnesses who attested to Cayley's considerable appetite for liquor. The owner of the Poodle Dog restaurant looked apologetically at Cayley when he told the court, "She's my best customer—free with her money and her bottles. When she comes in, all the waiters hop to, 'cause they know they'll be pouring a lot and they'll get a big tip."

When Jackson questioned the man as to Cayley's "rages," he said, "By God, no! She's as merry as Sinter Claus the day after Christmas!" The crowd roared, and even Cayley managed a smile.

As the afternoon wore on, the judge advised the prosecutor that he was allowed one more witness that day. "I call Michael Pearson to the stand."

Cayley's mouth dropped open and she looked at her attorney, eyes wide. Sam could see her whispering frantically to Jackson as he shrugged his shoulders and patted her hand.

"Michael," the prosecutor began, "you are the brother of Catherine, or should I say Cayley Duarte, is that correct?"

Michael was sweating and red-faced. He nodded, drew one of his hands across his forehead then quickly moved it to his lap out of sight.

"I take that to mean yes?"

"Yes." He croaked out the word, and carefully avoided looking in Cayley's direction. The courtroom crowd, restless and shifting in the late afternoon heat grew icily silent.

"So I suppose you would be in a position to know her habits, temperament, and business, would you not?"

Michael began to nod again, then stopped and said, "Yes."

"Michael, has you sister ever struck you in anger?"

"Yes. More than once."

"Have you ever seen her temper explode against her husband, Mr. Duarte?"

"Yes. Many times."

Cayley stood up and shouted, "Michael! How could you!" before Jackson pulled her down to her seat.

"Sweet Jesus, she's only making it worse," said Opal under her breath. "Shut up, Cay."

"And what business is your sister—Mrs. Duarte—in, Michael?"

"I'm 'shamed to say she runs a whorehouse. She's run one for years, before the fire and even today."

The courtroom erupted in a wave of noise that bounced off the ceiling, a flurry of excited voices. The judge banged his gavel for order as the prosecutor turned away, smirking at Jackson as he took his seat.

Jackson patted Cayley's shoulder as he stood up and walked to the witness stand. "Michael, you must be very upset with your sister to say things like this about her, is that so?"

"Objection!" said the prosecutor. The judge agreed.

"Michael, do you know that your sister has given a great deal of money to your mother and sisters and brothers over the years to help them out?"

"I never took a red penny from her."

"Maybe that's why you're so upset with her."

"Objection. Leading the witness."

"Your honor, I request that I might continue cross-examining this witness when we reconvene tomorrow."

The judge nodded. Cayley, looking more dejected that ever, was led off by a woman officer.

Opal pushed against the crowd descending the stairs. "I need a drink. Now how do you suppose Duarte got Cayley's brother to testify against her?"

Sam, right behind her, was grim. "It's a payoff or something worse."

Outside across the street from the courthouse, Opal pinched at the tops of her pale kid gloves, pulling them up her wrists. "It doesn't look good for her right now, does it?" The new electric streetcar glided past them, stuffed with workers on their way home.

Sam sighed, his shoulders slumping forward. "I must talk to Jackson. It wouldn't do well to question Michael further. Do you mind waiting a moment?" She shook her head; the Chinese man crossed the street and began a hurried conversation with the attorney just emerging from the wooden door. Opal collected their carriage from the livery and waited for him to mount up. She handed him the reins. Evening was closing fast, the hour when the streets are nearly deserted before bar and restaurant patrons infuse new life into them. They clopped up the hill to the Green Street house. The mare startled as a horseless carriage careened around the corner and came toward her; Sam tightened the reins, and the animal settled down once the noisy contraption passed.

"Do you ever think about buying one of them flivvers?" said Opal.

Sam smiled. "All the time. Nothing to feed or clean up after—not that I do that. But Cayley says,…" his voice drifted off, and he shrugged his shoulders.

Manuela met them at the door, obviously excited. "Mr. Sam, wait 'til you see who's here!" She plucked at his sleeve and tugged him into the drawing room. A tall young woman with fiery hair stood up.

"Hello Sam. Long time no see."

With a huge smile on his face, Sam grasped both of Beatrice's out-held forearms. She dropped her arms, and with a burst of a laugh threw them around his neck and hugged him to her. She then put her hands on his shoulders and held him at arm's length.

"You've come," was all he could manage.

"Yes, I have come," she said, grinning from ear to ear. "No promises. But I will visit Aunt Cayley."

330

Behind them, Opal put her gloved fingers to her lips. "My God, you're Ellen's girl, aren't you? You look so much like her!"

Sam turned from Beatrice. "Miss Beatrice Leary, this is Miss Opal Boone, a very good friend of your Aunt Cayley's."

Beatrice stuck out her hand, and Opal shook it. "I'll bet you don't remember me, do you? You were just a little tyke the last time I saw you."

"A lot of years in between," said Beatrice. She reached down for her traveling bag, nestled against the side of the red ottoman near where she stood.

Sam stepped over and grabbed the handles. "I'll take this up to your old room," he said. "Welcome home!"

Manuela prepared a light dinner for them of onion soup, roasted chicken and fried potatoes. Opal and Sam shared news of the trial with Beatrice, including the betrayal of Cayley's brother Michael. "She could use encouragement," said Sam. "I can take you to her tonight, if you're not too tired from your journey."

"It's the reason I'm here. Let's go."

"I'll sit this one out," said Opal. "You two can use the time together."

On the carriage ride downtown to the prison, Beatrice confessed, "I'm not sure I know what to say. It's not like I'm meeting the parson for tea."

"Don't let the jail overwhelm you," said Sam. "It's not made to make people feel happy." He smiled at her. "You'll be fine. She will be so glad to see you she probably won't remember a word either of you say."

Sam tied up at one of the posts in front of the building in the narrow alley. He took Beatrice's elbow and walked with her into the chilly anteroom, where they signed their names on a ledger as visitors. He sat to wait as Beatrice, after a single nervous backward glance, was escorted by a matron into one of the dimly lit visiting room.

Chapter EIGHTY

Cayley, head down, walked into the room on the arm of a woman officer. She fully expected to see Opal, and was ashamed of the state of things as they now were. When she sat down at the chair across the desk, she inhaled deeply, raised her head and nearly fell over. For once in her life, she was speechless.

"Hello, Aunt Cay," said Beatrice softly.

Cayley put both hands on the front edge of the table and peered forward as though it was difficult for her to see. She took in every detail of her grown-up niece and shook her head in small arcs. "It's really you," she whispered. Beatrice nodded. Cayley reached across the table with one thin arm and Beatrice clasped her hand. The contrast of her blush pink skin and frilly cuff against Cayley's pale and bony fingers nearly brought tears to the young woman's eyes. The guard looked the other way. The two women sat in silence, empty of words and full of emotion. The electric light overhead threw sharp shadows onto their faces. "I'm not dreaming again, am I?" said Cayley.

"No, Aunt Cay. I've come to be with you for a little while."

"Is Sam outside?"

Beatrice nodded.

"Sam...." Cayley let the sentence trail off and smiled without showing her teeth. She seemed to wake up. "What about your studies? Is everything all right at school?"

"Everything is fine, thanks to you. I know you paid for school and my living. No more secrets about that now."

"Oh!" Cayley waved her free hand in front of her face as if fending off a fly. "It wasn't all me. Your...Bill...Bill choked up some of it, but it was really all the money your mother would have had if she lived. She'd be busting at the seams with pride." Cayley raised her hand to indicate all of Beatrice. "Her own beautiful daughter, almost a doctor!" She covered their clasped hands with her own. "I'm so proud of you...for both her and me."

They sat quietly again for a moment. Beatrice shifted in her seat. "I'm giving a letter to your attorney—a character reference. I don't know if they'll be able to use it."

"I'd welcome a good word, after today." Cayley rolled her eyes. "My own brother…"

"I heard. I'm sorry. Sam said you've been really good to your family."

"I've done my best. I don't know what it's all about, with Michael. But it's damning me for sure." She patted Beatrice's hand, still clasped in her own. "I'm not expecting much, I guess. But I thank you for your letter. I hope it softens up the jury a little. At least I've got one respectable person on my side."

'I wish I could do more…" Beatrice turned her attention to her reticule, arranging it squarely in her lap with her free hand.

"You're here, and that's plenty for me." Cayley raised their joined hands and shook them as if she were erasing a bad thought with a clean rag. "Well, that's enough of the sad stories. Tell me about Philadelphia. Do you have a young man yet?"

Beatrice put her head down and smiled. "Too busy."

For the next half hour, Cayley quizzed Beatrice about her life, school, and plans she was making until both of them laughed like schoolgirls. They didn't unclasp hands until the prison matron stepped up to separate them and take Cayley back. Cay put her arm jauntily through the matron's and said, "That there handsome girl is going to be a doctor, Edamae," as they turned to leave the room.

"That's real nice," said the matron and nodded in Beatrice's direction as the young woman stood up and gathered her skirts around her.

***

Back at the Green Street house, Beatrice sat at the table in the dining room, her hands around a hot cup of coffee Manuela had produced from the kitchen. Sam and Opal sat across from her.

"She seems to be taking it well," said Beatrice, staring fixedly into her cup.

"Don't fool yourself," said Opal. "You don't become a success in this business without being able to make a street sweeper believe he's the King of Sweden—and she was the best little actress I've ever seen. When her family turned on her, it nearly killed her."

Beatrice looked up quickly then once again examined the contents of her cup. Tendrils of steam filled the kitchen with the dark, earthy, bitter scent.

"I cannot help but think it has something to do with the night your mother died," added Sam, passing the ceramic container of sugar to Beatrice. "Though this is probably not the time to talk about it."

"No, I want to hear it. I've been avoiding it long enough." Beatrice held up her hand to say no to the sugar. "Tell me what happened."

"Her brother Michael was in the alley with your mother that night—Cayley knows that for sure. But he claims he left and a tall, slim man came in. She believed him; I'm sure Cayley thought that man was Bill, which is probably one of the things that set her off. She didn't want to think evil of either of them, but ...."

"Cayley's husband knew my mother?" Beatrice moved her hand across her forehead quickly as if clearing it. A lock of flaming red hair dropped and looped around her ear.

"We all knew each other, even back then," said Opal quickly, and gave Sam a look. "Your ma and Cayley used to work as bar girls down at the Blue Rooster on Market—it's long-gone, thanks to the fire. Bill used to come in once in a while. Isn't that right, Sam?"

"Before my time," Sam muttered into his cup.

"So Bill Duarte would have been the last person to see my mother alive. You don't think he...?"

"No, I don't," said Sam.

"He and your mother were friendly," Opal interjected. "But they had a falling out years ago. Nothing serious, though." She sipped her tea, and coughed. "Jesus, Sam, where do you keep the whiskey locked up in this museum?"

"So no one knows what really happened." Beatrice toyed with the handle of her cup while the trio sat silently. Stifling an exaggerated yawn, she said, "Long day; I'm exhausted. I'm going up to bed. I'll see you all in the morning." She bid the others good night, and pulled herself up the stairs hand over hand on the railing as she did when she was a child.

She took in the smell of the old house—not much changed from those happy early years. Manuela, considerably grayer and more stooped, still polished the furniture with lemon skins. Cayley had changed the wallpaper in the upstairs hall. Beatrice hesitated for a moment in the doorway of Cayley's bedroom. An enormous, elaborate ebony-wood and gilt bed took up much of the room. There were a number of pictures, all with their faces turned down on the nightstands on either side of the bed. Moonlight pooled on the coverlet, made lacy by the window curtains. She crossed the Aubusson carpet, stepping from one full-blown rose to another, again reclaiming her childhood, and sat on the bed. She turned up one picture and looked at a handsome fair-haired man standing in profile, his straight nose the most prominent feature of his hairless face. He was wearing a light-colored waistcoat and vest, his hand casually in one pocket, the other holding a cigarette. He seemed familiar; Beatrice recognized him as an older version of the man who came to New York with Cayley years ago. She picked up another portrait, this one equally posed, a frontal view of him and Cayley arm-in-arm, dressed in somber clothing. She didn't see brutality in his face—if anything, he emitted intelligence, pride and a confident presence: a man who might listen to reason. She set the picture down and continued to her room.

It had changed little since she left; embarrassed, Beatrice noted that Cayley kept it almost like a shrine. She turned off the lights and shed her shirtwaist and skirt in the near-darkness, recalling the morning she so righteously marched down to the newspaper office to reclaim her family honor. It seemed a lifetime ago. She smiled a little and tipped her head forward to take the pins out of her hair. That daring little girl still lived in her. In the few days she planned to remain in San Francisco, she would speak to Bill Duarte and ask him to drop the charges, for old time's sake. What harm could it do?

Chapter EIGHTY-ONE

Beatrice attended the trial the next day with Wo Sam and Opal. The prosecutor continued to produce witness after witness who testified to years of temper, free-spending, and Mrs. Duarte's questionable nocturnal habits. In the late afternoon, the prosecuting attorney turned to the jury. "I wish to point out, ladies and gents, that I do not intend to paint Mrs. Duarte as someone completely out of control, but very much IN control, in every circumstance. Mrs. Duarte is a very calculating woman. The next witness will prove that once and for all. I call Mr. Henry Wallace to the stand."

The crowded courtroom swung as one to watch as Henry, felt hat clutched in both hands, shuffled to the testimony box to be sworn in. Cayley traded mystified looks with her attorney.

"Mr. Wallace," the prosecutor began. "You married Catherine "Cayley" Pearson in the year of our Lord 1887, is that correct?"

Henry cleared his throat heavily. The drink had changed him: he was swarthy in color, and heavier around the middle. He leaned forward in his chair, "Yes."

"And you are STILL married to this woman who claims to be the wife of William Duarte, isn't that so?"

Pandemonium reigned in the courtroom. Everyone seemed to be talking at once, causing Henry to hold back his answer until the judge pounded his gavel several times and threatened to clear the court. Henry had a pained expression on his face as though his stomach hurt. He leaned forward in his chair again, "Yes."

"That would make Mrs. Duarte a bigamist, wouldn't it ladies and gentlemen?" The prosecutor projected his voice over the crowd.

Henry stood up. "It's not her fault. I never told her." His words were drowned out by the sound of chairs scraping and risen voices. "She didn't know. It's a sin to divorce. I made it seem like I did it." His words were lost under the sound of the gavel and the judge shouting for adjournment of the court until the following day. Henry looked plaintively at Cayley as he was being led out of the courtroom by the prosecutor's assistant.

***

Opal sat across from Cayley in the dimly lit visiting room. Someone had mopped the floor earlier and the stench of stale water sullied the air. "You really didn't know?" said Opal.

"On my child's grave, I did not." The bluish glow from the overhead light made Cayley feel distant and sleepy.

"This is a fine mess."

"Jackson will get him to tell the whole story tomorrow, but the damage is done, isn't it?" Cayley sighed.

"And you've got not one but two husbands, girl." Opal tried to sound playful.

"All that and a hoo-er house, too," said Cayley. They began to laugh, hesitantly at first; then they reached across the table, grasping each other by the shoulders and roared until tears rolled down their faces.

Chapter EIGHTY-TWO

Beatrice found the whereabouts of Bill Duarte easily enough—it was in the newspaper. Though his room number at the Palace wasn't given, she brought her doctor's bag and claimed she had been summoned but misplaced the room number. At the trial, Bill certainly looked as though he needed a doctor's care. The clerk called his room to confirm—apparently a doctor was summoned. She went up to the second floor and, pacing back and forth, rehearsed what she would say to him several times before knocking on the door.

Duarte's attorney answered it. "Where's the doctor?" he said, looking behind her.

Beatrice fought the temptation to say, "I AM the doctor, you fool." Instead, she said, "This is personal business regarding my deceased mother."

"Miss, I don't mean to be rude, but this is hardly the time to be discussing mystery relatives with Mr. Duarte," the prosecutor said, his eyelids lowered in derision.

"Who is it?" Bill Duarte's voice sounded from around the corner.

"A friend of Ellen Leary," Beatrice shouted over the head of the prosecutor. Silence.

"Let her in," said Duarte. "And leave us."

Beatrice made her way tentatively around the corner, holding her black bag in front of her. She found Duarte sitting in one of the upholstered chairs next to a table covered with legal papers. She stepped squarely in front of him. "I'm Beatrice Leary. How do you do."

Bill Duarte said nothing. If possible, he had become even more pale, and stared, his face slack with astonishment.

Beatrice, growing increasingly uncomfortable, avoided his eyes. Finally, she said, "Sir, you are staring."

"By God," he finally croaked out. "I'd swear Ellen Leary was alive and walked into this room today. You look so much like her." He blinked rapidly several times. "Please," he said, gathering himself together and indicating a chair across the table.

"So you knew my mother?"

"Oh yes. A beautiful, beautiful woman."

"I do have some questions for you about her. But that's not the reason I'm here."

"Would you like tea? Are you still in medical school? Yes, I see the bag…"

"Mr. Duarte, please." Beatrice sat down and placed the bag on her lap. "I'm not here to trade pleasantries or discuss my current situation. I certainly understand how upset you must be with my Aunt Cayley…"

Bill Duarte made a gesture of disgust, pounding his open palm on the table between them. "Is that what you're here for? To talk about that crazy woman?"

She turned to face him. "Mr. Duarte, Cayley can be difficult, as we both know. But to put her away in prison for the rest of her life because of your indiscretion hardly reflects well on you."

"Did she ask you to come here?"

"She has no idea I'm here."

"Ah," Duarte ran his finger over his mustache, smoothing it down. "You two didn't have a conversation about me I take it?"

"No. Why would we? She would never ask me to come to you and request anything. She's filled with regret as it is, and takes full responsibility for her actions. I'm only here to ask you to do the right thing and set her free."

"I wanted to set her free. I asked for a divorce and she wouldn't give it to me."

"Wo Sam told me she thought you would reconcile. I believe she's still in love with you."

Bill snorted and held a white kerchief to his mouth briefly. "Strange kind of love, if you ask me. I've got a hole in me that's going to fester for the rest of my considerably shorter life."

"I'm not saying what she did was right. It wasn't. I'm here to ask for mercy for her. I'm only in town for a few days, and there's not much more I can do." She turned and looked hard into his eyes.

His face softened. "You look so much like your mother."

"So you said." Beatrice lowered her eyes to her case, and then focused on the botanical print of a red Dutch tulip on the wall across from her. "I understand you were one of the last to see her alive," she said evenly.

"That's true. Me and Michael Pearson." He said Michael's name with such disdain she nearly turned to face him, but merely closed her eyes for a few seconds.

"Tell me what happened."

"I'd come to see your mother at the O'Farrell house and I saw her in the alley before I went in. She was talking to someone. I turned toward them and saw it was Michael Pearson; I passed him on his way out. He was in a hurry, and had something in his hand. I'm ashamed to say your mother and I had words. She was angry with me for something I did. Something foolish, and she was right to be angry. She asked me to leave."

Beatrice caught her breath, but still did not look at the man.

"I wondered myself if Michael had anything to do with…what happened. I don't know, and that's all I'm going to say. Other than it was a terrible tragedy to lose such a fine woman."

"I still miss her." Beatrice's long neck curved down.

"I'm so sorry, my girl." He started to get up, but Beatrice rose quickly.

"Please think about my request," she said. "Cayley was very kind to my mother and me." She stepped swiftly toward the door of the hotel room and let herself out.

Chapter EIGHTY-THREE

Beatrice and Sam were in the courthouse the next morning when Jackson asked for a day's delay due to Cayley's weakened state; he cited a doctor's visit to the prison the night before.

"I'm going to the prison to examine her myself," Beatrice said, hurrying into her gloves and cape.

"She was barely strong enough to stand up yesterday morning, hanging on the arm of the matron," said Sam. "I was concerned, but she insisted she was fine. She may resist your offer to examine her."

"I won't let her slip through my fingers."

***

Later that afternoon in the parlor of the Green Street house, Beatrice told Wo Sam. "Cayley hasn't been eating. She's given up, it seems. Maybe Opal can talk sense to her."

"Opal's gone back to San Jose to have her lawyer draw up plans for the buy-out." Sam rubbed his forehead with his left hand. "The trial will go on, anyway. Jackson will not cross-examine Henry Wallace. Cayley is indeed still married to him. I agree with Jackson; there's no need to keep it on the minds of the jury. Cayley is the only person to speak on her own behalf. Jackson will call her to begin the defense tomorrow."

Beatrice fretted, twisting her hands together. "She's so weak. I'm not sure she can do it."

"She'll have to," said Sam. "I'll go to the jail, and persuade her to take the stand for herself."

***

Sam signed the ledger book in the musty waiting room. "She's already had several visitors today, including her mother," the clerk said. "We're supposed to limit visits."

"Please, sir," said Sam, in his most appeasing voice. "She is ill, and I bring news from home that will comfort her."

The clerk leaned back in his chair until it balanced on two legs. His cheap, rumpled suit jacket bunched up around his middle like a sash. "Was that there fancy house as grand as they say?"

"It was a palace," said Sam. "A house full of music, laughter and pleasure. Any type of food or liquor you wanted, it was there. The women were very beautiful. I would invite you to come in, but it's all gone now. Mrs. Duarte has nothing left. It's all been taken from her."

"Waaal, I don't have the coin for it anyway. It must be nice to be rich, even for a little while."

"I wouldn't know," said Sam. "I am merely a servant. But I will tell you that she is a good woman, and does not deserve to be treated so poorly."

"The guards like her well enough," the clerk said. "Too bad." He drew a small jackknife from his pocket, opened it and began to pick his teeth. Wo Sam stood, silent. "Ah, g'wan in," the guard said. "Won't do no harm, considering."

"Thank you, sir." Wo Sam bowed deeply.

Cayley was brought in, supported by the guard, Edamae. Sam remained standing on his side of the table. "Your mother was here?"

Cayley sat down heavily in the plain wooden chair. She waved the thought away as though it were a fly. "She asked me to forgive her for not coming sooner. Said Bill had some kind of hold over my brother to make him say the things he did about me—I'll bet he took the glove I hid. She said she was afraid to cross Bill—he could make plenty of trouble for everyone. He made her choose one child over another." Cayley laughed bitterly. "She said she'd speak up for me anyway, my old ma."

"That's a good thing."

"I told her to go home and count her live chickens—that I was pretty well done for."

Wo Sam cleared his throat. "I've never thought of you as a coward. Until now," he said evenly.

"Oh Sam. What's the point?" She looked away from him as if searching the walls for solace and sighed heavily. "I'm so damn tired of everything. I'm tired of fighting."

"Remember the old days when you were competing with Madame Maude? Do you think she would sit in a cell and starve herself to death? She's probably laughing at you right now, over a twelve-course meal on Morton Lane."

Cayley looked up angrily. "That's a damn rude thing to say, considering the circumstances."

"The circumstances you brought upon yourself, do not forget. And now you sit full of self-pity. Opal still thinks Montrose is the Ripper. Perhaps it was he who killed Ellen after all. If that's so, Madame Maude and Montrose are having a good laugh at your weakness. You'll have let them win in the end. You have let all the people who looked down their noses at you win, too."

Cayley pulled herself up by the edge of the table, "What do you think you're doing, talking to me like this? You, you Chinee! Fancy accent and all; showing your true colors and turning on me too. All of you can go straight to hell."

Sam rose up to stand across from her. "Chinee? How about 'yellow devil bastard'? Have you fallen so low you must insult me and my years of loyalty? Are you truly unable to tell when someone actually cares about you? Have you no pride left? No memory of the many triumphs of your life?" Sam raised his voice. "Perhaps you deserve to starve to death and die in humiliation after all. Perhaps nothing you have done, or anything I have done for you means anything!"

"No," said Cayley, her voice breaking. "Not so."

"No," Sam said softly, struggling to keep his voice and face expressionless. "Not so at all." He lifted his hand to touch her face, but kept it inches away from her, knowing the guard would step in. She felt the heat from his hand and angled her face toward it, closing her eyes.

"Please stop destroying yourself. Please remember who you are. Remember this for me. And for Beatrice, and Opal, and all the women you have known." He paused. "They are all still with you. As am I."

"Oh Sam." Cayley lowered her head, and wavered dangerously on her feet. Sam checked the urge to go to her side. She slowly brought her hand up to almost touch his raised palm, and looked into his eyes. "Edamae," she called to the guard. She dropped her hand to the tabletop, but kept her gaze steadily locked into his. "Got any of that slop from lunch? I think I've got an appetite after all."

Sam brought his lips up in a tiny smile as Cayley continued to stare at him. "If I'm going down, I'll do it in style," she said. "If you please, Mr. Wo; send something decent for me to wear tomorrow. The red one with the jet trim—and the hat." She paused for a breath. "I appreciate your help—and you—as always. I'll see you in court." She linked arms with the guard and started to leave the room. Just before the doorway, she turned and said in a near whisper: "You're a devil all right." She locked eyes with him for a long moment, turned and was gone.

Chapter EIGHTY-FOUR

Beatrice paced restlessly after Sam left for the jail. She considered telling him she paid Bill a visit, but chose against it. It would only embarrass Cayley and would further depress her since it made no difference. Beatrice had hoped to hear from the court that the charges had been dropped, but no word came.

She felt powerless to stop the fast-moving train of Cayley's destruction. If her aunt couldn't speak for herself, all that was left was Beatrice's testimony on Cayley's behalf—immediately, the thought was replaced by the knowledge that the newspapers would tear her apart, exposing her as Ellen Leary's daughter the minute Bill Duarte's lawyer cross-examined her. A lifetime of denial made her stomach churn. She paced more quickly, angrily pushing aside the dainty furniture in the parlor. Suddenly, she stopped. Her black bag sat on the mirrored sideboard, lit from behind with reflected light. She was an accomplished medical student in Philadelphia, close to getting her degree. Her future did not depend on making a good marriage, receiving an inheritance, or approval of her womanly virtues. She drew herself to her full height and looked about for her hat, which she pinned on quickly, glancing in the hall mirror before she rang up a cab. Tapping the toe of her kid boot impatiently, she buttoned and unbuttoned her jacket until the hack arrived.

In the half-hour it took to get to the Palace Hotel, a calm descended on her, as if she had slipped into a warm bath. When she knocked at Bill Duarte's door, he answered, smiled when he saw her and ushered her in. The legal papers were gone from the table, replaced by a coffee service and a few empty dishes with crumbs on them. He cleared them, and placed them outside the door as she seated herself.

"Mr. Duarte," she began, her voice reasonable and direct, "I've decided to testify on behalf of my aunt."

Duarte rubbed his chin. "That's mighty noble of you."

"Thank you. As I expect your attorney will be eager to point out that my mother was Ellen Leary, who was widely supposed to be a prostitute…"

"Nothing could be farther from the truth."

"Nonetheless, Mr. Duarte…" Beatrice lowered her eyes and smiled, "I intend to beat him to the punch, so to speak, and give the court that information myself."

"Now why would you do that?"

"I have an excellent reason. You see, I intend to also say that my father, who deserted my mother and I, leaving us destitute and alone, was none other than…you, Mr. Duarte."

Duarte shook his head in disbelief. "Who…who told you that?" he stammered.

"Oh, no one told me that, Mr. Duarte. I realize that you have no intention of backing off from your suit against my aunt, so I hoped the threat of ruination—the destruction of your reputation, and perhaps the end of your political career—might persuade you."

"But saying those things would ruin you too!"

"Actually," Beatrice smiled, "it would do nothing of the sort. I'm not dependent on a perceived pure reputation as many women are. If word of this reaches Philadelphia, I expect there will be damage. But nonetheless, I will return home, finish my education, and proceed with my life as a doctor." She hesitated a moment. "And what will you do? After I publicly shame you, of course?"

Bill Duarte brought both hands to his forehead. "I can't believe this is happening."

Beatrice jumped up and straightened her jacket. "Your choice. The opportunity to be known as the soul of mercy, or a devious scalawag." She did not look at him as she marched out of the door.

Chapter EIGHTY-FIVE

In the morning, Jackson began his defense. He told the jury how much he appreciated the hard work the prosecution had done proving that Cayley was indeed a competent person. "The contrast between this smart businesswoman and the irrational act she fell prey to was due to an irresistible and uncontrollable impulse. She lost the power to choose between right and wrong, and to avoid doing the act was beyond her control. And no one can tell you about it better than Mrs. Duarte herself. For my first witness for the defense, I call Mrs. Catherine 'Cayley' Duarte."

Cayley, still shaky, took the stand on the arm of her guard. True to her word, she wore her scarlet dress, its jacket worked with a fleur-de-lys design in fine jet beading around the edges of the peplum. She held her head up proudly when being sworn in, sat down, and began her testimony:

"Your honor, ladies and gents," she nodded to the judge and courtroom. "Respectable. That pretty word don't mean much when you're starving to death. I don't expect mercy from you. Most of you cross the street when you see me coming. It's true that being disrespectable made me rich once. I was in business selling something men wanted—no different than any other merchant since the beginning of the world. But for some reason, for a woman to offer herself with no strings attached for an even exchange of money, it's seen as a crime. Well, everyone has to have someone to look down on, and I'm that someone right now. You can call it whatever you choose, but what I did was a public service. Yes! Contemplate that for a moment. If it weren't for me, a lot of girls might have died of starvation or worse down in the Barbary, and a lot of high-class marriages would have been mighty miserable, and I'm talking about a few marriages in this very room." Cayley paused, inhaled deeply, and fixed her eyes on the ornately carved courtroom doors so as not to focus on any of her former patrons.

"I've had my sorrows, just like you. I lost my own baby to sickness and my dearest friend to a murderer's knife. But I'm not

348

making excuses. Me being here today isn't about what I did for a living, so holding that against me just don't make sense." She paused again.

"I'm here because I love Bill Duarte, who wanted to be 're-spectable' more than he wanted to honor the promise he made me. It's about love gone wrong, that's what. I was raised right. Had I known another man had a claim on me I never would have said yes to Bill when he asked me to marry him. More than anything, I wanted to grow old by Bill's side. He loved me too, once; we had a real church wedding. So when I found he was romancing that young gal and wanted leave of me...well, I just went crazy. Can you understand that? Can you understand the very heart being torn out of you?" She took a deep breath.

"I lost the most important person in my life, and I just couldn't take another hurt. I'm sorry for what I did. I'm talking to you, Bill. I am truly sorry." She looked at him and nodded, a small rueful smile on her lips. "Looks like you got that divorce you wanted after all." She dropped her eyes to the floor and her hands went up to adjust the hatpin on her hat. "That's all I got to say."

A silence fell over the crowded room. Bill Duarte appeared distracted, his hand on the arm of his attorney. He leaned over and whispered in the other man's ear.

The prosecutor shook his head and shrugged. "No questions, your honor," he said. "Permission to approach the bench." He and Jackson made their way to the judge's podium. After a short conversation, they returned to their chairs.

The judge banged his gavel. "The prosecutor has informed me that Mr. Duarte has chosen to drop all charges in this case. Mrs. Duarte, you are free to go. The jury is summarily dismissed. This trial is over."

The murmur of the crowd reached a crescendo; attendees were standing, milling about, talking among themselves. The newspapermen left the room, coattails flying. Cayley's guard Edamae came over and gave her a brief hug. Cayley herself looked dazed. Jackson had hold of her arm, and Sam and Beatrice pushed their way to the front of the room to reach her. As they walked her toward the door, they passed Bill Duarte. Beatrice lowered her eyes and shot him a grateful glance. He stood up, stared straight ahead and said, under his breath, "It's not what you think." Cayley and her crew swept past him into the bright morning light and the sounds and smells of a new day on MacAllister Street.

"Now what just happened? What did he mean by that?" asked Cayley, breathlessly.

"No idea," said Beatrice.

Chapter EIGHTY-SIX

Cayley's famous smile returned to her face within minutes of reaching the Green Street house, and every bush, plant stand and cup seemed to be infused with joy. "I just can't believe it," she said. "I still can't believe I'm here."

Manuela let out a scream and a stream of rapid-fire Spanish when she saw Cayley. She grabbed both her hands and kissed them, then ran back to the kitchen to prepare food.

"Do you think he just wanted an apology? Was that it?" Cayley removed her hat and threw it across the parlor where it landed half-up against a chair leg.

"Maybe that was it," Beatrice smiled sweetly.

Jackson came in the door, having followed their carriage in his own. "Just a few formalities to take care of, Mrs. Duarte. You are one lucky woman, is all I can say."

"You don't know the half of it, Jackson," she grinned at him.

"There is that little matter of bigamy to straighten out however."

"I suspect Mr. Wallace will be very cooperative—he looked pretty beat-up on the stand. It seems odd, I know, but I feel sorry for him. All this time, and he's lived without getting married again. Poor lonely man. NOTHING could bring me down off this cloud right now."

Manuela called for them to come to the table. They sat down and enjoyed a feast of cold roast beef, breads, fruit and other tidbits. Cayley insisted Manuela sit with them, but when the old woman seemed hesitant and uncomfortable, Cayley let her return to the kitchen. The conversation lapsed into silence, rose like a bubble and burst as quickly.

"Aunt Cay," said Beatrice, "I want to suggest something. What do you think about coming back with me to Philadelphia, then New York? Starting over in a new place. Nobody has to know about your past any more than they know about mine."

Cayley smiled and looked down at her plate. "Your intentions are good, Bean, but I have to say this," she looked up at the younger woman: "I'm not ashamed of anything I did to survive in this world. In fact, I'm mighty proud of it."

"Oh, no, I didn't mean it like that...exactly." Beatrice dabbed at her mouth. The gathering was silent. "Now I've gone and ruined the moment."

Cayley got up, came round the table and put her arms around the young woman. She squeezed her shoulders and kissed her cheek. "You haven't spoiled one damn thing, sweet." She turned the young woman to face her, and kept her hands on her shoulders. "It's just that when you bury the horseshit under a load of shiny straw, it's still going to smell, even if you're the only one who's digging around in it. My theory is, you got to own up to what you are and what you've done. Even if it's the stupidest thing you can imagine." Cayley dropped her arms and stood up straight. "Like taking a gun to a man just because he doesn't favor you anymore." She returned to her seat. "Now I suppose the offer of a visit is withdrawn since it looks like I'm going to blab about what a happy fallen woman I've been."

"I'd be embarrassed, surely. I won't deny it." Beatrice retreated into thought; after an awkward moment, she spoke again. "The carefully constructed story I've told others would be seen in a different light. I told the truth, you understand, but I left a lot out." Cayley started to speak but Beatrice held up her hand. "Not because anything you'd say would embarrass me, because I know you wouldn't do that. I feel foolish because I'm asking you to be someone you're not, and that's not right."

"Well you have grown up into a fine young woman, haven't you?" Cayley regarded her niece with respect. "I don't think you have one thing to be ashamed of, meaning what you told everyone back there about your upbringing and such. It wasn't any different than your mother and I planned for you. As for me, I'll consider your offer and how it would work best for both of us. I just might take a short visit out east, to let things cool down here. Fact is, though, I can't stay away from this city, and I don't intend to." She looked meaningfully at Sam. "Sam and I have some things to discuss after we eat."

When the meal was finished, Cayley pulled on a shawl and drew Sam by the arm into the garden in back of the house. This late in July, the air was chilly as the fog moved stealthily into the bay in the afternoon. Waning golden light caught the top of the maple, covered with brilliant green leaves. The ground was littered with spent blooms from the Confederate Star jasmine Cayley had planted against the wall. They sat on the white wrought-iron chairs, knee-to-knee.

"Here we are Mr. Wo."

Sam fumbled with the crease in his pants. "I expect you wish to discuss the sale of the business."

"Oh, Sam. Neither of us is any good at this sort of thing, are we?"

He looked up into her eyes. His were so dark there was no difference between the pupil and iris.

"We're way past the business discussion, unless I'm sorely mistaken." She put her hand over his and he clasped it.

"This is a difficult situation. For both of us," he said quietly.

"You'd think I'd laugh off what people would think about the two of us together out in the open, considering my business. But when I'm face-to-face with the real possibility of being unwelcome anywhere…well, it makes a difference, doesn't it?" She looked down at the ground. "I'm ashamed of myself. It's that old longing to be respectable. It won't let me be."

He caressed her hand, gently running his fingers on the back of it. "You're not alone…in any of your feelings. It's equally bad for a Chinese to take a white woman as a wife. I would not dishonor you by offering less. The rebuilding of Chinatown and my freedom from Wing Yee has given me the opportunity to be welcome among other Chinese once again. For you and I to be more than business partners would destroy that. It would also destroy the opportunity to rejoin society for my sister and Mei Mei."

Cayley laughed ruefully and pulled her shawl closer around her shoulders with her free hand. She brought her forehead close to his while still looking down. "Well, this is a hell of a situation, isn't it?"

He slid his face against hers until their cheeks met, and tenderly placed a kiss just below her ear. A tear slid down from the corner of her eye. She noted the sandalwood scent of his shirt collar and the silky smoothness of his cheek.

"I've told a lot of men they're the best I've ever known," she whispered. "But it's only true for one." She drew herself back and wiped her eyes with her wrist. "Maybe things won't always be like this. Someday…." She held her free hand out, palm up, imploring the universe. "I've been so selfish. I don't really know much about you at all, and I want to know everything. I never hid anything from you."

"Nothing would turn me from you. I've proven that many times. You know me better than anyone. Like most men, I am what I do."

Cayley clasped his other hand and held them both to her breast. "You've given me so much, and I've returned so little."

Sam smiled sadly and looked down. In the silence that followed, Cayley leaned forward, and their lips met, awkwardly, just brushing against each other like a butterfly wing on a petal. She sat back in her chair. "Maybe I'll take Bean up on her offer and visit Philadelphia. It'll give you and me time to get used to this, maybe figure out what it's all about."

"And the business?"

She sat up straight and looked at him impishly. "Business! Now we're back on solid ground! Quite a pair, aren't we? Anyway, I've given it some thought. I still want to sell to Opal, but retain a percentage, so I'll get the pay-out and a share's income, too…better for everyone."

Sam rocked backwards and shook his head from side to side, feigning despair. "I'm out of a job!"

"No, you're not. I've got it all figured out. Opal will want to keep you on, but you've got a choice. I'll sell one of the properties in the East Bay—that'll bring a pretty penny these days. With that money, you could set yourself up in Chinatown with your own building and business—maybe go into the medicine trade like that cousin of yours—or just rent it out, anything you want. You'll be the equal of any of them that you used to work for, and Lilly and Mei can hold their heads up high. Of course…." Cayley tilted her head to one side, "I'll be taking a percentage of the business. I don't think you'd stand for being a kept man." She turned her face to him and smiled, "But the down payment isn't a loan; it's your back salary plus a raise. It's only money, not what I really owe you. No one deserves it more."

Sam bowed from the waist. "I should be humble and refuse, saying, I am not worthy of such extravagance, Mrs. Wallace!"

Cayley laughed and brought his face up to hers. "Cut it out, Sam. None of that foolishness between us."

"Of course I accept; I'd be a fool not to. To be partners at least in this way—it makes sense. One thing, though…"

Cayley leaned back expectantly.

"I will probably marry Mei Mei. It will guarantee the safety of us all in Little China."

Cayley sighed and shook her head, placed both her hands over his. "We always seem to be marrying other people." She reached up and laid her palm against the side of his face. "Sam, you're mine no matter what. And I'm yours. I'll be back. San Francisco is OUR town, after all."

~THE END~

A special request from the author:

If you enjoyed the book, please give it a brief review on Amazon. Thank you, and much appreciated!!

Fact and Fiction in SHAKETOWN

Cayley Wallace is based on a real and very unapologetic madam, Tessie Wall, who crept into my research while I wrote sections of the *San Francisco* and *USA DK Eyewitness* travel guides. Once she appeared in my reading, she persisted—and finally inspired her own story. I made up almost all of the details of Tess/Cayley's life, and moved a few facts around in the service of fiction. For instance, Tess was actually widowed from her first husband, though she did take a pistol to her second, famously saying, "I shot him because I love him, damn him."

Because I wanted to be true to Tess Wall's actual life dates, I played fast and loose with historical events and personages: Donaldina Cameron—a heroine to girls of the Chinese slave trade—was a contemporary of Tess Wall's, as was the "modern" dancer Isadora Duncan. Ambrose Bierce—celebrated for his short story, "An Occurrence at Owl Creek Bridge" and "The Devil's Dictionary"—wrote for the Examiner at the time. Bierce was an exceptional writer with considerably more heart and social conscience than he appears to have in *Shaketown*. He never shied away from a tough story and disappeared while traveling with Pancho Villa's army near Chihuahua, Mexico in 1913. The Fairmont Hotel on Nob Hill wasn't built when I placed it in the novel, and my apologies to L. Frank Baum fans, who have undoubtedly picked up on the fact that the Oz book mentioned in the text wasn't published until 1900—however, being an Oz fan myself, I included it.

Cayley Wallace's early years, background and time-line are entirely fiction, as are most of the other characters that appear in the book, including Ellen Leary and Opal Boone. Wo Sam and his sister were created from an amalgam of the trials and tribulations of Chinese immigrants of the period and stories from my own Chinese relatives. Most of my research is from non-Chinese sources, so I offer an apology to those who find holes in my story. I've thrown in a few of my own experiences with San Francisco's Chinese culture—chiefly the visit to the street temple, a dim childhood memory of a seventh-grade field trip that I hope was recorded correctly.

Most of the physical places in Shaketown still exist, and many events are based on fact; a walking tour is entirely possible! The devastation of the 1906 earthquake and fire has been heavily documented, and I've tried to duplicate the wonder and terror of being caught in a +5 'quake from my own three experiences—fortunately, not even the 1989 Loma Preita earthquake was close to the "big one" of 1906.

This book would not have come together in its present form without the excellent input of my workshop team of writers: San Francisco historian Daniel Bacon, Ginny Horton, Greg Smith and Ann Hyman, and the superb editing of Zoe Zuber.

All illustrations are from my personal ephemera collection of chromolithographed trading cards, calling cards, postcards, and advertising cards. The photograph of Chinatown and a version of the photograph used on the cover are courtesy of the San Francisco Public Library's superb history collection, where much of my research took place.

The Real Tessie Wall

About the Author

A freelance writer since 1992, Joanne Orion Miller's work has been published in both print and e-zine formats; she is a recipient of the Raymond Carver Award for short fiction, and was among 20 international fiction writers chosen to attend the annual Spoleto (Italy) Writer's Conference. *Shaketown* is her first novel. A psychological thriller, *Power Lessons*, is in the works, as is *Harvest,* a "semi-rural romance" set in the California Delta.

Her non-fiction work appears in *Writer's Market, Fiction & Short Story Writer's Market* (both Writer's Digest Books), *San Francisco and Northern California, USA* (both Dorling Kindersley) and many other publications. She wrote and photo-illustrated comprehensive guidebooks to Pennsylvania, Maryland/Delaware, Chesapeake Bay (all Moon Handbooks/Avalon Press), Maryland's Eastern Shore, Delaware (both Moon Spotlight Books/Avalon Press), and authored guides to Marin County (Sasquatch Press) and Maui and Kaua'i (Peter Pauper Press).

Her recent solo trip around the world – illustrated with pictures and stories of touching down in India, the Galapagos, Amsterdam, Spain, and more - is documented on 1Woman1World1Year.blogspot.com.

Photo: Bonnie Kamin Morrissey

Joanne Online:
Websites: JoanneOrionMiller.com and AboutJoanne_Miller.com
Facebook: www.facebook.com/AuthorNews
Twitter: @JoanneOMiller
Goodreads:
www.goodreads.com/author/show/7159723.Joanne_Orion_Miller

Made in the USA
Las Vegas, NV
19 June 2022

50444827R00203